ULTRA-BOILED

ULTRA-BOILED

Gary Lovisi

RAMBLE HOUSE

Acknowledgements:

ULTRA-BOILED: Hard Crime Fiction by Gary Lovisi_is © 2010 by Gary Lovisi and contains the following: "**Introduction: The Ultra-Boiled Way**" by Gary Lovisi, the first half of which is from "The Hard-Boiled Way" by Gary Lovisi which originally appeared in *A Shot In The Dark* #3, and is ©1995, the second part is original to this collection and is ©2010 by Gary Lovisi. "**New Blood**" by Gary Lovisi originally appeared in *Tense Moments* #3 and is ©1991 by Gary Lovisi. "**A Rat Must Chew**" by Gary Lovisi originally appeared in *Hardboiled* #23 and is ©1997 by Gary Lovisi. "**Point of Origin**" by Gary Lovisi is original to this collection and is published here for the first time, ©2010 by Gary Lovisi. "**No Satisfaction**" by Gary Lovisi originally appeared in *Kracked Mirror Mysteries* #10 and is ©1996 by Gary Lovisi. "**Fast**" by Gary Lovisi originally appeared in *Hardboiled Detective* #11 and is ©1991 by Gary Lovisi. "**Live and Learn**" by Gary Lovisi originally appeared in *Hardboiled* #19 and is ©1994 by Gary Lovisi. "**Vortex**" by Gary Lovisi originally appeared in the Australian anthology *Hardboiled*, ©1992 by Gary Lovisi. "**Love Kills**" by Gary Lovisi is original to this collection and is published here for the first time, ©2010 by Gary Lovisi. "**Demonology**" by Gary Lovisi originally appeared in *Hardboiled Magazine* #17, and is ©1994 by Gary Lovisi. "**Not Much Joy In Prison**" by Gary Lovisi originally appeared in the online magazine *Plots With Guns*, and is published here in print for the first time, ©2003 by Gary Lovisi. "**Finders Keepers**" by Gary Lovisi originally appeared in the online magazine *BlueMurder.com*, and is published here in print for the first time, ©1999 by Gary Lovisi. "**Dry Run**" by Gary Lovisi originally appeared in the British anthology *New Crimes III* and is ©1992 by Gary Lovisi. "**Service**" by Gary Lovisi originally appeared in *Flesh & Blood: Guilty as Sin*, ©2003 by Gary Lovisi. "**Evil Forces**" by Gary Lovisi originally appeared in the online magazine *Hardluck Stories* and is published here in print for the first time, ©2005 by Gary Lovisi. "**SBC**" by Gary Lovisi is original to this collection and is published here for the first time, ©2010 by Gary Lovisi. "**The Mission**" by Gary Lovisi originally appeared as half of *Gryphon Double* #16, and is ©1998 by Gary Lovisi. "**Teeth**" by Gary Lovisi is original to this collection and is published here for the first time, ©2010 by Gary Lovisi. "**The Cure**" by Gary Lovisi originally appeared in the online magazine *Hardluck Stories* and is published here in print for the first time, ©2003 by Gary Lovisi. "**The Hardest Time There is**" by Gary Lovisi originally appeared in *Extreme Measures* and is ©1996 by Gary Lovisi. "**Axis**" by Gary Lovisi originally appeared in *Hot Blood #13: Dark Passions*, ©2007 by Gary Lovisi. "**War**" by Gary Lovisi is original to this collection and is published here for the first time, ©2010 by Gary Lovisi. "**Political Year**" by Gary Lovisi originally appeared in *Dirty Dogs* and is ©1999 by Gary Lovisi. "**Do Something About It**" by Gary Lovisi originally appeared in the online magazine Yellow *Mama* #15 and is published here in print for the first time, ©2009 by Gary Lovisi. Entire contents ©2010 by Gary Lovisi. All Rights Reserved.

ISBN 13: 978-1-60543-436-0
ISBN 10: 1-60543-436-1

Cover Art: Joseph Cali
Back Cover Photo: Laura Cali
Cover Design: Gavin L. O'Keefe
Preparation: Fender Tucker

www.ramblehouse.com

ULTRA-BOILED

CONTENTS

INTRODUCTION: THE ULTRA-BOILED WAY

Gary Lovisi

Ultra-boiled is hard-boiled . . . *on steroids.*
So then, what is hard-boiled? To be sure, hard-boiled is a term, and a genre that means different things to different people. The way I describe it is that hard-boiled is pure attitude. *Attitude to the core.* It's also a lot more. Some may think it's only fiction about violence, often very brutal violence, but that's not a necessary ingredient. Violence is there because we're talking about realistic crime fiction when we talk hard-boiled, and that means you lay it out truthfully to the reader. Don't sugarcoat the truth, don't play it cute. The attitude comes from realizing *that* truth. No matter how truly rotten or violent it may be. Knowledge of that truth can not help but affect the writer, or his characters, and if done well, the reader as well.

There's a lot of tough-guy talk and action in some hard-boiled fiction, but that's not all there is to it either. Others think all that's important is style, all that wonderful Chandleresque chit-chat which a lot of readers and critics like perhaps too much, but too often these days has entered the area of nostalgia, pastiche, or cliché. However, the real hard-boiler, Dashiell Hammett is, to those in the know, still on top. Carroll John Daly had *real* heart. Mickey Spillane *made* you read him. Jim Thompson, David Goodis, Cornell Woolrich (in his William Irish noir days), Chester Himes and Charles Willeford lived lives no writer could ever make up and their work soared because of it. Or, in spite of it. And modern hard-boiled fiction is all that and more.

Part of what hard-boiled is about is the adherence to a moral code in a world without any moral code or moral values at all. Hammett and Chandler wrote about it in the old days. However today, it can be a moral code as minimalist as that of Andrew Vachss' Burke, or as twisted as one of James Ellroy's cop heroes.

Today, more than ever, hard-boiled fiction is relevant fiction that has meaning and stands for something, unlike the broader spectrum of literature, and most other mass-market entertainment. Modern authentic hard-boiled material (not Chandler clones or blood and guts retro-pulp), seriously examines crime or social issues, often taking us to places and depths we'd rather not be taken into at all. The world is a cruel place, but for the hard-boiled hero (and the writer and the reader by extension), it's far crueler than anyone can ever imagine. And that's part of the real story most people who do not read hard-boiled fiction do not want to face. Escape is, after all, so much more pleasant. And comforting. And easy. It can be so . . . *cozy*. And all the answers are laid out for you at the end. What could be nicer? Well, folks, that ain't the way it is with authentic hard-boiled material. Oh, you might get a tidy answer at the end of the story, but if you do, there'll be little comfort in it, I can assure you.

Hard-boiled fiction is not just about private eyes either. Even in the past, some of the best hard-boiled writers; W.R. Burnett (*The Asphalt Jungle*), and James M. Cain (*Double Indemnity* and *The Postman Always Rings Twice*), were certainly *not* writing private eye fiction. They were writing hard, cold truth. The way it was back then, the way they saw it every day of their lives. Dashiell Hammett did the same thing as a Pinkerton, he took that life he'd lived and molded it into his Continental Op stories, later on into Sam Spade and the stuff that dreams are made of. But the core truth and attitude is always there in Hammett's work. And it is no less true today than when his work was first published over 80 years ago.

Today the hard-boiled tradition comes on strong, in some ways even bolder than ever. Today there are serious issues and debates in hard-boiled work that you don't see any place else. And certainly not at this level of detail and intensity.

Hard-boiled deals with crime, naturally. But it goes deep down into the black heart of crime. The corruption crime can bring into a person's life, or into our society. The pain and decay it spawns on so many levels. The effect on the criminal *and* the victim. The reasons for it all.

Authentic hard-boiled fiction is also about real people trying to live their lives, to make it in the day-to-day and getting smashed down inch by inch, lower and lower. But they still hang in there. They refuse to go down for the count. They're not giving up a damn thing, because they've had to fight like hell every day of their life for what they've got—and they'll fight like hell every day of their life *to keep it*. And I'm *not* talking materialism here, folks. Not at all. I'm talking pride, honor, dignity, respect, the truth—going out of your way to help a friend, or going out of your way to fuck the enemy—days of blood and rage, a gut full of hurt—stand-up people in a sit-down shut-up world! That's hard-boiled, to me.

I think that attitude comes through loud and clear in each of these 23 stories—my best and wildest hard crime and noir tales—collected together for the first time in book form. They are violent, maybe even brutal. In some cases the characters even revel in that violence. However, the point of view is always with the victim, or the character who is getting back at the thief, the murderer, the rapist or the child molester—that criminal who did you dirty in the first place. Revenge, pure, but not always so simple.

Some of these stories were previously published in book anthologies or magazines as far back as the early 1990s, or as recently as last year. Five stories are original to this book and have never been published before, while four others originally appeared only in online publications with this being their first-ever publication in print.

Some of these stories contain three of my favorite hard-boiled heroes. Vic Powers, is an ex-cop thrown off the force for being "unstable" and he appears in contemporary crime stories (so far with one novel, *Blood in Brooklyn* and one short story collection *Dirty Dogs*). Griff & Fats, are two retro-pulp tough-guy coppers whose stories take place in the early 1960s in the fictionalized Bay City (with one novel so far, *Hellbent on Homicide*). Joe Dillon, is a reluctant warrior who fights the evil he sees perpetuated by modern day religion. He is a work in progress.

Along with the other heroes, or fools, who are the main protagonists in the rest of these stories, these crime tales are replete with wicked femme fatales, crooked grifters, crazy punks, vile con men, vengeful vigilantes, evil child abusers, plus the usual array of killers, thieves and worse. The broad spectrum of crime in many manifestations. In other stories, for instance "Teeth" and "Vortex", crime straddles the thin line between bloody violence and madness. In some stories, a really bad guy or gal gets a well-deserved comeuppance. Wicked people, getting theirs, wickedly. You may even cheer a bit at their demise, maybe even as much as I cheered as I wrote it.

I want to take a moment to also thank Gavin L. O'Keefe, and Fender Tucker at Ramble House for having the guts to put out such a politically incorrect crime collection and to master artist, Joseph Cali, well known in Japan for his fine art and design who created the fun pulp-flavored original painting especially for the cover of this book.

I hope you enjoy the stories in *Ultra-Boiled*. They're not for the faint of heart, they're not even "nice" stories, but they are some of the best crime fiction I've ever written and they are definitely full of heart and . . . *hard-boiled attitude!*

Gary Lovisi
Brooklyn, New York
January, 2010

NEW BLOOD

HE ONLY HAD ONE MORE TO GO. One more and he'd be in the record books. One more and he'd be Number One! One more and he'd be the greatest of them all.

But it wasn't easy. With every killing the cops closed in on him more and more. The noose circled and constricted. His scent grew warmer and the chances of getting caught came closer. And he still had so much work to do. There was so much left unfinished.

It wasn't as easy as all the papers made it look either. No one seemed to understand. The victims, they all had to be just right. They couldn't be just anyone. That was the hard part and it was getting impossible now. There weren't that many accessible nurses in the city hospital system. Everyone was on the lookout. They were all so careful now, and the police were watching. Many of the best prospects didn't even go to work anymore. It made it hard to find out where they lived. Many others were guarded day and night. He knew. He checked. They were not accessible.

He preferred long-haired blondes. He knew he'd have to get at least one more of these to break his record. The papers said it all in big bold headlines:

NURSE KILLER STILL AT LARGE!

12 NURSES SLAIN IN 12 WEEKS!

TERROR GRIPS THE CITY!

WHO WILL BE NUMBER 13?

It was not easy. One nurse a week. Twelve long weeks. He'd wanted to give up weeks ago. Stop it all. Maybe turn himself in? He had actually hoped to get caught—but then the record stared him in the face—the newspapers and TV news played it up so big—he was almost the greatest mass serial murderer of nurses of all time—it was a challenge he could not ignore. The pressure was incredible.

But enough musings. He had work to do. Tonight was the last night of the 13th week. He'd have to do it tonight. It must be tonight. He had to stay on schedule.

He had found another nurse. He had this one picked out yesterday. He'd followed her. Watched her. Found her address where she lived on First Street in Park Slope. It was a short walk from where she worked at the Medical Center. The giant Methodist Hospital had plenty of nurses to choose from. But too many were Puerto Rican, a lot were black or from the Islands, too many were Indian or Paki's. All not right. Not right at all. Then he saw this nice Irish blonde. And she was just right.

He'd noticed her. Her hair so long. So blonde. He'd never seen her before at the hospital. He figured she was new. She was. He liked that. Laughed about it in his twisted mind. New blood. He needed new blood.

He stalked her. She was a harmless young doe. He was the big bad wolf. He felt the sharpness of his knife, as he did so he touched himself, feeling himself grow. He anticipated the time. It would be very soon now.

This was just what he needed. A new girl. She'd be one of the prettiest he'd ever had this way. He was getting more excited minute by minute. Anticipating.

Moving fast he followed her down the dark and lonely streets.

She looked back now! Thought she saw someone. He ducked behind a stoop; she saw nothing and kept walking. He followed again.

She reached Number 127. He'd cased the apartment building yesterday. There were ten floors. Her place was on the 7th floor, apartment 7A. He moved in quickly and carefully behind her.

She startled, jumped.

"Oh, hi, I'm sorry," he said so cordially, with such a smile, "I know I've got the key here somewhere . . ."

She turned, she looked at him. Sized him up. Wrong.

She held the door for him. Smiled.

She smiled! He liked that!

"You're the guy from 8C, Mr. . . .?"

"Sure. Johnson. Can never find my key."

She held the door open for him to enter the building. They walked together to the elevator. They got in the elevator together.

She pressed 7.

He remembered just in time and pressed 8.

She relaxed.

He got that weird feeling. Kept quiet. Watched her without letting her see him watching her. She turned and smiled. He smiled back.

The doors opened on the 7th Floor. She got out and walked across the hall to her door. He watched her put her key into the door. Turn the knob. Saw the door open a crack and before she could open it further—before the elevator doors closed and took him up to the 8th Floor—he was upon her. Pushing her into the apartment. Throwing her down to the floor. Closing the door behind him. Locking it quickly. Tight shut. Like a vault. So she could never escape. Never!

Then he turned to the girl. Blonde. Long hair. Pretty.

Very pretty. Laying on the floor at the other end of the room. Motionless. She was all his now.

She was laying there face down. She still didn't move. He came closer to her. The shadows of the dark room making his movements mysterious. Fearsome.

He touched himself in anticipation. Looking at her laying there. Helpless. Touching himself. Imagining.

He drew out the knife. It was long, sharp; the steel called out to him.

Then the lights went on! From out of nowhere a dozen armed men came at him. Knocking the knife from his hand. Grabbing him tightly. Holding him roughly with guns to his head while they frisked him for other weapons. He could not move.

The girl got up from the floor then. She took off the long blonde wig. Her real hair was short and black.

She held out the wig, "Here. Is this what you were after!"

"Liar!" he yelled at her, "You were so pretty. Instead you're just a disappointment like all the others."

"All those others you've killed?" she asked.

He didn't speak.

The girl held his knife so he could see it. "This is what you used to torture them. Such a terrible weapon. Why?"

He was quiet for a second, then smiled, said, "I know my rights. I want to see a lawyer. You can arrest me, but I don't have to tell you anything."

The girl smiled back, "Why darling, what makes you think we're the police?"

A RAT MUST CHEW

JIMMY DONGEN WAS A STATEN ISLAND WISE-GUY with his dirty hands into more dirty crap than even he could keep track of. Anything and everything to make a buck and not just gambling and other soft vices, but nasty stuff like teen-age hookers, drug dealing in schools, selling guns to kiddie gangs. The guys under Jimmy saw him as a greedy fuck, the guys over him saw him as a greedy fuck who brought in the cash. He was a good earner so they all put up with Jimmy Dongen while he tried his best to smart-ass double-cross them all when they weren't looking. He figured he'd end up with everything he ever wanted. I don't think he even knew all of what he wanted—he just *wanted*.

My name is Vic Powers. I came into it originally back in the old days when I'd been on the job. Before they threw me off the force for being "unstable." Hell, I wasn't unstable, I was just damn angry that a lowlife creep had killed my partner, Larry, and I wanted to do something about it. Larry was the best damn friend I ever had. The best damn cop I ever knew. Damn right I was angry. I was fit to be tied! But I wasn't unstable, leastways any more unstable than I'd ever been. But then again, I guess I could see their point, and it probably all worked out for the best. I wasn't cut out to be a cop. Not the kind of cops they want. Yes-men, ass-kissers, sell-outs and politically correct rats—a lot of them no better than the criminals they are supposed to arrest.

Well, all that was a lot of water under the bridge now, but over the years Jimmy Dongen had moved up, turning into one of the biggest of the bad guys. But he'd made a lot of enemies along the way.

He told me once long ago, after I'd saved his ass, that he wanted to go straight.

I told him he was full of shit.

He had acted all serious about it back then.

I just looked at him and said, "Rats must chew, that's just the way it is, Jimmy."

He got all upset, thought I was calling him a rat.

I smiled, said, "No, Jimmy, you're not a rat. Least far as I know, you're not. You're a scumbag, but you ain't no rat."

There is a difference.

Then I told him that to live a rat must chew. Rats—the four-legged kind, that is—have huge incisors that keep growing in their mouths and if the rat doesn't constantly gnaw at things, constantly chew, cut and grind with those teeth to wear them down, the damn teeth will grow right into the rats brain and kill it.

"Nice way for a rat to die," Jimmy had said.

"It's like that with a scumbag like you, Jimmy. You'll never stop. You'll never go straight. It's in the blood. Rats must chew and scumbags like you will never stop what they do."

Then Larry and I cuffed him and brought him in.

Well, that had been a long time ago. Like they say, a lot of water under the bridge, a lot of blood too. Now Larry was gone and I was on my own.

Now I was a two-bit no-one in a world that had dreamed me out of its dreams a long time ago. So I did the next best thing, I hung in and survived. I did my best to make it day to day. Trying to beat the odds but coming up craps with every throw. In the meantime I never dared to hope.

It was after Larry had been killed, but before my wife, Gayle, had been murdered. That's how I usually remember events in my life, I date them from who it was who was close to me—and when they were taken away from me. Killings, murders, my partner, Larry, my friends, my women, my enemies, my wife . . .

Anyway, Gayle was still alive back then and we were trying to have a real life. I was playing the hubby and loving it. Thinking of opening an office again, maybe a husband and wife P.I. team? A dream I shouldn't have let enter my mind.

Then Jimmy Dongen entered my world again.

He was on the run.

The cops—crooked and otherwise, the mob, a Jersey biker gang that dealt drugs, an upstate Aryan Separatist group that paid Jimmy a lot of good money for some very bad guns. They were all after Jimmy and I was in Jimmy's car parked under the West Side Highway while he was telling me all this crap.

I said, "Why, man? You had it good; you could have stopped the crap, taken it easy. You play so many games, so many sides against each other you were bound one day to get caught in the middle."

"I know, Vic," he said. "I guess it had to happen sooner or later. You know how it is. I got to do what I do. I can't stop. I could never stop. Once I started a life of crime, Vic, once I started playing The Game, I just couldn't stop it. I love it too much. Now I know there's only one end for us all, eventually."

"You know all this shit and you still fuck around."

"Yeah, I know all this shit, and it doesn't help me by knowing it."

"Not if you don't do anything to stop it, Jimmy."

He smiled, "A rat must chew, Vic."

I nodded.

The gun slipped into my hand.

I pressed it up against Jimmy's temple.

Jimmy's eyes blew up into big circles of surprise, and then understanding.

It was quick.

I pressed the trigger.

One.

Two.

He fell away from me.

I whipped the gun and placed it in his right hand, melding the fingers to the grip. Opened the door. Locked the passenger side as I got out of the car and walked away.

A rat must chew.

This was one rat that would never chew again.

POINT OF ORIGIN

STUART WAS CREEPING ME OUT AGAIN.

I caught him watching me and finally told Bert about it.

"I wouldn't be worried about him, Catherine." Bert's reassuring smile did much to soften my jumpy nerves. Bert had a calming effect on people, and on me in particular. His tan, FBI-Quantico good looks made me feel more secure than even the weapon holstered at my hip. That weapon which I was required to wear as a city police officer, but which I had never fired at a perp. Not even once. It's just that I've always been sensitive to things like being watched, and Stuart—I know he's really harmless and besides, he's a valued member of our team—makes me feel uncomfortable sometimes and I don't know why.

Bert picked up on my nervousness—he's so perceptive. "I'll speak to him, Catherine." Bert glances up at Stuart, we see him quickly dart into his cubicle. Bert shrugs, laughs, "The guy's weird, but you know how these computer geeks can be. No social skills at all."

"I guess," I said, but this wasn't the first time I'd noticed Stuart's eyes upon me, and I was hoping he wasn't developing some unhealthy obsession. That can happen when a small group works as closely together as we do. Our work, violent crime investigation, also can make things difficult. I just hoped that if Stuart had any little fantasies about me they didn't effect his work as a member of our team. He was an ace computer guy and we needed him.

There are four of us. We were put together by Commissioner Wallace after receiving special training, some of it from the F.B.I. Bert, Bert Singleton, was our nominal leader, at least in experience and seniority. He'd had Quantico profiling. He had the aggressive instincts needed in a leader. There was also Dennis Gomez. Dennis was short and gruff but he knew criminal gangs—from street thugs to organized crime. It was all his background as a street cop. They said he had real "magic" in that area. Dennis said that's what happens when you have an Irish mom and a Mexican father—you get a Chicano leprechaun! Stuart Rogers was our computer specialist, everyone called him a geek and he was kind of like that. Quiet, he often got lost in the background. And then there was me, Catherine Polk. I was the scientific member with a crime lab background and training as a blood spatter analyst.

The four of us made up the Violent Crime Task Force. We'd cracked some good cases since our inception a year ago, but lately things had been dry. Oh, they were still killing each other out there like there was no tomorrow—but we hadn't gotten a good bite on any of the half dozen cases we'd been working on the last few weeks. At least, not the kind of bite we could sink our teeth into—something that might lead to an arrest.

Then a new case opened up and changed everything. It began with the murder of a Jane Doe who turned out to be named Roberta Torres. It happened near the Planetarium, and it was especially vexing since we'd just canvassed the area for a gang-related killing two days previously.

"Right here, right under our noses!" Dennis muttered his frustration as he read the prelim report. "And it was vengeance, or a crime of passion, you can see the anger in the killing."

"She's been tied and then killed," I began, giving my prelim report. "Autopsy shows there was no rape, or at least no penetration, all three orifices were clean of semen. Nor were there any semen deposits elsewhere on her body. Her face had been detached . . ."

"Detached?" Stuart said incredulously. Sometimes Stuart did that, he didn't pay attention and then blurted out facts he was surprised to hear, as questions.

"Yeah, little geek, you know, like in an Indian taking a scalp—he'll cut the hairline and peel away the scalp. Our boy made a cut at the face line, then peeled off her face!"

Stuart looked like he was going to puke.

Dennis and Bert smiled at his discomfort, I almost felt sorry for him.

Back to business now, Bert asked, "Why do you think he did that, Catherine?"

That's what I wanted to know. I was considering an answer when Dennis jumped in with his usual helpful hints, "Who the hell knows? Maybe that broad was so damn ugly that the killer just couldn't stand to look . . ."

"Dennis, stop it! Your disgusting outbursts of gallows humor aren't required," I said sternly.

Dennis shrugged at my rebuke, adding one of his more common hand gestures as an accent.

Bert smiled, nodded, said, "Well, I wanted to make a couple of calls before I gave you my thoughts on this one. I think it's clear we're dealing with a highly organized killer and a controlling killer. The way he tied her up, not just tied, but he hog-tied her, like an animal. That indicates a complete disregard for Roberta Torres as a person. A human being. We've seen this before. The absence of a sex act of any kind I think extends that further—he's making a point."

"What the hell kind of point?" Dennis blurted.

"We don't know yet," Bert replied a bit testy. "Anyway, I haven't seen a killer this organized and focused since Bundy. His MO indicates high intelligence, college education, and discipline, such as what you might get with a doctor or lawyer. But he's certainly not a lawyer and probably not a doctor either. He could also be a military man, but not your average grunt or leatherneck, someone with intelligence, education, discipline, certainly an officer—however a Master or Gunny Sergeant with years of seniority couldn't be ruled out. However, my best early guess of a profile is that he could be a cop, highly intelligent and trained, maybe in some specialized field."

Dennis shook his head dubiously, "Yeah, that's helpful, that means it can be almost anyone."

"Not really," Stuart offered, softly. Then he looked at me, smiled and said, "What do you think, Catherine?"

He was in full work mode now, it enabled him to deal with us in a work setting that imitated a social one.

"We still don't know what this girl even looks like, but analysis of blood spatter patterns may tell us more information soon. Were you able to get a photo of the victim yet, Stuart?"

"It's downloading now."

There is a moment of silence while we are all waiting.

Stuart utters a little gasp, looks over at me, then turns the screen of his laptop around so we can all see the photo.

No one says a word. I'm unable to even breathe.

"Damn!" Dennis blurts finally, "She looks a lot like you, Catherine. You know, she could be your sister!"

I just nodded remotely, trying not to freeze up inside. I took a deep breath as I got up from the table, "I'll have a detailed report on the blood spatter later today."

Then I got the hell out of there.

I was still at my apartment two days later trying to finish that damn report. Still trying to jibe what I had discovered at the scene in the blood spatter with what I now knew of the murder. The face of the girl had been torn off, so I was a little freaked out when her downloaded image bore a striking resemblance to me. It sort of made it seem personal—and made me uneasy—but I knew I had to put those feelings aside and do my job.

I collected my crime scene photos and collated them. They showed all the rods I'd set up to better indicate blood spatter trajectory and direction. It helped me determine the weapon, the number of blows, location of the killer at the scene, and other things that drew me a map of what happened during the attack of Roberta Torres.

The first thing the blood spatter indicated, backed up by the autopsy, was that Roberta Torres had been killed first, quickly and efficiently. Then her face had been peeled off and taken by the killer. Only afterwards, had she been bludgeoned in the head and body with between 70 to 75 blows. Certainly rage overkill. The killer used a hammer, for the first couple of blows to the head which broke the facial bones, destroying any possible view of her facial appearance. Then he put down the hammer beside the body and used his fists. He beat her viciously.

Bert was certainly correct, this was one of the most highly organized and brutal killers we'd ever come across. It was a murder of incredible rage and hatred and perhaps even some kind of sick and twisted obsessional love.

I couldn't help thinking about Stuart and all his statistics and numbers and computer programs and wondering if the killer could be someone like him. Maybe, but then I smiled to myself, for I knew I was being foolish. So I put that thought out of my mind and finally finished my report.

Not soon after, the phone rang. It was Bert. He asked how I was feeling. I told him seeing the face of the Torres woman had been a pretty big shock at first, but I was over it now. Mostly. He asked if I wanted to join him and Dennis at his place for a few drinks. I said no, I didn't think it was a good idea. Then he asked if I wanted him and Dennis to come over for a few drinks. I said I was too tired, going to hit the sack as soon as I finished one last item on my report. He said that was probably best, but to be ready to roll next morning at 8 AM sharp, because the team was waiting to hear my report. That night I slept like a baby, putting all the silly uneasiness and thoughts I felt out of my mind.

Next morning we were in our conference room at Police Head-quarters. Stuart was late as usual. Dennis was pissed and eager to get started. He was being his usual cranky self, mocking Stuart when he wasn't there to defend himself—not that Stuart would have had the guts to utter a word in his own defense. I think he was scared of the gruff street cop.

Thank God Bert was our solid rock, a grown-up I could count on. He was such a sensible leader and got us focused. Stuart came in a moment later.

"I know! I know! I'm late again," he said setting up his laptop at the end of the table farthest away from everyone else. "Sorry."

Bert just nodded, said, "So let's get started. Catherine, I think you have your report . . ."

"Yes, I did a detailed analysis of the blood spatter and some interesting things came up. Not what I expected at all."

Bert and Dennis were looking at me expectantly, Stuart, head lowered as usual, seemed to be busy doing something with his laptop—downloading porno, no doubt.

I took a deep breath and tried not to think about how much the murdered woman looked like me, and switched into full business mode. For the next half hour I gave them my full report, afterwards there was silence around the table.

Finally Dennis broke in, "The killer cut her face off after she was dead—then he beat her? He began using a hammer then switched to his fists? I don't believe it. Bert, what the hell is going on here?"

Bert seemed surprised at the question, his mind may have been wandering, it was so unlike him. He said, "I've never seen this extent of anger before, or such hatred in any of our cases. We're looking at someone very intelligent and very seriously enraged."

"What about . . . I mean . . ." Stuart began, "The fact that the victim looks so much like Catherine? I mean, shouldn't we be concerned about that?"

Dennis shrugged, "I don't think it means much. Coincidence, that's all."

I didn't say a word but I could feel Stuart's eyes upon me.

Finally Bert spoke up, "It's something we should keep in mind, but it's way too early to get bogged down in suppositions and conspiracy theories. We need to stick with the hard facts we know and find this killer before he kills again."

Bert looked at me and a playful smile crossed his lips. Stuart looked at me also but said nothing.

I nodded at Bert. I guess that settled that. Bert wasn't buying the look-alike theory.

Stuart's eyes left me and shot to Bert. "You think he's going to kill again?"

"Yes, numbnuts," Dennis interjected, allowing his exasperation to flower. "That's the pattern. Right, Bert?"

Bert, to his credit didn't continue Dennis' tone. "Unfortunately, that appears to be so. This kind of intelligent and highly organized killer does what he does for a reason—his reason doesn't have to make sense to us and usually doesn't—but it makes sense to him. He's trying to make a point, and we have to find out what the origin of that point could be."

That seemed to be that.

Until the next dead woman showed up. Jane Doe #2.

This time the face was still attached, but she'd been beaten and battered so any visual identification was impossible. She was also hog-tied and left in an almost identical position as Roberta Torres, leaving little doubt this was the work of the same killer. If I felt a little 'uneasy' before when the victim turned out to resemble me, you could say I was now terrified when I learned that the new woman also looked like me.

And she looked amazingly like me! What the hell did that mean? What it meant, I didn't even what to think about. I was terrified. She was the same size, the same body type as me. It was uncanny and scary. I had that creepy feeling again, but this time squared. I told myself it meant nothing, just some weird coincidence. I knew I looked like a lot of women and a lot of women looked like me. But I still couldn't shake a creepy feeling like the murderer was watching me, maybe even talking to me through this murder, maybe even through the blood spatter.

Roberta Torres was dead, and now this new woman, but I had the nagging thought that he hadn't really wanted to kill her—he'd wanted to kill *me*. I know it was crazy, but while my mind told me one thing my feelings told me another. And I was scared. I was afraid that the face of the girl combined with the blood spatter told me a killer was watching me, following me, mocking me!

"Well, I think he's trying to build himself up to do something, something that he might not want to do, but something that is much, much worse," Stuart added.

"Like what?" Dennis asked defiantly.

"Like, maybe kill Catherine!" Stuart blurted.

Both Dennis and Bert just laughed at the little computer geek but I felt a cold chill come over me now, and noticed that Stuart was looking at me intently.

Later on, when Dennis and Stuart went out to get our lunch I confided in Bert about my unease about Stuart.

"He's really getting on my nerves," I said, almost feeling like a rat talking about my co-worker behind his back, but I didn't care that much now about protocol or office politics.

"Yeah, well, that last comment he made, it was totally uncalled for. Did it scare you, Catherine?"

"Well . . ."

"I mean, the fact of what he said, that the killer might be after you," Bert said seriously, looking into my eyes.

"Yes, yes of course it scared me. It made me very uncomfortable."

Bert didn't reply right away.

"Did you ever talk to him, Bert?"

"I laid down the law, threatened him with possible sexual harassment, told him his sick little twisted obsession was not appreciated, but he denied it all."

"Denied it?"

"He told me he thinks he is in love with you but doesn't know how to show or express his love. It was pathetic, actually."

"Oh, God!"

"Well, I told him he better not try anything with you, and that it had better not affect his work performance. Anyway, I think I'm going to put in a request to get him off the team. Dennis can't stand him. You're scared of him . . ."

"Well, not scared, but just . . . he seems so weird sometimes . . ."

"Scared, I think, Catherine, I can see the fear in you. He's gone in a few weeks, once the paperwork clears."

I felt better until Stuart asked to speak to me alone. Well, he didn't exactly ask me, it was through a note. We were finishing up another meeting when I saw it mixed in with my papers. I had no idea at first where it had come from, but once I realized it was from Stuart I became immediately nervous. How had he gotten the note in my papers without my knowledge? I held my panic, retraced the last few hours. I had left the room for a Coke. I left again to use the rest room. I sighed, it wasn't that weird, just strange. I opened the note when no one was looking. It said, "Catherine, don't say anything to Bert or Dennis, but I have something important to tell you that is for your ears alone. I will come to your place tonight, at 10 PM. Stuart."

Well, I hardly knew what to make of it. I thought it was merely his pathetic ploy to get into my bedroom once we'd finished up our round of meetings for the evening. It wasn't going to work, of course. And if he thought he was going to get anything in the way of sexual favors, the boy had another think coming. Stuart would find that he'd have a sexual harassment suit on him faster than white on rice. If he planned something more sinister—I had my service gun to take care of that . . .

Just before 10 PM my home phone rang. It was Bert. He wanted to come by right away and discuss something that he said was very important. I thought of Stuart and that he was coming by at the same time. This could become difficult.

"Can't it wait until tomorrow, Bert?" I asked.

"I'm afraid not, Catherine, it's about Stuart." His silence after he'd said this was ominous.

"Stuart?" I said, carefully. I wanted to tell Bert that Stuart would be here any minute, that he had slipped me a note to meet me here at 10 PM also, but something made me hold back. I don't know what it was exactly, I certainly can't explain it. Maybe I didn't want Bert to know I had gone behind his back to meet with Stuart alone? It was probably just guilt from not telling Bert or Dennis as I should have done.

"So what about Stuart?" I asked.

"Can I come over?" Bert said. "It's important, Catherine."

"Sure, Bert, come over," I said, knowing somehow that Stuart would never have the guts to harm me now. If he was planning to do something tonight, he'd never try it now, not with Bert here.

When he came in Bert looked tired and nervous, ill at ease, like I'd never seen him before. "I wanted to tell you face-to-face, I think Stuart's problem, his obsession with you, may have turned very . . . unhealthy." AM

"What do you mean?" I asked.

"I believe he's become dangerous, Catherine, and that he wants to do you ill," Bert said carefully.

"Stuart, do me ill? You really think he's dangerous?"

"He's obsessed with you, and well . . ."

"What are you trying to tell me, Bert?"

Bert signed, "I found something in his papers. I think Stuart could be the person responsible for the murder of Roberta Torres, and Jane Doe #2."

That admission hung in the air between us like an elephant about to do a double somersault on a trapeze right there in my living room.

Finally I said, "I can't believe he's capable of murder."

"Well, I couldn't either, at first," Bert added. Then he pulled out some papers and set them down on the coffee table in front of me. "Look at these."

I stared at the photos, many were full facial close-ups of Roberta Torres, police evidence taken from old family photos. Nothing special about that. However, next were similar photos of me! Not stock Department photos either, but all surreptitiously taken, without my knowledge or consent.

"He's been stalking you, Catherine."

"That little geek's been talking pictures of me!"

"It gets worse, I'm afraid," Bert added, handing me a composite photo that showed my face superimposed upon that of Roberta Torres, there were cross hatch marks and notes in the margins in Stuart's own hand. The images had obviously been printed from a file in his computer. Was this what Stuart had been working on during our meetings?

I felt a sudden chill, "Oh, Bert, Jesus!"

Bert pointed to a pen scrawl on the photo at the bottom that read, "The first one was a warning to let out the rage and scare her—the second was just for fun—but the next one to be killed will be Catherine."

I felt dizzy, terrified. If Bert hadn't come here with this, I'd be with Stuart now and vulnerable. Then who knew what he'd do to me. Maybe it wasn't *only* sex he was after? Maybe it was more, to hurt me, or my death? It was all so sickening, but could he be that twisted? That obsessed? Stuart was weird, but after the initial shock of what I'd just learned, I couldn't see him as a killer. But that didn't matter either. In our line of work we all knew that the most successful predators and killers always seemed to be the ones no one ever figured on. Meek little banal bastards, masters of camouflage. It was a sobering truth to me.

"I just thought you should know, Catherine," Bert added, bringing my thoughts back to him and the present. "We don't have much to go on. I'm sure Stuart could explain away any of this as notes taken during the investigation. A bit odd but nothing against the law and certainly nothing that could link him to murder. But we should keep a watch on him. And don't let him get you alone."

I nodded nervously.

"He's off the team for sure now, I'll make some calls tomorrow. I just thought you should know."

"Thanks, Bert," I stammered. This was all so unreal and scary.

He smiled, "I know you're distraught. You want me to stay a while, Catherine?"

I didn't reply right away, still trying to figure this all out in my confused mind.

Bert moved towards me and wrapped his arms around me, looking deeply into my eyes. I'm afraid I started to cry and he held me close.

"It's all right, Catherine. I'm here now, I won't let you go."

I tried to dry my tears, get my bearings.

Bert was holding me tight, so tight I could hardly move. I guess it was comforting at first, then . . . I felt his lips brush against my cheek, seeking my own lips, his hands cupped my breasts . . .

"Bert!"

"Catherine, I could take you now, make you feel what I feel, how long can we deny what we want from each other."

"No!"

He held me tighter, wet kisses on my lips.

"Stop it! Now!"

I tried to push him away but he was so much stronger than I.

"What the hell are you doing?" I said, "No!"

He wasn't stopping, I realized he wasn't even listening to me.

Then my anger surged ahead of my panic and I gave him a sharp knee into the crotch. Bert doubled over, his face full of pain, and something else . . .

"Get out! Get out now, dammit!"

Bert stood up as if the pain had suddenly disappeared and looked at me full of anger, with a rage I had never seen before. He walked toward me again, his eyes looked demonic.

I stepped back, drew my service weapon and leveled it at Bert's chest.

"One more step and I'll put a bullet into you, Bert! I swear it!"
That stopped him. Seeing the gun sobered him, I guess.
"Now get out! Get the hell out!"
When Bert was gone I sat down on my bed and cried. What was happening to my life? I was scared now, Bert had practically raped me! In fact, I was damn sure that he would have raped me, had I not drawn my service gun. I lay down and cried myself to sleep.

Next morning the phone rang early. It was Bert.
"What the hell do you want? You have some nerve . . ."
"Just listen to me, Catherine, please," Bert said calm, almost soothingly. "I'm sorry about last night, I made a bad mistake. It won't happen again. But I'm calling you because of the team, I need all team members to meet right away. We have a big problem. There was another murder last night and Stuart is missing. Please, Catherine, put your personal feelings aside and let's try to be professional."
"Look who's talking!"
"Okay, you're right and I deserve that, but I need you and Dennis working with me on this. I told you, we have another body, and Stuart is gone."
I sighed, a cauldron of conflicting emotions, with anger predominant. I struggled to keep it all in check and spoke in a very formal tone, "What time do you need me?"
"Be at the conference room by 10 AM," Bert said.
I didn't say another word, just hung up the phone. It was the only satisfaction I was likely to get for some time.
As I got dressed my mind was awhirl with what a mess this was becoming. Another dead girl? This was the third one! And where the hell was Stuart? Was he involved? Why didn't he show up last night? Had he actually killed this latest girl, perhaps realizing that Bert had the goods on him, and then fled? And what about Bert? He was my team leader—and a damn good one—but he was also a sexual harasser, at the very least. Perhaps even a rapist. It just seemed so muddled and on top of it all Bert was my supervisor in this operation and on the team. It made everything so complicated.

Dennis was at my place early. When he got out of his car he was furtive, agitated, it was barely 9 o'clock. He was an hour early. I was up and ready and we left immediately in his car. Once we got driving he got down to business.

"Will you tell me what the hell is going on?"

"What do you mean?" I said carefully, I wasn't sure how much he knew or whose side he was on.

"With Stuart, where is he?"

"I don't know. Didn't Bert fill you in?"

"Catherine, he didn't tell me a thing other than we had to be at the conference room at 10 AM sharp and that it was important. I haven't been able to get in touch with Stuart since last night. He doesn't answer any calls or pages."

"That's odd," I replied, at the same time trying not to let my imagination run away as I proceeded to fill in Dennis about the new body and the fact that Stuart was apparently missing.

As we entered police headquarters two uniform officers we didn't know came over to us, "Ms. Polk, Mr. Gomez, Stuart Rogers sent us to find you and escort you to the crime scene."

"Stuart sent you?"

The smaller cop nodded.

"Where's Bert, ah, Detective Singleton?" I asked.

"I don't know," the officer replied.

"He told me he was going to meet us here at 10 AM," Dennis added.

The big police sergeant shrugged his shoulders, "I don't know anything about that. I was ordered by Mr. Rogers to bring the two of you out to the murder scene."

Dennis shrugged," Okay, lead on."

I had a bad feeling about this. I looked over at Dennis and whispered, "Please, stay close to me, and keep a sharp eye on Stuart. Something's wrong and I don't know what it is."

Then we went with the two officers.

It was a short drive over to a bad part of town, and my mind was a cauldron of conflicting thoughts and fears. Dennis sat quietly, his usual taciturn self. The two uniform officers said nary a word other than Mr. Rogers would fill us in when we got to the crime scene. Stuart? Yeah, he'd fill us in, all right!

The crime scene was loaded with cops, brass and crime lab people. All the usual. The media hadn't arrived yet, but we could smell them on the way.

The sergeant brought us over to the body, where I found Stuart on his hands and knees, looking closely at the blood spatter and then entering data into his laptop. Where was Bert? I couldn't see him anywhere. I looked again at Stuart and a creepy feeling came over me. Had Stuart murdered Bert? Maybe because Bert had suspected him? I shook that thought out of my mind and forced myself into professional mode.

"Stuart, can you fill Dennis and me in?" I asked formally, as if I knew nothing about what was going on.

Stuart got up, brushed off his clothes. I could see the victim's body was located in a small ditch in what was an open lot full of refuse. This third victim—another female, of course—had apparently been beaten beyond any visual identification. My cursory view showed many blunt trauma injuries to the body and face, blood spatter in a conflicting array of patterns, but difficult to initially determine because of the rocky ground, grass and dirt that made up the crime scene. The patterns, in fact, seemed to conflict with what they were telling me. I could see this because of the indentations made into the soft ground around the victim by the knees of the killer. This showed me he had gone down to his knees to beat the woman viciously from at least four directions. Giving the killer at least four different points of origin for the murder. It was almost ritualistic. I gulped hard and wondered what Bert would make of it.

Stuart finally said, "I was beeped at 5 AM by the crime lab, they were on their way to the murder scene. A local precinct prowl car found the body about 4 AM. I've ID'd the body, from a purse found nearby. She is Susan Jennings, a local woman."

Police Commissioner, Jack Wallace, was close by and held out a newly faxed photo of the victim to show Dennis and me. That's when I fainted dead away. Susan Jennings was another woman who looked remarkably like me.

They brought me around fast enough. EMS guys were still there waiting on the lab people—who were waiting on us.

"You all right, Ms. Polk?" Commissioner Wallace said. He put a plastic cup with water to my lips. I drank slowly, hardly knowing I was being held by Stuart. His hand was softly caressing my forehead.

I jumped, startled at that. "I'm all right. Let me get up!"

Stuart moved off, but I still felt shivers all over my body from his being so close to me.

"So where the hell is Bert?" Dennis asked.

Stuart shrugged, "I'm sure he was beeped when I was. I haven't seen him since last night at the hotel bar. We had a few drinks before we went home. He left early, said he had a date with a hot chick," Stuart blushed.

"What time was that?" I asked curious now.

"About 9:30 or so," Stuart replied calmly. Bert had been at my door before ten. Could it be? I wondered if Stuart had been embellishing with the 'hot chick' remark. "I don't believe you, Stuart."

Stuart looked at me, and he actually looked hurt. That was strange.

Dennis spoke up then, "Nah, it's true, just the way Stuart said it. Bert left 9:45 to see some hot chick. I even asked if she had a friend for me and he said yeah, then he pointed to numbnuts there—to Stuart. I didn't understand what he meant by it though. Why?"

"Because Bert came to my apartment last night just before 10 o'clock, that's why." Then I looked at Stuart, said, "And why didn't you come to see me last night like you said in your note?"

Now Stuart not only turned red faced, but he grew tense. I'd obviously struck a nerve. He didn't reply, just gave me a sad, betrayed look.

"Well, Stuart?" I prompted, both Dennis and the Commissioner were looking at him now also.

"You weren't supposed to tell anyone," he said sadly, disappointment in his voice, but there was no anger.

"Well, I'm tired of all this bullshit, Stuart. I'm tired of you always looking at me like that, the staring, the stalking. You know, Bert showed me the photos that you took of me. I never knew about them. They were taken without my knowledge or permission. Did you take naked ones too!"

"Whoa! What the hell's going on here?" Dennis said, looking from Stuart to me and back at him. "Little guy, I knew you were horny for her, but this . . ."

"What is this all about?" Commissioner Wallace wanted to know now, I guess he could smell a possible lawsuit brewing against the department and wanted to head it off. We were beginning to draw a crowd. "You people should sort this out quietly. Use the prowl car over there. Get this personal stuff sorted out, privately—now! You know what I mean?"

I nodded, led Stuart and Dennis to the prowl car. We rolled up the windows. I sat in the driver's seat, Dennis beside me in the passenger side, Stuart in the back. I motioned for Dennis to keep his weapon ready.

"Okay, Stuart, it's private now, just you and me, like you wanted it last night. Forget about Dennis. Tell me what you wanted to tell me. And why did you take those photos of me? Why the stalking? Are you the killer?"

"Am I the . . .what? Killer! Of course not!" Stuart stammered in fear now.

I could see Dennis' finger on the trigger of his weapon, all he had to do was bring it up and shoot if Stuart tried anything weird.

"Then what the hell are you doing? Why did you want to see me last night? What was so damn important I couldn't tell anyone? And then you never showed—but Bert does!" I said, trying to hold back my anger.

"Bert really showed up? He actually came to your apartment?" Stuart said in surprise tinged with concern. Either he was the best actor I'd ever seen or really was surprised by Bert's visit to me the night before.

"Yes," I said forcefully, "and he almost raped me."

Dennis looked at me disbelieving. I nodded to him that it was true.

"I had to draw my service weapon on him, that's the only thing that stopped him from raping me," I added.

"That son of bitch!" Dennis growled.

I took out the composite photo showing my face juxtaposed over the face of Roberta Torres, "So what's this all about?"

Stuart blushed, "I'm sorry. I did take the photos without asking you. I do look at you, I like to look at you, Catherine, but I only took the photos because I had a theory about that girl looking so much like you. I'm afraid this latest murder proves that theory. These killings are moving in a line that leads to you. You are in great danger."

"Stuart?" Dennis asked suspiciously. "Where's Bert? Did you kill him?"

"Kill . . . Bert, of course not!"

I didn't know whether to believe him or not and I knew Dennis didn't believe him at all.

"Look, Catherine, I don't know what went on between you and Bert," Dennis said finally. "Lover's quarrels aren't my business."

"They're not lovers, idiot!" Stuart blurted, and while I could hear jealously in his voice there was also truth in his words. He was actually defending me.

"Well, I don't know or care, but if you killed Bert, you little weasel geek, I'll blow your freakin' brains out. I swear I'll find a way. You'll never see prison, Stuart!"

"Stop it!" I shouted.

Dennis continued to glare at Stuart but remained silent.

"Dennis," I asked, looking forcefully into his eyes, "Stuart didn't kill Bert. But maybe the real killer did."

That got his attention, as I had intended it to do. Stuart also looked at me curiously, and I could see that the little guy knew something he wasn't telling me. There was only one way to get it out of him.

"Dennis," I said calm, "It's okay now. Could you go and check the crime scene, I want to talk to Stuart alone for a minute."

"You sure?" Dennis said, making sure I got a look at his gun.

"Yes, I'll be fine," I replied with a confidence I did not entirely feel.

Dennis got up, reluctant, giving Stuart a look with the promise of cold, hard death in it if he even thought of hurting me.

I smiled at Dennis, "It will be okay."

When Dennis was gone I turned around, looking at Stuart carefully where he was seated in the back seat. I seemed to see him really for the first time then. We were alone. It was quiet. There was an almost peaceful feeling between us. He was relaxed now, happy we were alone. I think he was enjoying it.

"Stuart, tell me what's inside you that you couldn't tell me. I want to know what you are holding inside," I asked softly.

Stuart smiled, looking into my eyes with a warmth I'd never seen before from him, and I knew then he truly cared for me. He sighed, "If I ever thought you were in imminent danger, Catherine, I would lay down my life for you. I thought the best way to protect you was to find the killer. I was coming over to give you my theory . . ."

"Why didn't you come over then?"

"Bert. He told me I wasn't keeping up with the team—that I needed to organize the files and prepare a presentation for Wallace today—or he'd place a letter of warning in my file. I was out all night in the office getting it ready."

I nodded, waiting for him to continue.

Stuart shuffled in the seat uncomfortably, "I guess I was scared. I lost my nerve. I realized you would probably just laugh at me if I told you my theory. After all, I'm the computer guy, I set software parameters and type in the data so you guys can form the theories and . . ."

"And what?"

"I also wanted to tell you how I felt about you . . ."

I hardly knew what to say but I could see now that this man wasn't a killer and I needed to find out more.

"But why me, Stuart? There's so many better-looking women out there, unattached, looking for a good man like you. You make good money, have a good job. Why me?"

Stuart looked me in the eyes, bold and warm, "I'm not very good with people, worse with women, I guess. I've been hurt in the past, Catherine, I'll tell you honestly, and that has made me very careful and cautious. The truth is, I'd given up on women for years, concentrated on my work. That's been rewarding, fascinating, sometimes. Then when they set up the team and we worked together . . ."

"Stuart, since we've worked together you've hardly said more than a dozen non-business words to me over the entire year. And, well, you keep looking at me. I've caught you, and it makes me nervous."

"I know, and I'm sorry," Stuart continued. "But sometimes when you work close with someone you get to see the real person, Catherine. I very much respect and admire you. I'm sorry, but I couldn't help but fall in love with such a woman."

I couldn't help but smile at him, he was like a lost puppy, "Don't be sorry, don't ever be sorry for loving someone."

"I screwed this up so badly. I wanted to tell you my feelings last night, but they were all mixed up with this case, and Bert, and what I'd discovered in the photos."

"Yes, it's become quite a mess."

"I won't bother you any more, Catherine. In fact, I put in for a transfer last week. I've just been waiting for the paper work to come through. I was gonna tell you that last night, too."

"You put in for a . . .*not* Bert?"

"No, but I told Bert last week, I figured as team leader he should know. I didn't say anything to Dennis or you about it. Frankly, I didn't think anyone cared if I left."

"Stuart, you have to stay on the team and we have to solve these murders."

"I don't know, Catherine. It's hard for me to be here with you, to work with you and all . . . I know there's no chance for me with you, so maybe I should just go . . ."

I don't know why I said it but he'd touched me somehow, so I said, "Stuart, you're a good man, an intelligent man, don't sell yourself short."

He looked at me and I smiled at him, and I saw the hope in his face. I liked what I saw there, he was a good man. Not strong, not perfect, but true. I realized suddenly, I actually liked Stuart. I didn't understand him all that much, but that didn't seem to matter as much now.

He smiled then, his face brightening, as I'd never seen it before. He actually laughed. It was a warm and infectious laugh. Truth be told, when he looked at me in that warm way of his, he really looked quite attractive.

I shook my head to break the mood, we had to get back to work and where was Bert and what was he up to?

"Do you have any idea where Bert could be or what he could be doing?" I asked.

Stuart shook his head, then looked up as someone was knocking on the glass of the rear window of the prowl car to get our attention. I saw an image blurred and thought it was Dennis, but it was Bert!

"Come on you two, we have work to do," then he was off talking to Dennis and Commissioner Wallace.

Stuart and I quickly left the car to join them.

Once there was a lapse in the conversation, I said, "Bert, where the hell were you?"

Bert just smiled, "Police business, Catherine."

I looked at Commissioner Wallace, he had a grim look on his face. "I sent him out, Catherine," Wallace said. "Bert had a hunch about the identity of the killer and I think it has proved true. In fact, we're about to make an arrest in the case right now."

I looked at Bert and he had a wicked grin on his face.

I looked at Dennis and he just looked away, he couldn't meet my eyes.

"What the hell is going on here?"

Wallace called over two uniform officers and asked them to draw their service weapons, and Bert and Dennis drew their weapons as well. They all aimed them at Stuart.

Bert said, "Stuart, hand over your weapon and assume the position!"

"What?" Stuart stammered taken totally off guard.

"Stuart Rogers, you are under arrest for the murder of Roberta Torres," Wallace said, then he began reading him his rights as Bert took his gun and handcuffed him.

Stuart stood frozen and gave no resistance. I was enraged and said so.

"This is outrageous!" I cried. "Stuart's no killer!"

I watched dazed as Stuart was placed in a prowl car and soon taken away to a jail cell downtown.

I looked at Commissioner Wallace, Bert, "You have the wrong man!"

"Evidence was found at Stuart's apartment, Catherine," Wallace stepped in with the official version. "That's what Bert was doing this morning, executing a search warrant."

"I'm sorry, Catherine. This is hard for all of us. He was a member of our team, but he has problems, serious problems," Bert said softly with just a tinge of victory.

"I don't believe this shit," Dennis added, gruffly. "He's a cop for christsakes!"

"Believe it, Gomez," Wallace added. "We have the evidence, victim clothing, jewelry, all found at Stuart Rogers' place of residence. It pretty well conclusively links him to the murder."

"Not if it was planted!" I barked angry and full of rage.

"Now, Catherine!" Bert said softly, smoothly.

"Ms. Polk," Wallace said, "I understand your frustration, believe me we all feel it. I approved Stuart Rogers for this team, just as I did each one of you. I too feel your sense of his betrayal of us."

"His betrayal of us? What about *our* betrayal of *him*? He's not a killer!"

"Then who is?" Bert said with a confident smirk

I looked at him sharply, I knew I couldn't just walk into his trap. By making unsubstantiated statements in front of the Commissioner I'd look like a kook and that could only hurt Stuart's chances. Wallace would never believe any accusation against Bert without hard evidence. Right now, the evidence showed Stuart was the killer. I bit my tongue and saw a thin satisfied smile cross Bert's lips.

"Well, Catherine? If you have another theory or some other evidence let us hear it now," Wallace prompted, impatient.

I looked at Dennis, he just shook his head.

"No, I don't have anything," I said. "Not yet."

The phone rang and rang.

"Come on, pick up!"

"Hello?" said a man at the other end of the line.

"Dennis?"

"Yeah, that you Catherine?"

"Yes." I took a deep breath. I was determined to tell him what I had on my mind trying to think of the best way to say it. Finally I just blurted it out. "This is bullshit! Stuart didn't do it!"

There was a long silence from the other end of the line.

Finally, skeptical, "So you say."

"Yes."

"Evidence says he did do it."

"It was planted!" I snapped back.

"That's your theory?" Dennis asked, surprised, almost laughing at me.

"It's not finished yet, I'm still working on it," I said, then it came to me. "We have to get in and see Stuart. He has a theory but never told me what it was. Maybe he can put the pieces of the puzzle together."

"I don't know," Dennis replied, still skeptical.

"We're still a team, Dennis. Can we get in to see Stuart?"

"That shouldn't be hard," Dennis replied, "but I don't know if it is worth the trouble. Wallace seems to think they've got Stuart dead to rights."

"Yeah, on evidence Bert planted!"

"How can you be so sure of that, Catherine?"

"Because I know Bert and I know Stuart," I said. "And Dennis, you know them too. Come on, think about it!"

"I don't know," he replied hesitantly. "Why would Bert plant evidence?"

I had no reason, but I had to think fast. "This is a big case? If he solves it he's the hero? Maybe he's jealous of Stuart because of me?"

"That's ridiculous—you better have more than that!"

"Come on, come with me! At least let's see Stuart, give him a chance to tell us his side of it."

"Yeah, I guess we owe the little numbnuts that much."

"I'll pick you up. Be ready tomorrow morning at nine sharp."

Stuart was alone in a holding cell at police headquarters. He was morose, feeling betrayed and scared, looking at a long term in prison.

"Do you know what they have on me?" he asked, he hadn't seen a lawyer yet and I could hear the desperation in his voice.

"Wallace and Bert won't show us the evidence, they won't talk about it other than to say that it was personal items of the Torres girl. Jewelry and some clothing. Wallace is supposed to make a statement to the media later today."

"Then I'm sunk!" Stuart collapsed on the hard jail bed of his cell.

Dennis didn't say a word and I was stymied.

"We have to do something, Stuart. Tell us everything you suspect, your theory. What did you find out?" I asked quickly.

"I think Bert is the killer . . ."

Dennis and I looked at each other.

"Let's get the fuck outta here!" Dennis growled, he called for the guard.

"I knew you wouldn't believe me, that's why I didn't tell you," Stuart said.

"You're right!" Dennis shouted, angry now.

"No wait!" I cried, firmly holding Dennis back, as I looked at Stuart. "Why do you think that?"

"I put together the figures you gave me on the directionality of the blood spatter. The tails indicate direction and I created a computer model to recreate the crime virtually. The angle between the long axis of the bloodstains and a predetermined line on the plane of the target surface—in this case Roberta Torres—gives us some added information on the way the killer performed the murder, the angles of attack, his size, weight. When I put Bert in the model—he fit perfect."

I looked at Dennis, "That would explain how the evidence got into Stuart's apartment."

Dennis wasn't admitting it but I could see he was interested now.

I looked at Stuart and hugged him, "That could work, now if we can convince Wallace."

Dennis shook his head, "You'll have to prove Bert planted that evidence first—or Wallace won't bite. He's an old-time copper. But I have a hunch. If Bert did plant that evidence, that means he took if from the crime scene after the crime was committed—so he might have more. More of the girl's clothing or jewelry he kept as trophies. Somewhere. Hidden."

"It could be—it fits the pattern of this kind of killer," Stuart said hopefully.

"We'll just have to find it, Dennis," I said.

"If it exists, Catherine."

"Yes, if it exists," I replied thoughtfully.

"This is so totally illegal, Catherine. We'll not only get kicked off the team, we'll be fired from the Department and maybe even get jail time," Dennis said, seriously concerned.

"Yes, and Stuart could spend his life in prison," I said sternly, adding, "And worse, a killer will be free and out there—a cop. Bert would have effective immunity, free to kill again. How many more victims, Dennis?"

My partner nodded solemnly, "I don't like this but if Bert's got trophies—then he's the killer. So I guess we'll find out whether or not your theory is true or not today."

Easier said than done. Bert's apartment was clean. I mean really clean, well-ordered and spotless. No garbage, no papers, no files. It didn't even have much dust.

"Doesn't even look like he lives here," Dennis said perplexed. "I'm a guy, you know, we're slobs at heart. My place has beer bottles, pizza boxes left on the table, dirty clothes on the floor, a pile of dishes in the sink. This place is spotless. It's like he doesn't live here at all."

"Maybe that's because he doesn't live here," I said thinking it out.

"Yeah, he has to have some other place, some place more personal. But where the hell is that?" Dennis blurted.

"I don't know."

"Think, girl! If Bert's got another place, where could it be? A girl friend's house? Her apartment?"

"No, he's a rapist, freak at heart, he couldn't keep a real relationship for long. Anyway, it could be risky."

"He's a slick dude though," Dennis countered, which was true.

I could see Bert having some naïve woman on the hook somewhere—but that could cause complications. Bert didn't seem like the type to put up with complications.

"What about a brother or sister?" Dennis offered.

"No brother. There's a sister, but she's out of state."

"Well?" Dennis prompted. "Parents still living?"

"Father's dead, but his mother is still alive. She's in a nursing home, though."

"That won't work," Dennis said. "Too dangerous to hide this kind of stuff there."

"If he put the mom in a nursing home, maybe she had a house of her own at some point? Maybe it wasn't sold. That could be the place we need to search."

Dennis looked at me shaking his head, "Babe, I think you got it."

We did the requisite research on Bert. We knew what we were looking for. It didn't take us long to pin-point a one family house in the old Polish section of town that seemed just right.

The street was in one of those everyone-minds-their-own-business parts of town—or you could end up hurt.

It was dark inside and quiet as we entered the house. I drew my weapon, looked at Dennis, "If Bert's our guy, he's murdered three woman so far, cut the face off one, beat them viciously, framed Stuart, he's extremely dangerous."

Dennis nodded, he didn't need to be reminded, he drew his weapon also.

The house was dark. We kept the lights off and just used a searchlight. It was an old house. Our steps creaking on the floorboards. Shadows played upon the walls all around us. It was spooky.

"Looks like he hasn't changed the place at all since the parents left," I said softly.

"Where do we look?" Dennis asked, the house was big.

"I don't know. Bert grew up here, right? He probably had his own room as a kid," I said.

"Yeah, upstairs. Let's try it."

We walked upstairs. We found what looked like a boys room at the end of the hall. There, on the outside of the door was what looked like some kind of Halloween mask. When we got closer we saw that it was the face of Roberta Torres.

"Damn!" Dennis whispered.

I had to force down bile so I would not puke right then and there.

I felt a chill down my spine. Bert really was the killer! A part of me had never truly believed it before. Had never wanted to believe it of a cop. Now I knew it was true. I was scared, frozen in front of the closed door to a child's bedroom. Scared of what we'd find inside.

Dennis led the way, opening the unlocked door slowly, carefully. It creaked, the sounds seeming to us so loud in the total silence. Dennis entered, I was right behind him, our weapons out and ready. My hand was shaking. The room was dark. Pitch black. There was a terrible odor.

Suddenly a loud dull thud hit Dennis and I saw him drop to the ground, his gun clattering across the floor. Then I felt hard powerful hands upon me, my gun wrenched from my grasp, and rope quickly tied around me. I was hurled to the ground hard, a large and heavy figure tying my arms behind my back, my legs bent back and up behind me hard and tight and tied to my wrists.

Oh my God, I was being hog-tied!

Then I saw the same was being done to Dennis. When he was done, our attacker got up and turned on the light in the room. It was Bert, all dressed in his work suit, smiling at me with that demonic grin. He held Dennis' and my gun.

"Hello, Catherine. I knew you would come. I knew you couldn't resist," he said.

I looked from Bert's confident face over to Dennis on the floor beside me. He was effectively tied, out cold or dead. I couldn't tell which. I saw blood coming from his head. I looked back up at Bert, "What have you done?"

Bert didn't say a word, he just stared at me. It was that same look from those demonic eyes that I'd seen when he'd attempted to rape me days ago.

"What are you doing, Bert? Let me go! You have to let me go! Dennis is hurt!"

I looked around the room, a boys room full of boys things from his youth—but those were all covered in layers of dust now, not having been touched for years. The newer more recent additions to the room were very different: bloody women's clothing, large color gruesome crime scene photos—I recognized some of them from our own murder books—and photos of myself. They were blown up large, like posters. They showed me in shots taken from various locations, including in my own apartment! Some were nudes. My mind reeled at how he had come by them—I didn't have to connect the dots. I felt ill.

I puked then. Coughing and retching all over myself and the floor. Crying and coughing and shaking with fear. The smell was awful. It soon led to dry heaves once I was empty inside.

Bert took out a handkerchief and wiped the vomit from my face and chin. Delicately, almost lovingly.

I looked up at him, trying to get control of myself.

He was smiling. He was enjoying this!

"You fucking bastard!"

He was a stone. The smile melted from his face. It was a dangerous look.

"What kind of monster are you to do this?"

He didn't say a word.

"Answer me, you bastard! You coward!"

Bert stared down at me intently. It was as if his eyes were trying to penetrate my soul.

"I knew you would come to me, Catherine. I knew you would figure it out once I set up that little geek, Stuart. Now I have you here, all to myself, like I always wanted. You see, now I can do anything I want to you."

"Why? You're a cop, highly trained, educated, why are you doing this?"

"Fair enough, you should know. I am a cop, trained at Quantico, highly educated—all that says, Catherine, is that I fit—the profile."

"But why me?"

"Why, indeed," he looked down at me carefully, studying me. "I don't know if I can explain this, it's hardly normal, I know. One reason I became a cop, took the courses, went to Quantico, abnormal behavior and serial killer profiling, was that I was looking for answers."

"What answers!" I yelled.

He looked off into space then, somewhere else, "Mother has been ill. She went downhill soon after father died. Father died violently. He deserved it. But it got so bad I had to place her in a home. I think she's dying."

"What the hell does this have to do with me!"

"She's old now, Catherine, very old. But she was young once, very young and vibrant, just like you are."

"Jesus!"

"When you came on the team last year I hardly knew what to make of it. It was an incredible shock to me. You and her. Looking so much alike. I immediately loved you and hated you at the same time. I think it may have unnerved me. It was certainly very disturbing. And then there was that little twerp, Stuart, always talking about you to me, asking about you, his obvious infatuation for you was just disgusting. It nauseated me. I hated it. Hated him. Hated you. I think I hated you even more than I hated her because of what you were doing to me."

"Bert, stop it!"

He went over to the windowsill and brought over a framed photo. He put it in front of my face so I could see it clearly. It was another photo of me! It was an old time photo in an old frame, but it was me. Then as I looked closely at it a dread feeling came over me. It wasn't me at all! It was just some woman from sixty or seventy years ago who looked like me. Exactly like me! Same face, same hairstyle, same eyes, lips, nose.

"My mother, many years ago, Catherine."

I hardly knew what to think but I knew I had to say something. "Bert, you can't do this. You need help. I can help you. You have to let Dennis and me go. We can get you the help you need."

"It's too late for that, Catherine. I know I'm not . . . normal. That used to bother me once, but now I've learned to embrace the fact that I am . . . different. And I am not going to prison. Now, I just have to get rid of the evidence—you and Dennis—and let Stuart take the fall. Then it will all be over. Then I can go away and everything will be forgotten. I'm . . . sorry . . . ."

"No!"

"I'll shoot you with Dennis' gun, and Dennis with your gun. Then stage the scene. After a day or so, I'll come here to close up my mother's house and find you both. It will be a tragic shame. Don't you think?"

"I think not, Bert!" a deep voice boomed from the hall. It was Commissioner Wallace and he had his gun out and aimed at Bert—and right beside him were two sharpshooters from the Department SWAT team.

Bert wheeled and fired, and so did Wallace and the two sharpshooters. Bert's slug entered the doorjamb right by Wallace's head. Wallace's slugs went wide. But the sharpshooters lived up to their billing, they put a slug nice and neat right into Bert's forehead, and another in the center of his chest. Bert looked surprised, eyes wide as he fell down to the floor dead.

I cried as Wallace and his men came over and untied me and Dennis, others secured Bert's body. Bert was dead at the scene, Dennis had a bad head wound but he'd survive. I was just getting over being terrified within an inch of my life.

The emergency service guys got there soon. They came in with Stuart behind them. He was fearful but relief was spreading across his face when he saw me. I was surprised but happy to see him.

"Catherine!" he shouted, coming closer, hugging me gently but with warmth.

I looked at Commissioner Wallace and then Stuart.

"What? How?"

"I'm not as much of a bull-headed old copper as you might think, Ms. Polk." Wallace said. "I can smell a setup. Bert being too damn helpful on the case. Everything just so damn pat for Stuart being the killer."

I nodded, sighing in relief with new understanding.

Wallace looked at Stuart, then back at me, adding, "I had my suspicions. I had a tail put on you and Dennis. When you both showed up at Bert's apartment I knew something was up. When you came out here and found this house I figured there might be more to this than met the eye. The rest, as they say, is history."

They took out Bert's body then and Dennis was helped into an ambulance.

Wallace looked around the room, saw the victim's face hanging from the door, more victim clothing, blown-up photos of me and the murdered women, "Damn shame, he was a great cop but he had serious problems. Serious problems he let get the better of him."

Well, that was certainly the understatement of the year, but I kept mum.

Stuart and I walked out of the room together, silent, thoughtful. We couldn't wait to get out of that house.

"I'm glad you're cleared now," I said finally, as we approached the stairway on our way out.

Stuart smiled, then laughed nervously, "So am I."

"Well, we did end up solving this case," I added, for lack of anything else to say.

"Yeah, I guess."

"So I hope you'll stay on the team, Stuart. We need you. I need you."

"Polk! I need both of you!" Wallace barked from the doorway. "You're taking over the team from here on. Rogers, you'll help her. We'll discuss the details tomorrow. My office, 8 am, sharp! Now go on home and get some rest. You deserve it."

NO SATISFACTION

A VIC POWERS STORY

IT WAS A HOT SUMMER MORNING and I was doing the beach thing like I do every day now. It's what people with nothing to do, do these days. So I lay out in a chair on the sand taking the sun, oiled up like a greased pig. Ex-pig that is, I'd recently been "retired" from the force after what had happened with my partner's killer. Mandatory retirement. I had no choice. I'd shown "poor judgment" in what I'd done by chaining Larry's killer in his back yard so his wife and kids could have a go at him. It was a stupid thing to do. I know that now, but it seemed so right then. I'd lost my pension over it but didn't get the jail time. That's all in the past now, it's month's back in my previous life. Now I just hang here at Lude Beach during the day with all the off-duty cops, firemen, night workers at the Post Office, school kids off for the summer, bored housewives, and the other broken badges with nothing going for them anymore since they were thrown off the force. Most of them do stuff at night, I even had an okay bouncing job at a Bay Ridge bar, but the days of summer are beach days and Lude Beach was the place for me.

It's been called Lude Beach for more than 30 years; it's the only white section at Coney Island, all the way at the extreme left. Some people that don't know call it Brighton. It's fairly clean and crime free. With so many damn off-duty cops, firemen, correction officers and court officers hanging there, you can imagine we don't have much trouble—except what we ourselves make. And take care of ourselves. But believe me, that's enough.

I wiped the sweat off my face. Sucked down another cold brew from the cooler beside me as I watched all the bikini girls. They were all over the place. It was a good day. It was dreamlike. The sun, the sand, the heat, the girls. Love the damn beach.

Lude Beach wasn't a good place for an outsider to pick up a girl. There were a lot of cliques, a lot of different groups. Everyone knows everyone else. Outsiders stay outside. Insiders got it made.

There was this Israeli girl today that was driving the whole beach crazy. Every male here today had hot flashes and it had absolutely nothing to do with the searing rays beating down at them from the fiery overhead sun. Her name was Juna and she'd had a spread in Penthouse recently. She was really something. Long, curly brown hair, gorgeous smiling face, dark sun-tanned skin, browned to perfection, hot oily body in one of those leopard-skin bikinis right out of Tarzan and Jane.

She had five guys following her around the beach like lap dogs. They only wished. It was like a damn parade. I laughed. She wasn't attainable, by them, or me. That kind of stuff only goes to the big money. I finished my beer and turned over on my side, my eyes looking up into the pock-marked face of Gino Pintazzi. Another damn broken badge.

"Hey, Powers, word is you're looking for work?"

"I take my own jobs," I told him. "Now go away."

"Don't be a hardhead. Everyone knows how bad it's been for you, Larry killed and all. You being the dumb one."

I shot him a look.

"No sweat, Powers, I ain't here for trouble. We're all behind you for what you did, having those dogs grind up Larry's killer into low-grade Alpo was cool stuff."

"Look, shithead, you got me all wrong. But even if I was hard up for work, I wouldn't bother with the likes of you and the gangsters you hang with."

Pintazzi bristled but then smiled confidently, flexing his muscles like some stupid beach dink trying to impress a broad, thinking he was hot stuff on muscle beach.

"Think you're a wise guy, Powers! Well, I got news for you, you're just another broken badge. Just like me and them guys there, all trying to make out the best we can."

I got out of the chair. I stood up tall, looked Pintazzi right in the eye. "You're wrong, Pintazzi, I may be a broken badge, but I'm not like you and your gang. I lost my job on the force for being stupid, for doing unstable things, but you and your boys got kicked off because you were on the take. You're nothing better than the criminals Larry and I used to bust *every fucking day!"*

Pintazzi growled, glowed red in the face.

"Don't ever put yourself or those bags of shit you hang with in the same category as me. And especially Larry. I can be called a lot of things, but crooked was never one of them. You guys are lucky as hell to be out here on the beach. You should be doing prison time. Now get the fuck out of my face!"

"You're a moron, Powers! A loser!" His face glowed red, the bright sunlight making it appear as though he was boiling over inside. "Too bad no one didn't frag your fucking ass when you was a cop—like we did them do-good boy officers in 'Nam. They thought they was going to run things by the book too. We showed them. You're another loser, Powers, another go-nowhere fool."

Well, I couldn't let that pass. "I've taken all I'm going to take from you. Get the message, asshole!"

Pintazzi didn't get the message. I made sure he felt it. My fist came up in a wild swing that slammed into his face like a cement mixer. Blood sprayed all around. Pouring out of his nose now. Out of his lip. He was down in the sand, coughing, spitting, more blood, a little white nugget. One of his teeth.

I picked up my stuff and moved to another part of the beach where it was less crowded. I nursed my hand by sticking it in the ice in the cooler. It was a lot less messed up than Pintazzi's face. My hand came out of the cooler clutching a cold beer. I popped the top. I drank it down, the best damn beer I've had in a long time. A satisfying brew.

I was away from the rocks now, back by the wall with the wrinkled-up old folks. It was quiet, no morons around to bust my chops. I put the radio on, it was playing "Satisfaction."

What a damn true song! I cracked open another beer as a dressed-up young woman came over to strike up a conversation. She was pretty cute, your basic Brooklyn bimbolina, but she also had rough eyes with a lot of hurt in them. Trouble in a blue dress.

She said, "Mr. Powers, I was referred to you by a cop friend who said you'd be at the beach today and might help me."

"I have no friends on the force. Now go away and leave me alone, I'm not interested in helping the world."

She stood her ground. Guts or stupidity. I couldn't tell which. Didn't much care either. "Then fuck the world, just help me. I want you to do something for me."

I smiled, "Girl, everyone wants me to do something for them. Now get lost."

"I hear you're a private detective?"

"No."

"I have money," and she showed me five hundred-dollar bills. New. Crisp.

I admit I was interested. "Yeah so, who do I have to kill?" I said it kidding. It was a joke.

She got all serious and said, "I don't want you to kill him, just beat him up, beat the shit out of him. Like he did to me."

This is just what I didn't need. Boyfriend-girlfriend crap. To get in the middle of that could be a hell of a lot more costly than a short gain of a measly five hundred bucks. People get killed that way.

"Look, girly, what you want is a thug, a guy who breaks bones for a living. Not me."

"Please, Mr. Powers," she opened the top buttons of her shirt, pulling it low on her shoulders, turned around to show me the marks. Black and blue, some cuts, wounds still fresh. Recent. Ugly. She hiked up her skirt, this was with some of the old people looking on.

"Mind your own damn business, you old bastards!" I barked.

They turned away.

The girl continued. Her skirt was high, thighs full of welts. Real ugly shit.

"He never does my face," she said it proud.

I popped another beer. I felt like puking all over the sand. Instead I chugged it down. What can you say.

"So what the hell you want me to do?"

"Take care of him, like I said. Don't kill him, just teach him a lesson."

"No way. Look, I sympathize with you, but I don't want any part of this. Go to the cops. That's what the idiots are paid for. They'll hold your hand. Put your boyfriend in jail, if that's what you really want. There's women's groups to help you, courts might give you action. The justice system will prevail. Just get the fuck outta my face!"

She was gone. My day was turning into real shit. I looked around on the beach for Juna the Israeli vixen. She was nowhere in sight. Too bad, I could have used a look at heaven just then. I'd seen her *Penthouse* pics, real nice, way over my head though. Hell, if she'd been dead six months I still couldn't get a girl as fine as her. Maybe someday I'll learn looks aren't everything in a woman. Maybe. Someday.

I didn't see Juna anywhere, but I spotted that ball-busting moron Gino Pintazzi talking tough to a bunch of other broken badges and losers I always tried to stay away from. Every other minute he'd crack open another beer and shout purple as he barked at his buddies. I knew the shit was coming when he started barking so loud his big mouth drowned out all the talk and radios on the beach. Then he pointed at me and started to come over. A bunch of his boys came with him.

I finished my beer. Broke the bottom of the bottle against the cooler. The jagged glass would make a good weapon if it came to it. Christ, I felt like a damn punk in some grade B West Side Story, but I didn't have my gun, and I saw trouble on the way with no place to run. Not much else to do. So here it came, the shitbag moron and his crooked cop buddies. I gripped the bottle neck, had it palmed as much as I could with my hand behind my back.

"Big man, Powers! I'm here to kick your ass all over this beach!"

Pintazzi came closer. He was stinking drunk, crazed, and very dangerous.

"Careful, Gino, he's got a broken bottle in his hand."

Pintazzi stopped.

I showed him the beer bottle, the jagged glass was just itching to dig into him.

Someone pulled a gun. One of Pintazzi's buddies said, "Drop the bottle, Powers. This will be a fair fight."

"Yeah, twenty on one!"

"Drop the bottle! A fair fight, just you and Gino. That's how he wants it."

"Why should I trust you? Another crooked cop with a gun in my face."

"Because you have no choice, that's why, Powers. You have no place to run. Chicken out now and sure as hell all twenty of us will kick your ass. Be a man, fight Gino. One on one, no shit."

I threw the broken bottle to the side. Gino came at me like an out-of-control freight train.

He was pretty big, real mean, and could fight dirty as hell. Just like me.

It wasn't just a fight. Hell, neither of us could stand the other, and I'd messed him up just an hour before, but this was different now. It wasn't just an argument like before. It was personal. Gino was out to kill me and the idiot was so crazed and so sure of himself from the booze that he wanted to do it by hand. Putting his life on the line—for the sheer pleasure of taking mine.

He came at me with wild swings, trying to get me to hit back, but what he really wanted to do was get me in a clinch, bear hug, squeeze me like a tube of toothpaste.

I gave him a roundhouse swing that missed, ducked his return, and got out of the way when he came at me again.

There was a big crowd, all the usual beach bums and a pile of kids cheering and booing and having a real fun time. I hardly noticed it all. Gino was giving me some serious trouble.

Like I say, he wasn't that tough normally, but something had fired him up and he was out-of-control crazy. I knew I'd have to put him away fast or he'd wear me down. My best weapon against him was his own rage and anger—it was causing him to do stupid things.

"I'll kill you, Powers!" he yelled into my face as we rolled around the sand punching the crap out of each other. "I'll rip your damn balls off and shove them up your ass!"

"You shitbag moron, you couldn't find my ass with your tongue!"

"You double-dealing me!" Three punches in rapid succession to my head, face, stomach accentuated his point.

I ducked the fourth punch, came back with the sand-in-the-face routine and a foot in his face an instant after. I had him down on the sand again now, plastering his face with punches.

"I'm gonna mess you up good, Gino. I don't like morons bugging me. I got no patience for you and your crooked buddies. If you don't want to listen—you'll learn the hard way."

"Not me, Powers!"

"Yeah, you!"

"Stay away . . ." he growled, blood all over his face. His eyes were cut, how he could see was beyond me.

" . . . from her!" he finished.

Then I knew. Five hundred dollars. She'd saved her money and got what she wanted. I got real crazy then. I don't like to be used. I mopped the beach with Gino. His buddies finally had to pull me off him.

I was ready for them too by then. I'd retrieved the broken bottle, the ragged glass gleamed in the sun. I wiped the blood off my face with a sore arm.

"Who's next!" I shouted, crazed, the bloodlust boiling.

No one said a word.

I looked hard at the guy with the gun. "Got a gun and a big mouth. Shoot me, you'll be up for murder, shithead. If I don't die I'll mend real fast and get you back. You can count on it. Come at me and I guarantee I'll kill at least one of you guys. Mess you up real good before you can take me down. Don't be stupid. Gino ain't worth it."

They backed off. Picked up Gino and left.

I was in no mood just then. They could have jumped me, I didn't care, I was so out of my mind just then I might have welcomed taking them all on. I don't know. I'd get at least one of them for sure. Kill him! They knew it and had no stomach for that. They wouldn't take that kind of a chance for an idiot like Gino. They carted him off to their part of the beach and left me alone.

I wiped my face. Looked for the girl. I knew she had to be somewhere nearby.

I saw her past the concession stand. At the ice cream truck. She had her back to me now, buying an ice cream cone, probably very satisfied with herself. And she'd saved five hundred dollars too.

I took a walk over.

"I really hate being set up," I told her.

She turned around and jumped when she saw me. I admit I was a mess, would have scared the hell out of a dead man. Gino gave me a good beating. I was sore all over and pissed as hell.

"You owe me five hundred dollars," I told her.

She took a lick of her ice cream cone and started to walk away.

I grabbed her arm. "I'm talking to you!"

"I don't owe you anything. You turned down the job. Now let me go or I'll call the police."

My turn to laugh. I grabbed her purse, took out the five crisp hundred dollar bills and stuck them in the pocket of my bathing suit.

She slapped my face then. That bugged me. I grabbed the ice cream cone out of her hand and jammed it square into her face. I think a lot of ice cream went up her nose. She didn't like that but she'd deserved it. She started crying and I left her there. That's what happens when you play games with people—sometimes they play back.

I went back to my beach chair, sat down and cracked open another cold beer. Sat back and tried to relax and catch a few rays for a change without people bothering me.

The rain came down five minutes later. Real hard. Sheets of it. That was it for the beach that day.

I picked up my chair and cooler and went back to the car as the rain came blasting down. All in all a pretty lousy day. The beach just ain't as much fun as it used to be.

I'd messed up Gino good, stood up to his crooked cop buddies, and was still in one piece. Relatively. I never got a tan but I was five hundred dollars up so that made up for it, I guess.

It's like they say, today is the first day of the rest of your life. I hocked a phlegm out the window as I drove back to the dungeon where I live. I blasted the radio all along the Belt Parkway. "Satisfaction" was on again. I could relate to it. Good song.

FAST

I'M A FAST GUY. I've always been fast. I'm fast on the make, fast on the take, fast on the draw, and fast with money. But I wasn't fast enough with Betty.

She told me she wanted the money. Not all of it. Just her share. I told her to forget it. She didn't rate a share. It was all mine. I took the risk. I keep the cash. She should stay in the hotel, look sexy, dress up good, look real hot for me. That's what she was good for. That's the way it always was with her, that's the way it should be with us. I do the thinking. I make the rules. I'm the fast one.

Tom got all that cash. All that money. I want my part. It should be all mine. I'm the fast one. I keep my eyes open. I'm the one that sees all the angles. I don't know what the deal was. With Tom there was always one deal or another. One scam or another. One cheat or another.

I forgot all those past cheats for now. Now I was dressed in my hot little bitch best, and would give the fool just the welcome he was looking for. You can bet this little slut knew her stuff. I just kept thinking about all the cash in that old suitcase. I knew Tom was trying to keep it from me. That made me want it all the more. You could bet that by the time this little girl was through with Tom, he would be bed-ridden-exhausted for a week.

That's when I'd cut myself in. Get my share. Tom always was a cheap date. This time I'd take the suitcase and all the cash. It wouldn't make up for all our past cheap dates, but it was a start.

We screwed until my brains almost poured outta my head. I mean, Betty was so damn hot, so tasty, I couldn't keep my hands off her—she couldn't keep her hands off me either. But man, what a little tramp! Moving around like an animal in heat, moaning in Spanish—*I didn't even know she knew Spanish*—licking my fingers, telling me to do her real good the way I knew she liked it.

When I was so spent I couldn't stand it anymore she worked on me. Holding me tight. Showing me what a little tramp could do to her man. And when I was wiped out, physically wrecked and exhausted, she put me to sleep. Rubbing my brow. Using her body, inserting it in front of me. Her butt firmly thrust into my crotch, like we were a matched set of spoons. She was keeping me warm. Warm while I slept. Warm while I slept—alone.

When I woke up I found a note saying she'd left town.

Tom is like all the men I've known—a damn fool. Cock for brains and no sense. Now I've got the suitcase and all the cash. He can kiss my sweet little ass goodbye. All I have to do is make my connection with Dave and soon I'll be far away. Maybe sun myself on some tropical beach, no men around to give orders—only to take them!

My scam! My game! My damn money! And she took it all! I want it back! All of it! Now! The note said she was taking the first plane out of town.

I got dressed and went after her.

There was only one place she'd go when it got down to the nitty-gritty. She'd make it for Big Dave's place, start in with the "I dig you, baby, I nevva shoulda left you, I want you back," game, and she'd offer him half of the money in the suitcase. My money! All Dave had to do was get his thugs to wipe me out. They'd do it too, just for the time of day. At least they'd try. But I'd get to Big Dave first. Fast. Send him, and anyone else that got in my way straight down to hell, and then have a serious talk with my charming little Betty.

"You were real stupid to come here, Betty," Dave Hornsby said, moving close, taking the heavy suitcase out of her hand, setting it down. His snakelike arms embraced her, rough hands touching her soft shoulders, fiddling with the straps of the too-tight, too-short dress she was wearing. Dave's leg brushing her buttocks, his eyes looking deeply into hers, darting to her pouting red lips, looking back into her eyes, meaningfully.

"You look better than ever."

"I know."

"I want to help you, Betty."

"I just bet you do, Dave."

"No, really. I can see you're in a jam."

"Yeah, trouble just follows me around."

"I know. You can't blame it either. I mean, the way you look, it just starts everything bubbling over."

She didn't say anything. She was thinking. Fast.

His lips were on her neck, his big honker of a nose breathing in the scent of her perfume, the unwashed sweat and smell of her sweet young womanhood. His fat hands ran across her outer thighs, up the curve of her waist, and meandered upwards ever higher. Betty slapped him off with a loud whack. A fast slap.

"Come on, Dave, be serious. I need some protection. And not from you!"

Dave feigned disappointment, sulked a bit, then said straight-faced, looking her hard in the eyes, "What's in it for me, Betty? Tom can be a pretty nasty dude. I don't want to have my boys coming up short on this if there's no good reason for it. If there's nothing to gain from it. Make it worth my while, baby, and I can turn Tom DiCarlo into a small pile of dirt that'll just be a bad memory."

She tried to fool me with that leaving-town-crap. Running-away-stuff. Going to the airport and taking the first plane out-anywhere garbage. I didn't bite. I knew my Betty. I knew her wanton ways, her hot little fantasy-scams—and I knew all about her and Big Dave Hornsby. They'd had a thing going long ago. I thought it had ended. I guess it hadn't. I knew that now.

That's the place she'd be at!

That's the place I'd go to!

They wouldn't be able to stop me and I'd get my stinking money before any of them knew what the hell had happened.

I would be fast, man, real fast—too fast for any of them.

"Betty, I don't like the idea of Crazy Tom coming down here," Dave said. "My boys'll do the job you want, but not for free. Not as a favor, baby, as much as I still like you. You know what I mean?"

"I got something else, Dave. Something you'll like even better than me."

"The only thing better than you, baby . . ."

"It's green, Dave. Know what that means?" She didn't have to say more. Dave's eyes perked up. Betty opened the suitcase and all those neatly wrapped bundles of new twenties, fifties and hundreds stared back at him—whispering "Take me", "Take me",

"I'm all yours", just like a hard-up little slut on the prowl. Dave drooled, caught himself, hardly noticing Betty now.

Dave closed the suitcase, but before he could pick it up, she pulled it toward her. When Big Dave tried to slap her away, he found himself looking into the barrel of her .32 pointed right between his eyes. Betty smiled, sweetly. Just like she always did when she wins.

"You're dead if you make a move, Dave. The money's mine—I took it from Tom. He'll be after it—like a madman. You take care of him, honey, and I'll take care of you. You can have half. If you try for it all, all you'll get is a bullet. You know how I am, Dave. Take the easy half. What do you say?"

Dave oozed, like a snake coiling around itself.

"Betty, how could you pull a gun on me. That's not nice. If we can't trust each other, we have nothing. Of course I'll help you. Look, baby, half is good enough for me. I ain't greedy. I'll have the boys take a ride. They'll take care of Tom. No problem."

"He won't be there, Dave. Tom won't be anyplace your goons would think to look for him. I know Tom, he's on his way here right now—like an out-of-control freight train—fast!"

I heard the two guards walking out on the terrace; one telling the other how Big Dave wanted to make sure no one got into the house. To expect Crazy Tom DiCarlo. And to kill him on sight.

Okay by me, if they were fast enough.

I watched from my place of concealment. They talked about which way they thought I'd come at them. I didn't have the heart to tell them I was there already. Five damn feet away from them—on the roof just over their heads—with them in the sight of my gun.

I didn't have the heart to tell them. So I didn't.

The silencer gave the first shot a whispered swish as the bullet plowed into the back of the head of one of the goons. The other looked around, for a bare moment wondering where the hell the shot had come from, catching the blood oozing out of his partner's face where his left eye had been. I popped a slug into this guy's chest, just above the heart. He didn't even have time to unholster his gun.

Then I moved. Fast.

Down from the roof. Into the house. Saw one guard on the steps. Dropped him before he could say a word. Caught another coming out of the john. He'd left his rifle leaning against the wall outside the bathroom when he'd gone in to take a leak. Dead give-away.

Moving fast as hell now.

Running down the steps. Saw the wooden oak doors of the library. Big doors—closed. Excellent. I knew they hadn't run. Not yet. They wanted me dead first. They were under siege and they both knew it. They wouldn't run until I was out of the picture. Too dangerous otherwise. Unfortunately for them that event wasn't going to happen.

I went into the kitchen. Out the window and around the outside of the house to a window where I could look into the library. There they were. Betty, Big Dave, and two more of his boys. The goons had Uzis and were facing the oak doors. Waiting expectantly. Waiting for me to enter. Waiting for nothing.

I took out the two goons first. It was almost too easy. Two fast, well-aimed shots and their heads exploded like ripe melons dropped off the back of a truck.

I was through the window and in the room then. Real fast. My gun leveled at Dave and Betty as I moved to the two bodies and lifted their hardware, putting them in a desk drawer.

Betty screamed, said, "I knew it! It's him!"

Big Dave turned paler than a dead man. It was a good imitation. He wouldn't be imitating for long if I had anything to say about it.

"Wait, Tom! Don't do it! We're buddies, remember? We've done jobs together. Hell, man, we're both doing Betty! Don't ruin a good thing. Kill me and she'll hate you forever."

I wasn't buying. When you're scared shit you say some pretty absurd things. I smiled, said, "Maybe I'll kill Betty too."

Betty was shook up now. Didn't like hearing that kind of talk. Out-of-control scared. Thinking fast. Thinking for her life.

"No baby, I love you. Please, don't be mean. I meant no harm."

"No harm! You took my money!"

"He made me do it, honey!" Betty screamed, pointing the finger at Big Dave, turning the tables on him, much to his surprise and my own. My Betty was nothing if not inventive. "That bastard made me do it, honey! I didn't want to."

"Sure," I said.

"No, it's true. It's all his fault. Don't hurt me. If you've got to kill someone—kill Dave. He's the one you want—not me. Go ahead, Tom. Kill Dave. Now. It don't matter to me."

I had to smile at that, "Don't matter to me, either."

Dave cursed, almost jumped Betty then, but I slugged him down to the floor. He got up angry and scared. Shaking.

Big Dave was near panic. Maybe his life didn't matter to Betty or me, but it sure as hell mattered to him. The sweat was rolling down his face like from a broke faucet. He was shaking as he looked to the mess his two dead guards made on the floor. He looked back at the large oak doors, expecting his other men to rush in at any moment, finally realizing that there would be no one coming to his aid. He was up shit's creek and it was getting near high tide for Big Dave Hornsby.

Then Betty took a hand in the situation. She slapped Big Dave across the face. Again. Hard. Fast. Dave's lips bled. He took it good though. He knew what was coming. Betty was setting him up for the fall. And there was nothing that Big Dave could do about it.

I figured my sweet little Betty was working on me to kill Dave—to, in effect, blame him for everything. Betty could be real persuasive when there was something she wanted. Like life.

"You gotta believe me, Tom," Dave said hopelessly, knowing that I didn't give a damn about anything he had to say.

"He doesn't believe a word you're saying, Dave. All your damn lies!" Betty said, moving near him slowly, dangerously. Like a pantheress set to strike. "Tom believes me. Don't you, Tom? Don't you, honey? You're a louse, Dave. A liar! Always were. You use everyone you come in contact with. You used me. You used Tom. You came between us. Between our love. Now you tried to come between Tom and all that money he worked so hard to get for us. Well it's too late, Dave. Your using days are over. If Tom won't take care of you . . ."

"Betty!" I shouted, "Don't do it!"

" . . . then I will, Dave!" Then Betty pulled out a tiny .32, pulling the trigger and sending a slug into Big Dave's brain. It happened so fast. So damn fast. One shot did it, she was at point-blank range, and Dave Hornsby lay on the ground bleeding like a stuck pig clutching for breath, dying as we watched.

I motioned for Betty to put the gun on the table. Fast.

She did, came over to me, gave me a big kiss.

"Oh, honey, you saved me. I love you so much."

She hugged me, her sweat mingling with my own. I held her, but not hard. I wanted her, but there was something I wanted a lot more just then. She knew it too.

"You stay right here, honey. I'll get the suitcase and bring it right back here to you. Okay?"

I nodded. She was gone in a flash. fast.

I let her go. I always let Betty go. Sometimes I let her go too far. This time I let her go just far enough.

She wasn't stupid. She was back fast. With the suitcase. She opened it up so I could see it was still full of my money. Nothing had been touched.

"See, honey, I didn't let Dave have any of it. I had to fight him off from taking it all himself."

"So he wanted the whole thing. You only offered him half, right baby?"

She didn't answer.

"What does that tell you, Betty?"

"What do you mean, Tom? Don't be so cruel to me now that we're together and have all this money."

"You wanted half, baby. I told you no. It was for a good reason."

"Sure, Tom."

"The money's not mine, Betty. I'm just holding it. It's all gotta go back."

"Oh, honey, all that money. What if we take it? Who will know? We could run away and live great. Go to some little island, lay in the sun. I'll get that thong bikini you like me to wear and you could rub oil all over me. Everywhere. Get me all wet and slippery. Just like you like me. It could be real nice, honey. Don't give all that up."

"The money has to go back. If it doesn't go back I'm a dead man. Understand?"

"Oh, Tom, who's to know?"

"People will know."

"I don't believe you."

"Believe what you will, baby. In the meantime, let's get outta here. Too many dead bodies around and Big Dave's leaking all over the place."

Betty didn't say anything, but when she moved over to Dave's body I saw her draw close to the table where the .32 was laying. I let her. I wanted to see how far my darling Betty would go.

"Wait, Tom!" Betty said, ordered. Now I saw the .32 in her hand. She moved closer. "Put your hands up! If you go for your gun, I'll shoot, Tom. Believe me. Don't make me do it."

"I believe you, baby. Why you doing this?"

She laughed. "I want the money, Tom. The money's the only thing I care about. You should know that. After all, we're a lot alike. You're just not as fast as I am, Tom. Too bad."

I laughed now. "Baby, it's not even real money. It's all bogus. It looks good, but it ain't."

"Come on, not another story."

"You think I'd have that much money if it was real?"

She hesitated, then said, "I don't believe you."

"It's true. It's all counterfeit. I'm just holding it for someone."

She quieted for a long moment. Still holding the gun on me but thinking it through. Fast.

"That's all right, Tom. I don't believe you, but even if what you say is true, good counterfeit is almost as good as real. And now that I know it's fake I'll just be more careful how I spend it."

"And that's it, baby?"

She smiled. Tough. Victorious. "Not quite, Tom. I'm sorry, but I can't have you coming after me again. I know how you can be. A damn hardhead. If I let you go now you'd just track me down."

"Yeah," I muttered, "that's me, I just can't let no one get away with taking what's mine."

"See. So, goodbye, Tom. It's been . . ." she smiled and laughed a bit, " . . .it's certainly been financially rewarding."

"Don't do it, Betty! Please! I want to live! I'm begging!"

"And that's not very becoming. Go out like a man, Tom, I'll remember you better for it."

"Betty?"

"Goodbye, Tom."

Then she pressed the trigger.

For a split second the world seemed to stop. Then:

CLICK!

It was a telltale sound made all the louder by the intense quiet in the room.

I smiled. Laughed. "Must be a dud, baby. Go ahead, try it again."

Betty's face registered shock. Confusion. Then determination. She pressed the trigger again.

CLICK!

Anger clouded her features. She pressed the trigger in rapid succession.

CLICK!

CLICK!

CLICK!

I just laughed. "Tough luck, eh baby?"

She screamed, "You son-of-a-bitch!"

"I took the bullets out when you went to get the suitcase. Appears it was a good idea."

"You lousy bastard!"

"That's me, baby. It takes a lousy bastard to be able to live in the same world with people like you."

I pulled the suitcase out of Betty's hand.

Then she drew the knife, trying to slip it into my back as I walked away from her and I shot her dead before she could find a home in my back for her blade. My patience had finally reached its limit.

Yes, I knew my Betty. She couldn't resist a rip-off. I couldn't resist a little tramp cheat that finally got what she had coming to her. I knew Betty, and for the first time in my life I was faster than her, when it counted the most.

LIVE AND LEARN

GET OVER HERE!"
    You don't move.
    "Did you hear me?"
You're scared. Too scared to move forward. Too scared to run away.
"Stop whimpering, you damn son-of-a-bitch!"
You stand like a statue. Dying inside.
"I told you . . .!"
His hand is so big.
"Jump when I talk to you!"
It makes such a big fist.
You hold your breath. The fist swings but misses you.
Finally, you can breathe again.
"Get over here you lousy bastard!"
You move one inch closer. Scared to death.
"Get over here now!"
The hand opens. Hard and flat. Like a 2 x 4. Ready.
"I told you to get over here!"
You move one more inch. Closer. Hoping it will not hurt too bad this time. You tell yourself you're used to it by now. You can take it. Maybe it won't hurt too much?
"Come here!"
You inch forward.
"Closer!"
You freeze.
"Now don't move!"
The hand goes up. It makes a shadow over your face. The darkness from it consumes you. You shiver.
"Come here when I'm talking to you!"
You cannot stop shaking.
"That's better. Now don't move!"
The hand comes down.
Describing a perfect arc.
Full of energy and power.

Flat palm, smacking your face like a hammer. Hitting hard on the left side of your face. Pounding your small head. So hard you can feel your brain rattle inside your skull. The hand quickly moves back and upward for another slap.

"Now don't move!"

The hand slashes down again. On the right side of your head this time. Like a battering ram. You take one step back Reeling. Shivering.

The hand comes down once more. Hard. Harder than before. Harder than anything you've ever felt before.

"You're no good!"

You don't say a word.

"You're no damn good!"

The hand goes up again and then comes back down again. You feel the impact of it on your face. Again and again. And forever after. For as long as you live.

"I told you to get over here!"

You stammer.

He barks, "I'll show you!"

No words can come out of you.

"You'd better do what I tell you!"

You can't reply. You don't know why he hates you so much.

"Listen to me or you'll be sorry you stupid bastard!"

You're not stupid, you're not a bastard, but you cannot reply.

"You better not move!"

You can't move.

Your face is sore now, and there are drops of blood mingled with the tears. New tears mixing with older ones. Your eyes burn red with hatred.

There's the promise of death in those eyes.

But you do not reply.

There can be no reply.

To reply would only make it worse.

Worse than if you just stood by and took it.

Like you always do.

And fighting back would be worse still. Futile. You're so small. Defenseless. You can't fight him and you can't run.

Running would be useless. There is no place to run to. No place to hide. No one to help you.

But the promise is still there.

In your eyes it shines.

Full, burning-red, powerful.

Someday you'll make him pay.
Someday you'll get him back.
Someday that promise will be realized.
Someday . . .
So you don't cry.
You don't scream.
You don't fight or run.
You just stand there and take it. You bide your time and . . .
smile.
"Get up, dammit!"
You slowly get to your feet.
"I'll slap that stupid smile right off your damn face!"
Another slap, but this time your smile only grows, because now
you know something.
You know you'll get him back someday.
And knowing it comforts you.
"Stay there!"
You stay there.
"Don't move!"
You don't move.
One more slap. The hardest of them all, but it cannot wipe that
smile from your face. Nothing can wipe that smile from your face
now.
"You're a fucking no good stupid bastard!"
And you feel that hand slap you down again and again.
"You worthless piece of shit!"
But this time you smile bold.
Strong with anger.
You ignore the blood-taste in your mouth.
You ignore the lose teeth.
You ignore the trickles of red from your nose and lips.
"Stupid damn kid! You'll never learn!"
And you just smile and think . . .
. . . you're learning.

VORTEX

THEY HATED PAINTING, but they painted. They had to. They had to do it. They made sure they painted well. But they ran out of paint. They must have put too much on the walls and now they'd run out of paint.

That would make mommy and daddy mad. That was not good. They could not leave the room. They could not get more paint. But the older brother had an idea. So they made the cuts, mixing their blood together with what remained of the paint, and binding themselves together in blood.

And mommy and daddy didn't get mad at them that night.

When police detective Bill Crow and his partner Clyde Burkshaw entered the old tenement in Brooklyn they had no idea what they would find. They were on the hunt for a killer and they'd finally found him, but so had the press and what looked like half the curiosity seekers in New York. The block had been closed off by uniform cops, but there were still people everywhere. Nosing around. Full of rage. Crying at the horror that rumor said lurked within the apartment. Hundreds of people, dazed at this latest urban horror. The media everywhere sticking their cameras in everyone's faces.

There was the sickly sweet smell of blood heavy in the air, thick as gravy, hanging in the stagnant summer breeze like a vise around everyone's neck. Growing tighter. Just about to pop the top of everyone's head off. Tension and anger were growing. It was hot and it was getting hotter.

Right in the center of all it were Crow and Burkshaw, trying to figure out what the hell had happened. Why it had happened? How could such a thing occur?

They'd have to go back now, piece it together bit by bit, try to get some meaning or reason. They knew it was impossible, but it was their job.

The Voodoo Stranglers owned this section of the city. Roaming the streets in packs, talking the talk, walking the walk, taking what

they wanted to take, doing what they wanted to do. Hurting anyone they felt like hurting. It was a great life.

They usually went out hunting Friday night. Scare the people.
Get off on the fear. Rob and steal to buy drugs and booze. Do the
stuff they got and get crazy. Then go out on a spree for a few days
more. Sexing.

They weren't widely known. They weren't a big gang. No one
spoke of them much. But the other gangs knew who they were and
sidestepped for them, the other gangs called this a serious gang,
intense dudes—off the fucking wall crazy!

*The rage burned deep, like the seething coals of a blast fur-
nace. Hot and red. Firelike. Consuming—the darkness—the
light—the life that flowed and ebbed in the city like a rusty dripping faucet in the sink of a sleazy burntout tenement. A faucet that
was never fixed.*

*The Fixer would change all that. He was on the prowl. Work-
ing. After the hated transgressors, entering the vortex of life and
purifying it.*

Police detective Bill Crow looked at the photos again. There
wasn't much to tell from the mess depicted. You could barely determine the sex of the remains without a scorecard. He read that
scorecard now. Read the preliminary report and the Coroner's determination.

Victim: Alonzo Ruiz, member of the Voodoo Stranglers, the
gang rumored responsible for the kidnapping of the Thompsons—
that nice young white yuppie couple captured on Riverside Drive
after their car had broken down in the lonely hours of predawn.
They'd been abducted and forced into an old van. Then driven to
an abandoned tenement in Harlem. Then . . .well, you get the idea.
The girl was eventually butchered, but not before they had their
fun with her—and the husband was forced to watch it all. He was
later found nude and chained in the basement of the abandoned
building almost starved to death. Deranged. Later institutionalized.
The officer on the scene said the husband had been trying to rear-
range his wife's body parts as though she were a big jigsaw puzzle. Trying to put her back together again, but he was so far gone
he couldn't even get that right.

And now Alonzo Ruiz, member of the feared Voodoo Stranglers was dead the same way. Sliced and diced.

Clyde Burkshaw wiped the sweat that glistened from his old black face. He knew that coincidences don't happen like this in real life without reason. But sometimes reason has very little to do with certain situations.

Crow sat back sucking on a Marlboro and waited for his partner to drop the other shoe.

Clyde had a table full of photos and rap sheets spread out before him. It was a grim assortment of human tragedy.

"Lot of dead people listed here, Bill. A lot of the usual, some unusual. Some strange coincidences. I figure our boy is responsible for killing some of these guys that deserve killing. Guys the law can't get, guys that got off from soft-bellied judges on technicalities. First class garbage that they set back on the streets. It looks to me our boy is going after them."

"Yeah, at least members of the Stranglers. He's a fixer, no doubt, but he's still a psycho. Look at what he does to the ones he's caught. He's just a serial killer—who hunts down other killers—but he's still bad news."

"Sure, Bill, still and all I kinda like him. You know, I thought I'd seen it all by now."

"Me too, Clyde, but he's gotta fall, man."

"I know. He's gotta fall."

The Voodoo Strangler awoke to find he was tied and hanging above an old vat. The vat was one of those industrial metal containers and it was full of foaming, boiling water—the burning embers underneath causing the water to churn and bubble as if in furious rage.

The Voodoo Strangler's mouth was taped shut, his hands and feet tied with heavy chain. His face and body bleeding heavily from numerous razor cuts. His blood dripping down into the bubbling water, mixing with it, giving it a pretty pink hue.

"I have to go now. I'm sorry we can't play more but you have more friends I have to see yet."

The Strangler squirmed, tried to talk, yell, cry, tried to do anything—anything at all but watch as the crazy one slowly lowered him down into the churning fiery waters below.

Clyde fished around the hole in his molar with a toothpick. Worked it around a little bit and then looked to his partner with a face full of disgust.

"Well, he sure cooked that son-of-a-bitch. Not a bad end for Juan Garcia, really. A kid that likes to rape children won't get any sympathy from me, Bill."

"But it's getting out of hand, Clyde," Bill Crow said. He studied the scene again, went over Garcia's record. It made for some heavy reading. "We got a problem here. We gotta watch these Voodoo Stranglers and they don't want us watching. Someone's evidently after them—or at least the ones we think are involved in the Thompson mess. I'd like to know why."

"Yeah, Bill, but I've run checks on the Thompson family and relatives and they're clean. It looks to me our fixer is not involved with the Thompson's at all. He seems to be a free agent, an outside agency. I figure he's a psycho who heard about the case on TV or something, was so incensed by what he'd heard, he decided to fix it right himself when we couldn't make an arrest. Anyway, it's our best bet so far."

"Lovely. You might be right. Which just means we've got a very deranged and dangerous guy running around the city offing gang members. We gotta get him before the lousy papers turn him into a damn saint."

The clubhouse of the Voodoo Stranglers was in a run-down abandoned tenement on the outskirts of Harlem. A barrier between Harlem and the Barrio—a no-man's land that even the cops tried to stay away from if they could.

There were only four Voodoo Stranglers left from the original group of a dozen or so. Of course Ruiz and Garcia had met The Fixer already. The others had been killed in various rumbles and drug disputes. Two were upstate in prison for murder and drug charges. The attrition rate in a gang like the Stranglers was always high and going up day by day now.

The Fixer made it worse. Being a Voodoo Strangler just wasn't as much fun as it used to be.

"Police protection for the likes of this trash is a damn insult to every victim of crime in this city," Crow grunted. He and his partner, Clyde, sat their shift across the street from the Stranglers clubhouse. Watching. Waiting. Doing nothing and drinking a lot of beer. Just like the night before.

The Stranglers refused to have a cop stationed inside their clubhouse or anywhere near it. Most people thought it odd, but the gang claimed discrimination and police harassment, and actually had the spineless politicians downtown supporting them—after all, they said, weren't they the victims? Two of their members had been murdered by a killer that was supposedly gunning for the rest of the gang. Their leader, a big tough named Roche, actually accused police death squads of being behind it all. The media ate it up.

"That logic sticks up my ass like a month-old turd. Here we are protecting these slimeballs, and not only are they not cooperating—they're blaming us for the whole mess." Clyde hocked up phlegm and spit a juicy bit of it out the window.

"And they're crying about being victims," Crow added, "that's what bugs me—and they may be right! It looks like they are victims, at least with the Ruiz and Garcia killings. What a world! And they accuse us. It stinks."

"Well I hope this Fixer fixes their asses, but good, messes them four up like they never been messed before. They deserve it, if not for this crime, then for all the others. I'm sure they've got enough under the belt to each hang if we had any kind of justice in this city."

"Meanwhile we just wait it out, Clyde. And if this Fixer is here when we are, we'll let him do the dirty deed—then put him out of commission—afterwards. The world won't be in any worse shape minus four Voodoo Stranglers. In fact, we'll be doing everyone in this city a big favor."

The Stranglers had the clubhouse set up like a fortress. They brought in guys from an out-of-town gang to stand guard. They trucked in weapons—heavy-duty stuff they didn't usually keep close to hand. They had plenty of firepower and plenty of muscle—but when the bomb went off in the early morning hours the entire building was obliterated. Only a small crater was left.

"Son-of-a-bitch must have had a damn suitcase full of explosives," Crow growled once he and Clyde were able to get out of what remained of their car. The whole area looked like a scene from Hiroshima; rubble and fires everywhere, broken glass and shards sent in a 360-degree maelstrom. It was a miracle they'd lived through it. The blast alone took out every window on the block, knocked down the abandoned buildings on either side of the clubhouse. It was a scene from Armageddon. There wasn't anything left of the block or the Voodoo Stranglers.

"I thought it was all over."

"So did I."

"It's been a week. The gang guys are dead, but something is wrong."

"I guess we were both wrong on this one. Do you see how he did it? See what he did? That guy, the one called Roche. His body was never found. That didn't mean much at the time but now I've heard hints of talk, hints he's still alive and hiding out somewhere in Brooklyn."

Crow nodded, "The last of the Voodoo Stranglers. Roche. Alive. It has to be, just has to be when you think of it. An inside job, by one of the gang's own members. Who else could pull off an explosion like that, and who better to do it than Roche himself, the leader of the gang."

"We've been shitted. The guy who wouldn't accept police protection," Clyde said, "did this just to screen himself. Who's he hiding from? Now everyone thinks he's dead. But I wonder?"

"We gotta track him. A dozen people died in that clubhouse—even if they were only gang members—even if they were only Voodoo Stranglers—they were still people and it looks like Roche murdered them all in cold blood. If he did it—he's gotta be made to pay."

Crow and Burkshaw dug around on the streets in Brooklyn. They had a lot of contacts there from previous days. Set them to work. They didn't mind snitching on an outsider if the price was right. They got a tip on where Roche was staying. A girl friend in Bed-Stuy, she'd been Roche's main woman a year ago, now she was just another crack whore. Her mother moved her in with the grandmother in Bed-Stuy hoping to get the girl away from gangs and drugs and into a better environment. Silly idea, if you know Bed-Stuy.

My eyes are on fire.
My hands twitch with anticipation.
My brain cries out, "Kill them! Kill them all!"
I just laugh and get ready.
The knives are sharp. They glisten so pretty, even by the dim light of a dirty bulb in a grimy tenement. I have two knives. They are called Mommy and Daddy.
Mommy likes to cut up top. She likes lots of blood. Always so much blood.

Daddy likes to rip down low, open stomachs and intestines until the guts flow onto the floor and you slip on them and fall into the mess. Daddy is mean and nasty. He means business.
Mommy and Daddy are angry. They want to go after a bad boy. My brother is a bad boy. A very bad boy. Mommy and Daddy are going to fix him.
I'm going to help.

"There's something just came in."

"What's that?" Crow said, he and Burkshaw were on their way to an address in Brooklyn's Bedford-Stuyvesant section. A run-down demolished part of a dying city that long ago should have been put out of its misery.

Clyde said, "This kid, Roche, has a half-brother. From what I make out he wasn't an actual member of the Voodoo Stranglers but he did hang with them. Everyone figured he was away, upstate at a mental hospital for the criminally insane. He's not. He's been loose in the city for the last six weeks, hanging with the Stranglers. He's not on the sheets. Not listed in the records. He's Roche's half brother with a different surname and he's been missing for a couple of weeks. He seems to have left the gang after the Thompson's were murdered."

"Got a rep?"

"Yeah, they say he's real crazy. Serious. He also likes to play with knives. His brother, Miguel, El Roche he calls himself now, used him to handle problems in the gang—until he got out of hand. It seems even they couldn't control him. He's a cutter, Bill."

"Sounds like a natural to be the cutter on the Thompson case, Clyde."

"Just what I'm figuring."

The neighborhood in Brooklyn was old and run down. So were the houses. So were the people. So were their dreams. If they had any left that hadn't turned into nightmares yet.

The mother was at work.

The old lady, grandma, was at the Seniors Center, losing her money at bingo.

Miguel, El Roche, was in bed with the daughter, Clarise. They'd just finished doing the dirty deed—now they topped it off with a pipe of crack.

"This really makes it good, baby." Clarise said, toking on the pipe, taking the warm smoke deeply into her lungs, and feeling it move up within her, blasting her mind, setting her flying. This was better than sex, but Miguel was a man, and men only wanted one thing from a girl. At least afterwards he always turned her on to the best stuff. It was all worth it once the pipe was lit.

"Yeah, baby, you're so hot . . ." and he moved closer, rubbing her small hard breasts with one rough hand, while the other reached over and pulled the pipe out of her sucking mouth.

"Oh, wait, baby," Clarise protested, but Miguel already had the pipe, toking away madly on it himself.

"Ease up, girl, we got more. Don't get greedy or I'll kick your ass." Then he pulled her close to him, hard, down low, and held her down there—near it. She knew what he wanted. She didn't like doing it.

"Do it!" he said.

"I don't like that," she said.

"You like it. Come on, baby. We'll have a little smoke afterwards."

He is a very bad boy. He has always been a very bad boy. He makes me do bad things, like the things I did to those people we took off the highway. That bitch was so pretty and he made me rip her face off. Bad thing. I had no choice, I had to do it. I always have to do it. I always have to do what Roche says. He's the older brother. He made me bleed when we painted the room. We mixed blood together. You cannot deny that. So I do as he says—unless Mommy and Daddy tell me different.

Everyone laughed while the woman died. We all watched her. Roche laughed the hardest, the Stranglers laughed very much, and I laughed . . .but for some reason her husband did not laugh at all.

That upset me. It started strange thoughts in my head.

Then the husband began crying and he could not stop. I felt bad for him. Later I went out and found the parts for him, so he could put her back together again. It was no big deal. We tried to do it for a long time but we couldn't figure it out. I was there helping him, but I don't think he really knew I was there at all. After a while it got boring. Maybe some parts were missing, maybe I had cut some the wrong size. I couldn't figure it out but it was sure fun for a while. When I left him he was still trying.

And now Mommy and Daddy were mad at me for what I had done. What they'd done. What evil brother Roche and the others made me do.

And Mommy and Daddy talked to me. From where they live underground. Deep, from where I put them a long time ago, before I went away. They talk to me.
They told me more people had to die.
Mommy and Daddy told me so. It had to be done. Now they were all dead but one. Now I come for the last one.
"Roche!"

When Crow and Burkshaw got to the scene the smell of blood was heavy in the air. Everywhere. They saw the girl, Clarise, her mother and the grandmother being taken out on stretchers. They were all tied down. Clarise was hysterical. So were her mother and grandmother. The girl was still hyped-up on drugs. No one could get a coherent sentence out of any of them. They looked shattered. They'd seen things. It had affected them.

But the detectives didn't need to get a statement just then. One of the uniform guys called them over to a room down the hall.

"It's the girl's room," he said, holding a handkerchief over his mouth. "it's pretty terrible in there. We found the girl; her mother and the grandmother all tied up in there. They were forced to watch it. They saw it all. It did something to them. I think he did it purposely so they could watch, almost like he did it for them. Like a show. Pretty sick, huh?"

"Yeah," Crow replied quietly as he and Clyde approached the girl's room.

Crow and Burkshaw had finally found their Fixer, but they were too late. They wondered what twisted cord connected the Fixer and his killings, with Roche, the Voodoo Stranglers and the Thompson murder. They were sure they'd find out soon enough.

They went inside.

Clyde closed the door behind him. They moved deeper into the tiny room.

It was dark.

The window was covered.

Crow bumped into something big, wet.

Clyde turned on the light.

Bill Crow stood looking at an indistinguishable form about five inches from his face, suspended by bound wrists from a ceiling light fixture. The body had been stripped of its clothing—then stripped of its skin. If that wasn't bad enough, all the blood had been drained out of it, leaving a wet, pulpy hulk, a twisted rictus leering insanely at the two detectives.

Crow swallowed and took a deep breath. Calmed his nerves. "I guess we've found Roche." He said.

"Jesus!" Clyde said starting to shake visibly now, "Why? What the hell . . .where's the blood?"

Crow moved around the hanging body, careful not to touch it, moving closer to Clyde as he pointed to an empty bucket and a trail of dark and dry brown spots on the floor.

Crow and Burkshaw followed the trail. The blood trail. To another door. It opened into another room like all these old railroad apartments that are connected to each other. An empty room. The furniture had all been moved out. But it was not really empty.

There in the room, his body propped up against the far wall watching them was another kid. He looked just like the mug shots they had of Roche. Definitely a family connection, definitely the lost half-brother. Definitely the true Fixer.

He sat there dead and cold now. Staring out with hollow lifeless eyes. Another hollow husk.

His left arm was out, extended, hanging over a big pan. One of those pans that painters use with a roller. The vein had been slit and a few viscous drops still hung from the incision threatening to drip into the pan. They never did. Nearby was a paint roller. It was full and stiff but whether it was with dried paint or dried blood they couldn't tell. But something told them it was the later. They knew it was human blood. Come to think of it, it still smelled sickly sweet. In fact, the entire room had been painted with human blood!

Clyde lost it then. Would have lost it all if he had eaten yet. As it was he got the dry heaves and had to get out of there.

Crow stayed. Looked around. He knew he'd never understand this stuff. How could it happen? Why did it happen? The kid had painted the entire room with his brothers' blood. And his own blood. He'd forced the three women to watch it all. Made sure they saw it all. And they weren't talking. They were all too gone at this point. Maybe for good.

Crow looked around in wonder. The walls were still a little wet in places. Dripping unevenly in one spot. Probably the last to be painted. And yet, it was done rather neatly. No spots missed. And it appears he'd had just enough paint—blood!—Crow reminded himself—to finish the job.

The kid was dead. Suicided out. Not from the bleeding though. He had two knives dug deep into his heart—and written on his chest in his own blood was—"I love Mommy and Daddy!"

Crow looked at the words.
They began to dance in front of him.
He had to leave the room too now.

LOVE KILLS

TODAY THE GROUP WAS LISTENING to another heart-wrenching story of violence perpetuated against women by men. Janet and her ten female companions had formed a support group for battered women and their mission was to out-source positive emotions and healing through group therapy discussions to victims of violence from boyfriends or husbands.

The anger in the room, even hatred, was growing second by second with each word the young woman up front spoke, outrage becoming a palpable creature in their midst. The latest victim was named Sandy, a petite blonde housewife from Scarsdale. Nice home. Not so nice husband. Not her fault, really. In fact, none of this was her fault—she'd just picked the wrong guy like so many women do.

His name was Roger.

He was a bad one.

"The hitting didn't start until a month after we were married," Sandy said holding back her tears. She nervously dredged up the horrible memories, seeing it all and reliving it all in her mind, her anger mirrored in the faces of the 10 young women who were listening to her so earnestly.

"We got through the honeymoon without any incident. Roger gave me that saving grace at least." Sandy suddenly broke down in tears. Janet, the leader of the group came over and tried to comfort her.

Women in the audience grew angrier, curses flew, "Bastard! Men are all bastards!"

"The first time," Sandy continued bravely, regaining her composure, "he only broke my nose. There was a lot of blood, so much blood. I was terrified. He never gave me a reason, or told me what I did wrong. Another time he broke my arm and leg. None of that was as bad as when he threw me down the stairs. Roger told me it was because I had become a 'fucking fat bitch' by getting myself pregnant with his child. I lost the baby . . ."

Sandy broke down as a growl of outrage grew from the throats of the women, followed by a moan of deep sympathy, for many of these women had also gone through the same horrors.

"I really wanted that baby, oh God . . ." Sandy stammered, fighting bravely to regain control.

"Do you want to stop? Take a break?" Janet asked softly.

Sandy took a deep breath, steeled herself, "No, I want to get through it, finish it."

"You're a brave woman," Janet said.

The other women applauded Sandy for confronting her horror.

"The beatings had been going on for months, any day, any time, for no apparent reason. I know he blamed me for losing the baby. Roger wouldn't let me go out, nor meet with my friends or family."

"Typical male control freak!" one of the women shouted.

Sandy continued, "He wouldn't allow me to leave him either. He said he'd kill me, that he'd rather see me dead than with some-one else. When the police questioned Roger about my 'accident' falling down the steps—the hospital reported older broken bones on my x-rays consistent with physical abuse—then he blew a fuse. That night he came home and beat me so badly I had to be rushed to the hospital emergency room."

There were sighs and cries of rage from the women, Janet mo-tioned them to be silent so the speaker could continue her story uninterrupted.

"Finally," Sandy signed, "I just couldn't take it anymore. I did not go back home. I'm in a shelter now . . ."

Some women nodded knowingly, others cheered her, shouting words of encouragement and empowerment. Sandy smiled awk-wardly.

" . . . but now Roger is after me, stalking me. He told me he would kill me." Sandy blurted, full of terror and allowing it to show now. "I have an order of protection against him but . . ."

"We all know how that goes!" someone from the group re-sponded. Shouts of agreement accompanied her words.

Sandy nodded sadly, she stood in front of the group like a deer caught in the headlights, like someone who knew she was doomed and was just waiting for the executioner's ax to fall.

There wasn't a dry eye in the room once the young woman had finished telling her tale.

They took Sandy back to her safehouse, then they got down to business.

"Well, ladies, are we going to help Sandy with her problem?" Janet asked, for now a private meeting of L.O.V.E.—Ladies Overcoming Violent Exploiters—was in session . . .

"I think Sandy needs to know that she is not alone in this," a heavyset woman named Amanda said forcefully. She wore an eyepatch, covering the eye her husband had poked out with a screwdriver. He was in prison now, where he belonged. Amanda hated men and hated husbands in particular.

"All right ladies, so let me see a show of hands," Janet asked carefully.

Ten hands flew into the air.

"Then it's unanimous."

Three nights later a friend of Roger's let it drop where his runaway wife Sandy could be found. She was living alone in a house at 124 Mercer Street.

Roger made his way to the front door. This abuser certainly seemed bold, so cocksure self-confident like all men when confronting a lone and helpless female. He walked right up to the front door of 124 Mercer and calmly rang the bell.

"Sandy? Sandy, I know you're in there. Open up! I just want to talk to you."

The door slowly opened, inside was dark and no one seemed to be there.

No sooner had Roger walked inside when he was stunned by a sudden blow to the head. The door was slammed shut behind him and a dozen pairs of grasping hands pummeled him with baseball bats and fists. Blows reigned down on Roger mercilessly as he cried out in pain, pleading for them to let him go, to stop hitting him. His face was scratched bloody by long nails while hard blows beat him into submission and then unconsciousness.

Roger awoke in a bed in Mercy Hospital—but by the look of him his attackers had shown no mercy at all. He was in what amounted to an almost full body cast with multiple broken bones, fractures, sprains and contusions. His nose was broken, an eye was covered in gauze and oozed green pus, a feeding tube ran in his nose and down his throat while the ventilator was all that was enabling him to breath. That wasn't the worst of it by a long shot. The doctors said the extent of blunt force trauma indicated serious internal in-

juries and he would be going back into surgery soon to stem more
bleeding.

Sandy sat close by, looking down at Roger. Whether he knew
she was there or not was unknown, so bad was the extent of his
injuries. Sandy smiled for she could see that Roger was not long
for this world. Once he kicked off, all his money would be hers
exclusively. She couldn't believe her good fortune. This had
turned out so much better than the mere 50/50 split of the bitter
divorce she had planned. Better yet, she now would be able to cut
out all those annoying and expensive lawyer fees, $200 per hour
bills for expert witnesses on abuse and victimization. Who needed
that? Sandy didn't know who had attacked Roger but she was
thankful. Roger moaned painfully. Sandy whispered, "Don't
worry, honey, it will all be over soon."

The next day Janet and the sisters of L.O.V.E. received a visit
from Roger's sisters, Gloria and Cathy.

"We heard that Roger's wife, Sandy, came to talk to your support group," Gloria said with obvious distress and Janet didn't
deny the fact. "We wanted to tell you our side of the story. Roger
is a good man, he was a wonderful husband, and Sandy made up
all those vile accusations so when she divorced him she could play
the victim and win a big part of his estate in the settlement. Now,
it seems, it will all be hers."

"You people should really be more careful who you believe and
what's told to you." Cathy, the younger sister said in anger. "Do
you verify anything? Do you just accept any wild, unsubstantiated
story some woman having marital troubles or involved in a child
custody dispute tells you? Women lie too and Sandy is a liar."

Janet flushed angry then grew thoughtful. Had they made a
mistake? She looked carefully at the two young women confronting her now. They appeared sincere, truthful . . . sane. "We did see
the police reports, and Sandy had an order of protection against
your brother. I can assure you Sandy's fear was real enough, all of
us here have gone through similar victimization from men and can
relate to what she went through."

Cathy laughed derisively, "Sandy faked the fall, she never
wanted that baby. Roger was the happy one when Sandy got pregnant, he doted over her so, he wanted that baby more than anything in the world."

Gloria said, "Sandy told me she hated what the baby was doing
to her figure. I know she murdered that baby!"

"Now hold on!" Janet said trying to get control of the situation.

"Sandy's 'fall'," Cathy blurted, "and other injuries were all made up. She got that broken arm and leg from a skiing accident shortly before she met Roger."

Gloria added, "And you know any woman can go to any judge to have an order of protection granted. The mere fact one is granted means nothing. It's only later during the trial that the man even has a chance to defend himself and demand the woman substantiate her accusations."

Janet nodded to the truth of that but said nothing more, allowing the man's sisters to talk through their anger and feelings. Of course they were bitter, she thought . . . but . . .

"And as for Sandy being so scared of Roger and fearful for her life—Roger, who by the way, wouldn't hurt a fly—that was her usual excellent acting job. She is using you, just like she used Roger, and he didn't want to believe it either."

"Roger didn't deserve that evil Sandy, or that beating. He will probably die from it. Sandy probably hired them. She's just the type to do that sort of thing." The other sister said. "If my sister and I ever find out who did that to Roger we'll see to it they're in prison for the rest of their lives."

Janet didn't say much when the sisters left but they had given her a lot to think about. Had her valiant band of over-zealous sisters been duped? Was Sandy the aggressor and the abuser, while Roger was the true victim? It seemed impossible to Janet but the thought nagged at her inner and most basic instincts. Had they made a terrible mistake? Janet resolved to find out.

Janet met Sandy alone a few nights later at the empty L.O.V.E. offices where she hoped to get some answers.

"It's just the two of us here, we're alone," Janet said, offering the younger woman a seat at the conference table. Sandy stood, nervous, anxious.

"You said you had something important to tell me?" she asked.

"Yes," Janet said, taking a deep breath, for she knew once she began this, who knew where it might lead. Perhaps prison for her and the girls and the end of L.O.V.E. itself? "I spoke to Roger's sisters the other day and they . . ."

"Those witches!"

"They told me quite a different story of the relationship between you and Roger."

"I'll bet! It's all lies," Sandy said carefully. "Why are you asking me these questions anyway? You're supposed to be *my* support group, you're supposed to be on *my* side."

"We are on your side, Sandy. More than you could ever know."

Sandy looked at Janet deeply, curious, "Well then, why don't you act like it!"

Janet said it short and simple, "It was my ladies—L.O.V.E.—that put Roger in the hospital."

Sandy looked back at Janet with genuine shock and then began to laugh wildly at the admission. "And here I thought it was just a mugger, or some guy Roger owned money to for gambling! So it was you and the L.O.V.E. girls? That's precious!"

"So you see, Sandy, we really are on your side."

Sandy smiled, this was just too good to be true and better yet, Janet's admission placed her and all of her girls under Sandy's thumb now. "This is priceless!"

"Yes, I thought you'd be happy to hear the truth about how Roger caught his beating."

"Well, good, I'm damn glad to hear it. I just hope you made the little wimp squirm. Did he cry out? Was he in pain?"

"Yes," Janet said softly, "he cried out and he was in terrible pain."

Sandy's cold and bloodthirsty laugh was terrible to hear. "Did he ask for . . . mercy?"

"Yes he did," Janet replied soaking in the younger woman's words and demeanor and not liking any of it one bit. But Janet still had to get to the bottom of this, she needed to hear it all from Sandy's own lips.

"Good," Sandy said confident now. "That's the only kind of support group that's really effective. The revenge type. So now that I know what you and the girls did . . ."

"It's truth time, Sandy. Now I want to know if any of what you told me and the girls about Roger was true?"

Sandy laughed boldly confident. She shrugged unconcerned, "Sure, I guess I can tell you now. It was all made up; none of it was true. I planned to get a large chunk of Roger's wealth all along, but now, after your attack, he's not expected to live much longer. Now I'll get it all. But don't think I'm not appreciative, and I'll keep your little secret, if you keep mine. I'll even give L.O.V.E. a sizeable donation once I get my money."

Janet smiled, "Well, then, that's all I really wanted to know, Sandy, because you know it's important that the good work we do here at L.O.V.E. continues. I hope you agree."

"Absolutely," Sandy replied. Then the two women shook hands and went their separate ways.

Sandy proved as good as her word. A month after Roger passed away, Janet received an impressive five-figure check made out to the Ladies Overcoming Violent Exploiters non-profit organization.

That night as Sandy took the private elevator in her new apartment building down to the garage where her new Mercedes was parked, she was surprised to see a woman she recognized standing beside her car.

"Janet? What are you doing here?"

"Unfinished business, my darling," then Janet withdrew a stun gun that shot a massive bolt of electricity into Sandy that quite painfully incapacitated her. Sandy collapsed, helpless, unable to speak.

"All right ladies," Janet called.

From out of the shadows, from behind parked cars, came Roger's sisters, Gloria and Cathy. Both of whom were holding baseball bats, as they closed in on Sandy.

DEMONOLOGY

THE STUDY OF DEMONS is thought to be merely a supernatural concern relegated to religion and the church, but the only real demons I've ever found in this world of ours are the two-legged kind. And there's plenty of them. Sometimes the very people anointed to protect us from the supernatural ones.

The clergy.

To most people today's mainline religions seem harmless enough, some even appear to do good. I wasn't misled. I knew they extract a price for anything they give. And the cults are much worse. They demand much more.

All those Reverends, Priests, Rabbis, all those fundamentalist sects and bizarre cults so full of blind fanaticism and irrational hatred. Too often they turn into what they say they hate the most.

Evil.

Then they become the demons.

That's where I come in. My name's Joe Dillon and I fight them. I know all about religion. How bad it is. How it destroys the human spirit and only offers excuses for our evil acts.

Never solutions. The religion I've seen never advocates responsibility, self-reliance, and freedom of thought, only subservience and obedience.

It's the biggest lie there is in a world full of big lies.

There is no God for me anymore, no more religion of any kind. To me God is just so much fantasy, no more real than Mary Poppins or the Easter Bunny. But don't think for a minute that I'm not certain the idea isn't dangerous, and don't think the idea of God hasn't been responsible for most of the evil in our world either. But only the idea—it's people who have carried out the evil. It always is.

So much in this life is crap. Seeing it for what it is, is what's difficult. But you live and learn. I've learned the hard way. Now I'm doing something about it.

There was another person who knew the score and was ready to kick the scales of injustice right in the ass. She was just a wild-eyed kid trying to hold onto herself in a world of fools and maniacs. She was a hell of a fighter. I admired her.

Her name was Annie. She'd been brought up strictly religious. Too damn religious. The religious sickness, I call it. She was raised in a rigid home that gave no love and poured on the guilt because the Bible said to. At least, that's the way her people interpreted things.

She'd been packed off to a special Christian school in Alabama when she turned eight. I knew all about such places.

They all practice stern discipline. They lock the kids up at night. They treat them like slaves. Like property. They hurt them just about every way a kid can be hurt. Some are less harmful than others—they only fuck your mind. But that's bad too. Mess you up so you can't think straight ever again. So you'll be just like the adults. So you can't stand on your own two feet. So you'll be just another religious basket case. Of course, as if that isn't bad enough, there are those that do even worse.

Annie told me all about Reverend Powell. How he ran his "school". Locking the students away at night so they couldn't escape, making sure the "sisters" checked each girls' panties in the morning for discharge. Just to see if they had any latent sexual arousal during the night. Bad thoughts. Evil thoughts. The kind of thoughts that interfered with their studies and always led to punishment. The students were degraded, guilt-ridden, some became suicidal, all were punished severely if they spoke up or tried to run away.

Those were the lucky ones. You've got to fight that crap or it will destroy you. Most just went along. They kept quiet. They didn't want to speak up or conflict with what was said to be "The Lord's" will.

There were whippings in the shed behind the big farmhouse. Other "exercises" to rid the body of the Devil. You see, Annie was one of those said to have the Devil in her. Annie questioned what Reverend Powell said about a lot of things. She questioned the beatings. She questioned the sex. She questioned the hatred all neatly wrapped up in religion and force-fed to the kids. She questioned why any decent God would want his children treated so badly, punished and hurt so much. She even questioned the guilt that came with merely asking such questions. She was a dangerous child and they tried everything they could to teach her the error of her ways.

The harder they tried, the more she fought them.

Annie finally got away before they totally destroyed her but if she thought she'd had it tough before, it was a whole lot tougher now. A lot more ugly.

Annie ran straight into the warm, hungry bosom of New York City, the hot festering sore of Times Square, and into the fetid grip of a man-of-means called Slick.

At first she thought she'd found someone who would finally listen to her, talk to her, even comfort her. Not perfect, but he was there for her at least—when no one else had been. When no one else ever listened. And Slick was a slick guy, a fun guy, and knew not to push in the beginning. He had a nice smile too—even though it looked like he had razors for teeth.

Annie knew Slick was a pimp, and that his "family" was nothing more than a stable of young bitches for sale. But she'd been so wrong about all those religious bastards from her former life—people supposed to be so damn Godly—that Slick and his crew of 'ladies' were like a breath of fresh air for her. They were open in their ideas and lifestyle, and the concept was initially liberating. They didn't make judgments about people. In fact, they didn't seem to care an awful lot about anything except having fun and getting paid. They excelled at that.

The girls weren't bad once you got to know them. No one bothered her. They gave her food, a place to sleep, Slick bought her nice clothes. And she dressed up for him. It was fun. She was his special girl.

Annie finally found a place where she could stay awhile. That was until Slick told her it was time to go out on the street and make some cash by selling herself.

Annie refused to do that.

No matter what he said, how he threatened, she refused. He used all his powers to control her.

It didn't work.

Most girls were happy to "help out".

Not this one.

Not Annie.

She fought him. She fought him word for word. Sentence for sentence.

"Ungrateful bitch!" Slick called her.

She still refused.

He slapped her. Slapped her hard.

Annie wouldn't budge.

Slick had the girls 'talk' to her. But that didn't work either. Annie 'talked' back.

Then the women held her down and Slick raped her. The whores cheering him on. Annie crying and full of rage.

They thought they'd broken her spirit.

The next day Annie lifted one of the whores' knives, and cut Slick's throat from ear to ear.

I met Annie on the New Jersey Turnpike. I didn't pick her up. My car had a blowout. I was changing a tire when she came up to me from along the shoulder of the road. Curious. Hard. Sizing me up.

She told me later she'd jumped from some creep's car after she'd hitched a ride. He figured it was a license to do whatever he wanted to her. He figured wrong.

She said, "I need a ride. South. You going that way?"

I said, "No. Sorry. I'm going North. To New York. Brooklyn. You're welcome to ride with me if you want. Won't be more than an hour or so before we're downtown."

She was quiet for a long time.

I didn't press it. I tried to get the tire off. One of the bolts was giving me a problem. Something always gives me a problem.

She said, "I've killed a man back there. I don't think I can go back. He was a pimp. I slit his throat after he beat me and raped me. He wanted me to go on the street. Sell myself. I wouldn't. What do you think of that? Do you still want to give me a ride, Mister?"

I dropped the lug wrench. I looked at her closely. It was one hell of a statement. She was pretty young. Just a kid really. She should have been in school with her friends. She wasn't. I could see she wasn't kidding about what she'd said either. I can tell those things. It's part of my work. Reading people. She had a hard, severe look, a sparseness to her very being. I'd seen less wear and tear on old folks waiting to drop dead in retirement homes. But her spirit shone forth strong and bold. She'd been beaten, but she'd never been broken.

Then I saw the act replayed in her eyes. And others even more vile. I could feel her pain, see it there moving in waves across her face like a shadow of death. A haunting. It was terrible to see. I didn't look away.

"I'm sorry that happened," I told her. Then I looked over to the blown out tire, trying to get the tire off. Her eyes followed me. I said, "They looking for you?"

"The cops?"

"Yeah," I said.

"No. They'll never know. Don't care anyway."

"Help me get the spare out of the trunk. The faster we get it on the faster we can get going."

"You heard me, Mister?" she said. "I killed a man back there."

"My name's Joe, and you didn't kill no man back there if you killed a lousy pimp. That's a pile of garbage that only appeared to be a man. It wasn't. It was a monster in human form. Not a man."

"They'll be after me for it, Joe. Slick had friends, business associates he called them. Mob guys. Other pimps. They won't let me get away with it. They can't, it would be bad for their business. Funny, they calling it a business. I call it by its real name—slavery."

She was right of course about it being slavery.

Well, that's how Annie and I met. We liked each other right off. We had a feeling about each other. We knew we could trust each other. She had guts. I had a mission.

When she found out what I was up to she liked that too. She wanted to join in. I told her it was dangerous but I needed someone like her right now, especially someone with her previous religious experience and cynicism. It made her strong. Immune.

"Here's how it works," I told her one night after we had some pizza, drank a couple of beers. We looked over the photos that had come in that morning from a friend. They were good, clear shots of a secluded estate outside Atlanta.

It was a big, beautiful place. An Antebellum plantation. A protected, guarded place. A special religious school. Pre-teens and teens. The demons ran it. They called themselves "The Holy Ones". They weren't. They were only fanatics and maniacs.

"I've heard of the place," Annie said. "My parents were going to send me there for a 'proper' religious upbringing. Instead they packed me off to the Alabama school. It was cheaper. I was only eight years old."

I couldn't say anything.

"I've heard of the Atlanta school," Annie added. "It was in the news. I heard they killed a kid, beat him to death—though they naturally made out it was an accident. I think they said he was a drug addict, he had to be restrained by the staff. He fought. Somehow he died. They said he had the Devil in him."

"Annie, that kid was on a job for me investigating that school. He was only 18 years old. His name was Steve. Just so you know. Busting this place open is dangerous, but it's important."

"I know how bad these fanatics can be," she said, remembering.

"Yeah. I can never figure the parents. Don't they know what goes on in some of these places—to their own kids? Kids should be protected from this kind of stuff," I said.

"Some of the parents know. Some don't. Most of them don't care. The parents are fanatics too, Joe. Some of them even think the Devil possesses their kids. They're scared of them. Some of the kids have drug or alcohol problems, some are abused. The parents see the kids as the enemy. The kids never have a chance."

From what Annie told me about her own past she knew how bad it could be. Her own demon went by the name of Reverend Jeremiah K. Powell. He carried a brown switch. It was his favorite weapon. It was brown from all the dried blood soaked into it over the years. It wasn't his only weapon, nor the worst one he used, just his favorite. He said using it brought him closer to God. God may not know it but he's got one hell of a communication problem.

Annie told me that Reverend Powell said the Devil always had to be exorcised, especially from the bodies of children. Children are so devilish. So evil. He used to tell Annie that Satan was everywhere.

The son-of-a-bitch must have been looking in the mirror.

I promised Annie we'd pay Reverend Powell a visit after Atlanta. Right now Atlanta was a prior commitment. It was my mission. It was called the Christian Paradise School. These were the self-righteous maniacs who murdered Steve.

I had a friend enroll Steve in the school in late 1992. He enrolled him as his son, a wild boy who needed straightening out and to be given proper religious values. They were only too happy to take him and the check.

This was a Southern Baptist Fundamentalist school, but it was no different in its treatment of students than many other religious schools I had investigated over the years. And these are mainline religions. The cults are much worse.

This particular institution was heavy on punishment, guilt, degradation. Sleep deprivation and brainwashing were not uncommon. It was a wellspring of all types of abuse shielded under the guise of religion and God.

Most kids are resilient, they bend with the wind, just like any good tree does to survive. Some can't. When a tree can't or won't bend it breaks. All you get is lumber. But a kid with his or her own mind—a kid who won't bend, who won't accept all the nonsense and lies—they'll break him. And they'll love doing it. They'll think it's a holy thing they're doing. And they'll do it every damn time. Most religions can't allow you to have a free mind. A rational, skeptical mind. A scientific mind that wants to see evidence and not rely merely on faith. A mind that can ask questions, that has the guts to ask, "Why"?

These days in America that type of person is more dangerous than a loaded gun.

Steve had been in the school a month before they were onto him. In that time he'd collected enough data and pictures to put the director and his staff away for years. Close the school forever. Discredit the leadership of the church. But Steve had been found out.

They murdered him in cold blood—but the bastards never found the material he'd collected about them. Steve's notes and film were well hidden. Before Steve was killed he told me where it was. All Annie had to do was go in and get it.

I gave her a day or two to get the stuff. She'd call me when she was ready and the next day I'd come down to the school, an indignant "daddy" taking his daughter back home where she belonged.

I shook Pastor Brother MaKee's hand. It was cold and slippery. Like a dead fish, or a serial killer.

"The Lord moves in mysterious ways, Mr. Arnold. Your daughter has seen the wild wantonness of the outside world. The debauchery that exists in this Sodom and Gomorrah surrounding us. Here, within the saintly walls of the Christian Paradise School His Kingdom has come to a very small, but important part of this sorrowful world. Glory to His name!"

I nodded. I smiled. Fighting the bullshit. I thanked him and gave him the big check.

He didn't even look at it. He knew the suckers always paid up. Fought for the opportunity, in fact.

"You're lucky to get Annie into our school. There are so many difficulties in raising a proper Christian young lady these days," Brother MaKee added. He smiled like a saint. "We do the best we can, in His name, but we are mere mortals, my son. We try to do His holy work as surely as great Abraham."

I smiled back, thinking about Abraham. A wild-eyed fanatic who almost murdered his own son in an evil sacrifice because his deluded mind told him God wanted it done. A meaningless sacrifice, to a meaningless, petty, jealous, being. A deity unworthy of our devotion for asking such a thing. He is with us still. Right there in your Bible. I knew all about him. Annie knew about him. I didn't say a word. I turned my back and walked away.

Annie went inside, settled in, met her roommate, got into the routine. I didn't hear from her for three days. I was getting worried.

She wasn't supposed to make outside calls. It wasn't allowed. But there are ways. When I got into my hotel room her message was on the recorder.

"Hi. It's me, daddy. I have your present. Come and take me home. Please. I don't like it here."

Pastor Brother MaKee was firm in his denial. Annie was not anywhere on the premises. No one knew where she'd gone.

"Mr. Arnold, we deal with problem teens like Annie all the time. Many do not accept our stern character-building policies. Some can never be broken of that slim thread of rebelliousness no matter how hard we try. There is Satan's will at work here, sir. We see it all the time in these children. Drugs. Sex. Dirty language. Impure thoughts."

I thought that over for a moment. Impure thoughts?

"Let me explain myself clearly, Pastor Brother MaKee, so even you will understand me. If Annie is not brought to me in the next five minutes I'll go and find her myself—and if anything has happened to her I'll break you apart into so many pieces that God himself won't be able to put you back together again."

He stepped back indignant, bold, even angry. Then he thought better of it.

"Well, she is not here, sir. She's run away during the night. We are not responsible for her."

"And I suppose you're not responsible when I bring the cops here and have you arrested for murder and kidnapping."

Now it was his turn to smile. "Mr. Arnold, there has been no kidnapping or murder here. I don't know where you would get such a wild idea. You freely brought your daughter to us. Paid us, in fact, to take her off your hands. You cannot hold us responsible if she runs away. Some of them always run away."

"Or if she has been murdered?"

There was quiet for a long moment, then Pastor Brother MaKee said, "If, in fact, she is your daughter, Mr. Arnold?"

Pastor Brother MaKee didn't get a chance to press the button on his desk to call security. He had the snub-nose of my .38 brushing his teeth just then. He fell back and I jumped on his chest, forcing the short barrel of the .38 up into his left nostril.

"Now I'm finished playing. You understand?"

He turned sheet-white, sweat trickled down his forehead. His eyes as big as hens eggs.

"Blink twice if you understand what I'm saying."

He blinked twice. Fast.

"That's good." I pushed the revolver deeper. It made him uncomfortable and scared. That's why I did it.

"Now you're going to tell me where Annie is."

He didn't blink.

"You're not answering me, Pastor. That makes me very angry."

He said, "I . . . I don't know where she ran off to."

"You're lying. Most un-Christian-like."

"No! No, I wouldn't lie. God is great. God is good. God help me in my hour of need. Save me from this demon! Save . . ."

I slapped his face. That brought him around.

"Shut up! When are you people going to realize that if there really is a God he wouldn't have anything to do with monsters like you! You pervert and destroy everything you say he stands for. You destroy his children. You're the true demons. In your blindness you and your kind only serve . . . Satan!"

That gets them every time. Just the mention of the Evil One's name. But there's harsh truth to it. Too many religious leaders become exactly what they say they hate the most. They prove it everyday. We've all seen it too—if we'd only open our eyes.

"No! It's not true!" He would have shouted if my hand hadn't clamped down vise-like on his throat. Only a whispered gurgle escaped.

"Are you so sure. Demon!"

He started shaking. I shook him more.

"Where is Annie?"

"She escaped," he whispered, straining, petrified.

"You were onto her?"

"She is an agent of Satan. Your agent!"

"Oh, shut up you stupid bastard. I ain't Satan. I'm just a guy

who busts schools that destroy kids in the name of God and religion. I had a wife and family once. I lost them because I was stupid.
I didn't realize who the true demons were. Now I know. Now I do
something about them."

He squealed.

"I'm a guy who had a friend and partner named Steve Basil.
Remember him, parasite? Just 18 years old and you put him in a
grave!"

He was in full panic now. I encouraged his fear.

"I want answers!" I growled into his ear like a mad beast only
seconds away from ripping his heart out.

He shook his head.

"Where is Annie?"

"She's run—run away," he whimpered, afraid now even to answer me.

"You're not being helpful," I said. Either he was a good liar or
she actually had run away. I just hoped she'd run before they came
to get her. That might mean she was still alive and hiding somewhere on the grounds.

MaKee shivered. I cold-cocked him, sending him deep into
dreamland. It was a hell of a lot better place than he'd sent Steve.

I locked his door from the inside, then stepped out the French
doors behind his desk onto the vast lawn of the estate. I walked
around trying to look as if I belonged. No one seemed to notice
me.

I saw numerous outbuildings on the grounds. There were students with Bibles, all probably going to and from classes. No one
talking. All looking very serious. And certainly no laughing. No
horsing around like real kids do in school. They were sad kids.
Sold out kids. Lonely kids with that fake blankness on their faces,
a phony glow only skin deep. It hid vacant smiles. It was weird.
They all wore guilt like it was clothing.

"They're not like regular kids," a voice whispered behind me,
"at least not once these fanatics get through running their guilt
trips and demonology on them. Then they just become basket
cases. Worse than any slave, for they love their slavery, and believe it to be God's will."

I turned around and saw Annie hiding near a doorway behind
some hedges. She stood there like a mannequin.

I ran over frantic. "Are you okay? I thought . . ."

"I'm okay, I guess. They figured I was a plant from the beginning and had my roomie watch me. She was like female Gestapo, but by the third day I'd gotten away from her long enough to get to where Steve had hidden the evidence. She caught me after I made the phone call to you. I've been hiding out until you got here. The grounds are enormous in this place, but fenced like Stalag 13. You can't get out. They even have guard towers. But now I'm getting out. Right Joe? You brought your gun?"

"Yeah," I said.

"You might need it, Joe," she said.

"I know. Used it already."

"Oh, Joe, you didn't . . .?"

"No. I didn't shoot no one. Not yet. Just banged around Pastor Brother MaKee. He'll be dozing for another hour yet. I should have killed the bastard for what he did to Steve, but I didn't. It's more important to expose these people for what they are. They don't need any more martyrs for their rotten cause."

"Good, then let's get out of here, Joe. Please."

"Sure thing, kid."

The stuff Steve found was dynamite. Photos mostly. They showed everything from beatings, to downright torture, and whippings that Torquemada himself would have been proud of. A real sadistic band of ultra religious creeps. Nazis with Bibles.

Steve also found information on two other "supposed" runaways from the school. Steve noted where the bodies were buried. They had been beaten to death. One of the girls had been raped and then killed. We gave it all to the media and they did all the rest. The scandal was outrageous. The Christian Paradise School was closed down and MaKee, his staff, and the Board of Governors were all up for murder. They did not post bail, fearful that some of the parents might be gunning for them.

Annie and I had some time before the court case.

"You promised, Joe. I helped you. Now, you'll do something for me?"

"You really want to go through with this?"

"Yes."

"You know it could get messy?"

"I know."

I didn't say anything for a moment.

"It's something I have to do, Joe," she said slowly.

"Okay, Annie. A deal's a deal."

It was a two-hour drive to the Alabama border. From there another hour to the farm that served as the Glory To God School. Where "Jesus and Fundamentalism are one". Or so the sign said.

It looked like a nice place. It was a big place. In a desolate area. There were crosses everywhere. Big neon things. I guess the more crosses, or the bigger the crosses were, the holier you had to be. In that case, these were very holy people. It said so all over the damn place.

These were also the people who'd beaten Annie near to death. She'd been a normal young girl. Her only crime growing up in a land of narrow-minded fanatics and religious blockheads. But these blockheads had guns. Whips. Bibles that made whatever they said and did true—and holy, and just, in their eyes. But only in their eyes.

"Reverend Powell said I had the devil in me." Annie said, "I didn't, Joe, not until he got through with me I didn't. But I'm not so sure now, after he hurt me so much. Now I'm going to put the devil right back into that self-righteous son-of-a-bitch. Right back where it belongs."

"Just so you don't kill him, Annie."

The big house was quiet. It was after midnight on a moonless evening. Real dark. Real quiet. No one on the grounds. Lights-out had been hours before. The lights were still out. All the good little Bible-belters sleeping and dreaming pure Biblical thoughts.

A big guard dog roamed the back of the house. We drugged him with laced meat. He'd be sleeping for hours.

Annie and I didn't have much trouble getting through the front window of the house. It was a warm summer night. All the windows open. I pulled the screen right out. Nice and quiet. These country places are never that secure, their inaccessibility offered more security than any hi-tech alarm ever could. Or so their owners thought.

The Most Reverend Jeremiah K. Powell was asleep in socks and boxer shorts. Next to him in the bed was another form. A smaller form. Laying stone still, eyes open wide, watching us, mouth shut tight. You could hardly hear him breathe.

Annie moved close to the boy.

She whispered into his ear. "Joey, it's me, Annie. Remember? I came back, just like I said I would."

He didn't say anything. He just stared at her.

"It's okay, Joey. This is my friend. His name is Joe. He's a good man. We're here to save you."

I nodded at the kid. He was a stone.

Annie put out her arms, wide, waiting for Joey to come to her. She waited. Patient. It would take time, I could see him thinking it over. Wondering if he dared ever trust again.

Joey moved then, slowly. Delicately, slipping over the edge of the bed. Then he fell into Annie's arms and they hugged each other tightly—like they were halves of the same person. It lasted a long time and tears flowed from their eyes. The Reverend just kept sleeping like a cold brick, but it was time to wake him up now.

That was my part. I like rousting rats. Making them pay for their deeds. I'd take particular pleasure in teaching this one a lesson after what I'd just seen, but this was Annie's show. I was just the help on this one.

I moved close to him. It amazes me how the truly evil sleep so soundly. Like they've never done anything wrong. Like they haven't a care or regret in the world. Perhaps they don't. Perhaps, being truly evil, they wouldn't.

Annie ushered Joey out of the room into the connecting bathroom and closed the door behind them.

I used the snub barrel of my .38. A glancing blow on the back of his head. Reverend Powell was in sleepytimeland before he knew what hit him.

I had work to do now. I took out the tape.

It didn't take me long.

Soon I had the evil Reverend stripped down nude on the bed. He lay on his stomach, arms and legs spread out and tied tightly to the four posts of the big old bed. His mouth taped over so he couldn't make a sound. I slapped him a couple of times and he came out of it. His eyes looked like big, red melons as the terror caught hold of him.

The door to the bathroom opened. Annie came back into the room. She had a long switch, supple, thin, but very durable. It was a green wood switch. Newly cut. Never used.

I spoke into Reverend Powell's ear, whispering my words. They were the clearest, sharpest damn words he'd ever heard in his life.

I said, "You're going to mend your ways, Reverend. You've been an evil bastard, now you're going to get what you deserve.

After we're finished with you, you're going to close this school. Tomorrow. I want you to resign and be out of here. Understand? No more of this shit. If you don't leave I'll kill you. Understand?"

He nodded, petrified, not knowing what was going to happen. He was agreeing to anything and I knew it. That was okay, his words didn't mean shit to me anyway. I'd watch him. Make sure he left. Make sure he didn't go back to his old ways. I'd be back this way to check up. I always do. That's part of the mission.

"Before I leave you, there's someone else who wants to "talk" to you. Someone you've hurt a lot. Now she's going to hurt you back. A lot. I believe there's a passage for that in the Bible, Reverend. It has something to do with Justice."

Then Annie got to work. She was young and very strong. Had good wrist action. The switch caught the Reverend's flesh, snapping it apart. Once. Twice. And, finally . . . . dozens of times. The evil Reverend's back was awash in blood.

"It's time, Annie."

She nodded and stopped. Spit upon the Reverend and threw the bloody switch to the floor in disgust.

"See what I have to do, Joe. There's no court, no police, no God to help people like us. That's only for civilized crimes, problems between civilized people. It doesn't work with monsters like this. We have to handle problems like this ourselves. Each one of us. In our own way. So it never happens again."

I nodded. I knew she was right.

We made ready to leave. Joey came out from the bathroom. Looked at the Reverend. It bothered me for the kid to see this, but it couldn't be helped. He'd seen worse—been forced into much worse.

Annie took his hand and was taking him out the door but Joey held back. Quiet. Firm. Still as a statue. Staring down at the Reverend's bloody form. At the switch on the floor where Annie had thrown it.

Then Joey shook his hand loose from Annie, picked up the switch, and used it on the Reverend.

Once.

Twice.

Three times as hard as an angry child was able. Putting all his strength into it.

When he was finished Joey threw the switch to the floor, took Annie's hand and walked out of the room with her.

I left the room, closing the door quietly behind me.

NOT MUCH JOY IN PRISON

WHEN I WORKED IN THE FACTORY, it was like a prison. They let you go home but you had to be right back at the grind the next morning. It was a good-paying union job too, so you couldn't quit—it was hard to get fired—and with little education and no connections I had nowhere better to go anyway. The bosses knew that and rode your back with vicious hatred because of it.

Prison is far worse but at least you don't have to take the crap you do on the outside if you don't want to. There's no joy in prison except one thing; the dreaming, thinking and planning of getting back at the person who ratted you out, framed you, or did you dirty. Now, if the person who did you dirty is in prison with you, then you can experience the joy immediately. It's payback time and there's nothing anyone can do to stop you. You have the opportunity to get back at him like you never could on the outside, I mean, what are they going to do to you—send you to prison?

True, they'll add more time to your sentence, but tacking on another 30 or 40 years when you're already in for 50 don't seem to make much difference. Payback's the only joy in prison and it can be a real bitch.

This is a death penalty state. But I got that figured. We all do. It takes them almost twenty years to actually execute anyone, so I take full advantage through all the endless appeals. Hell, when you're locked up, it can help keep you sane to keep busy. Sometimes, even make you hopeful. Especially if you're innocent; of which there may actually be one or two, though from what I hear every one of them say, they is *all* innocent, *every single one of them!*

Everyone but me. I *am* guilty. *Guilty* as sin. I am a killer and proud of it. I killed for pay, and sometimes, if you pissed me off real bad, I killed for free. That's just my way.

Mostly I took contracts, but I also killed crooked cops, pedophiles, and rapist bastards, if I saw some righteousness in it. I was a bad son-of-a-bitch, but not an evil one. The evil ones really pissed me off. All the ones I did, I figured they deserved it.

Even on death row, during the endless appeals process, I was able to squeeze the last drop of joy out of life. There was this sadistic guard called Long Tom who liked to beat black prisoners. He especially had it in for Wilson Jones, a retard a few cells down from me who didn't like getting raped. Long Tom was aptly named. Long Tom was a Nazi guard, Aryan Brotherhood connections, an all around prick until I put a shank in his throat and he drowned on his own blood.

Which caused my execution to be postponed for an inquiry and eventually another trial. And many months later another death sentence. I appealed. Wilson committed suicide. Long Tom was given a distinguished service medal by the Brotherhood, posthumously. I continued my appeals and another year passed.

Then another year after that and then one more. They wanted to execute me so bad but the process was long and laborious. I had found another loophole in the system. They tacked on another 50 years for Long Tom's murder. I think I was up to about 250 years by then.

There's also a lot of time to think in prison. Sometimes I think about what got me here in the first place.

I'd taken a contract a few years back to kill a pimp that had stolen one of Slim's girls. This new pimp was some retro hippie skell selling runaways on the street. He did it like a commune; the girls used the money for food, to feed their kids, and for drugs. One big happy family. I killed the pimp for cash; he'd stolen away Jasmine, Slim's prime girl. Not so, I found out later. Jasmine left for a better life. Still *in* the "life" you understand, but being away from Slim, anywhere is better than being anywhere *with* Slim. Working for Slim was just hard and nasty. When I brought Jasmine back to him and got my pay, Slim was so happy we did a few lines and then he told me he had a surprise for me. We went downstairs in the basement where his boys had Jasmine all tied for the torture. Slim was going to teach her a lesson and he'd invited me to watch the fun. I didn't like that. I began to realize I'd made a mistake. One thing my Mama taught me was that a man will always make mistakes in life, but a *real* man will always set them right. I always listened to my Mama.

I told Slim, "You don't need to do this, man. Let's forget it and go back upstairs, have a few beers, chill."

Slim was serious and determined. "Gots to teach the bitch a lesson. Make an example."

I knew what that meant.

Slim was determined it was going to happen. He pulled out a knife and prepared to get to work. Jasmine squirmed against her bonds and tried to scream but she was bound and gagged tightly. She wasn't going anywhere.

Enrique and Solomon smiled in anticipation.

Slim was determined this would happen.

I was determined that it would not.

I drew my gun and killed all three of them. Slim got it first. Enrique and Solomon were next.

Fast, one, two, three. The word "remorse" never entered my mind.

I cut Jasmine loose. Of course, she's the one testified against me at the murder trial. Sometimes you can never figure.

I think back on things sometimes. It's amazing how things can get to the point that they get to. Here I am on death row awaiting an execution that had been put off three times already. There had been three additional murder trials. I even considered copping to some of the hundreds of unsolved crimes like the serial killers here do. They know they can delay the process by adding a murder here or there to their list. Sometimes they did the killing, sometimes they just watched, sometimes they borrow a murder they just heard about.

We had one guy here whose specialty was kids. Simon copped to 12 but insiders said he'd done as many as fifty. Maybe a hundred. Simon gave up a name and body location from time to time. He'd been on death row for 20 years and it looked like it would be the death of him too—*not* from an execution—but *from old age!*

I did not like Simon. I did not like what he did and I did not like him playing my game, even though to be truthful, I was playing *his* game. In any case, I began to have a thing for seeing Simon dead.

This would be tough to accomplish. I planned it for months. It's amazing the focus and concentration you can have in prison if you let yourself over to it. You can accomplish incredible things. It gives you a kind of power.

They watched Simon real tight. The guards and cons hated him. Pedophiles are the lowest form of scum in prison but child killers are ten levels below that. Every con would love to kill one if he could get the chance. Ask Jeffrey Dahmer. The guy that killed him should be a national hero—he did what society and the justice system couldn't do—he gave Dahmer the death sentence he deserved—cold, hard, violent, nasty, painful. Better than anything Dahmer ever gave the young men he'd killed, that's for sure.

Simon was a tough nut to crack. He still had DAs, retired cops, and family members interested in him. Everyone looking for closure on an old case or a missing kid. He almost never admitted anything, but on one or two rare occasions, when he thought they were going to execute him, he'd cop to a new kid. It would be one he'd say that he had forgotten. Then he'd give a name and a body location. They still tried to pump him for info and he played them for all they were worth.

Simon made like he was some master criminal too. Like he was some big brain who fooled the system. He got special privileges, even on death row, but not everyone in the system was fooled.

I had found that a guard had a sister whose kid had gone missing. Whether Simon had anything to do with it didn't matter. It's what the guard thought. I told him, give me two minutes. One day I noticed the cells were *not* locked down. I'm not saying how this was arranged. A malfunction in the locks? Who knows? Two minutes was all I needed.

I pried open my cell door, walked to Simon's cell. Simon and I were the only inmates on death row then. He was laying in bed, sleeping, or day dreaming about kids most likely.

It was over in less than a heartbeat. I went back to my house and went back to sleep. I slept like a baby too.

My execution had to be postponed again until the investigation was begun and another trial was set. A court of inquiry found there had been a short in the electric locking mechanism of the cell doors. I told how I had discovered it all quite by accident while exercising against the bars. I said that I instantly realized what it meant. I told them I saw I had one chance to kill Simon and I took it. I freely admitted my guilt. They added another 50 years to my time. That was fine with me. The guards in the block were all transferred. Then it was over.

Weeks later a new guard entered my house. He had a bag with him and set it down at the foot of my bed. He pulled out coffee, chocolate, a couple of cigars, candy, a few porno mags.

"We appreciate what you did," he said as he left.

I nodded. I wasn't ever getting out. No way. But now I had my perks, and sometimes that's enough in a place like this. Sometimes in a place like this, a little joy is the best you can hope for.

FINDERS KEEPERS

YOU KNOW, we got another call coming in over the box. It's on the edge of Blacktown."

Fats only nodded. He knew it would be trouble.

That's the way it began back in the bad old days of 1962 in a town I'll call Bay City. Even today, years later, I don't feel right—or safe—using real names in all this stuff I'm telling you. But that's the way it was in those days, being a cop, doing what we had to do to hold the line. Even then the slime was taking over, doing their damnedest to bust us down, destroy law and order, twist justice, kill cops. They'd get away with all kinds of crime then just do it all again *the very next day!*

I was being much too thinkful. Fats had a thing against too much "thinkfullness." He said I did that too much. He was right, of course. He was always right. My partner was a man who hardly ever did any heavy thinking, hardly ever talked, but when he did, it always meant something important. That's the man I teamed up with back then. Sergeant Herman Stubbs, 290 pounds of blubber with an attitude. I'm Lieutenant Bill Griffin, one of the lone survivors from the old days, still left alive to tell our stories.

"Hey Griff?" Fats asked, interrupting my mental meandering with his mouth full of Cracker Jacks. He was driving, but every so often he'd upend the box and pour a glob of caramel coated popcorn glop down his gullet. Then crunch it into oblivion.

"Yeah?" I said, watching as we flew by all the hookers on Dumont Avenue.

"You know what I think?" he said, sorta thoughtful. Fats never got that way unless he had something on his mind. Which, not counting food, wasn't often.

"I don't know. I'm kinda afraid to ask." I said, and meant it.

Fats just laughed as if to say, "You should be."

If you knew him that's just the way he was. But he only smiled at me and added, "What I figure is . . . I think we're about due. Ain't we, Griff?"

It had been weeks. Things going along smooth on the job. Kinda normal. At least for Bay City. No major problems. I knew what Fats meant. It *was* about time. We were due for another dose of some major-league weirdness, or some super sick crap, or any of the other stuff that gets thrust upon you in this job from time to time.

"Fact is, Griff, I think we're kinda overdue, so we may be in for some extremely super weird crap. What do you think?"

I grunted. He had a point—on that big fat head of his.

Fats grunted back, smiled. Knocked off the box of Cracker Jacks, opened another, and headed our Plymouth out to Livonia Avenue. We got the call there was a body laying in a yard waiting for us to give it the once over.

When we got to 426 Livonia Avenue—sure as the 'Square Mile of Vice' is the real center and heart of this hell town—there was supposed to be a man's body laying out on the lawn. What we saw was a white guy, mid-thirties, working-class clothes, and *not* very dead at all. He was wearing bracelets and very much alive and sitting calmly on the porch of #426.

"No one I know," I said to Fats as we walked over to the guy. He was with two of our uniform guys, our buddy Smitty, and his rookie partner, Billy Ryan.

"So what's up?" Fats asked.

Smitty gave us the nod, indicated the man in handcuffs on the porch. "That's Mr. Arnold Kroptic, who lives here. We were called to investigate sounds of gunfire."

I nodded. Fats burped, meaningfully.

Smitty produced a .32 handgun wrapped in a handkerchief, said, "The gun Kroptic used to shoot and kill John Strossen."

I nodded, "And . . . is Strossen dead? Where is he?"

"Oh yes, he is very dead," Kroptic chirped in, almost proudly. "I had to kill him. I just had to."

"And why did you *have* to do that?" I asked, giving Fats the nod.

Kroptic said, "I can't tell you that, officer."

"Detective," I corrected.

"Whatever," he replied.

I ignored his remark, looked over at Fats, "I think this may be the one. Our overdue case has arrived."

Fats smiled, then nodded like he'd been expecting it all along. Which, of course, he had.

Smitty looked at me and tried to stifle a laugh. He was a street cop, knew the score, said, "Just wait, Griff, it gets better."

"What do you mean?" I asked, waiting for the other shoe to drop.

Smitty smiled, nodded to his rookie partner Billy Ryan, said, "Why don't you take this one, Billy?"

Ryan chortled, said, "Detectives you caught a weird one right off. When Billy and I got here we observed Kroptic on the porch with the murder weapon in his hand. At his feet, over about there, just in front of the first step, was a very dead John Strossen. Billy and I disarmed Kroptic. He offered no resistance. Then we cuffed him to the porch post, and left to check out the house and grounds. We were gone for no more than five minutes. Swear it. When we got back, Strossen's body was gone!"

Fats just laughed and laughed, "Ah, didn't I tell you, Griff."

I looked around, said, "What about neighbors? Anyone see anything? I suppose Kroptic is mum?"

Smitty nodded.

Billy added, "He won't say a word, says the way we had him cuffed he couldn't look behind him anyway."

Fats said, "I mean, who'd take a dead body? Why would anyone steal a dead body?"

"Neighbors are all in their houses, behind locked doors, and covered windows. That's the kind of neighborhood over here on the border of Blacktown. No one wants to know nothing," Smitty said.

"And this Strossen, you sure he was dead? He couldn't have just got up and . . ." I asked. It was silly, but I had to ask, stranger things had happened after all.

"No Griff. I checked," Smitty replied. "Strossen was deader than dead. No pulse. Billy and I canvassed the area but we couldn't come up with anything. No one saw a thing or they're too terrified to speak up. It all happened so damn fast, but the crux of it is Strossen was shot dead, then someone stole his body!"

Fats just laughed and laughed.

I looked at him then, not finding it so amusing.

"Griff, this is better than the movies, better even than them old pulp magazines I used to love to read when I was a kid. Them crime horror stories with far-out titles like 'Captive Sex Slaves of the Hideous Ghoul Killer.' Now that was fun stuff, Griff."

I looked at him, "You used to read that stuff?"

"Sure, all the time. Great stuff. This is like them old stories, Griff. Totally weird. I think we're in for some fun with this one too." Then Fats turned to Kroptic, said, "Of course, Mr. Kroptic you had no partner in this murder? You killed Strossen on your own? And you never saw who stole the corpse?"

Kroptic smiled and said almost proudly, "The killing of Strossen was entirely my own idea. I had no partner or help in it at all. And no, I did not see who took the body, not that I care, now that he's dead."

"See, Griff, and I believe him," Fats bellowed, adding, "I think we got a real doozy here!"

Of course Fats was just playing in that odd sick, twisted cop way of his. He didn't like this kind of crap any more than I did, yet I had to admit that someone stealing that dead body out from under us had got my attention.

Besides that, Strossen was our only piece of hard evidence that a murder had actually been committed.

"Fats, I want that damn corpse!"

Fats nodded, laughed, "Yeah, Griff, it sure ain't right. Even kinda insulting. How dare someone steal our stiff!"

The rest of that day Fats and I, with Smitty and Ryan's help turned Livonia Avenue and the environs upside down and every which way but loose. If there was a hidden stiff anywhere in that section of town, Fats and I would shake it loose but as the day came to an end we came to a kinda different conclusion.

"He ain't here, Griff. He just ain't here. We woulda seen a sign, and I shook everyone's tree in this neighborhood and nothing fell out, because there was nothing there to fall out. You get it?"

"Yeah, nothing corpse-wise that is," I replied, but there was plenty of other crap, but all that was stuff we weren't interested in at the moment. Truth was a pissed-off 290-pound Fatman could do an awful job of intimidation, so that when he decided to shake someone's tree, every damn thing that person was hiding was sure to fall out. Everything, except the stiff that had been stolen.

"'Course Captain Landis is kinda unhappy about this turn of events," Fats chortled in what was the understatement of 1962.

"Yeah," I said, "we all is unhappy."

"So, there's gotta be something else, something we ain't figuring," Fats added. There he was, being obvious again. That meant he was starting to think, and that usually meant trouble.

I nodded, "You mean like the body wasn't stolen to impede our murder investigation? Or with us not having any corpus delicti . . . You mean it was . . . random?"

"Yeah, like random. Random Bay City resident drove by, maybe walked by for all I know, saw the corpse, put it in his car, maybe on his back and . . . You know? A real sicko. Took it home . . . or something."

"That's a special kind of crazy."

"Yeah, real special," he was silent for a moment, thinking. He reached into his pocket and unpeeled a Hersey Bar, consumed it in two quick bites, burped, looked at me and said, "Now, what sick, twisted, piece of human garbage would do a thing like that?"

I looked at Fats; "Bay City is a big, bad place. I guess we gotta start making a list."

And that's just what we did. The very next morning as we sat at Jackie's Diner on Dumont Avenue we went over the list of names Fats and I had put together the night before.

Fats offered his usual biting comment on each suspect. "What an accumulation of human vermin, lowlifes, parasites, degenerates, loosers . . . Damn, Griff, we gotta lotta names here."

I nodded. Lotta freaks.

Fats put a pencil mark through one name, said, "Cosgrove hung himself last week in his cell."

I nodded, "Or so they say."

"Whatever, for us it's just one less skell on our list," Fats laughed, showing his sensitive side again, I guess.

I said, "We gotta like a guy for this either knows Strossen or is into some weirdass death stuff, like maybe . . . necrophilia."

Fats shuddered, "You mean, like having sex with dead people?"

I nodded.

"Jesus," he said solemnly, then added a laugh, "I just thought of something. If he's having sex with that dead guy's body . . . Does that make him a homo too?"

I shrugged, laughed, what was I to do, that was just Fats' way of trying to cheer me up. "Appears to me he's got enough problems if he stole that body, chief among them are the legal ones. I don't wanna think about what he's *doing* with it. I don't wanna dig too deep into this stuff; I just want to get back our stolen stiff. You know, Landis ain't going to let us play too long on this one."

Fats nodded, serious now, "Let's see that list."

I handed him the list and he went through it carefully scanning each name. He said, "There's two here, two real demented bastards who might try something like this. Emilio Nardone, is just warped enough to do something like this as a joke. Then there's this other guy's, not what you'd think at all, a well-respected man, wealthy, family guy, business guy, big-shot undertaker. I hear he's some weird kinda S&M freak. Might be into making some new kinda scene . . ."

"Yeah? Gee," I said. "Hope it doesn't catch on."

Fats laughed, "So let's do it."

I said, "I'm giving the list to Smitty and Ryan, they'll track down each of the names, just to be on the safe side to see if any of these guys know Strossen. Maybe they took the body for revenge? Spite . . .? Who knows . . .?"

"You don't think it's the weird sex angle, Griff?" Fats said, a bit too hopefully.

I shrugged, "Who knows, whatever it is, we'll find out soon enough."

Fats nodded, "Sounds good to me. So, you wanna go visit Nardone or Simmons first?"

I looked at Fats and smiled, "Let's go see Nardone first, I gotta work my way up to dealing with a guy like Simmons and what we might find there."

"Amen to that, Griff."

Emilio Nardone had just got out of an upstate prison after doing a stretch for bank robbery. His trademark was defecating on the bank manager's desk before he left with the money. It kinda made his robberies memorable, but the crime lab never much liked dealing with the 'evidence' he left behind. But you had to give it to Emilio Nardone; he had a certain sense of . . . I guess in some circles you might call it . . . humor?

As we drove up to 410 Conastoga Drive, the residence he'd given his parole officer, Fats put it all into wonderful perspective, "Griff, I don't know how he does it! Now this guy robbed almost a dozen banks, and dirtied the manager's desk every single time. I just don't understand it. I mean, how could the guy crap on command like that? You know, you just can't do it when you want like that. Leastways, I can't. Like, just *do* it, when everyone in the bank is watching?"

I looked at Fats incredulous, asked, "We got this case of a stolen stiff and *that's* the burning question you got for Nardone?"

"Yeah, I mean, among others."

I shook my head, "Then why the hell don't you just ask him, because I certainly have no idea."

I was getting a bit testy, but Fats never seemed to notice at all. Truth is, he noticed sure as hell, but he'd never let on to me he noticed. That was the way partners worked on each other in the old days.

"You know, Griff, I think I will ask him."

He looked at me and smiled, and I could only shake my head.

"I'm gonna find out all about that. Guy could crap like that, on command, on schedule. I mean he's robbing a bank for Christsakes! He's gotta be under tremendous pressure . . ."

"Fats! I don't wanna talk about it."

"I mean, pressure doing the armed robbery. Then on top of that, he's gotta . . ."

"He's gotta . . . perform. Poop on command. Do his trademark," I added, trying to help out Fats with the words before he got us into a place I didn't want to go with this.

He smiled, "That's it exactly."

"You happy now? Okay, here we are. Let's go in and see Emilio and you can ask him yourself. Just remember, we're still looking for that stolen stiff."

Emilio Nardone was a thin, wiry man, dark hair, pencil-thin mustache, and eyes that gleamed like a mad man. With a smile to match. Handsome in a way, but a very strange way.

He opened the door after Fats pounded on it enough times making such a racket that if Nardone *had* copped the Strossen stiff even the dead guy would have woke up from all the noise.

Fats stabbed his BCPD badge in Nardone's face, said, "Emilio Nardone, we wanna talk to you."

Nardone said nothing as Fats bulled his way into the house, down the hallway, to sit opposite Nardone in the small, stale living room. Watching him like a hawk. I followed, casing the dive as the low rent flop that is was. I sat down across from Fats.

I said to Nardone, "You know John Strossen?"

Nardone looked at me, at Fats, shrugged, "Never heard the name."

I nodded, said to Fats; "He's lying. We don't have time for games. Why don't you take him out back and smack him around a little."

Fats smiled, hit a big ham fist into the palm of his other hand meaningfully and said, "Sure, Griff, that sounds like fun. Come on, Nardone, you need a little loosening up, and I'm just the guy to put you in a definite talkative mood!"

Nardone turned pale.

Fats just smiled at him in that special way he had with perps, which actually got Nardone even more nervous.

I just nodded, "Don't make too much of a mess, Fats, you know how much I hate cleaning up after you."

"Come on now, Emilio . . . Let me show you how I used to bust heads over in Blacktown when I was a rookie. Now them was some *violent* days."

Nardone froze.

I gave Fats a grim little smile. Fats never busted heads in Blacktown or anywhere else, but Nardone didn't know that. Nardone didn't know that at all. All he knew was that a 290 pound mean-ass copper wanted to break his bones unless he talked. Back in the old days that was known as giving the perp 'incentive'. Fats was big on incentive.

"L-L-L-ook, I, ah, okay, I lied." Nardone stammered. "I know Strossen, but I didn't kill him."

"I didn't ask you if you killed him, Emilio," I said. "I know who killed him. I want to know if you got the body?"

"What body?"

"Strossen's body, you dink!" Fats growled.

I could see Nardone was lost. He just didn't get it. So I said, "Spill what you know, Emilio."

Nardone nodded, sighed, "There's nothing to tell. I knew the creep. Can't say I'm sad he's dead. He had a lot of enemies, but . . ."

"Now we get it out, Griff," Fats said, but I wondered how much of it.

"Go on, Emilio," I prompted.

"Well, he was into some pretty weird stuff . . ."

"You mean sexually?" Fats asked.

Nardone nodded silently. He was terrified now.

I wondered why. I really didn't want to hear about it, but I said, "So, Nardone, tell me all about it."

Emilio Nardone shrugged, "He and a guy named Roger . . ."

"Roger Simmons?" Fats barked.

"Yeah, Roger Simmons. They were into certain, ah, peculiar sexual situations . . ."

Fats looked at me. I looked at him. We both looked at Nardone. None too happy.

I said, "You gotta be more specific, Emilio. Like, what kinda kinky stuff?"

Nardone did a bit of hemming and hawing, trying to figure out what to say, how to say it, and a way to get away saying the least possible. We knew the dance.

Fats looked at me and said, "Sons of bitches *are* having sex with dead people!"

I pressed Nardone now, "All right, Emilio, out with it. What's the story?"

Emilio Nardone shook his head, stammered, "Look, I only worked for Simmons. After I got out of the joint I got a job there. Strossen worked for him too . . ."

"And let me guess, Nardone, a guy named Arnold Kroptic worked with you there too?" I asked.

Nardone sighed, said, "Yeah, Strossen and Kroptic hated each other. They were always fighting, arguing . . . Roger tried to let them have equal shares, we all took turns . . .but they always complained, always . . .well, you know?"

Fats barked, "No, Emilio, I *don't* know! What the *fuck* are you talking about?"

Nardone looked up, embarrassed now, smiled a sick grin and said faintly, "You know, the grass is always greener and all that."

I wanted to smack him. "Can't we get a straight answer out of you, Emilio!"

"What the hell do you want!"

"The truth!" Fats barked, pounding the table now.

Nardone jumped, said, "Well, you know? Roger gave out the bodies, let us take turns with them . . . John and Arnold were very jealous of each other . . ."

"Of each other?" I asked, looking at Nardone with disgust.

"They were jealous of the corpses the other one got to have. Strossen had the corpse of Mary Jane Daughtry, a real piece, big woman, what a body! What tits! She was the absolute best, but beginning to go bad. You know? Spoiling. Strossen kept her around too long I think, but I couldn't blame him, not really."

"Of course," Fats growled, shaking his head in disbelief.

I shussed Fats and told Emilio to continue.

"Anyway," Nardone added, "Kroptic had the Jones girl, now she was new, fresh meat, young, and Strossen wanted to have a few turns with her. Roger did tell them to share. Roger was always fair, but John just didn't want to."

I looked over at Fats, his head was held down in his big hands, low, sad, he looked sick. He looked like he was going to puke.

Fats didn't say a word on the way over to Roger Simmon's place. It was in the best neighborhood. Big house. Nice lawn.

"Son-of-a-bitch!" Fats finally growled. "People die, they're your cherished loved ones, you pay to place them in good care. The best care. All so some sick demented twists can diddle them!"

"And fight over them," I said quietly. "And it seems, even kill over them."

"But why the hell would Simmons steal Strossen's dead body?" Fats asked as he pulled up the car to number 4428 Porter Lane.

"I don't know. This case has got me bugged. A necro ring is just too damn sick, too damn twisted for me. You sure were right. We got ourselves a real beaut of a case here."

"Yeah, and something else, Griff. I feel we're missing something. Important."

I had felt that feeling myself. You get it in investigations sometimes. You see all the pieces of the puzzle, except one—the one that matters the most and puts it all into perspective. The crucial, important piece."

"Something weird is up."

I laughed, "You mean something weirder than these ghouls having sex with dead people?"

Fats just looked at me all serious and nodded solemnly.

I hate when he does that.

We got out of the car and banged on the door to Roger Simmons' house.

A woman answered. She was pretty. She said she was his wife. Her name was Cassandra. She said, "Roger is at the Lincoln Street parlor, detectives. He's having the basement refitted for the new crematorium."

We nodded. I didn't know what to say. Fats could hardly look at her, could hardly say a word, which was pretty incredible for the Fatman when an attitude was upon him. I knew he was busting a gut to tell her. To warn her. She didn't know a thing.

I said, "Mrs. Simmons, you mind if we take a look around a bit?"

"What forever for, detectives? What is it you want?"

"We're working a murder case, ma'am," Fats said. "Man was killed that worked for your husband, by another . . .ah, employee."

"I am not conversant in any way with my husband's business, and certainly not with his employees. Roger handles his business as he sees fit with absolutely no involvement from me at all. I find the entire business, unsavory. I'm sure you understand, seeing as the type of business it is. Hardly fit for a lady's involvement at all."

I nodded.

Fats said, "Do you know Arnold Kroptic or John Strossen?"

"I have heard Roger speak the names, and not in a positive manner, but I have never met the gentlemen. I do not go to the parlor, detectives, and I certainly do not mix with any of the lower behind-the-scenes hired help."

"I see, Mrs. Simmons," Fats said.

We were walking into the living room when I saw the drop of blood. It was in front of a closed and locked door.

I looked at Mrs. Simmons, looked down at the door, pointed and said, "Closet or basement?"

"That's the door to the basement, detective," she replied, a bit surprised.

"What's down there, ma'am?" Fats asked.

"Basement," she said simply, then realizing what we meant she added, "Just storage. Boxes. A lot of dust. We never go down there."

We got her to unlock the door and let us in. There was a long wooden stairway leading downward. With Fats in the lead, and me following, and Mrs. Simmons behind me, we turned on the light and descended the stairway.

She'd been right, it was a mass of boxes, storage cases, old furniture. Junk. Dust. Over in a corner there was an old four-poster bed with John Strossen's body upon it.

Cassandra Simmons shrieked and fainted dead away. I caught a cold chill as I looked at the corpse. Strossen was a small man, almost a midget, ashen dead gray face.

I asked Fats to gather Mrs. Simmons, carry her upstairs and put her to bed. I told him to alert one of the servants to look after her. When Fats left I was alone with John Strossen's corpse.

"Good to finally catch up with you, shorty. You're Bay City's hottest ticket to track down. Pretty good going for a dead guy." I said, walking over to the bed to view him more closely. He was still fully dressed, still wore the bloody clothes he'd worn upon his murder, rigor had set in, but he didn't smell too bad. I wondered why. I turned him over easily, no crap stains. No wait, these were new pants. Had to be. Most of the time at the point of death, or shortly thereafter the bowel distends and evacuates, leaving quite a smelly mess. I realized now that someone had cleaned up John Strossen.

That got me thinking.

I wondered how the body had gotten here. I didn't want to think about *why* it was here, not right now. My mind centered on Roger Simmons, but somehow he didn't seem right for this. Why bring his sick little games home? I took a stroll around the basement as I waited for Fats. The dust was thick. Mrs. Simmons had been right, this basement had been unused—at least by her. I figured that Roger had done all his sick twisted necro games in the back room of his funeral parlor. I wondered if there might be a collection of photos behind this murder. Then I saw the footprints. Made by tennis shoes. Small. A woman's shoe. Or, a child's.

Fats came back, grunting, "She woke up, screamed again, took a pill, screamed, some more, told me to call her husband and to get that dead man out of her basement. I think we got a problem here, Griff."

I nodded, then put my fingers up to my lips, motioning for Fats to be quiet. I pointed to the footprints. I followed them around the room, leading Fats, to the stairs, back to the bed, where they disappeared—under it. I gave Fats a nudge and pointed under the bed.

I said, "You know if the Simmons' have any children, Fats?"

Fats said, "One child, Griff, a son named Bobby. He's supposed to be upstairs in his bedroom sleeping."

I knew Bobby wasn't in his room upstairs at all, he was here in the basement hiding under that bed. The same bed with the stolen corpse of John Strossen laying upon it. Now how the hell you figure that?

I looked at Fats and shook my head. This was not one of our better cases. We both knew it now. We had that fear, growing in us, about what this all meant. We both knew that in another minute we were going to have to bust this case wide open and that was something we did not really want to do now. It would end up destroying a young boy's life forever. That's the way things were back in 1962. You get involved in real weird stuff and get caught—your life is over. One way or another.

I sighed, looked over at Fats. The tower of blubber looked so sad I thought he was gonna cry. He just nodded, said, "Go ahead, let's get this over with."

I nodded, took a deep breath, said, "Okay, Bobby, you can come out from under the bed now. We know you're down there."

There was stone cold silence for a long moment. Like what I'd just said hadn't pertained to Bobby at all. Like he was hoping we'd just all go away. We weren't. We couldn't.

"Bobby?" It's all over now, come on out," I said.

I saw his shoes move.

Then I heard the shot.

Fats and I jumped out of our skins, scrambled down and under the bed to pull the boy out. Bobby looked to be about 16 years old, big for his age. In his hand there was a .38; in his head was a bullet that had his blood gushing everywhere.

"Dammit, Griff!" Fats shouted, "I never figured him for having a gun!"

We pulled the kid out and tried to revive him. Fats was just about to run out to put in a call for an ambulance when I grabbed his arm, pulled him back to me and said, "Won't be needing any ambulance, Fats."

He looked at me, his big fat face dripping tears, and he just collapsed in a heap next to me and the dead boy.

Fats and I sat there for a while, too stunned to move. The body of the dead boy Bobby for company, the rotting corpse of John Strossen looking on from behind us.

Fats said to our boss, Captain Landis, "Near as we can piece it together the necro ring began with Simmons. He hired freaks like Nardone and the others would play along, keep it secret. They did only the women first, kept them around, had their private parties in the funeral home basement, dressed them up, swapped them. Later on they began using all the corpses, male and female . . . kinda experimenting . . ."

I said, "Thing is Roger Simmons had photos of it all. He kept them in a secure place, tucked away in a locked dresser hidden in the unused basement of his house. A place where he knew his wife would never venture. That's where Bobby must have found them. It wigged him out; he began to spy on the men working in the back rooms of the funeral parlor his father owned. He saw a lot. Too much. He began to follow the workers. We have corroboration on this now from Nardone. Bobby was there spying on Arnold Kroptic when John Strossen came to his rooms to continue the fight from the night before about the Daughtry girl . . .ah, Daughtry corpse. Anyway, it was Bobby who took Strossen's body, Kroptic kept mum because he didn't want it to get out about the necro ring. Kroptic also figured that if we couldn't produce a body, there was no proof a murder had taken place and he'd be in the clear."

Landis scratched his head. He'd heard some doozies in his long career but this was the worst. And the dead kid made it a real tragedy.

"How the hell that kid get Strossen's body to his home, anyway?" Landis asked.

Fats jumped in, said, "Bobby was a big kid, Strossen practically a midget. The kid was sitting in his heap spying again—when he saw the action—the murder of Strossen. He just ran over when no one was looking, stole the body, dumped it in his car and left. The whole thing took, what, five, ten seconds?"

I just nodded, "Then he was gone."

"One thing I don't understand," Landis said. "This just never came out. I mean, we'll cover it up and all in the official report to protect the kid, but, what the hell was he gonna do with that body? He wasn't gonna . . . do anything like he'd seen in those photos? Was he?"

I saw the pained look on the bosses face. This was tough for him to deal with. He had kids. It was real terror. I didn't say anything, hoping Fats would answer, but when Fats didn't, I knew something had to be said. So it was up to me. I said, "Boss, I don't rightly know for sure. I've seen some twisted people in my life. You too. God knows, Bay City's got more than it's share these days. How do they get like that? I guess they start young. I don't really know what Bobby Simmons was going to do with that body, or what he intended. I guess we'll never really know now. But I know what I'd *like* to think. I'd sure as hell *like* to think that Bobby did it to show his old man how wrong it all was, how utterly sick, maybe shock him back into reality from whereever his disgusting perverted, degenerate ways had lead him. That's what I hope a good son, like Bobby, was trying to do. He was in way over his head. He had intimate knowledge of things no child should ever have to deal with. No adult, either. I'd like to think that's what it was all about, though. I think he was a good kid."

Landis nodded, I could see the relief in his face.

Fats looked at me and I dared him to say the unspoken question—then why'd the kid kill himself?

The wheels of justice creaked along. Roger Simmons and Emilio Nardone were on their way to prison for various offenses. Arnold Kroptic was on his way to death row for murder. Cassandra Simmons was admitted to a home for the mentally disturbed.

Landis told Fats and me to take a few days off. Actually, he ordered us.

We didn't see each other for a whole 72 hours after that. It was the longest stretch for us to ever be apart. I stayed home alone in bed for the entire three days, drinking myself to sleep, full of nightmaring dreams, until I just couldn't take it no more and had to get back to the job.

Fats never said what he'd done on his enforced 'vacation'. I never asked him. I only found out years later, that he'd spent every damn minute of every damn day and night at the grave of Bobby Simmons.

Simmons Funeral Home was closed down. Then it reopened under new owners. New name. It had some kind of special going the last time we passed by, first class funeral with all the trimmings for a new reduced rate. Fats and I hardly noticed it.

Sometimes you get a case that no matter how well you can tidy it all up in the end, no matter how you can get to the sick, twisted truth of it all, it still leaves a bad taste in your craw. Some things will go with you to the grave. Silent secrets.

I never told Fats or anyone else this, but Bobby Simmons muttered one phrase from under that bed before he shot himself.

When I'd been alone with him in that basement, while Fats was still upstairs, I asked Bobby why he'd stolen the body.

I heard his crazy laugh from under the bed.

Then in a whisper I wish I'd never heard, "Finders keepers."

DRY RUN

I COULDN'T GET THE THOUGHT of all that cash out of my head. Not for a moment. It had to be more money than I'd ever see in my entire life of driving a stinking cab.

I drive for Able Taxi, around the city, out to the 'burbs and airports, into the ghetto to get rich white kids their drug toys. I usually make $32,000 a year with the tips. Not bad really, but I wanted more. If I worked until I dropped dead I'd never make as much money as I thought I was going to make on the deal Fuentes was bragging to me about that day in the cab.

He said it was big money. I believed him. I knew he was some kind of mob guy, kissed the butts of the Italians that ran Red Hook. I saw it as a wild, one-time score that would set me up pretty for the rest of my life. Hell, man, I was pushing 40 hard; a chance like this wouldn't come along again. So I'd do the sure-fire smart thing—I'd knock off Fuentes and take the upfront money for myself.

"I've got a big deal going," Fuentes told me yesterday. "I hear you work cheap and ask no questions. That's good. I gotta make a delivery. I've got some heavy cash and I'm supposed to bring it to the back room of the Hermoso Bodega on 5th Street. You drive me there tomorrow. Just you and me. You park your cab outside the place, then take a walk with me inside."

I said, "Sure, whatever you want. What's my cut?"

"Oh, say one thousand. Cash. Not bad for an hour's work."

"Sure, man, not bad at all." I was drooling.

"Then you pick me up at ten tomorrow morning, sharp."

"Sure, Fuentes. I'll be there."

You can bet your ass the next day I was there. Five minutes early. Fuentes was there early himself so he liked that. He got in the back seat of the cab. I sped off to 5th Street.

The city was quiet that time of day. The streets looking deserted in the mid-morning chill. It was a frigid March day, unusually cold considering the recent mild weather, so it kept the people off the street. That was fine by me.

I saw the small briefcase Fuentes carried, resting so delicately upon his knees where he was sitting in the back seat of the cab. He looked nervous. Sure, with that much cash anyone would be nervous, I thought. That briefcase had to be filled with big money. Maybe all twenties. Maybe even all hundreds!

Soon all that money would be mine.

There was an alley back of 6th Street tailor-made for the job I had in mind. I'd drive down 5th Street, making it look like everything was going according to plan. Drive right up to the bodega. Then I'd turn around and slug Fuentes when he least expected it, then keep right on going into the alley back of 6th Street. I'd take the briefcase full of money and drop Fuentes back there with a welt on his head that he'd never forget. And that would be the end of that. By late afternoon I'd be on a nice beach in Bermuda with the best babe I could find and no worries.

I drove past 4th Street. The city was quiet. No one on the street but there was always traffic. The bodega was on the next block, but when I stopped at a red light on 4th Street Fuentes got my attention—by pulling out a damn gun.

"Keep the brake on, *amigo*. This is where I get out. You stay here and don't move." Then Fuentes was out of my cab in a flash, running through the traffic, down one of the side streets to be lost in the city.

It had all been so unexpected I hardly knew what to do. I watched him go, astounded by his actions. None of it made any sense to me then. He couldn't have known I was going to mug him. His actions really didn't indicate that, they indicated something however, but I just wasn't sure what it all meant.

Then I noticed he'd left the attaché case. My eyes riveted to the back seat where the case sat so innocuously. Not like Fuentes to leave behind a briefcase full of money—no matter how much in a hurry or frantic he was—unless the suitcase wasn't full of money at all!

My mind screamed, "Set-up!"

I flew out of the cab, rolling across the curb, managing to get under a nearby parked car just as my cab blew up in the biggest damn explosion I'd seen since a 'Nam napalming twenty years before.

When the smoke cleared and the screams of the people quieted down I saw what was left of my cab. It wasn't much, just a mass of smoking metal, while glass on every store on the block littered the street. My head rang like one of those giant Chinese gongs— but as far as I could tell I was still in one piece and I didn't see any blood.

I was alive and that's what was important. Once I was assured of that basic fact my mind focused on other items of interest. Like, where was the money? Where was Fuentes? Why the double-cross?

When you're planning to do someone dirty you never figure he'll do you dirty first, but it seems that's exactly what happened to me. It sure messed up my day.

Fuentes had disappeared into the muck of the city. No one I asked knew anything. I had a few contacts, but I guess Fuentes had better ones. It seemed to me he had gone deep and wasn't moving.

At first I was just happy to be alive after what I'd been through. Then it began to get to me. The thing was, I felt like I was supposed to have died in that explosion. Like it was actually meant for me. I just couldn't figure out why.

I took a drastic reevaluation of my life up to that point. Enemies. People I'd offended. Jealous or envious types. Not many of these. It just didn't jibe. I've always kept to myself since I came back from 'Nam. I've never been in jail, never arrested, never caused any trouble. Had an amicable divorce years ago, no money owed the sharks, and didn't use drugs. I was a 39-year-old working drudge, honest (relatively) and clean, you could tell because I was such a damn failure. I even paid my taxes.

Then why the set-up?

I began to do my own investigating when the cops couldn't get me any action. What did I really know about Emileo Fuentes? He was an up and coming hood, into loan-sharking and gambling, dabbling in drugs and women. Just a guy out to make a buck—any way that he could. The word said he was moving up.

I asked around. I didn't get much. Nothing concrete. No one seemed to know anything; they were shut as tight as a clam at a fish fry. There were a couple of Puerto Rican guys I knew down in Sunset Park. I went over to see them. One didn't know a thing. Told me to move on out. Right away. I moved.

The other guy was a small-time gangster named Pedro. He'd been an old time buddy. He said he knew all about it.

"Okay man, come on, spill it."

"You're not going to like it, *amigo*. I heard it from a very reliable source, a woman I'm doing." He laughed, a smile crossing his handsome face as he remembered his latest trophy. "It's Fuentes' wife, my man! Seems she'd be a good source, don't you think? She gets lonely for a real man. So we get together sometimes. Usually when Fuentes isn't around. Sometimes when he is. She is a very nice lady. Very tasty."

"What'd she say?"

Pedro shook his head, took a deep breath, "You're right, *amigo*, it was a set-up."

"But why? I've never done anything to Fuentes. Why does he have it in for me?"

"That's the thing, it's not what you think."

"Then what the hell is it, Pedro!"

"Easy, *amigo*. This is the story I heard from Rosa. See, Fuentes is a small player, but he's been climbing the ladder to success. He wants to be one of the big boys real bad, have a lot of fancy cars and hot young *putas*. Maybe he's been seeing too many gangster movies? He's on his way up but the spaghetti benders are in his way. They run things here and in Red Hook and extract a price for what's called 'upward Mobility.' "

"Get to the point, Pedro."

"So, *amigo*, you were the price. Or part of it. See, Rosa told me about this hit Fuentes has to do for his guinea bosses. A dangerous job. It's against a made man. So it's not 'legal' and has to be done just right. Fuentes is the only one to do it. It involves a big cash payoff. Fuentes is scared shit but has to go through with it. The plan is for him to meet with this big capo. They'll drive up to a corner in a limo somewhere in Brooklyn, Fuentes gets in and gives the capo an attaché case that's supposed to be filled with money. Then Fuentes jumps out of the limo and B-O-O-M! No more capo. Get it? It seems that you were the training, *amigo*. You're no one. A cabby without a family. Fuentes just wanted to see if he could perform the contract according to specifications. So he had to practice. You were the practice. The dry run. You screwed it all up though. You weren't supposed to have lived through it. Fuentes knows you're after him. He's in hiding for now, but he's still got the contract on that capo, so he'll have to come out pretty soon."

I didn't know what to say. All kinds of emotions were boiling over inside me, anger uppermost of all. Then that drifted off into a kind of numb apathy. Fuentes was right, I was a nobody. No friends. No family. No contributor to society at all. Nothing! I wouldn't be missed. No one even knew I was here! The reality sobered my thoughts. I didn't know what to do. I couldn't even think about it.

Then the door burst open and two of the biggest guys I'd ever seen rushed in, guns leveled into our faces before we knew what was happening.

They pushed me to the floor and told me not to move. I didn't. My lips kissed the floor, I shivered. Then they started to rough up Pedro. It was obvious he was the one they were after. I figured Pedro had sold them some bad dope or something. It got intense. Pedro cursed them in super-quick Spanish. The goons roughed him up more. Harder. I saw drops of blood hit the floor around me. Blood landed on my arms and face. It was warm and wet. I couldn't bring myself to look up at what was happening.

Then I heard another voice. Rough but commanding. It was Fuentes! I kept my face to the floor so he wouldn't see who I was; so far he hadn't noticed or cared who I was. He had more personal matters to attend to at the moment.

I guess the news about Pedro fooling around with Rosa finally got to Fuentes. People just love to talk and Pedro had a dick for brains when it came to women. And the one thing everyone without money talks about is sex and who's doing who. That talk gets around. It must have got around to Fuentes too.

I heard them mention me, the *gringo*. They glanced my way. Fuentes never guessed it was me. I made sure my face was hidden as I shook for dear life. One of the goons saw this and laughed. Fuentes said it would be a shame to kill such a fine coward. I just couldn't stop shaking.

Fuentes left the apartment, his two goons dragging the unconscious body of Pedro between them. I knew Pedro was going for a one-way, and I'd never see him again.

They were gone almost as quickly as they had appeared and left me on the floor alone sweating rivers. I counted my lucky star that Fuentes hadn't recognized me. I guess I looked like just another *gringo* buying drugs from Pedro. I'm sure he never would have guessed I knew Pedro.

I can be a gutless wonder when I'm scared, but when someone tries to kill me—and for no reason—it's amazing how that will stiffen even my backbone. I wanted revenge. I wanted to kick Fuentes' ass. Who the hell did he think he was anyway?

I knew Fuentes had to move on the capo soon. I figured to follow him and make my move when the time was right.

It didn't take long. The days moved fast, the time shooting by. I followed Fuentes. Stayed clear of his two goons. Watched and waited.

By the third day I could feel the time drawing near. Early that morning Fuentes left his house. He was alone. Not the usual routine and he carried a small attaché case tightly in his hand. He looked at it constantly. Carefully. I knew this was it.

Fuentes took a cab to Foster and 11th Street. I followed in an old beat-up hack I borrowed from a friend who used to drive nights, but was shot two weeks ago in the Bronx.

Fuentes looked nervous. Or maybe it was just my imagination and I was the nervous one. The cab let him off at the corner of 11th Street. He walked to the corner of 12th Street. A big black limo waited there. The chauffeur decked out in a too-tight suit uniform, and showing a noticeable bulge under the armpit, opened the door for Fuentes to enter the back of the limo.

Fuentes put one foot down on the velvet carpet. Hunkered down and slowly moved forward. I watched him move in. Saw him say hello to the capo, who was sitting there like a big Italian Buddha at the opposite end of the seat. They shook hands. Fuentes sweated. I could see it running down his face through the sites of the scope.

I pulled the trigger and Fuentes ate one in the back of the head near the stub of the neck.

The spray drenched the capo in blood and gray matter. He shouted in panic, tried to move Fuentes body off him, tried to get out of the limo but then thought better of it.

The chauffeur/bodyguard was taken by surprise but responded quickly drawing his piece, guarding the car, looking for me but unable to pick me out. The capo yelled for him to get Fuentes out of the car. The bodyguard helped him dump the Puerto Rican in the gutter. Then the capo saw the attaché case.

The bodyguard handed the attaché case to his boss, closed the door of the limo and ran to the driver side of the big car. He jumped in and gunned the car out into the traffic.

I watched them drive away. They'd gone about five blocks when the capo's curiosity must have gotten the better of him.

The explosion blew the doors and sunroof right off the limo. It mulched the capo and the bodyguard into a hundred red beefy pieces.

I watched the EMS workers gather Fuentes out of the gutter and place him onto a gurney, then roll him into the back of a truck. The guy in charge gave the thumbs down sign over the body.

The EMS workers put down their equipment and lit up cigarettes.

That's all I wanted to see. Maybe I lost all that upfront money, maybe it never was there to begin with, but Fuentes lost a whole lot more. He's one bastard who won't be messing with me again.

See, I didn't mess up on my dry run. I don't need to practice.

SERVICE

FIRST SAW HER in this low-life strip club on the boulevard. She was a dancer, but . . . You see, Clarise only danced in the private back room. She did special parties, but to see her you would never, *ever*, believe she was any kind of dancer. Especially not a sex dancer. She was young then, and beautiful, and just over three hundred pounds of pulsating female flesh. And with all that weight she still moved like a cat, every roll of fat quivering, straining, shaking over every inch of her sweat glistened skin. Her flesh bounced obscenely, lustfully. It shook, it beckoned. She was disgusting. At first I couldn't look at her.

Then, I couldn't look away.

I used to go every night after that to see Clarise dance. I know I was obsessed with her largeness. I was like a tiny moon revolving around her massive planet-sized body and I loved it and she knew it. I would stare at her jiggling flesh, drinking the hot odor of her woman sweat rolling off her body in waves as she gyrated before me. There was the look of fire in her eyes. When she finally stripped down to her G-string, I found myself fighting with other men in the room to touch her, to thrust bills between her massive private parts. She deftly took the dollars and placed them gently under her ponderous breasts or between the lips of her vagina where the bills stayed put as if in a wet, clammy vault.

Thinking about it now as I sit here in this cell, I don't know why I got into it with her. I just did. I went there every night after work, elbow to elbow with all the other chubby-chasers and losers in the place, watching Clarise in amazement. We were like jackals at a feast; each of us attuned to her every move as she danced. She was incredible. Standing above me on the stage, her huge body defiant, her foul language, taunting obscene gestures, the slaps and rants of her rage. The odor that abounded from her was terrible, and at the same time . . . intoxicating.

I remember when Bud and Joe at work first took me there, saying I needed some adult entertainment to take my mind off all the numbers in my head. I was good at numbers, being an accountant.

"And besides," Bud told me, "The fat chick that dances in the back room is a fucking laugh riot!"

Maybe, but not for me. For me she was beautiful, the most sexual woman I had ever seen in my life. People say a 300-pound woman cannot be sexy. Well, you've never seen Clarise; never felt the stage moan under her weight as she rocked back and forth like an elephant in heat, dancing to the howls of dozens of lust-crazed admirers. I can't explain it. It's not . . . healthy . . . It's not supposed to happen this way. In our culture of anorexic, toothpick-thin models or big-breasted blonde amazons, short and fat is not supposed to be what a man wants. Clarise's gross obesity was beyond anything most men would ever consider sexy. But it was more than that. Clarise was special. She had a way of pressing the right buttons on a certain type of man. From the first day I saw her, I knew that I was that type of man. I knew that I had to find some way to meet her.

It was a mysterious thing to me because the night that I finally got up the balls to speak to Clarise—to tell her I'd picked her out of all the women I'd ever seen as the most sexual and the most beautiful—she seemed to have picked me out of the crowd of her admirers. She beckoned me to come to her after her last set.

When I saw her afterwards, she was picking up her dirty, soiled clothes, ringed with sweat and odor. She rolled them into a balled up handful, looked at me and threw her dirty clothes in my face, saying, "Take these and follow me out back."

I grabbed each item greedily; they smelled of sweat and other rank odors, from her underarms, her genital area, her buttocks. I held them tightly savoring the smell. Then I followed her, watching her ponderous nude buttocks shake like mountains of jelly as she walked in front of me. She was like some obscene female version of a Sumo wrestler. It was disgusting but I was aroused all over again. Nervous. Anticipating. Fantasizing.

She turned around for a moment to see if I was following her, said, "Come on, God-dammit! We don't have all fucking night."

I hurried up, holding her discarded clothing tightly, feeling the rough fabric on my fingertips, against my cheek, breathing in the smell of her. I did not care if anyone saw the boner in my pants, I just hoped I would not have any accident that might embarrass me in front of her.

We reached her small closet-like dressing room and she pointed for me to go inside. Then she threw a large, tent-like robe over her dripping nakedness, and slammed the door behind her.

I took a deep breath.

"Sit down," she said. It wasn't an invitation, it was an order.

"I'll stand," I replied.

"Suit yourself. Tell me, what's your name?" she asked pulling her clothing out of my hands and throwing them in a corner of the cluttered room where they landed upon a similar pile of dirty and discarded clothing. The whole place stank of rancid sweat.

"Arthur Berger," I said, finally.

She shook her head. "That just won't do. Your new name from now on is . . . Let me see . . . Your new name now is 'Service'. Do you understand?"

I didn't understand but I wanted to play along. "Arthur Service?" I asked.

"No, dammit! Just, *Service!*" She barked, watching me closely. Her cold, dark, beady eyes darted to my crotch and she grinned, wickedly, licking her lips, rubbing her own crotch for one brief but intoxicating moment in front of me while I watched her. The way she did it, it was the most incredible thing I had ever seen in my life. She was so obscene, so animal sexual. I almost fainted.

When I smelled her juices I became hard again.

She said, "Very good, Service."

I was hot, feverish, I said, "I don't understand."

She said, "Yes you do. Come here. Closer." She disrobed. "I want to show you something, Service."

At first it was embarrassing; eventually it grew disgusting. I hated her. Just as much as I loved her. Even today, so many years later, when I fully realize all she did to me, how she manipulated me, hurt me, and used me, I still love her. Even after all the terrible things she made me do and the terrible things I finally had to do to stop her—I still love her.

"Service! Come here, we're going out," Clarise told me one day. This was weeks later. Now I was living at her apartment up the boulevard from the club where she worked. She had a lot of men callers. It was amazing. I tried to put them off, let them know they weren't wanted anymore because I was Clarise's *new* man, but they all just laughed.

"You're just the latest, young fella," an older man said to me one evening when he came by and asked to see Clarise. I'd seen him before on TV, he was some kind of soap opera star.

"You be the new babe in the damn woods here, boy," a tall black man named Bert said, laughing in my face. He left an envelope for Clarise that was stuffed with cash.

I went into the bedroom where Clarise was laying naked upon her big round bed. She'd just come out of the shower—she almost never took showers. Or baths. That had been hard for me to deal with at first, but after a while I didn't mind. In fact, I grew to like it. Clarise told me that I would. I guess she knew me better than I knew myself. I never realized at the time that that would be my undoing.

I realized later that her men never minded either. No matter what she did. I was just another of her admirers, of which I was the latest in a long line and probably the stupidest of the lot. That was when we had our first and last fight.

"What the fuck do you expect me to do, Service!" She'd screamed at me from the bed, "Men give me presents. If you were a real man you'd give me presents too!"

"Clarise, I love you."

She just looked away angry.

Then I got angry too, feeling that tightness around the top of my head. Jealousy, confusion . . .

"I want us to have a good normal relationship," I said.

She just laughed, bitter and cruel. "I don't do 'normal,' Service. Neither do you. You think you're here because you *want* to be here. But you're really here because *I* want you to be here. And don't *ever* forget it! You get it now? If you won't do what I want you to do, Service, you can just pack up and get the hell out!"

I was crushed, defeated, just the thought of being without Clarise set my mind in panic and dread I had never felt before. My eyes just stared at her. I didn't know what to think, say, or do. I felt tears run down my cheeks. "Clarise . . ."

She looked at me and laughed in my face, loud, callous, taunting me. "You are so damn weak! You worm! You little piece of crap! You dirty turd! You lying bastard! You said you'd do anything for me! *Anything!* Now you're going back on your word! And to think, I used to love you?"

Her use of the word 'love' for the first time to me shook me more than I realized. It was like a slap in the face, but it was also a thin strand of hope, a lifeline, and I lunged at it with all the desperation I felt.

"I meant what I said, Clarise," trying to hold back my tears now. "I really did!"

She looked at me boldly and shouted, "You said you would do anything for me, Service. Anything I ask! Will you lie, cheat, steal for me?"

I was quiet for a moment, knowing what I should not say, but knowing what I had to say.

"Yes," I said, defeated, trying to wipe away my tears.

"You mean it, Service?"

"Yes."

Clarise smiled now, patting the big bed, "Come here, Service, sit next to me. I want to show you something nice."

That was the first time we really talked. I told how good I was with numbers, and Clarise was very interested, asking me pointed questions on accounting, taxes, and money laundering. My answers made Clarise happy. She said, "Service, I've never let one of my special admirers into my business before, but I need a good accountant, money manager, cash flow expert. Do you think you are up to the task?"

I jumped at the suggestion, "Yes!"

"Will you do exactly what I tell you to do?"

"Yes," I replied.

"Anything? No questions asked?"

"Yes, anything . . . to be with you . . . to be of service to you."

Clarise smiled.

I found out Clarise had a mansion high up in the hills. It was a secluded estate with trusted servants and everything a rich person could want. She used the apartment in town and her club on the boulevard to recruit young men. A certain type of young man. Like me.

My life of crime began a few days later. It started with me going out on my own on jobs. Clarise would tell me what to do, and I would do it. It was as simple as that. Thefts mostly, at first. It began with petty shoplifting, and then purse snatchings, escalated to B&E, armed robbery and finally kidnapping for ransom. I did it all. Under her orders. Anything she told me to do. When she told me to kill a man I'd met months ago at her city apartment, the TV soap opera star, I did that too. She gave me a gun and an address. That's all I needed.

Clarise said he had made her mad, that he'd been slacking in his admiration.

I knew what that meant; he wasn't keeping up his gifts, booty, bribes, pay-offs, goodies to Clarise.

Clarise said, "Don't slack off on me, Service."

"Never, Clarise," I said and meant it.

It went on like that for months. I was Service now. Arthur was dead. I lived in Clarise's big house. I wasn't the only one there though. The big black guy, Bert—who'd made fun of me so long ago—who'd dropped off that envelope full of cash to Clarise— lived there too. There were half a dozen others. Sometimes Clarise had us work together as a crew on scams or jobs, but mostly we worked on our own, each one of us doing whatever we could do to lavish cash or jewelry at the large feet of our obese goddess. Each jealous and paranoid that the other would gain more favor in Clarise's eyes or some kind of one-upmanship because of his gifts to her. It was sick and twisted, but none of us cared, least of all Clarise who owned us all and used us any way she pleased.

I never questioned how this woman could have such power over myself, or so many other men. I was just a small satellite revolving around her largeness—one of many small moons caught in the power of her planetary orbit. Her heavy gravity threatened to crush me at any moment, along with all these others. And like all these others, I could not bear to live without her.

I soon discovered that Clarise's criminal empire—and that's in fact what it was—stretched far and wide, and ran deep. She had extensive interests. Businesses where she was a silent partner, modeling agencies, gaming houses, the garment district, Wall Street, legal and illegal drugs. She had a chain of brothels that poured cash into her coffers. Bert ran them for her. He brought Clarise a fat envelope stuffed with hundred dollar bills every day, gifts from the women that worked for her. It seemed Clarise also had female 'admirers' she put to work in her brothels. They too, it seemed, would do anything for love. Love of Clarise. It was like some kind of twisted cult, and I was in the thick of it, in a privileged position. I was happy. And that's all that mattered to me at the time. I lived in the big house with Clarise. I saw her almost every day. It was only when the time between visits to Clarise began to grow longer that I began to feel edgy. Jealous, paranoid, finally even angry. But I didn't want to express that anger or jealousy, or even ask questions. You *never* questioned Clarise. I didn't want to ruin the good thing I had or get her mad at me. So I shut up. But things were beginning to worry me.

When Clarise called me into her suite of private upstairs rooms a few days later I was surprised but delighted. She had an unusually pungent odor that morning, body odor mixed with the slickness of sex. Then I noticed the man in her room seated on the sofa across from her. I knew him as Riordan, a homicide cop, and another 'admirer.' He sat quiet and calm, eagle-eyed, watching me jealously, openly salivating over Clarise. I hated him. Clarise got up and stood before us rubbing her hands across her lush obeseness with a lust and venom that made me sweat. I wanted to reach out for her and devour her sex right then and there.

"Easy now, Service," she laughed, noting my mood, mocking me the way she always did. She looked over at the cop. "You know Riordan?"

I nodded. I'd seen him around at the house, like a lot of the others.

"You two are going to do a special job for me."

I waited. Riordan didn't say a word either.

Whatever Clarise wanted done, we were ready to do.

Clarise said, "Bert has been making plans with my little Black Lolita." The word 'plans' was a bad word in Clarise's book. Only Clarise made plans.

Bert was the large black fellow who ran Clarise's brothels; Lolita was her most prized girl, young, sexy, beautiful, ebony black. It was rumored she was Bert's own daughter from before he had taken up with Clarise. I should have known something was up when Bert moved out of the big house last week. Now he stayed in the house with Lolita. That looked like Bert was into doing his own kin, but before my thoughts went too far down that road, Clarise cut them off by saying, "It's not what you think. Bert's trying to take my darling Black Lolita away from me. Out of my service. He's not going to get away with that. I don't know or care what his reason is. He's not going to get away with doing that. Now this is what you two are going to do for me."

I swallowed hard, looked at Riordan. He smiled evilly. Waiting.

It was simple really. Bert was now living at the brothel on West 20th Street, a brownstone in the center of Midtown. The girl known as Black Lolita had a room upstairs and did her business there for Clarise. Sometimes *with* Clarise. Riordan was to get me in with his badge. A bogus bust or shakedown. We'd go upstairs. Then I was to put a bullet or three in Bert's head. Quick and easy. Riordan would take the gun and dump it. I'd go out the back way and head back to the big house to report to Clarise how Bert had died. She always liked to hear the details. Riordan would bring Black Lolita to the big house later to see Clarise. To make amends. She said I could watch if I liked. I didn't think so.

Problem was, I liked Bert. He always treated me good, even if he made fun of me that first time we'd met. He'd just been telling it true. Anyway, what I knew was that he had some kind of thing for Black Lolita, but I knew she was *not* his kin. Not exactly. She was his stepdaughter. She'd got herself involved with Clarise the same time as Bert. Similar situations but for different reasons. Clarise was powerful, she could bend will, manipulate minds, get anything she wanted. And she wanted it all. She had all of me and now she was going to have me murder Bert. Such was my mission for Clarise. A mission I could not deny. And I knew that Riordan was her latest man-toy and that once I killed Bert he'd draw his gun and kill me. And all the loose ends would be nicely tied up. I'd been noticing that Clarise had been getting a little tired of me lately. She got like that sometimes.

When Riordan gave me the gun I just gave it back to him, determined I would not kill Bert and that I'd have it out with Clarise once I got back to the big house. That was my thought, and my big mistake. Riordan just sneered at me with his big cop face and pulled out another gun.

"Big Mama told me you might be trouble, and to be ready, Service."

"Clarise? Clarise!" I cried.

"She's been watching you lately. She knows the signs, how her admirers are consumed with love and lust for her big juicy body, obsessed with the nearness of her large gross flesh, desiring to feast upon that flesh in an orgy of wet . . ."

Riordan stopped his fantasizing, smiled, licked his dry lips. His face was flushed, puffy, strange. He pointed the gun at me, said "Goodbye, Service."

Riordan pulled the trigger and I felt bullets tug at my chest. I felt shock and anger and then terrible pain. A warm wetness ran over my body. I saw that it was red and sticky and smelled like copper. I couldn't believe it was ending like this, alone, in a back alley behind one of Clarise's brothels.

Moments later I saw Bert come outside and suddenly Riordan took out the gun I was supposed to shoot Bert with—the gun I had foolishly given back to him because I refused to be a part of this murder plan. Riordan got off three quick shots and Bert fell down dead. One slug had entered Bert's head and torn his skull apart.

I screamed and cried, watching with fear and fascination as Riordan placed the gun he had used to shoot me in Bert's hand, melding the man's dead fingers to the gun stock. Next he took the gun he had used to shoot Bert and put it in my hand.

I looked up at Riordan as he was taking off his gloves and he just laughed, the fatty folds of his face bouncing with delight—in much the same manner that my beloved Clarise would laugh. That same cold evil laugh of doom.

I tried to lift the handgun, to get off a shot at Riordan but I was too weak and fading fast. It just made him laugh all the harder.

"Clarise?" I cried, dropping the gun, falling into darkness.

I don't think I was supposed to live. I know that now. At first, I thought everything would be okay once Clarise came to see me. I was up for first degree murder. We were in a death penalty state. My heart leaped with joy when Clarise came to see me that first day. She had a man with her who she said was to be my lawyer. A fellow named Sinclair, another of her admirers.

Clarise carefully placed her large body into a chair across from me and said, "Just play along with what Mr. Sinclair tells you, Service. Everything will work out all right."

"But Clarise . . .?" I stammered, full of tears.

She reached out and touched my arm, softly, "Don't worry, Service, it was all a terrible mistake and everything will be arranged."

"But why?" I asked. The DA was already putting pressure on me to make a deal and give up Clarise. But I wasn't talking.

Clarise smiled, beady eyes gleaming darkly, "Bert had to be made to pay, it was handled badly . . ."

"But Riordan said . . ."

She withdrew her hand from my arm, "Service, now don't make me mad. You know you cannot trust what anyone tells you, except me."

"Clarise . . ."

"I want you back with me, Service. Now you do as Mr. Sinclair tells you."

"Clarise . . ."

"Service!" she said sternly, then she took my hand again and rubbing it, said, "I wouldn't let one of my best boys go down without a fight. Don't you trust me?"

I nodded. I wanted to believe. I still loved her.

The court case was quick and conclusive. Riordan and his partner testified. They lied. I asked Sinclair to put me on the stand but he didn't think it would be a good idea. "Do you want to hurt Clarise, Service? If you testify, that will give the prosecutor the opening he needs to ask you all kinds of questions about Clarise and her business activities. You know Clarise doesn't like anyone knowing her business. I know you'd never tell, Service, but these damn prosecutors are all tricky rats. You want to help some damn DA looking to make a name for himself off of the love you and Clarise share?"

"No!" I shouted, but they were already offering me deals to talk.

"Then be quiet and let me handle everything, Service. You'll do a little time, then we'll get you out." He had such a reassuring manner. Sinclair added, "Do it for Clarise. She'd want it that way, Service."

I nodded and I never talked.

Clarise never came to see me again either.

I got twenty years to life in prison. I've only done a few months. I may get out someday on parole, or I may not, but there's really nothing to go back to now anyway.

Clarise won't return my calls, she won't respond to my letters. When I told Sinclair to ask her to come and see me he said, "Now, Service, you know Clarise can't be seen visiting a convicted, incarcerated murderer. If Clarise—a lady-friend of our gubernatorial candidate by the way—were seen coming to visit you, those damn Republicans would have a field day! You know he's leading in the polls? She's supporting Teddy Longerman for governor. Teddy's one of her 'boys' from the early days? Even before you, Service."

I said that I wouldn't want to spoil anything for Clarise. Last week I read in the paper Riordan had been appointed Chief of Detectives. I heard through the joint grapevine that Black Lolita ran all the brothels now—in a very roundabout way, of course—for Clarise. Lolita was convinced that I had killed Bert. I never let on different.

Now I sit here alone. Waiting. They say I'll get out in twenty years. Maybe. But I know that Clarise don't like loose ends. I'm a loose end that needs to be looked after. A problem that needs to be solved. Permanently.

"How does it feel, Arthur? To know it'll be decades before you're a free man," the guard said to me. He stood by the bars outside my cell. "That's a long time."

I hardly remembered the name Arthur now. I *had* been Arthur, once. Now I was just Service.

"My name is Service," I said simply.

"Sure. Sure, Service," he continued smiling at me.

"Some day I'll get out," I said. Some hope in my voice. "If I could just talk to Clarise . . ."

The guard shook his head negatively.

Then I saw the glint of the slim blade he pulled out from his uniform pocket. He threw it to me through the bars, where it landed on the mattress behind of me.

"She wants it done before breakfast, Service. She told me to tell you to do this one last thing to prove to her that you love her," then the guard walked away.

It was lock-down time. Lights out. The noise in prison never stopped but I didn't hear any of it now. It was all quiet for me.

It wouldn't be morning for eight hours yet.

I looked at the blade—your generic prison shiv, handmade, untraceable—I picked it up. The cutting edge was jagged but sharp. It would do.

I thought about Clarise.

I lifted the blade to my throat.

Then I lowered my hand.

What had she ever done for me that I should do this final deed for her? Nothing! Nothing at all. All she ever did was run my life and fill me up with a lot of empty promises. Promises about 'us'. Not one promise ever came true.

Now I'm locked away in here and she is out there. Away from me. I know she is with other men. Other women too, probably. Riordan! And she does not come to see me. Never a message or a good word. Now *This!* She wants me to commit suicide for her! After all I've done for her?

I was thinking about spilling my guts on Clarise when I heard a noise down the hall.

It was the guard coming back. This time he had two other guards with him.

I grew alert, nervous.

He was carrying an electric cord. He let me see it as he approached the bars of my cell. It swayed back and forth in his hand, like a noose. The image was not lost on me. He smiled evilly, like Riordan.

I looked at the shiv, and said, "I can't do it."

He said, "Here, try this." He threw me the electric cord.

I ignored it, shook my head, "I'm through with that, with all of it. I'm not going to cut my throat. I'm not going to hang myself either."

The guard shook his head, "Oh, yes you are, Service—whether *you* do it, or not."

They came closer, opening my cell door. They caught me and placed the electric cord around my neck.

Tight.

Tighter.

The first guard's lips touched my ears as he pulled the cord ever tighter. I couldn't breathe!

The other guards held me fast. I couldn't move!

He whispered to me, "By the way, Service, Clarise told me to tell you goodbye. *SUCKER!*"

The guards laughed loudly. Taunting me in death.

They laughed so loud I woke up.

I froze, horrified.

Then I was shaking with sweat, chills, my teeth were chattering cold.

I found myself mercifully alone.

I let out a peep of laughter like some madman, or some madman suddenly become sane.

I kicked the shiv under my bed.

"The hell with you, Clarise!

I tried to relax, savoring thoughts of how I was going to get back at her.

Then I heard footsteps approaching my cell. Two pairs of feet entered my field of vision. I looked up at the prison guards, who were smiling strangely. One carried something horrifyingly familiar.

EVIL FORCES

WHEN SHE TOLD ME to beware the evil forces, I just didn't think much of it at the time. You know, Griff?"

I nodded. That was my partner, Fats, saying those words to me back in 1963, in a town I'll call Bay City.

I'd never seen Fats so nervous. His big blubbery face full of sweat, his walrus-size body shivering and shaking like Jell-O with a bad attitude. I'd never seen him so affected but then the recent killing had affected a lot of us. By the end of it all, it got a whole lot worse and damn near cost Fats his life.

It began one rainy, cool morning. Fats' nose was running like a faucet as he drove our old war-wagon Plymouth down Dumont Avenue. He ignored all the hustlers, pimps, grifters and hookers plying their trade boldly out in broad daylight. Like it was all so normal. If you knew Bay City back then, you'd know that wasn't the half of it. We headed for Rosie's Diner for some morning eats.

I said, "You know Fats, that's pretty disgusting, rubbing your suit sleeve all over your wet slimy nose like that."

He just burped, rubbed his nose again. I saw the sheen of mucous on his sleeve. He said, "I got a cold, Griff. The damn faucet won't stop running."

I nodded. It had been uncommonly cold lately, like almost a supernatural cold. An evil chill. I didn't like that feeling at all, and when I looked over to Fats, I could see that he was thinking the exact same thing.

"Something's up, Griff. Something bad." He was driving slow, careful.

I shrugged, "Something's always up in this town."

We never got to Rosie's. A call came over the box and we had the siren screaming and lights flashing as Fats gunned our Plymouth across town to an empty factory on the border of 'the square mile of vice'.

The locals, mostly hookers sleeping off the previous night's dating action, and winos and junkies on the nod, hardly noticed us as we pulled up to a deserted section of fence surrounding a run-down factory that hadn't been open for business in years.

Our old friend Barney and his new partner were already there.

"Hey Griff, Hi, Mr. Stubbs," Barney said welcoming us to his nightmare, "You ain't gonna believe what we found! We got us another one!" He took us to the big double truck doors of the entrance.

Barney always called Fats Mr. Stubbs. I know he was intimidated by the Fatman. He wasn't the only one. Half of Bay City was intimidated by Fats in our heyday, including brother cops and our bosses downtown. Even the mayor kept away from Sergeant Herman Stubbs. They'd had a history in the early days that had put the X on Fats, ruined his career and made a lifetime enemy of the powers-that-be. That's why Fat's partnered with me now. The word was out. No one would partner with him; it was a career killer for sure. My career was dead from other sources. So we just naturally gravitated to each other, partnered up, and somehow it all worked. We even had Captain Landis in our corner on occasion. He liked results. Fats and I got results.

I smiled at Fats. He looked all-serious, then took out a Hershey bar with almonds, unwrapped it with one hand and packed the entire chocolate glob into his huge gaping maw, then he took a deep drag from a Camel with the other hand.

Clouds of cigarette smoke and the smell of chocolate swarmed over me.

"Appears to be an interesting case," Fats said.

"How can you tell?"

"I got the feel, Griff. Got's the feel."

I nodded and kept walking. I knew what he meant. Sometimes you just know. Then, as if to validate my thoughts, Barney spoke up nervously.

"Some weird stuff here, guys."

"In what particular way?" Fats asked, burping loudly. Nothing was going to take him away from food when the eating mood was on him.

Barney's gaze took in the huge abandoned factory. It had been a hangar-type building once. Dark, enormous, empty. But now not quite empty . . .

"Fats . . ." I whispered.

"I see it Griff."

"A blood trail," Barney said expressing our thoughts and trying to hide the terror in his voice. He slowly moved forward, Fats and I soon passed him up.

"It's up there. I ain't never seen nothing like it before. It's like one long . . . "

"Smear . . . a giant smear of blood. We're talking pints, Griff. Starts here, runs over to . . ." Fats said, following it. I followed him, Barney took up the rear.

I took the lead now and walked on ahead, counting my paces, "Thirty-five, thirty-six, thirty-seven, and it stops right here. Amount of blood indicates the body stopped here. Dragged itself, or was dragged here. That's strange."

"But where is it now, Griff?"

Barney said, "Ah, guys, if you don't need me anymore is it okay if I go outside and have a smoke?"

Fats held out his pack of Camels.

I knew Barney did not smoke.

Barney took a butt out of Fat's pack, gave the Fatman back the pack and left.

I smiled.

Fats just laughed to himself, then said, "Bulls! They all wanna be dicks, until they see the hard stuff."

"Ah, Barney's all right." I said, looking over the crime scene again. Looking for the body and wondering where it could possibly be.

"Sure, Barney's a peach, Griff, but this ain't his style. This kinda sicko crap is more like . . ."

" . . . more like *our* style, Fats." I finished.

Fats nodded, shaking his jowls, "Lotta blood, Griff. This fella—I assume it was a man—was literally tore apart. A bloody mess for sure. But interesting enough, if he wasn't dragged—and I don't think he was—he was sure as hell clawing the cement floor here to get away, or to stop being pulled . . . I wonder?"

We could see fingernail marks through the muck of the floor.

"Trying to get away from the killer?" I said simply.

"Or something, scared the hell right out of him!"

I looked at his big, fat, sweaty face, "Or *something?* What you trying to say?"

"Something scared this guy right to hell and back. A guy cut to ribbons like that don't lay down and die like a reasonable corpse but tries to get away with the last bit of strength in his body. What do you suppose scares someone like that, Griff?"

"I don't know."

I froze when I felt the drop on my cheek. I remember hoping it was a drop of rainwater from the leaky roof above—we'd had some rain lately. Fats looked at me and I watched his big sad face as I brought my finger to my cheek. When I brought it away, I saw blood. Then Fats and I both looked above our heads into the darkness of the metal rafters. There didn't appear to be anything up there in the shadows, until we saw a dark blob wedged far above us. Another drop of blood dripped down on me.

"I think we found the stiff," Fats said, being his usual wise-ass self.

"Yeah, now why don't you be a good boy and find a ladder and bring him down?"

"Ah, Griff, you really gonna make me climb up there?"

I said nothing, just made the call for the meat wagon and for Doc, the medical examiner, to take a ride over while we tried to figure how the hell the stiff got up there. Who put him up there and why, for Christsakes?

"So what happened to him?" I asked Doc Carten after he'd had a look at the corpse. Fats stood by looking over the body, it was shredded with lacerations, a mass of dried bloody pulp on a gurney.

"Interesting," Doc said re-examining the mess.

"Yeah, well, Doc, I'm sure it is, but you mind letting us in on it?" Fats bellowed. He was eating a large tuna hero. He'd forced me to stop off at Jackie's on the ride back to get him something to tide him over until dinner.

"This corpse has had almost all the blood vacated from the system. There was an attack here so violent, so intense, so devastating, the body was literally torn to pieces. Almost shredded. No human could do such a thing. There's something else, no human would be able to fling this mass of flesh so high into the rafters of the building. It was not placed up there, it was flung up there, blood spray indicates as much, but for the love of God I can't see why."

This wasn't what I wanted to hear just.

Fats asked, "So Doc, then what kinda animal could do this?"

I was thinking lion, tiger, maybe King Kong?

Doc shook his head, said, "No animal did this either."

Fats gave me a confused look, then said, "Doc, you're not being real clear."

"Doc," I asked, "if the killer wasn't human and it wasn't some animal—where does that leave us? And how did the body get up there? What could be that strong?"

Old Doc didn't say anything right off. He was examining, thinking, shaking his head. Looking nervous.

"Where does that leave us, Doc?" I repeated.

"Somewhere in between?" Fats offered.

I didn't know what Fats meant by that comment but it didn't do me much good when I saw Doc Carten reluctantly nod his head in agreement.

I said, "What the hell does that mean?"

Doc replied, "I don't know how to say it, Griff. It doesn't make sense. None of this makes real sense."

Fats nodded, "Evil forces, Griff. That what you're trying to say, Doc?"

Doc just shrugged, said, "Your guess is as good as mine Sergeant Stubbs."

When we left I was more perplexed than ever.

"How do we explain this to Captain Landis? What do we say, our perp is neither human nor animal? What's that mean, Fats, he's a freakin plant! And a damn strong one, because whatever it is hurled a full grown corpse 35 feet into the rafters!"

"No, Griff, what it means is something in-between human and animal, like a . . ."

I looked at him then, getting more exasperated. 'Like what, Fats?"

He didn't say anything. Which was unusual for him. He clamed right up. Most uncommon if you knew the Fatman.

I mocked, "Fats? Oh Fats?"

"Yeah, Griff?"

"Is there something you're not telling me?"

He didn't say a word. I could hear the wheels turning in his head though.

I barked, "You fat bastard! You got a clue or some idea about this! I just know it! Come on now, give!"

"You're not gonna like it, Griff."

"I don't like it already."

Then he said it.

"Werewolf, Griff. I think we got us a werewolf killing."

Well, with over five years to go before retirement, this murder was turning into one big stinker. I just hoped Fats hadn't finally cracked.

"Werewolf?" I asked.

"Yeah, werewolf."

"Fats, you're a trained police professional. What would ever make you think that?"

"Evil forces, Griff. I can feel them. I see them in the lacerations on the corpse, like dozens of tiny knife marks but made by some type of claw. Not human. A werewolf hurled the body up in the rafters."

"I don't believe it."

"Look, I'm just saying, that's what it *looks* like to me."

"Okay, I got you now, so you're not really going nuts. What you're trying to tell me in your own crazy way is that we got some sicko pervert or mental case out there who *thinks* he's a werewolf?"

Fats didn't say one word. *Not* a good sign.

"So what exactly *are* you saying? I asked.

"Either we have a madman, Griff, or something much worse . . ."

"Worse?" I didn't like that but I put it out of my mind for now, "So what do we do?"

"We begin with the evil forces. We go and talk to Zelda. She'll tell you what she told me about what was happening."

I shook my head but at least it was a place to start.

The Amazing Zelda had a place on Third Street off Dumont, right in the center of the Square Mile of Vice. She'd been a doll once, when she was young in the 20s, sexy flapper speakeasy dancer. Today, 40 years later she was *rough*. And tough. Former hooker and Madame, now doing the mind-reading fortune-telling scam. From what I'd heard, Zelda had been doing well at it too. Like she knew certain things she shouldn't have known. Or so some people said.

"I get feelings sometimes, Fats. You know what I mean?" Her wild eyes looked us over. There was something weird and mysterious about Zelda and I wasn't so sure that it was all an act.

Fats didn't know what she was talking about. He just said, "You mean like cravings?"

I laughed. Tried to compose myself. My partner, always thinking of food or sex.

"Detectives, we don't have to play no games with each other. You know I'm running a good scam here. I admit it. I pay off and no one bothers me. But sometimes, it seems too good. It scares me. I'm thinking of quitting, doing something else. I was telling that to Fats the other day."

"Zelda, tell me about the evil forces."

"They're everywhere, Griff. All around you. All around me, swirling around Fats. Hungry. Bloody. Ready and waiting."

Fats looked like he was getting the creeps.

I figured Zelda was certifiable but said, "Ready and waiting for what, Zelda?"

"To do stuff, to do evil. They scare me. I can see them sometimes. I see their forms, not their human ones, but their otherworldly ones. The ugliness is indescribable. There's one I've been seeing too much lately, in my dreams, now even in my waking hours. Dark fur, growling, bloody fangs and mouth, claws, wolfish . . ."

Fats looked at me nervously.

"Like a werewolf?" I asked.

Zelda just froze. Silent. "I can feel it, Griff, it's here!"

"Here? Now?" Fats pulled his gun.

"In Bay City, I mean," she continued, eyes glassy, her skin suddenly turned ashen. She was a good actress, I'll give her that. She was even spooking me.

"Zelda?" I asked.

She froze, her eyes growing larger like terrified yellow disks in her head, her face twisting in fear, then terror. She opened her mouth to scream but not a sound came out. She was frozen in total terror.

Damnedest thing I've ever seen whether it was an act or not.

Fats slapped her face. "Come out of it, Zelda!"

Zelda crumpled to the floor.

She didn't move. She was quiet, pale. It took me a minute to realize she wasn't breathing.

I checked her out. She was an excellent actress and scam artist.

I looked up at my partner, took a deep breath and said, "Fats, she's dead."

Fats shook his head in disbelief; "I didn't slap her *that* hard, Griff."

I nodded. I knew Fats' slap hadn't killed Zelda. Fear had killed Zelda. Sheer stark fear.

"She'd seen something, Griff. Somehow she picked up on the werewolf and that means something," Fats said. "I'll make the call, why don't you check out her place."

I took a blanket off the couch and covered Zelda's body. It was disturbing looking at her face, at those bulging eyes. It was like she was still looking, still seeing and connected to what, I wondered. For sure it was something that had truly terrified her, her old heart had just given out. Maybe the same thing that had tortured that unidentified body in the warehouse? I wondered. It gave me the creeps.

Doc Carten called us with an ID and time of death on the warehouse victim, "Ronald Meyer, male, white, about 25 years old. We got a partial print . . . of something. Doesn't seem human, I'll have to do some tests. Thought you'd want to know, seeing as he's the son of the most important man in Bay City and an escapee from a mental institution."

I told Fats.

"We're in a real mess now."

Captain Landis called soon after. We expected it. He said, "Look, guys, they want this cleared up. Yesterday!"

Fats growled, "Political pressure, as if we don't have enough crap to handle."

"Well, let's get cracking," I said. "Better go and take a ride, talk to Meyer's father. Then take a ride to that mental institution. Something very strange in all of this and we're going to get to the bottom of it by hook or by crook."

"I'm with you, Griff!"

Old Man Meyer wasn't much help. Rich, retired industrialist, clipped coupons, recluse on a secluded estate, quiet, lonely, desperate. His second marriage to a fecund showgirl 40 years his junior had produced one child, Ronald. Wife died in childbirth. His son had been his life, and that life had gone dark a year ago when Ronald had been diagnosed with a terminal brain tumor that brought on paranoia, dementia and sudden outbursts of extreme violence. He'd killed a man in a fight, but what had been kept out of the papers is that he had also cut out the man's heart and eaten it. Witnesses were terrified. Ronald was tried and put away in an institution for the criminally insane. That was our next stop.

We were driving out of Bay City. After a while Fats started getting chatty. Always a bad sign.

"You know what the problem is, as I see it, in this world of ours?"

I was afraid to ask.

"All the damn assholes, Griff."

I couldn't disagree. I nodded, I could see where this discussion was going. I knew it was going to be a long ride out to the nut-hatch.

"No really," Fats insisted.

"I don't know. Assholes are annoying, but I think if you really want to fix things it's the scumbags that really cause the problems."

If you've been in police work, or ever lived life with your eyes open, you'll know these are two very distinct types of trouble-causing people.

Fats cogitated on my words a moment and smiled, "You're right, you know."

"Thanks," I muttered.

"No really, I think I got it figured now. The assholes are bad, they're trouble sometimes, but the scumbags are definitely worse."

"Absolutely. Assholes usually are just annoying, and every one of us can be one now and then."

"Right you are," Fats bellowed.

"Yeah, but scumbags . . . Man, they're the guys that do the bad stuff."

"Right, Griff, except if you're talking about skells. Now you take your basic city skell and I'll peg him worse than a scumbag any day. And a lot worse than any mere asshole." Fats said, letting his words of wisdom scoot around in his brain.

"Right, but you know all scumbags and skells are also ass-holes," I added.

Fats nodded, driving, thinking some more, then adding; "Yeah, but *not* all assholes are scumbags or skells. See what I mean?"

"Absolutely," I replied, his logic was impeccable.

"Now, take your basic scumbag skell, some mother raping bas-tard or druggie whore, some thrill killer maniac lowlife only fit for the electric chair. That's gotta be the worst kind of combo there is," Fats said proudly. "That's where all our problems come from."

I shrugged, said, "Slow down, Fats, we're coming to Willow Grove."

Willow Grove didn't let on it was an institution for the criminally insane, but the high walls and discreet guard towers told us
this wasn't your average funny farm.

"They're coming to take me away, aha, aha, aha, la, la, la, de,
da." Fats sung as we got out of our car.

"Shoulda happened years ago," I muttered. We walked the
white pebble drive to the gate to announce our presence. Soon we
were in the main building and greeted by a pompous looking oaf
dressed all in white who said he was Doctor William Willard, the
high mucky-muck of the nut house.

We shook hands and then Fats and I got down to business.

"Doctor Willard," I asked, "the reason we're here is to investigate a murder and one of your inmates . . ."

"We call them patients, officer."

"Well, it's Lieutenant, actually." I responded.

Fats laughed, chugged down some Ju-Ju Bees. I guess he imag-
ined he was at the movies, waiting to see the main attraction,
which would be a tour of the asylum.

"Anyway, Doctor, one of your patients figures in a murder
we're investigating."

"I doubt that very much, Lieutenant. Regardless, we value the
privacy of our patients very seriously."

"Even when they break out!" Fats barked.

"Impossible, detective! Turner is held under the tightest security." Willard said.

I looked at Fats and he looked at me. I said, "Doctor, I don't
know who this Turner is. We're here because someone killed
Ronald Meyer. Meyer escaped from here last night and was found
dead this morning. Mutilated."

"Oh that? Of course, it was a terrible shame," Willard said
nervously, backsliding now.

Fats gave me his most meaningful nudge.

"We need your cooperation, Doctor Willard," I said trying to
play good-cop to Fats' Attila the Hun. "Do you have any prospects, especially in the werewolf area that we can talk to?"

That made his face grow serious, fearful.

"Come on, Doc, we need your help in this," Fats prompted.

Doctor Willard took a deep breath; nervously looked at us.
"Yes, one of my patients does have serious delusions that he is a
lycanthrope."

"A what . . .?" Fats barked.

"That's Doc lingo for werewolf, Fats," I said.

"We have him under constant lock-down and medication," Willard continued apparently ignoring Fats' outburst. "He is one patient that no one on my staff has been able to reach. Medication only tranquilizes the situation; it does not allow us to cure it. But this man is heavily tranquilized all the time, I assure you, and under restraint. He is certainly not leaving his cell or the grounds."

"Could that be this guy, Turner, you mentioned?"

Willard nodded reluctantly.

"Could he be faking it? Faking taking his meds?" I asked.

"Well, I suppose so, Lieutenant," Willard said thoughtfully, "patients do that from time to time, but my staff acts accordingly to ensure that all patients are amply medicated as the need arises. Whether they want it or not. We are quite aware that we have some dangerous people here, but most are ill and really just misunderstood."

"Yeah, right, Doc. They're misunderstood, like Al Capone was misunderstood," Fats barked. "Is this an institution for the criminally insane or not?"

I deflected Fats' question and asked, "Well, Doc, who is this Turner?"

Doctor Willard took a deep breath, said, "We house him in a special ward all by himself and he is under 24-hour watch. Elijah Turner is our most violent and dangerous patient here at Willow Grove."

"And that's gotta be saying a lot," Fats added.

I ignored his remark; "We'd like to see Turner right away."

"Impossible," the doctor said.

"Nothing's impossible, Doc, a murder's been committed," Fats bellowed.

"You can't do that!" Doctor Willard seemed shocked, surprised, he moved back a step.

Fats moved forward a step, Willard moved backwards another step.

Fats said, "Don't tell us we can't see him, Doc."

I put my hand on Fats' two-ton arm and more pleasantly said, "You see, Doctor Willard, this is a capital case now. A murder has been committed. We want to see Elijah Turner right away."

"You can't see him, it would be too traumatic. Why, when he sees people—anyone at all, even myself or staff—he flies into violent fits of rage that are almost impossible to control," Willard said nervously.

"I get that way myself, sometimes," Fats laughed.

I gave my partner a shake of my head; he wasn't being helpful.

"It can't be helped, Doctor. Now tell me, in which building and in what cell is this Elijah Turner housed," I asked.

"Spill it, Doc!" Fats growled. He was loosing patience.

Doctor Willard sighed, said, "Follow me, he's in Special D Block. I'll take you to him."

Willard led us to an ultra white building set away from the others in the complex. It was made of cinder blocks, not standard red bricks like all the other buildings. There was a billy-club-wearing member of the staff seated at a desk at the entrance. He was a big one; over six feet and he jumped up in surprise when he saw us.

Willard took us over to the desk, said, "Albert, these are police detectives. I've brought them to see Elijah Turner. Please unlock the door for us."

"Ah, Doctor Willard, I don't know . . . I don't think that's such a good idea now. You know what I mean? Turner's acting very strange lately. Violent. I wouldn't go in there if I were you . . ."

"Albert, the keys, please!" Willard said sternly, annoyed at having staff question his actions.

"But Doctor . . ." Albert stiffened.

"Keys, Albert!" Fats barked. Then to me he said, "Something smells awful peculiar here, Griff."

Willard blanched, looked at Albert with alarm. "Give me the keys!"

When Willard opened the door that led into the corridor he ran to cell #1. And we were right behind him. He looked through the little eye-level window in the door, gasped, said, "Oh my God!" and quickly threw open the door to the cell. Fats and I drew our revolvers and bulled our way through. The Doctor came in afterwards, Albert followed nervously.

Fats and I looked at each other, then at Willard. We all looked at Albert.

"Son of a bitch!" Fats growled.

I said, "Doc, you and your boy Albert here better have a damn good explanation why Turner's missing!"

We were back in Willard's Office in the main administration building. Fats had called Smitty to come by to take Albert into custody. I told them to sweat him for all he was worth but the worm seemed to be holding mum about the entire affair. Sacred to death more likely. Didn't want to end up like Ronald Meyer trussed up in a warehouse like a side of beef. We had an immediate search of the hospital and the grounds but Turner didn't show up. Somehow, Fats and I didn't think he would.

I said, "We've got to tell Captain Landis; get an APB out on Turner. We can't have that psycho running loose, God knows what he'll do!"

Fats nodded and took care of it.

I turned to Willard, "I think you better tell me now if you know anything about this. You did let Meyer out. Why? His rich father pay you off with cash under the table or did he just promise to buy you a new wing for your fancy hospital? And now Turner's gone too?"

Doctor Willard held his anger and stalled for time. He saw the way things were going. I smelled a rat. Bribery, professional ethics violated, scandal, and murder! I noticed a transformation come over him then. He was cornered and he knew it. Maybe we didn't have the whole story yet, but I sure had my suspicions and it was just a matter of time. Willard knew that too but we didn't realize how dangerous that would make him.

Fats came back and we stood in front of the doctor waiting for him to spill the beans. He was seated behind his big fancy desk, nervous, bug-eyes, telling us about the great strides a facility like Willow Grove made for his patients. I wasn't much interested. I got more interested when I felt the unmistakable cold steel of the business end of a revolver pressed into the back of my neck. I froze. I saw Fats had a gun to his head too. A voice from behind us said, "Don't move. Don't turn around. Go for your guns and you're both dead men."

We looked at Willard. We saw him nod to a man or men behind us. Then Fats and I were slugged from behind and fell into unconsciousness.

When I woke up I found we were in adjoining locked cells. Fats was slumped in a chair just coming back from his vacation in sleepy-land.

"Wha—happened?" he said drowsy, feeling the big lump on the back of his head. "Jesus, Griff, that guy sapped me good. Knocked me right into tomorrow!"

Fats was right, it probably was tomorrow, or the next day. I wasn't certain how long we'd been out but I noticed now that we were locked in separate iron bar cells, adjacent to each other.

Gary Lovisi

"You okay?" I asked, smiling at his obvious chagrin and discomfort. The Fatman had a hard head and for someone to give him a bump like that; he had been hit *hard*.

"You know, that wasn't nice. Totally uncalled for. I got a real beef with the guy that slugged me and when we meet—*and we will*—he'll damn well regret it!"

"Fine, I'm all for revenge," I said, "but right now let's figure a way to get out of here."

"Yeah, and get our hardware back," he said, feeling his empty shoulder holster.

I nodded, there was that. We were unarmed and locked up while one of Willard's little psycho freaks was running around his nut house with our weapons. Or maybe even out in public. Now we were locked up and not able to do a damn thing about any of it. Not a good sign of things to come.

It got worse when Willard and two of his goons, both holding guns—*our* guns by the looks of them—appeared outside our cells. Another man was with them, he was held in straight-jacket, chains and mask. Obviously the missing Elijah Turner had been found.

Somehow I didn't think they brought him to our cell to lock him up and let us out.

I recognized one of the guys holding the guns and gave Fats the nod. It was Louie the Butcher, a rape-killer from years back we'd arrested. He was supposed to have gotten the death penalty but instead got off on an insanity plea and had been placed here with the other criminally insane. Now he was working for Willard and held my own gun on us. I could see the gleam of sweet revenge in his eyes.

"The evil forces are at their zenith tonight, detectives," Willard said suddenly in an eerie monotone.

Fats looked at me as if to say, "I told you so".

"The forces of Darkness require a sacrifice, a blood sacrifice, for their hunger. Who shall it be? Which one of you will brave the beast of Hell tonight, and in doing so find the answers to all your questions?" Willard said boldly.

Fats and I didn't say a word.

"You are investigating a murder, actually, many murders, done through the darkness of lycanthropy. You do not believe? That is to be understood, even I did not believe at first, but you shall see. It is true. And when you see, it shall transform you, as it did me. You shall see and judge. Lieutenant Griffin, watch your partner tonight, observe what transpires, understand the true horror, and we shall talk in the morning."

I shook my head, not knowing what the blamed fool was talking about.

"Look, you better release us both right now!" I demanded.

Fats barked defiantly, "Let me outta here!"

However, Willard seemed beyond reason now. I could see he was gone from reality, a change had come over him. Something had pushed him over into the land of the mad. There was no reasoning with him.

Willard ordered his goons to take the chains and straightjacket off Turner. Next they took off the mask and the muzzle, unlocked and removed the handcuffs, and then they pushed him into the cell with Fats and locked the door!

Fats stepped back, rolled up the sleeves of his shirt and warned, "You even come near me, boyo, and I'll knock you into next week."

I stood alone in the next cell watching with concern. I said, "Fats, be careful. See if he's got any weapons, pat him down, then knock him out and tie him up with your shirt and clothes."

A brief scuffle and then Fats had Turner down and out and was in the process of tying him up tight and fast.

"He's immobile now, Griff."

"Good, just keep an eye on him," I added.

Willard, who had been watching the entire event with his henchmen laughed and said, "It won't do you any good. For when the power of darkness is exalted and the transformation takes place, nothing you have done can stop him. Your precautions are useless. Sleep with one eye open, I warn you. Pleasant dreams . . ." he laughed mockingly.

Then Willard and his thugs were gone leaving Fats and me alone. Me in my own separate cell and Fats in his cell with the maniac Elijah Turner who thought he was a werewolf. So far, Turner had not been a problem for Fats to handle. In fact, it had been almost too easy, but I felt things weren't what they seemed and I wondered what Willard had in store for us.

I was thinking what we were going to do about it all. I knew there was very little we could do. Maybe bribe or capture a guard? If one ever came by with food or water. But I had a feeling it was going to be a long night and that no one was coming here until morning.

"I know what I gotta do, Griff. Make a Cross and then wait for the transformation," Fats said gruffly, watching Turner's still form where it lay tied up quietly on the floor of his cell.

"Transformation?" I asked.

"Zelda told me about him. When she mentioned to me about the evil forces, she told me there's always a transformation. She said it was called extreme personality disorder in them fancy doctor books, but to the untrained eye it can be seen to be indistinguishable from magic."

I looked at Fats with surprise and a new respect. I didn't think he had it in him to understand these complex medical syndromes, but I still wasn't entirely sure what he was talking about.

"Griff, Zelda told me that evil forces emanate from a man who was made into a monster. It began from when he was a child, an infant. There had been horrendous abuse, torture, that had harmed the body and twisted the mind into something . . . something else. Something not exactly human. Something that we could never understand. But that incredible pain and torture upon a mind can change a body too, transform it. Evil forces, Griff, the ultimate rage of pain unbearable and unbelievable. The werewolf."

I shook my head.

Turner groaned and moved slightly just to remind us he was still there.

It was quite now, getting dark.

"I don't believe in werewolves, Fats."

"Neither do I, Griff, but no one told Turner that."

"Hah!"

Turner suddenly opened his eyes. They had a weird glow to them; the pupils were *yellow*.

"Jesus, Griff!" Fats whispered, "Now *that's* weird."

I nodded. I'd never seen anything like it before. It was supposed to be a full moon tonight. I knew we were in for a rough night.

"Fats, if he attacks you, move over to my side of the bars. If you can maneuver him near me, I can lend a hand through the bars."

Fats was busy tying two sticks together into a cross. When he finished he held it up and showed me. When he showed it to Turner, the man just let out a guttural growl. It didn't sound human at all.

"Be careful, Fats."

"Sure, Griff, I'm a big boy."

Time passed. No one came to our cell to give us food or water or even to taunt us. It just got darker outside the bars of our cells but the full moon gave some illumination.

As night became complete outside, I noticed a peculiar change in Turner. His appearance grew distinctly feral; there was a cunning glint in his eyes, a vicious and almost animal-like appearance to his features and posture. The mere five-o'clock shadow that had been on his face hours before now seemed to have grown into a dark matting of . . . *fur?*

Fats noticed it too, said, "I don't like this. His face, his hands, he didn't have all that hair when Willard put him in here with us, did he, Griff?"

I didn't know what to say. I barely believed the evidence that my own eyes were showing me. It was uncanny, but there *was* some kind of transformation going on!

I was glad to see Turner was still securely bound, for if he ever got loose I wasn't sure Fats could handle him so easily now. Especially if he was in that manic animalistic state where he felt no pain, knew no reason, and had the massive strength of the insane.

"He's struggling at his bounds," I warned my partner.

Fats nodded, he'd armed himself with a table leg. "He'll get loose soon. When he does, I'll be ready for him."

I wasn't so sure.

Another hour passed and darkness covered the sky outside our tiny window. A full moon shone partly through thick black clouds that raced across the sky caught on howling winds. It would have been a spooky night even if Fats hadn't been locked in a cell with a criminally insane homicidal maniac who thought he was a werewolf.

I noticed the change in Turner's physical appearance had now become incredible and profound. He hardly looked human at all any more. Fats and I were both astonished by this transformation and watched intently and with fear as it progressed.

Time passed. It was freaking us out to view Turner's transformation. Neither of us could conceive of such a thing happening to a man. It wasn't natural at all. And we knew it wasn't any trick or parlor magic. This was real and it scared us. And it had me worrying about Fats. Turner now actually looked like some uncanny mixture of man and wolf, some type of pre-human feral man at his most wild and vicious preparing to strike death at any moment.

"Damndest thing I ever seen, Griff," Fats said and I could hear the fear in his voice now for the first time. He was watching Turner intently; waiting for the attack we both knew would come soon. "He's turning into a monster right before our eyes!"

I checked my watch. "It's almost midnight, Fats."

"Yeah," he gulped, "they say the evil forces are at their height at midnight."

"Evil forces, my ass! Come on, Fats, snap out of it, he's just a freako mental case! Once Landis finds we're overdue, the boys will be down here and get us out. Then we'll put Willard and all his nut house psychos away forever. We just gotta get through the night."

"Yeah, easier said than done," Fats said.

I wanted to say something to calm him down but I needed to calm myself down first. My bravado of a moment before melted away when I took another look at Turner. There was something about him that was vicious, evil and hungry and it was showing boldly now. Unafraid. Almost taunting Fats and me. When he looked at me I knew real fear and, God help me, I was glad it was Fats in that cell with him and not me!

Suddenly Turner let loose with a heart-rending howl that seemed to break the night apart as he easily ripped apart all his bonds and was now free. With one swift jump he was upon my partner and had his hands at Fat's throat.

I yelled to warn Fats but Turner was on him so quickly I knew he was in a fight for his life.

Fat's tried to club the madman off him with the table-leg but Turner, the wolf-thing had apparent superhuman strength. He easily pulled the club out of Fats' hand, tossed it away, and was at my partner just as furious as before.

Fats screamed, sheer terror now as he looked into Turner's cold yellow eyes and noticed the long yellow fangs in his mouth that had once been teeth.

"Hold on, Fats! Fight him off! You can do it!" I shouted, enraged that I could not get in there and help my partner and friend, terrified for his life, frustrated that all I could do was watch. Watch a battle that I feared he would lose.

I tried to stretch my arms through the bars in an effort to hit Turner from behind, but he was too far from my side of the cell for me to reach him.

"Move him closer to me, Fats," I barked.

Fats, wide eyes white and obviously in the fight of his life shouted back, "Damn, Griff, this bastard is strong! I can't move *him!* He's moving *me!"*

So it went: the werewolf—I could hardly think of him as the human being Elijah Turner any longer—held Fats up against the cell bars opposite my cell and was pounding and tearing at him mercilessly. I was unable to help, reduced to a terrified spectator. I didn't like that at all. I watched in rage as crimson sprays of blood landed on the wall and flew through the air with each punch and tear Fats received. It was terrible. Fats would literally be beaten to death and torn apart before my very eyes if something wasn't done to save him soon.

"Fats!" I shouted.

There was no answer.

I could see my partner was still standing, still trying to defend himself, but it could not last. He was taking a massive amount of abuse and pain. I saw his face and he was terrified, almost transfixed as he looked into the furry face of Elijah Turner and saw only heartless feral yellow eyes, fangs, claws, wet with his own red blood.

Finally I had an idea. I could see that Fats was mortally terrified. If only I could use that fear to get that fat bastard mad—*mad as hell! madder than hell!*—then he might fight back!

"Fats! Fats!" I barked. "You gonna let a furry freak like that hit you without giving him a pounding back? What are you, a big pussy? You gonna just lay down and let this mental skell beat the crap outta you? Come on, man, fight back! Kick his hairy ass! Make a fist damn it! Make a fist and pound it into his face and never stop pounding!"

The werewolf pounded Fats' head. With each blow Fats took he still hung in there somehow. He was taking terrific punishment but Fats had the hardest damn head I've ever seen. Usually that's a handicap to a copper but in this case it was just what the doctor ordered.

I wondered what the hell he was doing. Why was he taking such a beating and not fighting back?

"Fats?" I barked.

"I'm okay. Bastard's getting me real pissed off, you know what I mean?"

"I hope so."

"Real pissed off, Griff!"

Then I saw my partner make a fist and bring it up in a pounding blow to the side of Turner's head. It was a blasting blow to the ear and Turner let out a loud yelp. The terror left Fats' face now. It was replaced by a rage and anger I had never seen him evidence before. His rage grew and mirrored the rage of the werewolf, and soon grew greater than that of the werewolf.

"My old man beat me, Griff! When I was a kid! He beat me bad, dammit! I ever tell you?"

He had not.

"It wasn't pretty!"

"Fats! Defend yourself, dammit!"

"I never fought back!"

I saw him raise his fist. It was a massive hammer; all muscle, sinew and bone.

Then he shouted, "Not till now. I'm fighting back now!"

Then Sergeant Herman Stubbs, massively pissed off and in a truly nasty frame of mind, let loose with a tremendous pile driver right into the face of the werewolf. Turner's head shot back, shook. Turner growled in pain, but before he could do more, Fats let loose with a constant stream of pounding head shots into the monster. It was a beating that broke bone and ripped sinew. It tore flesh and caused streams of blood. This time the blood was Turner's, the werewolf was in trouble and Fats just came on stronger with each attack. Fats never stopped, never relented. Both man and wolf were now covered in gore, bleeding form dozens of gashes and bites; both locked in a death duel that only one could survive.

"That's it, dammit!" I encouraged.

Fats was boxing the creature now, his massive fists smashing into Turner's face, into his head and breaking it apart. Turner—full of werewolf animal power—kept coming, but the tide of battle had turned. The animal ferocity in Turner had for once been met and overcome by the human anger in Fats. Human anger and pain that Fats was drawing on to make him win this battle. And Fats' well ran damn deep. Fats kept fighting, pounding away, bashing the werewolf's head against the metal bars of his cell, choking the life out of the creature, and finally forcing the battle over to the bars at my cell.

Now I saw the face of Turner up close, a mass of gore and broken tissue. I'd seen faces in highway head-on crashes that looked better. The feral ferocity in the werewolf's eyes was somehow dissipated now, rather than rage I saw fear. The fear of a cornered animal, a terrified beast hunted by a master huntsmen who would never give up and never loose the fight.

Turner growled like the ferocious beast he was but Fats only fought harder.

Then Fats growled back and his sounds even terrified me.

The two clenched once again, Fats pounding away at the flesh of Turner's body. Fur went flying in patches. They were trying to tear each other apart. The werewolf used his claws to tear and rip Fats' flesh. My fat partner had plenty of padding but was tore up bad. Now shorn of fear and righteous with rage he just reached out, grabbed the werewolf's clawed paw and snapped it like a twig. I heard the bone break and then a feral canine yelp of pain.

Fats had the werewolf up against the bars of my cell now. Finally Turner was in range and I had my chance. I quickly wrapped my arm around the creature's furry neck and squeezed tighter and tighter as Fats pounded away at him. Turner was caught now and we were not letting him escape. I squeezed harder, tighter; crushing the air out of his lungs as Fats pounded him mercilessly. After a couple of minutes of this relentless beating I could tell he was weakening. A few minutes more and the thing was gasping for breath. Then the struggle suddenly ceased. Turner's lifeless body fell to the cell floor dead.

I shook my head and looked up at my partner. He was a gore-covered mess.

"You okay, Fats?"

"I think so, Griff. I look a mess but I figure it must look worse than it actually is if I'm still alive and able to stand up on my own."

I nodded, glad he was just alive, realizing now that Zelda had been right. I was shocked and confused by what had happened. Had it actually happened? Already Turner's body had transformed back, loosing the fur and werewolf appearance.

Fats smiled as if he had been reading my mind. "Damn, no way we can tell the truth on this one, Griff."

It wasn't until morning that Captain Landis and a brace of harness bulls came to unlock our cells and let us out.

"Sure glad to see you and the boys, Cap," Fats said as Landis helped him over to where Doc Carten began to work on him.

Doc Carten took one look at Fats, said, "What the hell happened to you?"

Fats just smiled, said, "I'll put it all in my report to the Captain."

"So how you find us, Cap?" I asked.

"When you and Stubbs didn't report in," Landis said, "I figured you'd got yourself into another mess. Willard gave us a bit of trouble but we got him to talk and we got his staff of psychos all under wraps. He had a nice scam going here, using the criminally insane to pull jobs, having them kill anyone who gave him a problem. Ronald Meyer was going to tell his father what was going on here, so Willard used one of the patients to kill him."

"That was Elijah Turner. Willard eventually freaked out about Turner," I said. "he'd crossed the line, he believed Turner was a real werewolf."

"Yeah, Griff, the evil forces got him too," Fats added.

Landis looked at Fats. Doc Carten had him all bandaged up now. Then Landis pointed to the lump on the floor in Fats' cell.

"What's that?" Landis asked, trying to distinguish the mass of flesh and finally realizing with disgust that it was a man's body.

"All that's left of Elijah Turner. Homicidal mental patient. He suffered from some kind of personality disorder," I said. "I don't rightly know what it's called but it's in the medical books. He killed Meyer. He's the man Willard used to kill people who gave him problems. Turner thought he was a werewolf. So did Willard. Willard put him in the cell here with Fats. The two had a terrible fight, and well, Fats got the better of him."

Landis nodded, "Willard should have known better, he must have really been off his nut. Anyone can see the guy wasn't any werewolf, what's left of his face, looks like he barely even shaved yet."

I smiled. Fats didn't say a word.

Landis grunted skeptically and walked away. "Okay, you guys, why don't you go get cleaned up and take a couple of days. I want your reports by Friday."

"Sure, Cap," I said.

"Absolutely, Cap," Fats added.

Then Fats and I left to get our story straight.

SBC

YOU'VE ALL HEARD about the condition, syndrome, or whatever the hell mental health professionals call it, commonly known as suicide by cop. It is a last ditch, desperation measure by a person—criminal or not—unable or unwilling to commit suicide by their own hand. So they get someone else to do it for them. That means a police officer. They set up a bogus but apparently dangerous situation, usually with a gun or reasonable facsimile, and provoke the cops to kill them. Nice and quick. A legal cop shooting and the guy is dead, fast and relatively painless, the cop left questioning his actions . . .

I'm that cop. The shooter who was left behind by the man who set me up to kill him.

It happened to me a few months back. It was a department-cleared shooting and the newspapers eventually even called me a hero—coming to the aid as I did of a brother officer whose life was apparently in mortal danger. But it still bugs me.

My story isn't about the guy who got himself offed by me. I had little sympathy for him. It's about the people that coward left behind. The damage he did to his family—wife, parents, and most of all his children by suiciding out. Then there is what me and my family had to go through. Things were never the same again. I lost my wife because of it. It changed everything.

There's something terrible about killing another human being but some kills are worse than others. That sicko gave me no choice but to protect a fellow officer's life, he isn't worth worrying about, but what he made me do still bothers me. It's not the line-of-duty shooting that's the problem. It's being tricked, used, forced into a situation where I did the guy's dirty work for him. That bothers me. He *made* me kill him. I didn't want to do it, but he forced me to do it. We later found a note and a pink toy plastic water pistol—looked just like a .45, he'd spray-painted black. It looked real enough. It was *real* as far as my partner and I were concerned. The guy wanted to die and I'd obliged him.

Now I was back on the job but skittish. I didn't ever want to draw my gun and kill anyone again. So I kept my gun empty. Unloaded. I knew it was the wrong thing to do, but I just didn't want to shoot anyone anymore.

The truth of it was, if anyone knew this, I would have been taken off the streets. I was a danger to myself, the public and my new partner—the rookie from Sheepshead Bay. Like most people self-absorbed with guilt and depression—*like the guy I had shot, no doubt*—I didn't think about the consequences. I just didn't have the nerve or desire to pack it in then. And leaving the streets I loved, being out of the action and wasting away behind some desk, wasn't my style either. I went to work in the day-to-day and prayed, as I did my duty. After all, in 18 years of service I've only fired my gun twice.

The rookie and I had been called to a domestic disturbance. Typical. A couple fighting in a small row house near Emmons Avenue. One of their kids apparently made the 911 call. That must be some fun family for a kid to grow up in.

When we got there the husband and wife were going at it full tilt. They were both Russian and screaming and cursing up a storm. Throwing so many things at each other that they were running out of things to throw. Broken stuff was everywhere, it's a miracle no one was dead yet. Neither me nor the rookie could understand a word of it though.

We quickly separated the two adults. When we had them in opposite corners of the living room—with me between 'em naturally—I had the rookie take the two kids into the back room away from the battleground. They'd seen enough.

I looked over the husband and wife carefully. They glared at me and then each other. They gave me a hateful look for keeping them apart from killing each other. Well, I thought, wasn't that just too bad.

I noticed scratches on the man's face and arms, his left arm was bleeding. I saw dark bruising on the woman's face, below the right eye, and more on her shoulder. I told them to keep quiet and not move. When the rookie came back in from settling the kids in a back bedroom I called it in.

"We'll need an ambulance, and I'll tell Captain Hunter we need someone that can speak Russian," I added.

The rookie stood guard while I made the call.

The cavalry was on the way. We waited. It shouldn't take long.

The man and then the woman each spoke to us but they knew barely a dozen words of English between them. It was impossible to get anything understood. I was considering having the rookie bring back the older kid, the boy. He looked about 12-14—I'd see if he could speak English. Maybe we could use him as a translator?

That's when everything whirled right out of control.

The woman suddenly screamed at her husband. He spit at her and taunted her in return, calling her *blet* or something like that. It really set the woman off. From God-knows-where she pulled out the longest knife I'd ever seen and charged the man like a maniac. Pure murder in her eyes.

I ran to stop her. The rookie drew her service weapon and she was going to let go with a quick round to drop the wife when the husband suddenly grabbed the gun out of her hand. The man knocked my partner down to the floor with some kind of karate chop to the neck. Rookie was out cold. Then the guy turned and smacked his wife's face just as she came at him. She reeled, made a swipe at him with the knife, missed, and then he decked her with a power blow to the head. She went down like a felled ox. The rookie was down too now, she was obviously stunned, and the husband now had the rookie's gun in his hand.

"Drop the damn gun!" I barked, drawing my gun. Maybe he didn't understand English but he sure as hell knew what I meant.

The Russian turned to me suddenly, craziness in his eyes. The rookie's gun was still hanging limp in his hand down by his side. I ordered him to drop it. I hoped he'd wise up, not push the matter. My hope was short-lived. Suddenly a mad gleam of pure hatred came into the Russian's eyes and he lifted his hand upward with the gun, slowly, almost as if in a dream.

"I said drop the gun!" I pointed my weapon right at him.

I prayed this wouldn't go any further. Most guys with a gun who see a cop draw a weapon on them drop their gun fast. Some shoot. You never can tell for sure.

I pointed my gun at the man and meant business, ordering him to drop his gun again, but I was bluffing. My gun wasn't loaded.

The Russian raised his arm still holding my partner's loaded weapon and then pointed it. My partner lay on the floor frozen and still stunned. I hoped she wasn't seriously hurt. Then the Russian pointed the gun *away* from me—*to his wife*.

"Oh, damn!" I cried seeing plainly what was coming, "No! Don't do it!"

I dropped my useless unloaded weapon to the floor in my headlong rush to tackle the man before he pulled the trigger.

I hit him hard, running into him like a freight train. He fell
backwards against the wall with me on top of him. We were both
wrestling for the rookie's gun, which the Russian still held tightly
in his hand.

Suddenly a shot rang out.

More than ever now we were fighting for possession of that
gun.

I realized now I could be fighting for my very life, that damn
Russian was remarkably strong. I couldn't get the gun out of his
hands. I grew fearful that I might not be able to get the gun away
from him before he used it on his wife—or me.

Suddenly I saw the rookie standing behind me. She'd apparently collected her wits and I saw her holding a gun and pointing it
at the Russian. It took me a second to realize that she was holding
the gun I'd dropped. *My* gun. My *unloaded* gun!

Events like this have their own momentum. In a heartbeat the
Russian saw the rookie with a gun pointed at him, knocked me
aside, raised his own gun to get a shot off at my partner.

The rookie had a clear shot, she was set and ready. Under any
other circumstances she would have dropped the Russian flat before the man could ever get his shot off . . . But not this time.
When rookie pressed the trigger, the only sound was a loud and
very telltale click.

To say the rookie was shocked was the understatement of the
year.

So was the Russian.

I watched frozen, fearful of what was coming, astonishment on
all our faces.

The rookie pressed the trigger again and again, and it clicked
empty every time.

The Russian smiled now, ready to pull the trigger of the gun in
his hand. He'd aimed the gun at the rookie point-blank but at that
moment his wife came back to life. She suddenly flung herself
upon her husband, plunging her knife deep into his back. There
was a terrible scream and a gushing of blood. The Russian's shot
went off wild, thankfully missing the rookie, but putting a nice
hole in the ceiling over our heads that rained plaster down on us
like dusty snow.

I grabbed the wife before she could pull the knife out of her
husband's back and plunge it into him again. The rookie ran over,

checked the Russian, he was bleeding bad but thankfully quiet now. Then she cuffed the woman.

"Your gun was empty!" The rookie barked at me. "Why the hell didn't you tell me your gun wasn't loaded!"

She handed me back my gun like it was a useless thing and I quickly holstered it.

"I didn't have time," I said lamely.

She turned away from me, angry, still scared, mostly just disappointed.

That disappointment in her eyes gnawed at my gut and I'll never forget it.

We got the lovely couple under control and then the ambulance and back-up officers arrived. A sergeant came in and took over, told us to begin writing our report.

They took out the woman soon after, booked her for attempted murder.

The EMTs were still working on the knife in the Russian's back before they could move him. He looked pretty bad off.

The two kids had come in from the back bedroom, where the rookie had put them earlier. They must have seen everything.

"Mama? Papa?" the younger girl cried.

The boy, who was older just hugged his sister. He looked at the officers taking away his mother and at the knife still protruding from the back of his prostrate father with a strange detachment that I found disturbing. We'll be hearing from that kid someday, I figured. Five years or so, for sure.

What a mess this had become.

I took that desk job the next day.

A month later I quietly put in my papers. I'd almost got a good rookie killed, I'd almost allowed that crazy Russian bastard to execute his wife right there in front of us. I was drinking more now, but feeling it less.

I thought about my gun being unloaded because I didn't want to shoot anyone again. Citizens and mental cases committing suicide by cop—something that never even occurred to me when I'd been a rookie coming up. All the rules had changed these days. The job just keeps getting harder, while the people we deal with are more twisted than ever. Sometimes I wonder if there's a name for my reaction to all this stuff that effects cops. Some specific syndrome, with a fancy name. Some form of trauma, no doubt. I never went to the Department shrink after my shooting. I didn't want to talk about it, over and over, analyze it endlessly. But I think there might be something to it now. I should have gotten help, instead I drank.

When I retired I moved down South to a carry state but I never carry a gun. Mostly I hang out at a local bar and have a few drinks . . .then a few more drinks . . .

There's this rookie cop who comes into the bar most days, checks it out, chats up Sam the bartender and some of the regulars. Seems like an okay guy. He kind of reminds me of myself when I was young and began on the job. Most of the time I don't talk with him, or anyone else. Most of the time these days I'm passed out on the bar. Pretty good for a guy who can barely pay his bar bills.

Today there is some ruckus in the bar but I pay it no mind. I don't perk up these days unless Sam puts another drink in front of me. But I do notice the ruckus gets louder and I finally hear people scream and running.

Only then do I lift my head off the bar. What I see is the rookie to my right in front of the bar and some guy behind the bar, with a gun to Sam's head.

Everyone else has run out of the bar by then.

The rookie draws his gun, but hesitates. He doesn't want to shoot yet.

"Drop the gun!" he shouts harshly, his firm cop voice a deadly warning.

The intruder just smiles, makes sure the cop sees his gun is pointed at Sam's head.

Poor Sam, I think to myself. He looks scared to death. He may be a low-life prick but he didn't deserve this. Sam could be a bad guy. Knowing what I knew about Sam, if I was still on the job, I'd have pinched him long ago. But I'm not on the job now, I'm retired, and I need another drink.

"I said drop the gun!" the rookie barks again.

The intruder smiles cunningly, then suddenly lets Sam go. He just lets him go like it's nothing to him now. Sam runs out of the bar as fast as a racehorse going for the finish line.

Now it's just the intruder and the rookie cop.

And me, still in my seat and slumped down on the bar between them.

The intruder is behind the bar, the rookie is in front of the bar. Both pointing loaded guns point-blank at each other. I realize that we're at that particular moment in time . . .

That's when it hit me. This wasn't any robbery, not even a hostage-taking. The intruder never wanted Sam at all. Sam was just a pawn. I look at the intruder out of the corner of my eye. He's young, at loose ends, hyper, emotionally distraught. I know the signs. I had seen this all before.

I knew I had to do something. I had to stop this rookie from shooting the intruder. I had to save this cop from being forced to kill this sicko and having to go through what I had gone through.

I jumped up from my bar seat grabbing the gun held by the intruder. That put myself between him and the rookie. I tried to pull the gun out of the man's hand. He pulled back, he was young and strong, then the gun went off.

I was surprised by the weapon's report. It was loud, it was a real gun, loaded. I felt a searing pain in my side. I was hit.

Then I heard three quick bursts from the gun of the rookie, tightly-packed shots into the intruder's chest. Kill shots, right by the book. The intruder never got off another round, instead he just fell back, dead.

I slumped down to the bar top in pain. I'd been wrong about the intruder; it wasn't a suicide by cop after all.

I just held onto the bar, trying to get my breath, trying to talk. Finally the rookie came over to me. "You'll make it, old timer, hang in there."

Old timer?

I hear him yell out to someone, "Call for an ambulance!"

It's getting darker in the bar now, even though the Southern noonday sun is bright as fire outside. The rookie is at the intruder's body now picking up his gun. I smile to myself, even though I was wrong, I know my action gave the rookie the time he needed to bring down the intruder. That has to count for something.

Soon the rookie is beside me. I can't hear what he is saying, but my eyes can make out his words as I read his lips. He says, "Thanks for saving my life, old timer."

Old timer, my ass!

"Don't worry, you're going to be okay. The ambulance just got here," his lips tell me. It's not easy reading him, but my eyes open wide then he adds, "By the way, can you believe that freak *wanted* me to kill him? I found this note in his shirt pocket."

The cop shows me a paper. It has three words written on it.

'Suicide by Cop.'

I nod slowly, so I was right after all.

Then the EMTs arrive and begin working on me.

"Don't worry, you'll make it, old timer," a young girl tech says.

What the hell is it with all this 'old timer' crap!

The rookie cop smiles down at me.

Now I can relax. I know everything will be all right soon, and I don't even feel the need for a drink.

THE MISSION

THE OLD PRIEST WAS ON HIS KNEES AGAIN. Praying. Just as he did this time every morning. The cold stone floor of his tiny room, without even the tiniest throw rug upon the stone flags, did not offer him any warmth or comfort for his old knobbed knees. It did not matter. He did not care. He hardly noticed things like that anymore. After a lifetime of devotion, more than half a century of hard work and prayer, Father Alphonse Gaetano was above earthly pleasure and pain—his mighty spirit having transcended the mere physical world. And in doing so, he was now privileged to have touched upon something much more spiritual. And strangely, much more substantial. He lived within himself these last years of his long life, performing the work that the old Pope so long ago had demanded of him, the work he had been blessed to perform.

The work of guarding American's Holy Mother Church, his beloved Catholic Church, from the evil within.

He'd done well over the years, discrediting pedophile priests, seeing to it that their crimes were made public, that victims spoke up, that local and national news media responded with reports and investigations. It was not easy. The official church was allied against him and tried to cover up, pay off, or do anything to deny the existence of the evil. They denied everything. And though he loved his Church, and knew he was ripping it apart, he knew the evil must be exorcised.

And the worst evil of all was this terrible degeneracy and affliction that so warped that small minority of Mother Church's holy priests. The damage these few priests did was incalculable. Horrendous. It infected the anointed representatives of God Himself upon the Earth—breaking their scared vows, destroying their sacred covenant with the Almighty—and instead of fighting evil— these priests performed the ultimate blasphemy. As trusted priests of God, with the trust of His flock and worshipers in their hands, they initiated evil, and perpetuated it with God's most beloved and innocent. The children. The children who were the Lord's most ardent worshipers, who trusted in God, and his human servants—His holy anointed priests.

He was old now. Tired. The evil he'd seen, been forced to fight over the years—and its source, his own brothers and sisters in Holy Mother church itself—had done something to his very soul. Hurt it in a manner, and with such deep pain, that went beyond mere physical pain. He was a deeply sad man these days, but not a broken one. Never a broken one. For every time he found The Evil in the church, he had always found a way to destroy it, and this gave him the strength to go on. Even today, his old eyes still showed with that same fierce fire, that same sure knowledge and intense determination that men many decades his junior wished they possessed.

But knowledge and power never come cheaply.

Nor without consequences.

And the darker the knowledge . . .

The deeper the pain that knowledge can bring.

My name is Joe Dillon and I fight my own private war against those who use religion and God for power, profit, pleasure. I call it "the Mission" and it's sacred to me.

Annie helps.

She understands.

I said, "Annie, I think we had a very successful run last time. It was good. We hurt them badly. But I hate the violence. I was never that way. Never like that. I was a good man. Once. Just a . . . family man. Until . . ."

"I know, Joe," she said, trying her best to comfort me, but knowing that my family—my wife and young son—the only two things I cared about in my life, had been taken from me. My family had been destroyed. So had I. And it had been religion—a priest of all people—who had done it.

Annie didn't say anything more. She knew all about my past. I knew all about hers. It's stuff you don't want to keep thinking about. Finally she said, "What is really bothering you, Joe?"

"I've got another job."

"Okay. Joe, that sounds great. Let's do it."

"It's from an . . . uncommon source. I have to meet with the man tomorrow for the details."

"That's fine, Joe," Annie said. She was always up for anything to fight the enemy.

"I don't know about this, Annie. He wants me to kill someone. To kill a priest. I don't think I can do that. I used to be a Catholic. I never thought of doing that. Even to the priest who had hurt my son."

Annie nodded, sighed.

I said, "But I don't know any longer. I feel I'm being pulled into the darkness, pulled toward an extreme that I . . . I just don't know, Annie."

"You have a 'mission', Joe," Annie said.

"Yes, 'the mission' is everything for me, but, sometimes I wonder . . . I get scared. I don't want to become what I am fighting against."

The darker the knowledge.

The deeper the pain.

Alphonse Gaetano thought about all that now and understood the words like never before.

He was an old Monsignor now. High up in the church. Powerful. Well-respected. But still just a priest really. Just another shepherd for His flock. The fact that his particular flock was all the priests of holy Mother Church in America did not matter. Nothing mattered except fighting the enemy. Beating him back, pushing him away, keeping him down. And living one more day in God's Glorious Garden as He had planned for him to do. To serve Him in the holy war against the hated enemy.

But now he had to do something terrible. Simply terrible. He had to have someone killed. And the realization was shredding his old noble priest-heart into a hundred pieces. Breaking it terribly. For the man that must die was another priest, and not just any priest but one very high and powerful within the Holy Church. One moving up very quickly into that loftiest of pinnacles of the hierarchy. The man had only last year been exalted to the position of Bishop, now rumor boasted that soon he would be invested with the rank of holy Cardinal. It began to look as though nothing would stop this man's rise in the Holy Church. It was even whispered that he was a prime candidate to become that which the church needed so desperately in these troubled times—the first American Pope. After his present Holiness passed on into the glory of Heaven, naturally.

But other things were whispered as well. In the dark places where only Father Gaetano listened. Terrible things. But only

vague whispers after all. Words that none but Alphonse Gaetano
would pay attention to.

It fell to Alfonse Gaetano to seek the truth in these matters.
And what he had learned had broken the old priest's heart. Now he
knew he had to act. Quickly. To save the church he loved.

"Mr. Joseph Dillon, I have asked you to come here because there
is a service I would like you to perform for me. I make no bones
about it. It is a terrible thing that I will ask you to do. However, it
is something that if not performed would be ever more terrible
than the performance of the act itself. I am sure you will agree
once I explain it all to you," the old priest said in his kind manner,
trying to calm the intense-looking young man before him.

Joe Dillon looked hawk-like in the lair of his enemy. "Look,
priest, I don't like you people and I don't like what you stand for.
Religion. God. It's the biggest lie in a world full of lies. The only
reason I decided to even meet with you is because your messenger
said that you had some information about the Fruit of Islam
School."

"That is true, Mr. Dillon, it comes to me from one of our Afri-
can priests, who through a lapse in his faith, converted to Islam
years ago. He has since seen and documented some terrible things
that I am sure you will bring to the attention of the proper authorities."

"Why me? I've been trying to bust that school for years. It's
not even true Islam, more like some cult that's just an excuse for
anti-white racists and criminals to network. To organize and
spread their hate. It concerns me when they form a school and begin abusing children in the name of God and religion."

"And that is as it should be, Mr. Dillon," Monsignor Gaetano
said quietly. He liked this intense young man sitting before him,
but maintained no illusions about him. He was dangerous, and
could be a real danger to the church that he loved. He could also
be of use in the Monsignor's plans. Carefully the priest withdrew a
large plain white folder. "Here is the information I promised. Use
it well, Mr. Dillon. It was not easy to obtain. Save those children.
Please."

Joe Dillon sighed, took the folder and waited.

"And now the reason for this meeting. The terrible thing I have
in mind is murder, Mr. Dillon. Not a pleasant prospect. It is an evil
act, directly forbidden by the Lord I serve—specifically forbidden
by his own Holy Commandment—and yet not to act in this case,

Mr. Dillon—not to act would be complacency in a far greater evil."

Joe Dillon was intrigued; he slowly sat down facing the old priest. He could see the deep furrows in the old man's face, the sadness in his eyes, even as those eyes sparkled with fire and great wisdom. And strangely, a great kindness. He admitted to himself, he was intrigued, but said, "I'm not a killer, Monsignor Gaetano."

"I know that, my son. And were I a younger man, strong as in my youth, I would take care of this situation myself. In my own way. Believe me. But I am old and weak, and the evil one is young and strong. I am no match for him. I need your help. I need you . . . to kill him for me."

"How many times do I have to tell you, I am not a killer!" Dillon said with some anger now. "You priests, always playing God. Always making rules, telling people how to live, what to do, but you always seem to break those rules when they apply to yourselves."

Monsignor Alphonse Gaetano nodded sadly, acknowledging the general insult to all priests and the specific one, to himself. "Perhaps you are right, my son . . ."

"And I am not your son!"

"Be that as it may, Mr. Dillon, you are still correct. Some of us do play God. Sometimes it is necessary. I myself have been guilty of that conceit on more than one occasion in my special work. But it has to be. Sometimes. There can be no other way. Sometimes. Sometimes, Mr. Dillon, justice demands it. Men must stand up and make tough decisions—sometimes the toughest and most terrible of decisions. And if it means playing God, Mr. Dillon, then so be it!"

"How can you believe in God and say such things, priest?"

"It is because I believe in God that I say and do such things." Gaetano said. "It is what must be done. I shall quite probably be damned for it in the afterlife."

"I don't know what you are talking about. What is it you want from me? I tell you again, I am not a killer."

"I know that. And none of this is your fault. Only mine. I am an old priest, Mr. Dillon, and my days are numbered, but before I go I want to be sure that the greatest evil that has threatened my beloved Holy Mother Church for the last hundred years is destroyed. That evil man—that evil priest must die. And you, Mr. Dillon, must do it. Please."

The look Joe Dillon gave Monsignor Alphonse Gaetano was one of exasperation tinged with anger.

Gaetano nodded, "I know, Mr. Dillon, you are not a killer."

Joe Dillon didn't say a word.

"But you will become one, Mr. Dillon. Once I tell you what I must tell you—then you shall become a killer—and you will kill for me."

"Never, priest!"

"Please, I ask your forgiveness for what I am about to tell you," the old man said, and there were genuine tears in his eyes now, tears of great sadness and great pain.

Joe Dillon felt a sudden nausea and chill. His mind snapping back to thoughts of Thomas, his young son. Years before, Joe's ten-year-old son, Thomas, had been abused by a priest at the Catholic school he attended. There had been a hint of scandal. Nothing concrete. Most of it was covered up. The priest, Father Andre, while never actually admitting anything had been sent away for "treatment" upstate for what had been termed a "nervous disorder", but that hadn't done a damn thing to alleviate the damage done to Thomas. To Nancy, Joe's wife. Or to Joe's small family, which had fallen apart before his very eyes. Even while it was all happening, Joe had been too stunned, too hurt, too confused and disbelieving to understand what had happened or do anything about it. He watched his son slip lower into depression and fear, the sudden rages, the terrible dreams at night. Later there were the drugs, the stealing, and more terror. Finally, the suicide that had claimed Thomas, when he just couldn't take the pain any longer. He'd been only fourteen years old when he died by his own hand, but those last four years of his life had been a living hell. For everyone. Thomas's suicide was nothing less than murder—it had just been time-delayed four years—but it was still at the hands of Father Andre.

Joe Dillon's problems had not stopped there. His wife, Nancy, blamed herself for everything. Blamed Joe. It had put such a wedge between them that life, once a beautiful and hopeful journey, had become terribly dark and twisted. Nancy ended up drinking herself to death. The coroner had been astounded by Nancy's blood-alcohol content. She had so much alcohol in her that it was like she'd been poisoned.

Joe knew the truth. Nancy *had* poisoned herself. She just couldn't live any longer with the memories of Thomas. And there wasn't anything Joe could do to stop any of it. Joe's entire family, his entire life, had been destroyed. Torn into ruin and death. All because one degenerate who happened to wear the robes of a priest thought he could get away with whatever he wanted to do to a helpless, ten-year-old boy. A boy who had trusted him, and to whom he was entrusted to protect.

And Father Andre had abused the boy and gotten away with it too. It was only years later that Joe learned about the extent of pedophilia amongst the priesthood in the Catholic Church. The hundreds of millions of dollars in settlements and hush money the Catholic Church paid over the years to lawyers and families to quash investigations, court action, and publicity on this epidemic. The fact was, that in upstate New York, and many other locations throughout the United States, the Catholic Church had secluded "retreats," actually secret hospitals that tried to deal with the pedophilia epidemic amongst the priesthood. Joe never knew any of this back then. It was all kept quiet. Usually. But sometimes it came out. Against all the odds, it still came out. It was a miracle that as much of it came out as it did.

Joe Dillon looked over at Monsignor Alphonse Gaetano, at the black mitre and habit the old priest wore, and a bitter hatred welled up within him that he had not felt for many years.

He'd not felt like this since viewing Nancy's tortured face years ago, as the cops slid the drawer with her body lying so stiffly upon it out from the morgue freezer for his identification. Not since then had Joe Dillon felt this kind of anger and rage.

But Joe Dillon held back his worst impulses. Hugging the while manila folder closely to him. This was, after all, why he was here in the first place. He took comfort in the knowledge that the information within would in some measure avenge Thomas's death. Perhaps even save someone else's child from what Thomas had gone through.

Dillon said, "What is it you are trying to tell me, priest?"

"My duty is vast, young man. I was appointed by his Holiness, the Pope, to investigate the Evil here in America. Many years ago. So many years ago. Before even the present Holy Father. It has been a difficult fight. There are enemies all over, and worse, collaborators and sympathizers who cover for them, make excuses, use the law to obscure the truth and defame victims and witnesses. It makes my job next to impossible at times. But I have my victories."

"What victories?" Dillon asked.

"Against The Evil, my boy. The Evil we both fight against. Each in our own way. Those who abuse God's children. I have worked against the bad priests in my own church for years, investigating rumors, building up cases, bringing forth evidence and witnesses. Causing the media to spotlight the issue."

"Pedophile priests," Dillon said.

"Yes, my son," and this time Monsignor Gaetano was happy to see that the young man before him did not protest when he used that paternal appellation once again.

"In the old days, Mr. Dillon, I struggled to find evidence, to get the victims and their families to open up, bring charges; to get the media to pay attention to the tragedy. I would handle these things myself, in my own way. Quietly, from behind the scenes. And I was somewhat successful with all the perpetrators but one. There was this one priest so intelligent, so cunning, so unscrupulous and careful, that it has been impossible to link him to these crimes in any way whatsoever. But he is guilty. Mr. Dillon. Guiltier in fact, than all the others!"

Joe Dillon sat transfixed, the sweat of nervous fear running down his forehead as he listened.

"Today this priest has risen in the Church hierarchy. Some say he will be appointed soon to the College of Cardinals, and from there, it is not inconceivable that he may become the next Pope. The American Pope. A very real possibility, since the Church in Rome recognizes the importance of the Vatican's connection with the United States in these troubled times, as it did with Poland and the occupied Communist bloc in years past."

"Politics," Dillon said.

"Politics, on a global scale, Mr. Dillon. But if such a thing happens, this Holy Mother Church I love, will be destroyed. For you should understand, this man will not just be a bad pope, or an unprincipled or incompetent one. God knows we've had plenty of those through the millennia. This pope will be an evil unprincipled monster—but one with a golden tongue and great power and charisma."

"And you want me to kill him? To do your dirty work? Why me?"

"Because, Mr. Dillon, it occurred to me that you have a personal stake in this as well. Perhaps, even more so that I. You see, while Father Andre was rumored to have abused your son Thomas, Father Andre was only a small part of a much wider group of priests infected with this affliction. My investigation indicates that

The Mission

the planning and control of the abuse, and the recording of it—for I am sure that certain photos and films were made of this horror—was all directed by another hand. A higher authority. A priest, who is now called His Holiness Bishop Robert Brennan. He is the one who is responsible for what those priests did under his direction so long ago. It was all done under his leadership. And I believe that should you look hard enough, you will find the terrible evidence of his crimes secreted somewhere in his home or office."

"What proof do you have of his involvement, priest? I am not here to do your dirty work," Dillon barked, anger laced with terrible fear now.

Alphonse Gaetano took out a small while envelope, opened it quietly, withdrew a small Polaroid photo. It was old and looked a bit crumpled. Gaetano handed it to the young man before him and said, "Look at the photo closely. Study it. Tell me what you see there."

Joe Dillon flushed, felt his fingers tingle with electric fear as he took the photo in his hand and examined it. Once his eyes fell upon the images there he shuddered. Shaking involuntarily inside, and visibly outside. Dillon sighed with great sadness, memories he had wished to keep well-buried for the most personal of survival reasons. Then he carefully looked at the image shown there, from so long ago. From happier days. It was his son, Thomas, standing in front of St. Mary's Church, smiling, a proud ten-year-old dressed in the robes of an altar boy. Dillon's face darkened when he saw the image of Father Andre standing next to the boy, and next to him, another priest with his hand upon Father Andre's shoulder.

"A much younger Father Andre, and Father Brennan, from many years ago, Mr. Dillon. Please pay particular attention to the ring upon the index finger of Father Brennan's hand."

Dillon looked at the ring carefully, able to make out the unique style and image that was unlike anything he had ever seen before. Burning that image into his brain forever.

"A unique ring?" Alphonse Gaetano asked.

Joe Dillon nodded.

Monsignor Gaetano sighed, "And now, Mr. Dillon, I must ask your forgiveness for what I am about to show you."

Joe Dillon's gut tightened. He shook involuntarily.

Monsignor Gaetano withdrew another envelope. He deftly placed it upon the table before him, but he did not remove his old withered hand from covering the envelope.

"What I have here is another photograph, Mr. Dillon. It is an evil photograph. It is terrible. If you decide to look upon it, I think I can promise you two things. It will change your life forever, and it will cause you terrible, almost unbearable pain."

Joe Dillon sat transfixed now. There was sweat on his forehead. His temples beat like drums, hot blood pulsed into his brain like a hammer. He tried to calm himself by taking deep rhythmic breaths. It did not work.

"I tell you this, Mr. Dillon. If you look at that photograph, you will kill the man I want killed. For you will know who really was behind the pain your son suffered. And you will suffer more pain and anger than perhaps you may be able to handle. You will avenge your son, and by doing so save many other children and my Holy Mother Church from this monster."

Joe Dillon moved to grab the photo but Alphonse Gaetano held the envelope down upon the table with a strength Dillon could not believe his old withered hand still possessed. Gaetano brushed Dillon's hand away.

"This is no game, Mr. Dillon. In my capacity as investigator I often come across evidence against my priestly brothers—the depths of such filth and degeneracy few people could ever con-template—and in that capacity this evidence is often used to force these people out of the priesthood. At times, it is released to law enforcement agencies for prosecutorial purposes—though I am expressly forbidden to do this under Church law."

Joe Dillon brushed Alphonse Gaetano's hand away from the envelope—but then the Monsignor slammed his hand down upon Dillon's—before he could pick up the envelope.

"Wait! Think about it!"

"Let me see the damn picture!"

Tears began to run down Monsignor Gaetano's face, he began to cry as he said, "So be it, my son. May the Lord protect you with His infinite love and mercy."

Dillon's head pounded as he brought the envelope closer and slowly opened the back flap to take out the photo. His hands were sweaty and his pulse raced as he withdrew the photo, staring at the white back, staring at the words written upon it in black pen, "Thomas Dillon, ten-year-old white male, File #473021, Aug. 1985".

Joe Dillon stared at the writing on the back of the photo. It was all that was left of his son now. He stared at the words for a long time. Building up his courage. He was scared. He didn't realize he was crying. He tried to get a grip on his fear and rage.

Then he turned the photo over and looked at what was depicted there.

Then Dillon screamed, dropping the photo, covering his eyes, crying hysterically as the old priest came over to comfort him, whispering into his ear, "That is the enemy I am fighting, Mr. Dillon. That is my Mission. To stop this from happening ever again to another child."

The old priest let Dillon cry it out. Release was a good thing. After a time Alphonse Gaetano withdrew a long white handkerchief from his robe and handed it to Dillon. "Here, wipe your eyes, it is not seemly for a man to cry. We are warriors, Mr. Dillon. Warriors do not cry, warriors fight."

Dillon wiped his eyes and looked up at the old priest. Angry, insulted, full of fear and hurt and hatred for all things priestly, but above all, he felt ashamed. Ashamed at what he had seen in that photograph, for what had been done to that poor ten-year-old boy. At that point, it didn't matter to Dillon that it was his own son in the photo. Thomas was just one of many innocent children abused and caused to suffer by degenerate and evil adults. Just another abused child hurt and used by those older and in authority who used their age or power for evil purposes.

"I am sorry, my son. I am so sorry I had to show that to you," Gaetano said sadly, suddenly weak, looking so old and tired now.

"No, father, I had to see the photo. Now I think I understand. I understand why Thomas . . . Why he killed himself. My poor son . . ."

There were more tears now.

Monsignor Gaetano put his arms around Dillon and tried to comfort him. He said, "It's all right, Joseph. Cry it all out. It will never go away, but try to cry it out the best you can."

The old man hugged the younger man, trying to comfort him in his pain the best that he could, and as he did so tears began to stream down his old weathered face as well.

Some time passed and now the young man and the old priest sat facing each other talking.

"The proof, Joseph, is in the photos. Remember the ring on Father Brennan's hand in the first photo I showed you? Remember the ring in the second photo?"

Dillon gulped nervously, picked up both photos and studied them scrupulously. No longer was he a distraught father full of pain and fear, now he was the hardened avenger, out for proof, information, knowledge—to be used in his revenge.

"Of course you will not see Father Brennan anywhere in the second photo, Joseph, but if you look closely you will see the hand that is holding your son down. Only a hand. But upon that hand, Joseph, notice what you see there."

Dillon examined the photo carefully, compared it to the first one, then back again. There was no doubt, the ring was the same, the hand was the same. Dillon said, "It's Father Brennan, without a doubt."

"Are you sure?" Monsignor Gaetano asked.

"Yes. It's him. There can be no doubt."

"That is good, Joseph. You have discovered something. Now, what are you going to do about it?" Gaetano asked.

"Whatever I have to do to stop him."

"That is good, Joseph."

"The only problem is, I've never killed another human being before, Father," Dillon said carefully.

Monsignor Gaetano came over and put his hand upon Dillon's shoulder reassuringly; "There is a first time for everything, my son."

Dillon nodded slowly.

"But you must be very careful. Bishop Brennan is a very wealthy and powerful man now. He has hired a new bodyguard—a very bad man—rumored to be nothing more than a thug, a hired killer, and very dangerous. Be careful of him, he is with Bishop Brennan always now. He is an ex-cop, thrown off the force for being unstable. His name is Vic Powers."

Dillon nodded and sighed, he said, "Then will you do something for me, Monsignor Gaetano?"

"Of course, my son."

"Will you bless me in what I am about to do?"

"Of course, my son. Come closer. Nothing would give me greater joy."

All those religious hypocrites! So vast in number. Joe Dillon hated them all, knowing they were the ones who used the idea of God and religion to get power, to hold power, to justify all their rotten acts. To keep people down, degrade others, and to whip everyone into shape to serve them. Using God for their purpose.

Still and all, Dillon had to admit, there were some who believed, some who truly lived by The Word. Some who really were decent, living each day with love in their hearts and the true teachings of Jesus—the way Jesus had said things should be. Joe knew religion was bad, maybe even evil, but he also knew there were certain people—and they were in all religions, amongst all peoples—who lived by the truest and highest ideals and principles of their religious teachings—people who never compromised when it came to decency, love, compassion. Even if it concerned a person outside their own religion—outside their particular racial or ethnic background or, one who did not speak their language. Even one, who in their eyes, might be an enemy or sinner. Sometimes, even when a person did not believe at all. These people even respected that too. They were so strong in their faith. It perplexed Joe Dillon. Often times, these good people went outside themselves for another person, sometimes even someone they did not know at all. Or, perhaps, even a person they did not particularly like all that much. Just because it was right to do so. It was right to help. Joe knew that was true too. The other side of religion. What religion should be. What it was. Sometimes. What it, too often, was not.

Joe Dillon didn't believe in God, but he realized that if there were such a creator, that the love and Grace of such a being would shine down upon these people. Joe Dillon wished that some of that love and Grace would shine down upon him after he performed his terrible deed of murder.

Bishop Brennan was at his desk talking with his numerous minions; monsignors, priests, an Archbishop sent directly from the Cardinal. Word had it they were there to discuss an important matter concerning the succession of power in Holy Mother Church.

Behind Bishop Brennan sat a large man dressed in a dark suit, quiet, ever watchful, his eyes fire-red with alertness, scanning: faces, movement, gestures, mood, intentions. He was not a priest. He was not affiliated with the church in any way. Save one.

Alcera Redondo, the Bishop's major-domo announced the new visitor into the august presence of His Eminence.

"Mr. Joseph Dillon, to see you, Sir," Redondo said.

Brennan looked up with evident annoyance and distaste.

He obviously did not recognize the name. His eyes shot to his daily events calendar, did not see the name listed, and shot an angry glance back at Redondo.

"Sir, he carries a personal letter from Monsignor Alfonse Gaetano with the seal of the Holy See of Rome upon it."

Bishop Brennan was about to say something, thought better of it, motioned graciously to Redondo to show the man into the chamber.

To those clerics surrounding him the Bishop let out with a heavenly sigh. The perfect image of a humble man called once again to do God's Holy work. He said, "It seems some business of the Holy Father calls, good sirs. If you will excuse me please, my aide Alcera Redondo will escort you to the church garden for refreshments. It's only a short walk out of the compound and down the road. The blooms and flowers are particularly gorgeous this time of year and I will join you all there directly."

The Archbishop, the Monsignor, the priests and brothers chatting amiably, all filed through the large glass doors and out into the huge yard behind the house. When they had gone, Alcera Redondo closed the doors behind them, lowering the shades.

The man in the dark suit did not move. He still remained. Bishop Brennan did not acknowledge him or ask him to leave with the others. He was not of the others. The man in the dark suit was not of any group.

Redondo came back into the room, bowed gracefully and said, "My pardon, Holy Sir. I would like to announce, Mr. Joseph Dillon."

Joe Dillon walked into the richly appointed room. The place looked like a palace to Dillon, the richness and luxury were so evident as to be disgusting.

"Yes, Mr. Dillon?" Bishop Brennan said, curious, allowing his hand to dangle before him in what looked almost to be an obscene gesture, offering his guest the opportunity to kneel before him and kiss his ring.

Bishop Brennan allowed himself a slight smile. Practice for when he would become Pope. Then they would all be kissing his ring—and his ass as well!

Joe Dillon recognized the ring immediately, but he had been schooled well by Alphonse Gaetano. He walked forward carefully, slowly, eyes humbly lowered, as if awed by the magnificent presence of the man before him.

Redondo, the aide, backed out of the room quietly, gently shutting the huge oak doors as he quickly left to escort His Eminence's guests down the road to the church gardens.

Now Joe Dillon found himself alone with the monster.

His Holiness Bishop Robert Brennan smiled beatifically, hiding his raging impatience.

But it was the man behind Bishop Brennan that was the focus of Dillon's attention right now. Of course, Dillon had heard of the man, even before Monsignor Gaetano's warning. Vic Powers. A very bad man.

Dillon looked away and concentrated on the Bishop. Watching him advance, the evil man, the monster cleric, His Holiness Bishop Robert Brennan—High Priest of the Lord God, Defender of the One and True Faith, the man responsible for an innocent ten-year-old boy's suffering and death. Dillon's son, Thomas. Dead, but not forgotten.

Here he was, the hated enemy.

Joe Dillon held himself in check, the way Monsignor Gaetano had told him to do. To wait. To be patient. To allow himself to get close. So Brennan's guard would be down. So the bodyguard would not be able to crush him before Dillon was able to do what he had come here to do.

Dillon bowed low, and with a graceful gesture took the delicate pro-offered hand of the Bishop and with eyes down, and expression solemn, lightly touched his lips to the Bishop's ring.

"Bless me, Father," Dillon said quietly.

"Go with God," was the Bishop's stock reply.

Then the Bishop gestured for Dillon to rise and speak.

"Holy Father . . .?" Dillon said softly.

Bishop Robert Brennan said, "Now tell me, my son, what news have you brought?"

Joe Dillon slowly withdrew a small envelope from his breast pocket. Near the knife he had secreted there in a special compartment of his jacket.

All the time he felt the eyes of the Bishop's bodyguard upon him. Locked on him like a laser-guided missile.

The letter truly had the lofty imprinture of the Holy See of Rome. Bishop Brennan grabbed it out of Dillon's hand as if it were the gold ring in some celestial merry-go round.

The Bishop looked over the envelope, then noticed Dillon was still standing before him. Watching him.

A most unusual messenger, the Bishop thought. "You may withdraw," he said dismissing Dillon.

Joe Dillon stood his ground. He could feel Power's gaze upon him. Before it was too late he said, "I have been instructed to wait for your reply, sir."

"So be it," the Bishop shrugged, then he lowered his gaze and began to open the envelope.

Once eye contact had been broken, Dillon rushed Bishop Brennan. It was so sudden. So quick. Dillon's knife out, and at the Bishop's throat. Forcing him down. A burning glance over to Powers where the bodyguard stood with his weapon out, in police stance, aiming at Dillon's head. His finger on the trigger ready to fire.

Then the Bishop said, "Please don't concern yourself with this, Mr. Powers. I am sure I can handle it."

Powers eased, but remained in position to get off a shot if need be. Watching intently.

Dillon brought the short knife up to the Bishop's neck. The cold steel of the blade pressing against his rich black and purple vestments.

"What is it you want, Mr. Dillon? Is it money? Are you a thief? A sinner against God who will burn in hell for all eternity?"

"Shut up! Damn priest! I'm here because of what you did to my boy. Thomas. Years ago you molested him. And you got away with it. And Thomas committed suicide because of it. And my wife, Nancy, she drank herself to death because of it. And me . . ."

"I don't understand . . ."

"My life, it was destroyed because of you! You're an evil degenerate who uses God and the Church to mask your terrible acts!"

Bishop Brennan laughed. "Are you serious? You must be a madman! I am a Bishop in Holy Mother Church! You must be demented!"

"Photographs don't lie, scumbag!" Dillon growled, opening the envelope and stabbing the terrible photo into the Bishop's eyes. The same photo Alphonse Gaetano had shown him days earlier.

Bishop Robert Brennan turned ash white. His eyes grew wide and for the first time Joe Dillon felt the cleric growing nervous as the fear within him grew.

"You did it! I can feel it! I can see it in your eyes!

Brennan froze, silent.

You killed my son! Now, I'm going to kill you!"

"No!" Brennan cried, "Don't do it! Have mercy!"

"Go to hell!"

Then Brennan shouted, "Powers!"

There was silence. Hard. Dangerous. Dillon with the blade at Brennan's throat, Brennan shaking in fear, both men looking to Vic Powers, to see what he would do.

With his weapon trained on Dillon, Powers said to the Bishop, "You can take him. I think you should try. If it looks like it's going to go wrong, I'll still be able to step in. It's the way you told me you'd want it."

There was a long dead silence, confusion, then reevaluation.

"I can take you!" Brennan said, a dark smile coming to his face now. Then from somewhere within Brennan gained strength and determination. And something else. He knew now what Powers was trying to tell him, that since Dillon had not been able to kill him yet, Dillon would never be able to kill him. That, in fact, Dillon could not kill. That Dillon was not a killer. Powers knew it and now Brennan understood. One killer can always recognize another . . . Dillon didn't have the look, the feel, the way about him. That knowledge now gave Brennan great strength.

Bishop Brennan laughed then. Laughed right in Joe Dillon's face.

"Mr. Powers is correct. I don't know why I did not see it before. I am in no danger from the likes of you. You're not a killer. You have never killed before. You haven't the nerve."

Dillon froze. Brennan struggled, almost getting loose from Dillon's grip. Dillon could have made the cut at any moment, but he held back, and in doing so lost his opportunity. Another minute and the Bishop slapped the knife away from his throat, it flew out of Dillon's hand to fall to the floor with a loud clang. Then the Bishop punched Dillon on the side of the head, hard, again and again, then in the kidney area, again and again, bringing Dillon down, hurt, doubling over. Down to the floor. Golden Gloves and the CYO had kept Brennan in shape and he took full advantage of that experience and training now. Brennan then gave Dillon a vicious kick to the face, another to the back of the head. Dillon lay on the cold floor now, at the mercy of his enemy.

The rage and anger Bishop Brennan felt did not stop there. He went over, picked up the photo Dillon had shown him and tore it up into a dozen pieces. He sent them raining down on the fallen form of Joe Dillon like evil black snow. Then Brennan picked up the knife. It was that same small blade Dillon had not had the guts to use moments earlier.

Now it was Brennan's turn.

Brennan brought the blade up to Dillon's throat. Hard. Tight. It was so easy for him. Drawing blood. Drops of warm redness trickling down Joe Dillon's neck and chest.

It would do. For openers.

Bishop Brennan grabbed Dillon's hair with his free hand, while with the other he dug the blade onto Dillon's neck, then he snapped the man's head back with a rough jerk as he growled into Dillon's face.

"Where did you obtain the photograph?"

"You bastard!" Dillon whispered.

Brennan laughed. "You did not have the nerve to use this knife. Do not make the mistake of believing I would observe the same restriction. Now where did you obtain the photograph?"

"You killed my son!"

"And now I shall kill the father as well! Now tell me, before I shove this blade into your heart. Where did you obtain that photograph?"

"You're scared! That's because it's you in the photo! You hurt my son and I know it was you!"

"I am not in the photograph!"

"That's your hand, and your ring there in the photo. I know. That's why I kissed your ring when I came in here. To make sure. It's the same ring. Your special ring. A unique ring. The only one of its kind. And it connects you to the abuse of my son. The death of my son and wife. You killed them, just as certain as you're going to kill me now!"

The Bishop smiled. The young man was right after all. Dillon would be dead within minutes, and he knew it too.

Joe Dillon began to weep. Not for himself. For his son. For his wife. For his ruined life.

"You ruined my life!" he cried.

"And now, I shall take it."

"You caused my son to commit suicide! You caused my wife to drink herself to death! How can you live with yourself?"

"Very easily, Mr. Dillon. You must realize that for people like me, living is its own reward," the Bishop laughed, amused at this simple truth that applied to him so well.

"And you're as evil a bastard as there ever was!"

Bishop Brennan just smiled, "Evil, like so much in life, is relative, my son."

He was enjoying his control over the helpless man before him. It was most exhilarating. This self-indulgence. This instilling of fear and pain. There was much to be said for this. Then he pulled Dillon's hair back, roughly jerking his head up, the knife in his other hand pressed up against Dillon's Adam's Apple. Tight. There were more streams of blood now.

"And now the killing blow, Mr. Dillon. You will find yourself in the unique position of receiving Extreme Unction—the Rites of Death—from one of the most exalted Bishop's of the Holy Catholic Church—even as you die by that very same Bishop's hand."

Brennan readied himself for the cut. From out of the corner of his eye he saw his bodyguard moving up behind him.

"What is it, Powers?" Brennan turned to him with a short grunt.

"Do you want me to do it? It's what you pay me for, after all?" Vic Powers offered.

Without hesitation, Bishop Brennan smiled and said, "No, Mr. Powers, That will not be necessary. I believe I'll take a particular pleasure in killing Mr. Dillon myself. You may dispose of the body afterwards. But, before I kill Mr. Dillon, I think I will tell him just how much I enjoyed his lovely young son, Thomas. How beautiful he was, how so very innocent when I . . . ."

"No!" Dillon screamed.

Bishop Brennan's arm moved for the killing cut, then suddenly stopped when a huge fist covered his own hand and the knife he still held in it. From behind he felt the partner to that massive hand clamping down upon his mouth like a steel vise.

Somehow Joe Dillon was released, to fall to the ground weeping. He didn't know what the hell had happened and looked up now in amazement.

What Dillon saw was the Bishop's bodyguard, Vic Powers. He had one massive hand covering the Bishop's mouth holding him firm. His right hand grasped the Bishop's hand—which was still holding Dillon's knife, and guided it in a slow-motion arc—across the evil cleric's own throat.

Cutting once.

Cutting deep.

The movement was slow, almost like a slow motion replay as Dillon stared upward in disbelief and horror, watching as thick red blood poured out of the slit that had suddenly appeared in Bishop Brennan's neck as he gurgled, contorted, and finally drowned in his own blood.

When it was over, Powers let the carcass fall to the floor, and began wiping his hands clean of blood upon the man's own priestly robe.

Powers looked down at Dillon, who was looking up at Powers in amazement.

"Now what?" Dillon whispered in fear, trying to get to his feet.

"You screwed up." Powers said.

Dillon tried to get up. It was very difficult. "I couldn't do it. I'm not a killer."

Powers looked at Dillon and a chilling smile crossed his lips. He said, simply, "I am."

Dillon didn't say anything as Powers helped him to his feet. The two men taking stock of each other. Curious. Guarded.

Dillon sighed, shrugged. Wiped the sweat from his face. Looked down at Bishop Brennan.

Powers said nothing.

"Well, he's dead now. An evil end to an evil man. My son and wife are avenged," Dillon said thoughtfully.

"Revenge is good," Powers said.

Dillon tried to ignore that. Instead he said, "You know, I used to believe in God, believe in the Church before all this happened. Now I believe in . . . nothing."

Vic Powers did not reply.

"What do you believe in, Mr. Powers?"

Powers turned, looked into Dillon's eyes. Dillon was suddenly fearful, he'd never seen that kind of anger and rage before, never, ever looked through such a window to see such raw violence ready to erupt.

Powers suddenly smiled, the effect was chilling. He said, "Me? What do I believe in?"

"Yes, Mr. Powers. What do you believe in?"

Powers smiled, "I believe in homicide."

Joe Dillon shuddered, he couldn't comment on that, or at least, he didn't want to. But the thought chilled him to the bone. And yet, he thought he almost understood Powers in some essential way now. He did not like the thought. It was too disturbing. Instead, he quickly changed the subject. He asked, "Why?"

"Why?" Powers grunted back, "because I was paid."

Dillon didn't understand.

Powers laughed. "Not by him. At least not originally. One of the families had a hunch Brennan was behind the abuse of their son too. There was no proof. Just a feeling. I said I'd take a look.

In the course of things I was able to get myself hired by the Bishop as his bodyguard. Of course, he needed a bodyguard after the set-up I did on him. I just happened to be available. He was only too happy to take me on once he discovered my reputation."

Dillon nodded, trying to take it all in.

Powers said, "Of course I knew he was a first class hypocrite, louse, liar, and fake, so I figured working for him was the best way to find out what I wanted to know."

"Then I came along," Dillon said.

"And almost fucked everything up," Powers remarked.

"Why did you kill him?"

"Powers shrugged, "Someone had to do it."

Dillon sighed, "I couldn't do it."

"I know. It's all right. That speaks well of you. As for me. It's what I do."

Dillon swallowed, looking at Powers and for the moment had the uncomfortable sensation that he was in the presence of some primordial god of death, some mythical manifestation of rage and violence and revenge come to life. Then the feeling was gone and the fog cleared and it was just him and Vic Powers and a soaking wet, blood-red rug with an evil bishop lying dead upon it.

"But suppose, just suppose things had turned out differently?"

Powers smiled. "Like, what if you would have come after me? Tried to put me down, then go after Brennan?"

"Ah, yeah, something like that," Dillon nodded.

Powers smiled, ran his hand through his hair, said, "That might have been a sorry situation for sure."

Dillon winced.

Powers then moved over to the large bay doors, lifted the thick blinds, unlocked the latch and said, "Gayle, come in here for a minute."

A very beautiful, but hard-eyed woman entered the room, her face stone serious, her eyes cold and piercing, her hands holding a sawed-off pump shotgun.

Powers looked at the weapon, looked to Dillon and said, "Up close, it's the most effective weapon that I know of to turn around a sorry situation."

"But it can make one hell of a mess," the woman said.

"Gayle," Powers said, "I'd like you to meet Joe Dillon. A man with a mission. Joe, my wife, Gayle Armstrong."

Joe smiled. They shook hands.

Gayle looked over to the corpse of Bishop Brennan and said, "I see the world has one less scumbag in it now, Joe."

Joe Dillon nodded, then froze suddenly remembering something and shouted, "My God!"

Dillon ran to the back doors just as a young woman ran into the room leveling an Uzi.

"No! No Annie!"

Dillon ran up to her just as she came through the door, tackling her to the floor before she could get off a shot, quickly brushing the point of the weapon away from Vic and Gayle.

"Joe!" Annie screamed.

"It's all right, Annie! It's all right!"

They were in a loft in Soho, a Japanese restaurant that offered private rooms for food, and drink, and very private talk.

Vic Powers said, "So Annie was there all the time? Watching Gayle?"

"At the time we thought you and Gayle were on the other side, Vic," Annie said, smiling, taking another sip of the warm sake. "I saw Gayle standing guard outside the door, figured she might be trouble and needed someone to watch her."

Joe said, "Annie was watching Gayle, if she came into the house, Annie figured trouble and was going in after her."

"Shooting all the way," Annie added. "I'm not like Joe, you know that, Vic? Joe's a good man; I'm not a good girl. Get in my way . . . Sometimes I just don't know what I'd do . . . All I had to know was that Joe was in trouble, I'd spray that entire room and take everyone out, then get Joe the hell out of there."

"Cowboys," Powers said.

"Cowboy and cowgirl," Gayle added.

Vic laughed, "I love it!"

"So what do you do now?" Gayle asked Annie.

Annie shrugged, "Go with Joe. Where ever he goes, I'll follow."

"Why not work with us?" Powers asked. "Gayle and I are private right now, and we get an interesting case here and there. There's some money. We could use two good people."

Dillon said, "I wish I could, Vic. I like you and Gayle, but I have a . . . I have this Mission. It's more important to me now than ever. And I cannot deny it."

"And I go with Joe," Annie added. "We're a team, like bullets and a noose."

Vic nodded, looked at Gayle, said, "I know what you mean. Like blood and sweat."

"And tears too, Vic. Don't forget the tears," Gayle said, thinking of her own son now.

Vic nodded. Trying not to think of the tears and the reason for them.

It was weeks later. The mysterious unsolved murder of Bishop Robert Brennan was just now leaving the pages of the city newspapers and TV news, to be replaced by the latest scandal of child abuse at a special Islamic school. The Fruit of Islam School, a radical offshoot of a radical Black Muslim sect had finally been closed down by the police. The building was put up for sale, officials of the mosque under indictment for half a dozen charges. The information Monsignor Alphonse Gaetano had given Dillon had proved invaluable. Devastating.

When Joe Dillon had last seen the old priest, the man had been seated at his desk, some might say his throne of power and position, telling him about the evil in his Beloved Church.

Now Monsignor Alphonse Gaetano was flat upon his back, lying in bed, a comforter and blanket tucked up around his neck, his old wrinkled face a pasty-white. He coughed deeply, trying to focus his eyes upon his visitor.

"You have come, Joseph."

"I am here," Dillon said, watching the old man before him, sadly noticing how quickly his health had deteriorated. The once sharp, piercing eyes looked dull and tired now. So very tired. It was so very sad.

"Come closer, my son. We must talk."

Joe Dillon moved his chair closer, tilting his body so that his face was bare inches from that of Master Gaetano's.

"Ah, now I can see you. Such a young man. So healthy. Your whole life ahead of you."

"I am not that young, Father Gaetano."

Alphonse Gaetano laughed, coughed, got control back and said, "All things are relative, my son. Compared to me, you are as a child."

Joe Dillon bristled.

Alphonse Gaetano smiled, reached over and patted Dillon's hand with affection and respect. Then held it tightly. Like a lifeline. Grabbing the long fingers, pulling them apart, and then placing a ring upon the index finger of Dillon's right hand.

"What . . .?" Dillon asked.

"It is the Ring of St. John. A holy relic. A symbol of power and respect in the Church. It was mine. A symbol of my special office. Of my Mission, Mr. Dillon. Now, it is yours. A symbol of your power. Your duty. Your Mission, Mr. Dillon."

"But, Father . . ."

"I am dying. My time is short. Yours is long."

"I cannot work for the Church. I hate it. I hate the priests!"

"Then don't work for the church. Work for yourself. Work for justice."

"I don't know," Dillon said, he felt the ring on his finger. It was heavy, hard, cold. He tried to get it off. It would not budge.

"Did you take care of the matter we discussed?"

"I did not kill him, but he is dead nevertheless."

Father Gaetano looked at Dillon curiously. "I will ask you all about it later. If I have time. But for now, my son, there is something I want to tell you."

"Yes," Dillon whispered.

"The Mission." Alphonse Gaetano said quietly, "Now, it is all yours. You must continue the Mission, and I must bless you in the blood of Christ to protect you from all evil and temptation. Expected. Unexpected. Satanic. Man-made. Natural, and of your own kind."

"I understand."

"No, you do not understand. But I shall make you understand, Mr. Dillon. You have a Mission, and it is a sacred Mission. You may use the Ring of St. John to command any and all resources from the Church hierarchy. Even from the Holy Father himself in Rome. But you must understand, there are two sides to the Mission—you must fight the evil in religion and the Church—but you must understand that not all religion, not all aspects of the Church are evil. Can you accept that?"

"I'm not sure, Father Gaetano . . ."

Alphone Gaetano seemed to shrink, grow weary, grow sicklier.

" . . . but I will consider your words." Dillon added.

The old priest sighed, let go of Joe Dillon's hand, making himself sit back. So tired now. So weak. He said, "Then I leave it in your hands now, Mr. Dillon. My time is short. Yours is long. Use it well."

"Yes, Father Gaetano."

Alphone Gaetano smiled, "Go now, my son, leave me to talk with my Heavenly Father before I die. There is much I must say to him and much I must ask of his divine patience and goodness. And foremost on that list is for him to protect you in whatever you may do—and for him to guide you so that all your endeavors are good and right and just."

Joe Dillon bent down and softly kissed the cheek of the old priest. There was nothing but respect and awe in the way he looked at the old man now. Respect, awe, and maybe something else. A kind of love. The kind of love Jesus spoke about.

"Go with God, my son," the old priest said, blessing Dillon with the sign of the cross one last time.

"Go with God, Father Gaetano," Dillon replied.

"I know you will do well."

"I think I'm beginning to understand what it is all about now, Father."

Alphonse Gaetano smiled, looked up at Dillon for the last time and said, "I believe that you do, my son. Praise God Almighty. I believe that you do."

TEETH

Y NEW TEETH WERE FINALLY IN. Right from the beginning they felt strange in my mouth, like they didn't belong. They didn't. To begin with, I think they were too big. They certainly made my mouth dry, and I had to keep wetting them with my tongue so they would feel like they weren't glued to my gums.

I guess I should tell you about the time before I had my new teeth and what led up to them. It began with my body art craze; tattoos, piercings, and went all to hell from there. Yeah, it was popular in certain circles, the club set in the city, among many of the Goths, but there was also an entire substrata of underground people into it big time. The people I hung with. Sex freaks: S&M, B&D, other stuff. We all dug a new weird kink. Some added surgical enhancements and implants to accentuate their bodies, even their private parts, to make themselves weirder, more alien—if that was possible. Enhance the sexual. One guy had implants in his arms and back that gave them the hard ridges of a lizard. Another guy had two, one inch studs implanted under the skin of his head to make short, stunted devil's horns. Cool! He was popular with some of the ladies.

I had been planning on getting something like that, then I got the teeth. I thought it would be edgy and better, but now I'm not so sure.

It was a retired dentist who made the teeth for me. I just called him Doctor Henri. He never talked about his past. I never asked him. All I knew was that he came cheap enough that I could not pass up what he was offering.

You see, I had serious dental problems. I was in constant pain. Not only did I have a massive amount of cavities that needed filling—that was the least of it. I had to have root canals on almost every tooth, painful procedures that I would have to schedule every other week, for years. After that, there were caps and crowns, and all kinds of fancy, expensive bridgework. I was told that I also had serious periodontal disease, where I had to have more annoying and intrusive treatments. My gums were receding. I didn't know whether my teeth would all just fall out one day, or give me endless agony for the rest of my life from the rot that affected sensitive exposed nerves.

Some people in the 'hood said Doctor Henri was mad, others said that he was not allowed to practice dentistry because of some transgression in his past. He certainly seemed spooky. He only performed dental work before dawn. But since I worked nights, it actually worked out better for me that way. Then there were the rumors. Nothing definite, just weird stuff. I didn't pay attention to them, they just couldn't be true.

Doctor Henri told me he had a plan that would solve my dental problems once and for all and satisfy my desire for the implants. That's when he told me about the teeth he would make special for me. Immediately I dropped out of my dental plan at work. Even with the union discount, I would have had to pay thousands of dollars each month that I did not have for this dental work. The Mafia has nothing on the dentistry profession. Doctor Henri was going to do all the work for a nominal flat fee. He said it was part of an experimental plan and I would be getting a full set of quality choppers for practically nothing. It sure sounded good to me. So I said, "Sure, let's do it!"

Now looking back on it, I know that it was too good to be true. I was about to find out that Doctor Henri had some rather bizarre procedures and practices. He only did his work in gold, and I found out the strangest thing of all was that all his reconstruction was made in the forms of fangs, with points. When I came out from the gas my entire mouth was filled with these shiny gold teeth. I have to tell you, it was shocking but also really cool. My one care was to make sure I didn't bite my tongue or lips by mistake. When I did, drawing a few drops of blood, the teeth seemed to tingle with a strange sensation.

I don't know what kind of experimental plan this was. Doctor Henri wouldn't tell me, but it sure changed my life. Everyone hated my new teeth—squares that is, the dull folk who were mostly scared of them. However, there was a certain type of girl—the macabre kind to be sure—who found them interesting, attractive, even sexy. These girls were weird too, and into some strange stuff; they liked all kinds of sex, and for a while I was getting deep into dark things with them that I had never before believed possible. Looking back, I think the squares were right to be scared.

Right away I became a cool and scary cult star in the local underground.

It was the teeth that did it. I'm sure of it now. They *were* special. I began to feel that they had a power all their own, like they lusted for blood. At first I thought I was only imagining it. Then I wasn't so sure. After a while I could not say no to them. A while longer and I could not stop them. Eventually, I did not want to.

Everything began to go terribly wrong when I met Eloise. She came into my life like some macabre Goth princess. Dark and mysterious, waif-like, bitter and biting, but dripping with every kind of temptation I ever thought of—and a lot I'd never even guessed at. Her teeth were gold too!

She loved my teeth. She told me they really turned her on. She was so focused on them. Well, things just started out weird and got stranger. Eloise showed me the way. She was dark and evil and we used each other. I thought we had something special. Something new.

I quit my job. We took what money we had and moved out to the country. Eloise had a small farm and house. There we lured young women and men into nights of drink, drugs, sexual debauchery, depravity, and eventually death.

But it did not end there.

We started to gnaw the bones on the carcass of our victims. Blood and flesh dripping and running down our faces. My teeth's sharp gold points tore at the raw human meat, almost leading me, like it was their destiny.

"We are transforming into something special," Eloise told me one evening. "We are becoming a new species of humanity. Are you ready?"

Eloise explained the souls of the dead will become a part of our own. Their strengths would be added to ours. She grew to like the taste of flesh. I was growing increasingly aware that my teeth were now controlling me.

As the victims piled up, and the remains were buried away from the house in deep graves in the remote rural soil, I began to have serious doubts about what Eloise and I were becoming.

"You say we're transforming?" I asked her one night after I'd buried the leftover parts of another victim. "Just what are we becoming?"

"Monsters," she said simply, and I was stunned by the word. "Evil, disgusting, horrible, murderous, depraved monsters."

My eyes grew large, my mouth opened as if to speak, but I could not say any words. Finally I said, "You told me . . .we were supposed to be something special . . .a new species . . .?"

Eloise just laughed wildly, uncontrollably, in full madness now. Her eyes looking me over thoughtfully as she licked her gold teeth.

I think that's when I became scared of her. I was already scared of my teeth. And now I was scared at what I had become. It was one thing to fantasize about us as sexual vampire cannibals—some kind of new species; it was something very different to *know* we were only evil, disgusting, murderous monsters! Nothing special or cool at all in that, just freaks that needed to be put down. I blamed Doctor Henri. It was all his fault. And the fault of my teeth.

Eloise began watching me after that. She knew my heart wasn't really into the little games and torture any longer. I had lost my desire. I grew distant, irritable. She tried her best to coax me back to her by using every bit of depravity she knew. It just made me more distant and disgusted. I even tried to leave her, but I couldn't. And my teeth started to ache.

I no longer had the taste for human flesh. I began to vomit from it; even the smell of blood had a negative effect upon me. Eventually I would even vomit when I saw a new victim at the house, even when they were alive and unharmed, for I knew what was in store for them. It didn't excite me; it repulsed me, because I knew what Eloise would soon do to them. You see, she had now descended totally into madness and evil.

My teeth still yearned for flesh. Even in my disgust, I fought hard against their dark desire. The teeth had controlled me and brought me to all this. It was their fault. I was angry at them and had to fight their influence over me. I did that with the most recent acquisition, a girl from the village brought in by Eloise and drugged last night. Through her, I would try to obtain my freedom and defeat the curse of my teeth.

The girl was bound, gagged and bleeding, her eyes seemed to mirror the fear and utter terror in my own as I looked at them and was pulled within. My teeth seemed to tug in my mouth, the gums pulsing, the points seeking to bask in her warm, wet blood, desiring to cut into her body, to sear the meat of her youthful flesh.

I was sick inside, vomiting again at the very thought of what my teeth wanted me to do, and what Eloise had already done. I knew what was in store for this girl even after death mercilessly claimed her. Eloise was preparing a special feast. She had gone out for provisions, leaving us alone for a short time. I knew that now was my only chance. I went back down into the basement with a long cutting knife. As I approached the bound girl she wiggled and tried to scream in terror through her gag, a situation that would have excited me a month earlier. Now it repulsed me. I cut the girl's bounds, removed her gag. She began screaming hysterically. I grabbed her and slapped her back into sanity.

"Get out of here! Run! Now! She'll be back soon and she'll kill you and eat you!" I screamed at her. "Run! Get out of here!"

Once she was gone the vomiting stopped but my teeth began to ache as if a dozen cavities gnawed raw exposed nerves. I think they were angry at me. That had to be it. It was as if they were speaking to me. They would not leave me alone! Doctor Henri, and his damned teeth had brought me to all this. The teeth were punishing me. Now I would punish the teeth.

I went to the workbench and took a large pair of pliers. I opened my mouth wide. Then I began working at the bridges, caps, and crowns of all the teeth in my mouth, one by one. I twisted, wiggled, and pulled them all. Bloody, painful, I screamed and cried and cursed as finally I pulled the last of them out. It had taken an agonizing hour and now my mouth was a mass of bloody tissue and gums. Finally I just collapsed unconscious from the pain and trauma.

I awoke to see Eloise standing over me and she was not happy. She held a gun in her hand. "Look what you did to your beautiful teeth! And you let that bitch go! How could you do that? Do you know what you did? Now, they'll all be here, rooting around, asking questions, *finding* things! You've ruined everything! My father said you were a perfect patient—that you were ready. You think you can just pull them out and that's it? There's more of us—you can't stop us!"

"Your father?"

"Doctor Henri. Now you have to be punished," Eloise said coldly, detached, working her way up to her murder spree mood. "You have been bad. Your have turned against me. You betrayed me. You betrayed your teeth. Now you must pay."

I expected no less, then Eloise pointed the gun at me and pulled the trigger.

Everything happened so fast I can barely remember the order of it now.

The bullet grazed my head, and I slumped down, bleeding profusely, dying slowly. My life drifted away as the blood poured out of me. Eloise smiled and licked her teeth as she eyed my flesh with a new desire.

"They say former lovers always taste best," she said, laughing wildly, madly.

Then sudden and utter pandemonium broke loose. A dozen heavily armed police and SWAT team members barreled down the steps into the basement. Gun barrels broke through the glass of the basement windows. Eloise saw them and aimed her weapon. Shots were fired. She screamed and did a death dance from a dozen high-powered hits. Then she dropped down dead, silent, still.

The SWAT team rushed over to me shouting:

"Hurry up! He's dying! Stop the bleeding!"

"My God, he's got no teeth in his mouth!"

"That bitch pulled out all his teeth!"

"Unbelievable!"

"He's lucky that girl escaped, or he'd be dead too!"

"Yeah, too bad she didn't make it!"

"Yeah, but at least we can save this one!"

I gurgled blood.

"You'll be all right now."

I didn't think that I would.

"It looks like we got here just in time."

I still didn't think so.

"Come on; let's take him out. Ready, one, two, three, lift!"

That's the last I remember.

When I awoke I saw Doctor Henri standing over me.

I realized I was in a dentist chair.

I must have passed out.

"There you go, young man," Doctor Henri said with a sly wink. "All your teeth are back in and as good as new. Why, it's gonna be just like they were never parted from you at all!"

I screamed wildly.

Doctor Henri said softly, "No one can hear you, I'm afraid. My office is totally soundproof."

Then I saw his own gold teeth, the pointed fangs calling me as he smiled. "You thought it couldn't get worse? You are about to find out . . ."

Then he injected me with something and I lost consciousness.

I had the strangest nightmares, there were teeth all over me, chewing me, biting my flesh, and then . . .

I thought it was all over. It was really just beginning.

When I opened my eyes, I saw Dr. Henri smiling down at me once again.

"It was a long treatment, young man, but imminently successful," he said, almost happy, a twinkling in his little piggy eyes.

I shuddered, wondering just what he meant. I began to realize that Dr. Henri, my mild-mannered, friendly dentist, was in fact a monster far worse than I or even Eloise had ever been. Dr. Henri was a maker of monsters and I was his latest special project, his darkest creation.

I tried to move, get up, escape, but I was securely bound into his dentist chair, unable to use my arms or legs.

I shouted, "What have you done to me!"

He said, soft-spoken as he brought a small mirror to me, "Here. Take a look for yourself."

With dire misgivings growing to alarm, I accepted the small mirror he placed in my hand. My arms were still bound to the sides of the chair so I had to angle the mirror before I could get a good view of my face.

The teeth were back! So it hadn't been a dream.

Dr. Henri said, "Angle the mirror down to your waist and you'll see something I am particularly proud of."

What new terror was this? I slowly did as he said.

What I saw reflected in the glass caused me to scream and shudder, dropping the mirror to the floor where it crashed and broke into a hundred pieces.

I could hardly believe what my eyes had seen.

"What have you done to me?" I shouted.

"Simply made you better," he said, always the calm professional with the pleasant bedside manner. "You were always someone special to me. As was my own daughter. Now, you are even more special."

"I'm a monster! You've turned me into a monster!"

"Yes," he said, proudly. "Isn't it lovely."

"No! It's horrible! Look at me!"

Dr. Henri smiled. I noticed his own pointed gold teeth were now red. Covered in blood. My blood?

"I gave you back my dearest treasure, my darling daughter, Eloise, the only person we both love," Dr. Henri said dreamily, looking down at me with misty eyes. "Now you can have her with you for as long as you live. And even beyond."

My body strained with terror at the bonds that held me to the chair. I craned my neck up and twisted my chest so I could get a better view of my abdomen, and see now with my own eyes, just what had been placed there by Dr. Henri.

I looked downward and saw the face of Eloise; her eyes, her nose, her lips, and when they suddenly parted—her teeth! She seemed to be smiling at me—from where her face had been somehow surgically implanted into my own abdomen. It wasn't her head, just her face. It looked real, not a drawing or tattoo. It looked *alive!*

Then I saw the lips begin to move in what looked like an attempt to make words.

"I haven't hooked up the voice box and vocal chords yet," Dr. Henri quickly explained with some embarrassment. "We'll do that first thing tomorrow. I'm sure Eloise has a lot to say after all she's been through. Don't you think?"

She was dead, how could this be?

Then Dr, Henri gave me another injection, saying in a soothing voice, "Sleep now, young man, Eloise is back from the dead and soon will be all yours again."

I don't remember much after that. When I woke up I found myself in a hospital bed in a private room. All white walls, medical equipment, monitors. The door was shut. It was quiet. The sun was just coming up through the blinds across from my bed.

I tried to move, to sit up, hoping to get out of bed but I was too weak. My muscles didn't respond. There were no ropes or restraints on my arms or legs any longer and for this I was thankful. I took a deep breath and tried to relax, to calm my fears. The teeth, Dr. Henri, Eloise's face, all seemed to blend together. They must have all been some terrible dream. That must have been it. I steadied my nerves and tried vainly to get out of bed.

Then I heard it.

A voice.

Muffled and low.

Angry.

Female.

Do you hear me?
My eyes grew wide with alarm as my ears strained to discover where those words had come from. They seemed to have come from below me. Under the bed?
Get off me!
"What . . .?" I whispered. There was no one else in the room. No one seemed to be under the bed. And yet . . .
You're crushing my beautiful face! Turn around, lay on your back, dammit!
I gulped and did as the voice instructed.
That's better.
I recognized the voice now and my heart started to beat frantically.
I slowly pulled down the blanket and sheet that covered me and looked fearfully towards my abdomen. There I saw Eloise's face, her eyes open and looking up at me, her mouth displaying her pointed teeth, her voice speaking from the place that Dr. Henri had surgically implanted her into my own body.
You thought it was all a dream? Well, my friend, the nightmare has only begun!
My guts tightened as my heart raced now in fear.
It was her face, stitched into my abdomen that spoke to me. It was Eloise. She was back from the dead and worse now than ever.
"Eloise?" I stammered.
Yes, and I am not finished with you. You betrayed me. Now we are one, my father had seen to that. We will continue where we left off and there is nothing you can do about it.
"No!" I shouted.
Have much fear, because I will direct you from now on. I am in charge, can't you feel it happening within you?
"No! It can't be true! I will not help you any longer!"
Oh, but you will. You will do exactly as I direct. I told you we are one now. You see, your nervous system and voluntary muscles are now connected to my brain. Not your own. I control you now. Your body is mine.
I doubted that. I fought her. I had some limited muscle control and I was able to slowly turn my body in the bed.
Your control of your body and muscles is limited. Now see how I direct you. I will make you get out of bed. I will make you get dressed. Then we shall go and see my father.
"No! This can't be happening!"
Eloise only laughed madly.

I fought her control of my muscles with a determination I had never known before. Finally I was able to turn over on my side.

What do you think you are doing?"

I didn't say a word in reply. I just concentrated on controlling my muscles and gasping for breath, and I was finally able to roll over and lay on my stomach.

I heard the voice let out a muffled scream followed by muffled curses.

I bore down on my abdomen, forcing my waist deep into the smothering confines of the mattress. I pushed my abdomen and her face hard into the bed.

I could tell Eloise was frantic now. I don't know how she breathed, perhaps Dr. Henri had connected her mouth somehow to my own lungs. If so, I would do something to cut that connection now. I stopped breathing but I continued to force my abdomen into the mattress, down, deep, deeper.

I could feel Eloise struggling; my abdomen a mass of uncontrollable muscle spasms. Slowly, inexorably, Eloise was being smothered. The weight of my own body upon her face was cutting off her breathing.

It was all over in another minute. All struggle suddenly ceased. Finally she was gone.

I rolled over, now having complete control of my muscles again and looked downward into her empty, almost serene face.

"Goddamn bitch!" I cried, gasping for breath.

She was finally dead. It was over, and I breathed deeply and I tried to get the terror to leave me as I decided what I was going to do next.

I thought of Dr. Henri. He'd be back soon. Before he returned I made sure to take out those damn teeth once again. I used my hands and fingers this time to pry and bend them so they would loosen. Then I took them out one by one. It was extremely painful but I had to do it.

Next, Eloise. I looked down at the human face that Dr. Henri had surgically transplanted into my abdomen. It was incredible, utterly terrifying as I contemplated the thought of what he had done to me. And what I must do now. For Eloise's mouth was open and her own teeth beckoned to me evilly.

I hesitantly reached down and brought my hand towards Eloise's open mouth. Something told me these teeth, too, had to come out. I felt the sharp points of each tooth, and I was about to pull the first one out of her mouth when I suddenly froze.

Sharp piercing pain cut into my fingers. My eyes bulged with terror. I felt wetness and when I tore my bloody hand away I heard Eloise's sharp voice.

Get your damn hand out of my mouth and away from my beautiful teeth!

She was conscious again! Immediately her will took control of my body, my muscles. She willed me to get out of bed. She willed me to get dressed. I tried to fight her but it was no use. My muscles responded to her every desire. I tried to speak but I could not utter one word. Eloise was in full control.

He's only going to put your teeth back. You've only delayed us. The teeth are always ready, always hungry.

I did not want to think of the things she might make me do now. There was only one hope and I held onto it for all I was worth.

After all, Eloise had to sleep sometime.

Didn't she?

THE CURE

E WAS GETTING OUT. He couldn't wait. Prison had been an unending hell for him, but also a learning experience. He was a much better criminal now than ever before, but of course Arthur Ford never thought of himself in those terms. Arthur didn't see himself as a criminal at all. Arthur was a misunderstood victim of sexual preference discrimination.

They all said Arthur was cured. Teams of psychiatrists and expert social workers had poured through his mind over the years. Gone over each of his ghastly deeds in grim detail. Corrected them, shown him the error of his ways.

He told them all he didn't have those feelings anymore. He learned the definitions of words like "empathy" and "remorse" and used them in his speech patterns to the doctors. Even better, he learned how to show empathy and remorse in his actions. He was a stellar pupil.

They told him that because he was cured they would authorize him for release. They said that the evil compulsion that had seized him so many years ago and made mild-mannered Arthur Ford into such a terrible monster, no longer existed. They said it was a travesty of justice to keep such a patient who had worked so hard for recovery incarcerated. It was inhuman, Arthur's lawyers said. It was cruel and unusual punishment. Prisoner rights advocates agreed. Eventually the judge did also.

He was out now. Alone. Walking the city streets. Thinking about one thing and one thing only—the one thing he had thought about doing all those dark years in prison. It was the one thing that kept him going all those long years—the dream that he'd eventually get out—and that he'd have one more chance at another kid.

He'd learned well while inside. He'd studied at the feet of the masters: talked to other pedophile offenders, and learned from them. He knew how to play the game.

Now he was out and delighted as he heard the high-pitched voices of young children at play. Their sounds beckoned to him from the schoolyard across the street.

A smile crossed his face as he watched them; his tongue wet his lips as he approached the fence to get a better view of the children at play. There were so many of them and so many different types. All running around and playing so happily. They were all so young, so innocent. Of course he wanted them all, but he was careful to search out for that special one. He eventually saw him alone and off to the side of the sandbox. A boy of perhaps ten years old, who looked even younger for his age. Just the way Arthur liked them.

Of course he was not supposed to go near schools or school-yards as an agreed prerequisite of his release, but he did not see any cops around. No adults either. And besides, right now, he was just *looking*. Later, another day, when he had a car and his kit ready, he'd be back for the boy. For now he just stared and fantasized. Watching the sad, young boy. Dreaming.

He kind of lost track of time. A teacher finally called the children back into the school building and the sad young boy went with his classmates. In a minute the playground was empty.

That's when Arthur noticed the man. He was on foot, he didn't look like a cop, he just stood across the street smoking a cigarette in front of a candy store, watching.

At first Arthur grew nervous, but when the man nodded and smiled at him, Arthur relaxed. A cop would have busted him right away on a parole violation. This man could not be a cop. He must have been watching the children as he had. That might be interesting, he thought, someone else who understood and enjoyed his particular sexual fantasies. There were many like that in prison, but they did not fare too well in the general population. It might be a good idea to link up with a like-minded fellow on the outside.

As Arthur thought about it, the man casually walked across the street toward him. His movements were calm, in a non-threatening manner, "Mind if I have a word with you?"

"What do you want?" Arthur asked, as the man approached with a smile on his face. Arthur noticed the guy was short and stocky, he looked strong, but he had an unusual glint in his eyes.

"Lovely group of children, don't you think?" the newcomer said. "My name's John."

Arthur didn't reply.

"It's okay, I was watching them too. I even have mine all picked out," he laughed. It was a grim laugh that denoted sadism.

Arthur could relate and was immediately interested. He'd been fantasizing along those lines himself lately.

"My name's Arthur."

"Glad to meet you, Arthur," the man named John said. "You know, I hope we don't fancy the same one. That would not work at all. I had my eyes on the little girl by the slide. What about you?"

Arthur was buoyed by the admission, smiled and remembered, "the sad, lonely boy by the sandbox."

"Of course, I also considered him, an easy one to cut out from the herd, I'd bet."

Arthur nodded, "An easy opportunity."

"You have been away, I can see. Upstate?"

"I just got out," Arthur said.

"Bet you couldn't wait to be back out on the streets again," John said.

"You have no idea," Arthur replied. They were walking down a narrow and quiet street like old friends now. "They let me out. Can you believe it? They said I was cured."

"Were you?" John asked with a laugh and a wink.

"No," Arthur replied, "I tricked them all. I don't think there's any cure for what I got, except the next kid."

John laughed evilly, "Well, you know, there is one other cure."

"Oh, yeah?"

"Yeah," then John plunged the knife into Arthur's heart.

Arthur Ford shuddered in a painful death throe.

"That's for my son, Brian." John said. "And now, Arthur, you are finally cured!"

THE HARDEST TIME THERE IS

HE KILLED ELEVEN TIMES. At least that's what the cops figured. Eleven times—eleven children. One of them was my own ten-year-old daughter. Her name was Stacy. My name is Ben Walker.

I can't describe what he did to her. Even after I saw the body, I could not believe one human being could do such a thing to another. Certainly there was no reason for what he did. Stacy was a harmless, beautiful, helpless child. They all were.

Even now, years later, it still blasts the soul of each parent. We live with ghosts crying in torment. And we all cry with them—and wonder why.

He's in prison now. Serving hard time. But the time the parents serve is the hardest time of all. Even a lifetime in prison can't make up for all the young lives he's snuffed out. All the futures shattered—the families destroyed. All the weeping mothers—and the fathers, trying to be so strong—and failing so miserably. All the tiny pieces of life, the dreams and joys we had that will never be experienced. Now there's just an aching sad loss that seems to grow with the passing months and years like some gigantic black hole devouring each person's individual universe. My own universe died with Stacy.

He's in prison, but it's not enough. And the deal that had to be made to put him there was the worst affront of all. It scorns the dead and mocks the living.

It set the world upside down for me. Even more than the murder and mutilation of Stacy—the deal the authorities made to get this murdering filth behind bars is more bizarre and sick than the killings themselves.

His name is Judson Hastings. A young drifter who came to Montreal in early 1981. He worked odd jobs here and there. Had a cheap room in the French Quarter. Stayed to himself. And he killed our children.

I remember that day in June when Stacy was out playing in the front yard with the other neighborhood children. Laughing and running, playing tag with her friends in the warm summer sun. That was the last time we ever saw her alive.

Hastings put one over on the cops, on the law, on the politicians.

Although the police were sure he committed the murders, and he'd even admitted the fact in an early confession not admissible in court, there were no bodies. And everywhere the police looked they not only couldn't come up with a body, but they couldn't even come up with any hard evidence to link Hastings to the murders. Things began to look bad for the prosecution's case.

Hastings shocked the entire city when he offered to supply the locations of all the bodies for a fee! The bodies of the eleven murdered children for one hundred thousand dollars. It came to ten thousand dollars per child. He mentioned he'd throw in the location of the body of the eleventh child, our own Stacy, as a freebee.

The Province Prosecutor, the police, the parents were all astounded and outraged by this offer. It was the height of insult and arrogance. Yet some of us realized that without the bodies the PP might not get a conviction. With the bodies, they could put Hastings away forever. He'd never kill again.

"You'd best do it. It's a good deal," Hastings laughed in that arrogant manner he so often used. "Without the bodies I'll just get chump time. I can do five years standing on my head."

That admission gave us all bitter food for thought. No one doubted his words for a moment. Using that argument the Province Prosecutor was able to sell the deal to a shocked and disbelieving public and even some of the parents of the murdered children.

"I know I won't get the money," Hastings said confidently, almost soothingly.

"You're damn right you won't!" Prosecutor Stanton said, and that at least was some small consolation. "You'll never see a penny of it."

"That's all right with me," Hastings replied, and smiled almost beatifically. "It's really for my wife to live on. How would she get along without me to support her? She shouldn't suffer for my crimes. She needs the money—and you need the conviction."

So the deal was cut. A check was deposited into Elizabeth Hastings bank account in the sum of one hundred thousand dollars, and Judson Hastings gave the locations of the bodies of the children he had murdered.

A trial was ordered in lieu of the new evidence and Judson Hastings received a two hundred-year sentence without parole. He would be locked away forever and they would throw away the key. We all thought we were rid of him. At least that's what I thought at the time.

It was months later when disturbing rumors began to crop up in town; strange news items appeared in the back pages of the newspaper. The police, lawyers, and some of the parents who had been involved in the case began to talk of vague feelings of unease and concern about the deal that had been struck and what was now going on with Judson Hastings in prison.

What was going on was that Hastings appeared to be living the good life. Local news shows did stories on him. Now because of the money paid to his wife he had credit for the first time in his life—or at least his wife did—and it enabled Hastings to purchase a lot of expensive items that he should not have access to. He took out subscriptions to sex magazines and had them sent to him in prison. He had a TV and VCR in his private cell where he could look at hardcore porno films smuggled into him. He had pen pals all over the world, many of whom saw him as a kind of hero. He wrote letters, articles, and even did drawings that were published in small magazines around the country and down in the States. His wife and her new boyfriend, Hastings' defense attorney, used some of the money for a two-week vacation to Las Vegas. They took out credit cards in Hastings name. And there were other items even more disturbing—which showed us all how this lowlife child killer was living better in prison than he ever had on the outside!

"I hear he can have women brought in," a buddy of mine said one day. I didn't believe that but when he showed me a garish record album cover showing a wicked clown with a knife slashing a bunch of kids I almost vomited. It was an American punk rock record and Judson Hastings had done the cover painting.

"The band will be performing a free concert in the prison next month and Hastings arranged it. It will be in his honor. A legal aid benefit! Can you believe it!"

I could believe it. I was beginning to believe a lot of things I had never thought believable lately. I thought prison was for punishing criminals, but I began to realize we'd only given Hastings a free and secure base of operations to spread his sickness.

224 Gary Lovisi

The parents found out all this and a lot more. It was worse than we suspected. We formed a group and made our concerns known. We got a lot of lovely lip service but nothing else. It drove us all frantic. Where was the justice? We tried to sue Hastings, to have the hundred thousand dollars taken away from his wife. It wouldn't work. We tried to have Hastings given harsher treatment, but that would have been discrimination and not allowed under law. A group of the fathers even fought for early parole for Hastings, figuring that once he was out of prison they could take care of him their own way—that finally justice would be served. That wouldn't work either.

Hastings didn't want to leave prison. He was smart enough to know what the parents would do to him if he ever got out, so he refused release, even taunted us all by saying that if he was released early he'd probably just do the same thing all over again.

I believe he liked it in prison. He was a celebrity, a star, for the first time in his life. He got special treatment and protection. He was segregated from the other prisoners. He received free medical attention, free dental, free therapy and psychiatric counseling for anything that struck his fancy. All supplied by people eager to study him, eager to meet with him, eager to hear his words. And he was left alone to do what he wanted to do. No one interfered with him. He was a murdering savage and he was getting away with it—society was, in effect, rewarding him for his atrocities— and there wasn't a damn thing any of us could do about it.

Hastings would never get the punishment he deserved. It began to get to us. Eventually it got so bad I couldn't take it anymore. I knew what I had to do. I had to go inside and get him myself!

It wasn't as difficult as it appeared. Canada has only one Federal prison for lower Quebec Province. That was Bordeaux Jail on an island in Montreal. And Bordeaux Jail was where Judson Hastings was imprisoned.

The tough part was actually getting myself arrested, convicted and incarcerated for a crime sufficient to do the hard time at Bordeaux. I wasn't a criminal and all this was new to me. I tried the best I could. Of course I wasn't looking forward to what I might have to do to get myself arrested. To the lies I'd have to tell my wife and friends, to the crime I would have to commit. Something non-violent of course, but something serious enough to get me time in Bordeaux.

I did not relish the prospect of serving even a day in prison but if it brought me closer to Hastings, just for one minute, I'd be grateful of the chance to send that bastard to hell where he belonged.

The next week I decided to go through with the deed—a neat little frame-up—of myself. What I planned was to get myself busted for drugs. It happened all the time and the penalties are stricter here in Canada than they are in the States. I had it all figured out. I was proud of the plan. A first offense that had to be serious enough to get me time—but not more than a year or two. To insure the jail time I would arrange to get caught with a gun.

The Square in the old section of Montreal is a small plaza and park in the center of the old French quarter. It's rife with arty people and college students and tourists—and drug dealing.

I bought a hot gun from a guy in the Square. No questions asked. Next day I took my life savings and went to the Square to see if I could buy some coke. The stuff was everywhere, but not in the quantity I needed. I had to ask around. There were plenty of dealers, plenty of buyers, and plenty of cops. I still asked around. I knew sooner or later I'd get busted by an undercover narcotics agent.

It didn't take long. They got me for buying quantity as well as having an unregistered and loaded, concealed weapon.

"Okay, Walker," the narcotics officer said cuffing my wrists and packing me into the back seat of the prowl car, "it was a stupid stunt. I can see you're an amateur. Just another guy figuring to make a big score out here. We get them all the time. The yuppies up from Boston are the worse. All rich wiseasses. Well, Walker, all you've scored tonight is jail time."

I didn't say a word, but there was a grim smile on my lips as I thought about going to prison, to Bordeaux Jail, and finally meeting up with Judson Hastings.

"Another smart guy," the other cop said looking at me. He started up the car. "They'll wipe that smile off your face in prison soon enough."

The court case was quick. I didn't fight it. In the end the fact that it was a first offense almost got me off with probation, but having the gun gave the judge pause to reconsider. And then fate took a twisted hand in things. With the explosion in violent crime and all the overcrowding in prisons, getting caught with an unregistered and concealed weapon wouldn't get me time unless I'd actually used the weapon.

The judge eyed me with a steely gaze that said, "Don't ever let me see you in my courtroom again!" It was a sham. In a harsh even tone he said, "I order the prisoner remanded into the custody of the court for two years probation. Next case!"

They took me away for processing. Anger and frustration boiled over inside me. I just couldn't believe that the world worked so insanely—how a child killer was treated like a celebrity while no matter what I did—I couldn't get myself into jail to get at him. I began to wonder just what horrible thing I would have to do to get myself incarcerated!

Then fate stepped in once more. It turned out that the gun I had bought from a guy on the street had been stolen from a doctor in Toronto—and that it had been used in the killing of the doctor. A cold case reopened. I was the chief suspect in the slaying. I was arrested once more and held pending trial. The circus was starting all over again.

I made bail the next day. Explained to my wife that it was all a terrible mistake, but I realized here was the perfect set-up to get me sent away.

Cynthia is a good woman and she stood by me. She never figured what I was up to and I wasn't that cruel or stupid enough to tell her.

"I'll get a good lawyer, honey. I'll fight it. I didn't do it," I told Cynthia. All the time inwardly smiling at what I thought was a golden opportunity.

I wouldn't fight it. I'd just put up a token resistance. I'd take the fall for whoever the killer really was—take my place in prison—then get Judson Hastings!

The case dragged on and on, and though my lawyer did his best I'm afraid I didn't offer him much in the way of an alibi. The evidence looked entirely circumstantial, and a conviction looked tricky until the prosecution brought forth a surprise witness. It was the doctor's wife, and she placed me at the murder scene giving a positive ID.

I smiled to myself. Well, that settled who the killer really was. And it just about did me in.

I kept silent. The judge sentenced me to seven years with a reduced sentence on a plea bargain because there had been a problem with admitting the gun as evidence. With good behavior I could be out in three years. That was all the time I needed.

On the outside, Parthanais Detention Center is a huge gleaming skyscraper, a state-of-the-art processing center run by the RMCP. On the inside it is a cesspool of hatred and filth, a dangerous hellhole where prisoners are warehoused like cords of wood—dried up and ready to ignite into flames at a moment's notice. They all thought I was a killer and I allowed them to think so. It helped me get along and probably saved my life those first couple of weeks until I figured out how to act.

I was not ready for prison. I didn't know what to expect and my short stint in the city jail hardly gave me an inkling of what my world would be like for the next three years once they sent me to serve my time in Bordeaux. It would be cruel and insane, a terrible ordeal of pain and anguish, with the only thing holding me together being my plan to get Judson Hastings.

So I resigned myself to my fate. I had decided to pay the price a long time ago if it meant getting the killer of my daughter. And that thought gave me hope and courage to cope with anything that might happen to me in that dark world of inhumanity called prison.

I steeled my courage. I had purpose and strength. I was imbued with a good and holy mission. Then because of the overcrowding at Bordeaux Jail in Montreal the powers that be arranged for my incarceration—at Kingston Penitentiary in Ontario!

They sent me to the *wrong* prison!

I was transported deep into the Ontario backlands—far away from Bordeaux Jail and Hastings! And I would have to be imprisoned there for three long and terrible years!

Kingston. The name slit the throat like a jagged piece of glass cutting its way down into the worst hell I could imagine. This would be my new home for the next three years.

Looking back at it all now, I realize how naïve I was, quite stupid really, for even thinking I could pull such a stunt like going after Hastings. As the interminable months passed into years at Kingston I began to forget all about Judson Hastings and my plan—he might as well have been on another planet for all that I was able to get at him—and in Kingston I had more concrete and immediate problems to worry about. For day to day was a furious fight for life and dignity, the mad continuance of existence that drudged onward interspersed only with times of terrible danger and violence. I tried to stay out of things. I tried to have strong allies and find friends who would protect me—or at least leave me alone. I tried to get along—sometimes—to survive always—without losing my manhood.

I bunked with Willy Snyder, a mob accountant who'd taken the fall for James "Big Man" Andreatti of the Toronto mob. Willy was a smart guy. Willy had a lot of pull as long as he kept his mouth shut. And being Willy's friend offered me some real protection. But Willy was getting edgy in prison, with three years paid and twice as much to go. He wanted out, and he wanted out soon. And the only way he might be able to do that would be to talk to the province prosecutor and offer information in exchange for reduced time. Not a popular move in certain circles. I counseled Willy against it. He didn't listen.

I was asleep the night it happened. Willy was sleeping in the bunk above me, no more than two feet from my face. He never woke up. I discovered the deed after being awakened by the warm wetness of his blood dripping down upon my face. Dripping over my lips, running inside my nose. I jumped up screaming.

They'd just slit his throat, as quick and clean as a red-hot knife through butter. I didn't see or hear a thing and counted myself lucky and still among the living for that very reason. It was a sobering thought, but soon a new reality asserted itself, for with Willy dead my protection had suddenly evaporated. And a man without protection in prison is in big trouble.

The cell was empty and quiet now without Willy's boisterous words and good humor. When night lock-up came I huddled in my bunk, blanket drawn over my head. I shivered now and I knew that it wasn't from the cold. Already it was starting, I could hear the taunts of the other prisoners, the jeers, the whispers, and the looks that were cast my way. I was a paunchy forty-year-old white male alone and unprotected, and without Willy here it looked like open season on me was just beginning.

I sweated through that night and the next. A couple of the old-time lifers said they'd keep an eye open, call the guards if it looked like I might need help. I knew if I really needed help everyone would look the other way. A few of the muscleboy trash gave me the rape look. One came over and said, "I think you'll make someone a nice bitch, old man!"

I didn't say anything when he and his group laughed. I walked off, trying to look tough, and made a pact with myself to watch my damn back—and to kill the first one who messed with me. I had a knife and I'd use it if I had to. But I knew I was just fooling myself. No power, no status—no status, no protection.

Now that I was alone in my cell everything had become stark and gray. Willy was the last bit of humanity in my world and with him gone my fear and isolation grew.

On the third day one of the guards came by. It was Tomlinson, an old-time Brit and a regular guy for a guard. "Be getting a bit of company later today, a real nasty one if you ask me. Be on the lookout—and don't turn your back on this one for a second if you know what's good for you. Fair warning, alls I say."

"Jesus," I whispered.

It was the afternoon. A slow day. Not much happening. It was the slowest damn hell anyone could imagine.

Then they brought him in—my new cellmate—Judson Hastings!

Tomlinson opened the cell door; pushed Hastings inside, slammed it shut and was gone. Well, I'd waited for this moment for tears, had given up all hope of it ever happening, and now that it had, damn if I wasn't so taken aback I didn't know what the hell to do. Oh sure, my first reaction was to lunge for Hastings' throat and kill him right then and there, but I was so thrown off I hardly knew what to say or do for the moment.

I watched Hastings intently. Examining him. My eyes never leaving his form. My hatred building, and at the same time a small voice inside me counseling, "Wait. Wait and see." I waited.

He looked at me and smiled almost self-consciously, then went to pick up his stuff from where it had been strewn across the floor of our cell.

"Bloody bastards," Hastings said, "treating me like a damn common criminal."

I didn't say a word. Of course he wasn't a common criminal, he was a monster.

"They don't know who they're fooling with," Hastings added.

I said, "Yeah?"

"You're damn right, mate. I'm Judson Hastings, the guy what put the screws to those blockheads in Montreal—got off with a cool hundred thousand I did—and had them all wetting their pants before they got me behind bars."

I didn't respond. I took a deep breath, fighting with the fury in my mind and heart that was straining to break loose and take Hastings apart. But I held it in check; I held it in check, dammit! The one thing prison does to those who survive it is to give a man a lot of time to think. You use it or you die. You turn things to your advantage. One of those advantages was that Hastings apparently didn't know who I was. Didn't know I was Stacy's father. Didn't know anything about me. And since I'd kept things quiet since I'd entered Kingston, all anyone knew was that I was a guy who was in for killing a doctor in Toronto. And that's all I ever mentioned.

I realized the advantage. Dammit, I had him just where I wanted him! It was a dream come true. I actually smiled. Fate had taken a delicious twist in my favor this time and I would exploit it to its macabre best.

The next couple of days Hastings and I both kept to ourselves, which wasn't easy being cramped in such close quarters. I thought about the irony of the situation, him being taken out of a plush prison in lower Quebec to do harder time in Kingston where he and his crimes were just another statistic. There'd been worse in the two years I'd been in Kingston. He was just another killer. People's memories are as short as the nightly news. Mine wasn't.

I guess no one checked. No one figured one of his victims' parents might be in prison, and certainly not in Ontario. After all, the murders had occurred in Quebec Province. It was a strange situation.

The muscle boys stayed away since Hastings was bunked with me. Hastings was a big, nasty-looking creep, and he was a psycho killer—the rapers and muscle boys didn't want any part of that kind of action—and Hastings made it quite clear his first day in our block that he didn't like people who bothered him. Two of the rape boys from across the block tried the nudge and grab game on him; he grabbed each of their necks, yanked back their heads and then bashed them face first into the concrete wall.

Repeatedly. He did it with a calm nonchalance. It was chilling to watch.

Of course that brought on all kinds of threats, but Hastings didn't seem to notice, or if he did, he didn't give a damn. I realized that I could learn something from this miserable excuse for a human being, that in some aspects he might be useful to my survival in this place—so ironic since he was in a very real way responsible for me being here in the first place. Of course, I'd take care of him real good one day, but not yet. Not just yet. I wanted time to think and plan, and I must admit I was savoring the situation. Hastings didn't know who I was. He didn't know that all I thought about for 24 hours a day was better and nastier ways of killing him. That I had some really innovative, some really evil ideas brewing. He didn't know any of this, but he'd find out all about it in good time.

But there were times when other thoughts entered my mind. Stacy and her mother, my previous life. It all seemed a million miles away now, as if it had all happened to someone else in another life. It might as well have happened on another planet, so far removed was my present reality from my once happy past.

I heard from Cynthia today. Her letters have been coming with less frequency. I figured she was busy. I didn't really want to think about it. Hell, there wasn't much I could do anyway. We'd been having problems since I went away. She just didn't understand what I was doing, that I was the only one doing anything to bring justice to Stacy's killer, and though a couple of times I began lame attempts to tell her what I really was doing—I just couldn't. It was too crazy, and I could see that craziness and anger mirrored in her eyes. It scared me to tell her—it would have scared her to hear it. So I kept quiet, played the strong, suffering fool and another part of my life began to crumble as Cynthia and I were parted and began to grow apart. Now she wanted a divorce. Oh, she still loved me, but she just couldn't live with it all; Stacy's murder, my going away, her being alone all the time now. I really couldn't blame her. It was something I had expected over the last year. It was something that in the dark pit of my mind I felt I could clear up some day—once my 'job' here was done and Hastings got what he deserved—then I'd get her back. I guess at the time, I didn't realize all the damage that had been done. Thing about a death blow, it's something you never recover from, whether it's done with a gun—or more slowly with a lot of mean, cold words.

The days dragged into weeks. Hastings complained about everything. He demanded special treatment. He was, as he reminded me many times, "a famous celebrity," but when I asked him to elaborate, he'd shut up like a clam. He wasn't stupid. He was in with the general population now, if he ever bragged about being a child killer he wouldn't last the week.

I didn't get too close to him, but I watched him every minute. Watched him and boiled over inside. I wanted so much to pound

that fat head of his into mush. To crush the life out of him. To rip
him apart into a hundred pieces. But I held back. I tried to get
along with him, even tried to get him to be my friend, as disgusted
as it made me. I wanted his natural defenses to be low when I
made my move.

I'd have to make that move soon, I realized. Being exposed to
Hastings was just eating me up inside. The constant pressure I was
feeling, the deep-seated anger and hatred, and the frustration at
holding myself back from doing what I knew I should do was eating me up. Why prolong it! Get it over with! I'd enjoyed the irony
of the situation long enough, the endless fantasies of what I would
do to him. I couldn't stand it anymore. I'd have to make a decision
soon.

It didn't take me long to figure out what I would do. Something
quick and easy, something horrifying for Hastings. So I decided to
slit his throat, just like Willy had been killed. Only I'd do it when
he was awake. The very thought of Hastings running around the
cell in terror, clutching his throat as his life blood spewed out all
around him, gurgling for help—with no help in sight. That was the
gusto!

The perfect time would be tomorrow night. It was a month before I was scheduled for parole, and a time when the perfect diver-
sionary tactic was planned to go off.

Rumor was strong that Bobo Marchetti was going to get his
head split for beating a group of the Black Brothers in a drug deal.
This would happen somewhere between 2 to 4 am, the usual time
for payback. It would mean the guards would be diverted or paid
off to stay out of it—and the cellblock would be clear and open
from 2 to 4 am. It would mean the Black Brothers would be out of
their cells, roaming the block, hunting down Marchetti and anyone
else they wanted. Things like this happened during the night shift
sometimes.

Marchetti was a dead man and must have known it, but scuttle-
butt had it that he had a few tricks up his sleeve and that if the
Black Brothers came looking for him they'd get more than they
bargained for.

Hastings and I tried to stay out of it. I told him the best thing to
do was to stay in our cell. Try to ignore the whole thing, and don't
get involved. Under no circumstances leave the cell.

He agreed. He didn't care. He went to sleep like usual. He slept
so well, so peacefully. He was a monster and he slept like a baby.

The night it was supposed to happen I was ready. I couldn't sleep. I watched the last guard give a bed check. That had been an hour ago. No guard for over an hour now. Something was up.

I was waiting for the right moment. I had a knife, prison made, with a ragged edge that would do the trick. I was lying in my bunk below Hastings, dreaming of running that ragged edge across his throat.

Suddenly I heard a loud bang and crash. It was followed by two pistol shots.

The lights went on. The cell doors opened. The alarm buzzers and claxons blared like all hell had broken loose. It had.

"Breakout!" Someone shouted.

I saw five Black Brothers running down the block and Marchetti was with them.

He was with them. They were *together*. Marchetti was giving them orders and handing them weapons.

I realized now the drug hit was just a smoke screen for something much more serious.

Marchetti wanted out and so did the Black Brothers. They'd probably furnish the muscle he needed; he'd furnish the money and weapons. Then they'd breakout!

Things were getting hairy awfully fast. The cellblock was already closed off. The prisoners locked in, the guards locked out. Outside I heard gunfire, battles going on in other blocks between prisoners and guards.

Marchetti and the Brothers tried to fight their way out.

They had a few weapons, mostly small revolvers, but I saw at least one machine pistol that God knows how they'd obtained. But the block was sealed tight.

They couldn't get out. And the guards couldn't get in. It looked like a standoff. I waited for the tear gas that I knew the guards would start pumping into the block to rush in—but it didn't come.

Marchetti and the Brothers realized the situation before anyone else did. They'd disabled the tear gas system and locked out the guards for now—but in doing so they had locked themselves in as well.

There was just one way they could go with it then. They emptied the cells, gathering us all together. To cheers from his fellow prisoners, Marchetti stood before us defiantly. He shouted us all down.

"We're breaking out! You can all go with us!"

There was a lot more cheering, a lot of shouting, but a lot of tension and fear. We all knew what was coming. Marchetti and the Brothers now held their weapons on us. They had something in mind. It was payoff time.

"But first, some unfinished business," Marchetti said.

And then the guns spoke and four men dropped down dead—enemies of Marchetti who'd been paid back for whatever reason. The other prisoners moved away, forming a circle around the bodies. No one said anything. No one moved or blinked. The guns were still on us, and we were helpless, waiting. It wasn't over yet and we all knew it.

The Black Brothers shot down three of the Aryan Brotherhood. They shot two of the rape muscleboys. They put a bullet into The Worm's head. Then they picked hostages, motioning them out from the crowd with their guns and threats. These were guys Marchetti and the Brothers hated, guys the other prisoners hated too, guys that would probably be dead meat by the time this thing ended. They were Louie the Rat, Eddie the Thieving Bastard, and—Judson Hastings!

I almost choked. They were taking him away from me! Marchetti had already messed up my plans—now he was going to stop those plans! If I didn't do something soon Hastings would be out of my reach forever. There was only one fate for hostages in the hands of Marchetti and the Brothers. That meant I'd be denied my revenge and Stacy would be denied the justice she deserved.

Oh sure, Hastings would get his, but not the way he should—he wouldn't get it from me! It was important that I be the one to kill him, that I be the one to whisper Stacy's name into his ear as he died. That I be the one to say how much I loved my little baby and tell him I wouldn't let him get away with what he'd done to her.

The Brothers dragged Louie, Eddie and Hastings away with guns to their heads, screaming and begging, crying and struggling the best they could to get away. They couldn't get away, but they put up a fight. The other prisoners, some pals of Louie's and Eddie's were scared. They didn't want anyone else taken hostage. They all had knives and they didn't like the Brothers any more than they liked the muscleboys or the Aryan guys.

What was supposed to be a controlled operation turned into a wild melee when a couple of guys drew blades and began to gang up on one of the Brothers. They were helped by the Aryan Gestapo and soon a full-scale riot broke out with bullets flying and blades drenched with blood. It was a horror, desperate men fighting like dogs in the cramped hall of the block, cursing and killing, cutting throats, blood everywhere.

Then there was a loud explosion and the guards burst through the door, shots going off in every direction. Another of the Brothers went down, and Louie and Eddie and a half dozen other prisoners went down too. Marchetti grabbed Hastings—pulled him back, pressing his gun in his ribs—backing away.

I followed them. Moved in closer.

In all the commotion and smoke it took Marchetti a moment before he saw me.

"What the hell you want, Walker!" Marchetti shouted. I was blocking his path, "Get outta my way!"

"I want Hastings."

He gave me a confused, short-tempered look. He didn't understand what I meant. He didn't care.

"Help me," Hastings shouted, "I don't want to die!"

"Shut up, Hastings!" Marchetti growled, pressing the gun harder into his rib cage, "He's mine, Walker! My hostage outta here!"

I said, "I want him, Marchetti. I'm not leaving until you give him up."

"You crazy bastard!" Marchetti shouted. "Get the hell outta my way or you're a dead man!"

"Then do it, Pigface! I ain't moving and you'll have to kill me!"

Marchetti grew livid. "You son-of-a-bitch!"

Then he did it, just what I was hoping he would do—he took his attention off Hastings for a brief moment, moved his gun away from Hastings and out to get a shot at me. He got off two rounds, one missed, one grazed my shoulder, but by then Hastings knocked Marchetti to the concrete floor and was trying to bash his head into oblivion. I stopped that.

I had the gun now. Trained it on Marchetti. "Get up! Get the hell out of here! Move!"

When he was gone I helped Hastings get up. I had the gun on him now but he didn't seem to notice yet.

"Thanks," he said, shaken, genuinely appreciative.

"That's okay, Hastings. I wasn't going to let that pig-faced son-of-a-bitch kill you . . ."

"Yeah, that's damn good."

Then I showed him the gun. His face fell, and I motioned him over to a dark stairwell. " . . . because Hastings, I'm the one that's going to do it. Been waiting a long time for this. A real long time."

"No! No, you can't do it! I never done anything to you!" he shouted angrily, indignant, as if he was the harmless victim of a terrible unjust crime, some capricious evil he did not deserve.

I didn't say a word.

"What are you going to do?" Hastings asked near panic. He would have run, if there was some place to run to, and if he wasn't certain I'd kill him the moment he made a move.

"It's time you paid your debts, and I'm the collector."

"You're crazy!"

"Crazy, sure, just like the rest of our society that's let you get away with your monstrous crimes for too long."

His eyes brightened then. "You . . . know?"

"Everything."

"They were so young. So pretty. One of them . . .?"

" . . . was my daughter."

"Yes, but I, I do not know which one . . ."

At that point it didn't matter that I was Stacy's daddy, I was seeking revenge and justice for all of Hastings' crimes for all the dead children. At that point I could have been any enraged parent.

"It doesn't matter which one anymore, Hastings. There were eleven children you killed—one would have been one too many. It's time."

I pushed him further into the stairwell. It was dimly lit, but a safe, if temporary haven from the chaos all over the cell block as prisoner fought prisoner, finally to be cut down by guards storming into the block with riot gear, clubs and automatics. I would have to work fast.

I closed the door behind me. We were alone now.

"You're going to kill me?"

"Yes."

"But, but that's murder."

"Hardly."

The gun was heavy in my hand. I knew I'd have to get rid of it soon. I had a better weapon for the kind of work I had in mind. But I knew Hastings was a big and powerful man, a crazy man that I'd have to disable—but not kill—if I was to do my work properly.

I motioned him to the corner. "I'm not going to kill you yet, Hastings. Just disable you. So you can't get away, so you can't fight back, so you'll be just as helpless as the children you destroyed. It's not murder, Hastings, it's called justice."

"No! You can't!"

"And then I'm going to destroy you, Hastings!"

I pressed the trigger sending a bullet into his kneecap, shattering the joint into a mass of blood and pain. When he slowed enough from twitching and writhing I took out his right elbow, shattering that joint and causing it to fall apart in a mass of ripped flesh and blood that splattered the floor beside him. He was in terrible pain. He tried to stop the blood, and did a fair job of holding it back, but a lot leaked from between his fingers.

"You're helpless now, Hastings. And I don't need this anymore." I threw away the gun, took out my blade and moved in closer.

He was helpless, bloody, in terrible pain. But the pain he was in now was only a preamble to the terror he'd soon experience by my hand.

"Remember the name, Hastings. Stacy Walker. Blonde hair. Blue eyes. Innocent and helpless. Young and dead."

"I, arrgghh, I, I don't remember. No! Don't!"

"You did vile things to her. You cut her ears off. I'm going to cut your own ears off. You cut out her breasts. I'm going to cut off your genitals. Now you, you . . . you get the idea, don't you?"

"No! Please!"

"We are far beyond the time when 'please' will have any effect."

The ears came off first. It was not as difficult as I thought it would be. I told myself I was not doing this to a real person. It was just a monster in human form. Two quick cuts and a bit of carving and it was all over. I put them in his hands for him to hold. He looked at them in horror. Blood flowed like a fountain from the wound and I stopped it as best I could. I didn't want him to die just yet, so I worked fast before he lost consciousness or died on me.

I worked on the genitals next. I held his family jewels out for him to see. He screamed. I shoved them into his mouth, he was choking on the blood, on the mass of flesh, and he spit them out. They fell to the floor in front of him, a mass of wet, bloody flesh. He screamed.

"Why did you kill them, Hastings? Why!"

He didn't say anything. He just stared into space, gasping for breaths. His ears were still held tightly in his left hand. His crotch was a river of wet redness that spread across the floor in tiny trickles. He was drifting away.

I slapped his face. Did it again. He came back to consciousness for a moment. His eyes grew hard and sharp.

"Why?"

He smiled. Coughed.

"Why!"

He laughed at me.

"Why, Goddammit!"

He looked into my eyes then, hopeless, a vast emptiness.

"It was fun, Walker. Fun!"

"You're right, it is fun Hastings," I said, then I continued to cut and cut and cut, and he somehow lived through it.

I was avenging Stacy.

I was bringing real justice into the world.

I was performing my sacred mission.

I was killing Judson Hastings minute by minute, piece by piece, drop by bloody drop.

I don't know how long it was before the killing frenzy left me. The things I did to that monster are buried deep within me now; I can barely remember much of it. I suppose I'm pretty lucky about that.

All I know is that with the riot still in progress I somehow made it back to my cell. I quickly cleaned up, then buried myself in my bunk. Shaking, fearful, but strangely satisfied that I'd finally brought some justice to Stacy's murderer. Judson Hasting's last hour on this earth was a living hell. Still, it was far less than he deserved.

Once the guards took back control in Kingston there were searches, and bodies were found. Hastings was not the only one, nor the only one mutilated. Marchetti got his too, so now there was no one to link me with Hastings in that last hour of his life. There was an investigation later. The authorities tried to piece things together, to focus blame and responsibility for the deaths. It was like trying to spit and hit the moon. In the end they charged a couple of the obvious hard cases and swept the rest under the rug. Hastings death was just another "terrible example of prison violence" and soon things automatically set into the same old routine at Kingston.

I got out last week. Breathing the free Canadian air is the best part of my life now. My parole came up as scheduled. I'd been a good boy. As far as anyone knew I wasn't involved in the riot, but had stayed in my cell the way all good prisoners are supposed to—and besides, they needed the cell space.

I gave Cynthia a call.

She wasn't happy to hear from me. Said she was seeing a guy who owned a clothing store downtown. Said her life was different now. I said that mine was too. A lot of changes. A lot of memories. We started talking about Stacy. About us. What might have been. Maybe, what could be again?

I asked her if she'd see me.

I told her that I loved her. I missed her. I needed her.

There was silence from her end.

And then I heard the soft sobs. Heard the crying.

I felt the tears stream down my own cheeks.

She said, "Ben . . ."

I said, "Yeah, baby . . ."

"Do you have a car yet?"

I smiled, "I'm lucky I've got a life left."

She gave a jittery laugh, "I'll be right over."

"I'll be waiting."

AXIS

THE BLOOD SPATTER spoke to me of love and obsession and was born in violent sexual release."

I turned off my mini-recorder, put down my notes on the case, and thought again about what I had just discovered about the latest victim. That was Jennifer Kelly, murdered in a similar manner to the first victim, Wanda-June Esposito. But the Kelly murder scene showed some differences. The blood spatter was markedly different. I had to think over what that meant.

That was all before Ron was with me. He'd insisted on coming up.

"Julie," he'd called so forceful. "I have to see you."

"Can't it wait? I'm in the middle of a new case, a second homicide that appears to be connected to the Esposito murder. That may mean a serial murderer . . ." I tried to keep the excitement out of my voice, not really appropriate under the circumstances. However, that excitement was because I was a too young, too pretty, and too new blood stain analyst working for the police on a contract basis. I hoped this could be the case that made my career, you know, got it going to the big-time. Maybe even TV spots with Greta and Geraldo? Ron's insistence and negativity about my chosen profession only complicated an already complicated relationship. He was a hot-shot Wall Street trader on the way up and he didn't like what I was involved in. *Oh well!*

"No, it can't wait, Julie. I haven't seen you all week . . ."

"But I'm on this case . . ."

"I know. You're always on some kind of case. Look, I'm coming over," Ron was like that, he never took no for an answer. Sometimes I really liked that about him, but tonight I didn't.

I sighed, collected my paper work and prepared to put it away for the night. I tidied up the place and then I took a shower and waited for Ron. I knew he could be possessive and obsessive but the sex was totally incredible. Wild animal sex!

I waited in anticipation, wondering just what Ron had in store for me this time. Our first bout with rough sex had gone far over the limit. Ron had slapped my buttocks raw, calling me a mean bad bitch, punishing me, humiliating me. However, instead of making me angry it just got me excited, building me to a frenzy I'd never known before. Ron and I went on from there. He never slapped my face, and he always told me he loved me as he hit me. As long as he told me he loved me when he hit me, I figured that was okay. I know it was *out there*, but we liked being *out there*.

When he got to my place he attacked me like a rabid beast whose lust hadn't been sated in months. I love the attention, perhaps even require it. I melted under his power and let him take me hard and often. We both liked it rough. We often did it like this, so fast and furious. I realized that all the pent-up emotion these last two cases had brought out in me was coming out in our sexual bouts. If anything, once Ron initiated our rough foreplay, I continued it and even brought it into even more intense areas we'd never explored before,

Ron was surprised by my unleashed passion and it brought us both off like we'd never experienced with any of our previous lovers.

After our bout of animal sex, laying in bed exhausted, I massaged my welts. My only hope was that they wouldn't show or become black and blue. I got an antiseptic from the medicine cabinet for the scratches I'd dug with my nails into Ron's back. Many of those cuts were still bleeding and as I wiped up the blood I noticed the small drippings and spatters that ran down his back, onto my pillows and sheets. He was pretty badly tore up and I gasped, then smiled, hardly believing I had done that to him.

Ron didn't mind though. He never complained about anything I did to him, he said he liked it all. He said he enjoyed the pain. He liked to get it, and he liked to give it. Ron told me he wanted us to go farther in our sexual adventures and I was intrigued. I didn't know what that meant but he left it purposefully vague, a delicious and erotic surprise that I could fantasize about when I was alone and missing him.

When I awoke later I discovered that Ron was gone from my bed and noticed that the light in the living room was on. I figured he was watching TV but I heard no sound. Instead, I walked in on him sitting on the sofa looking over the Esposito and Kelly crime scene photos.

"What are you doing?" I asked, more than a bit perturbed that he was looking over my private notes and personal papers on a case.

"Couldn't sleep, found these and figured they'd be more interesting than TV so I took a look. Hope you don't mind."

"Well, no, of course not, but . . ."

"Interesting case," Ron commented quickly, "so you interpret the blood spatter at crime scenes. What does it tell you, Julie?"

"A lot of things, sometimes," I said.

"These crime scene photos, they're . . ." he looked up at me, smiled wickedly, "very graphic. Very bloody. Are they always like this? The woman naked, so vulnerable, so much blood all over . . ."

"Look, Ron," I knew he wasn't used to such things in his day-to-day Wall Street world, and his purulent mind could turn anything onto a sexual angle. But this? "These women were murdered, bludgeoned to death. I don't think you should be looking at the photos in *that* way. It's not pornography, Ron."

Ron smiled, "Of course, Julie, I didn't mean anything by it." He put the crime scene photos down, looked up at me and said, "Come over here, you."

Then he took me again on the couch, then onto the floor. It was harder than previously, more brutal. It hurt me a little but I actually enjoyed it. When it was over Ron left and I went to sleep exhausted.

The third murdered woman showed up next morning. Clarissa Roberts. She'd been killed the same way as the other two.

I was busy for the next few days and didn't see or hear from Ron until the murder was written up in the papers in a new article that used leaked information to connect the Roberts murder with the previous two. A task force was now formed and it took most of my time. I ended up having to do more extra work when I discovered I'd somehow lost or misplaced some of the photos of the two previous murders. That really annoyed me.

I was dog-tired and ready for bed when Ron called that evening and said he had to come over. As tired as I was, I became wet with lust for him anticipating our games. I told him to come up, but just for a little while, I had an early day at work the next morning.

Ron and I went right to it as soon as he entered my apartment. This time he brought handcuffs and he was wearing a mask. I didn't like it at first, but I was too excited to worry about it, and right away we were onto—and into—each other with a frenzy I'd never known before.

The problem was I could see where, sometimes, Ron seemed to get carried away with things. The cuffs were too tight on me, but his wearing of the mask seemed to bring out a hidden part of him I'd never seen before. Some of it I liked, it was beyond kinky, but some of it was weird . . . scary. But I guess I liked that part too. And Ron wasn't the only one, because I also got carried away with these new games. I wondered if either of us knew how far to take things before we stopped, how much pain was acceptable or not, and *if* we could stop.

Ron's newest kink was posing me. He'd force me down into various positions, bind me, then when I was helpless and scared, he'd penetrate me in all three orifices. It was rough, even brutal, normally I liked it. This, though was different and I'd yelled at him to stop. I asked him to leave.

"What?" he shouted, annoyed I was breaking the fantasy. 'The magic', as he called it. "Come on, you like this just as much as I do!"

"No! Stop! No more!" I shouted angry now.

I was nervous, fearful of the look I'd seen in his eyes just then, a lust I saw that was not sexual any longer, it was only violent. You see, I had the strange feeling that Ron was posing me in scenes from the Kelly and Esposito murders. Some of the positions were eerily familiar, from my crime scene photos. That was just too much for me.

"I don't think I like this," I said, but when he asked me and I told him what I thought he was doing, he just laughed.

"Julie, what's the problem? It gets me off, I find those photos . . .interesting."

"I think they arouse you!"

"All right, so what if they do. It's nothing any different from some of the S&M porno we watch, stuff we both enjoy sometimes doing."

"Those are movies, fantasies. You're posing me like the killer posed Jennifer Kelly's body at my crime scene. She was a real person, a murdered woman. How could you? That's . . . disgusting!"

"Oh, come on now! You do the same thing. You tell me to do you this way, that way, stand, or sit in a certain position . . .like you don't pose me! You don't hear me complaining, Julie. It's no big deal."

"Well, I don't think I like it," I said softly, thinking that maybe I'd been too severe with him. After all, Ron wasn't in law enforcement, or a victim, so he couldn't really understand.

Ron huffed about it, he looked angry, even hurt, but I think he was secretly pleased. I asked him to leave again, but mostly because I had a big day tomorrow. I had to give my presentation to the new serial killer task force. I had more evidence connecting the third murder victim to the previous two. Ron left and I prepared for bed.

Laying in bed alone that night before I fell asleep, I thought about Ron and our relationship. It wasn't exactly right I knew that, but I liked a lot of it. I don't know why I bothered with Ron sometimes. I'm sure really, down deep, he didn't like women—maybe not even me. But in spite of myself I couldn't resist our games. I liked them too much. In a way, I may have been too much like Ron for my own good. Anyway, it was just too deep and complicated to try to figure out that night, so I just decided to go to sleep and allow myself to enjoy it as long as it lasted. After all, it was just sex and games, and that was just too much incredible fun for me to pass up.

The next morning I looked over my notes before my presentation like I always did. I noticed that some of the crime scene photos for the third victim, Clarissa Roberts, seemed to be missing. I thought I'd had twelve 10 x 12 glossies in the file, but there were now only ten. I looked all through my files and papers, and the more I looked the more frantic I became. These were two of the most graphic photos of the lot. I never found them and a cold chill struck me, so I called Ron. There was no answer at his office. I left a message and then left for work and gave my presentation to the police with the information I had on hand.

"The blood spatter on the first victim, Esposito," I told the detectives, "was projected, it was gushing blood, mostly in arterial spurts from a blow or blunt force trauma. The blood spatter in victim #2, Kelly, created high velocity bloodstains, the pointed end of the bloodstain, the tail, indicates the directionality of the force. This victim was attached from behind."

There were questions from the detectives and I answered them as best I could.

"And that brings us to victim #3, the latest one, Clarissa Roberts. Again, we have projected blood, most of it is as I have already described in the previous victims, but I also found something else. Something totally different. With this victim we have projected blood spatter but of a unique pattern in one area of the murder scene, the wall behind the corpse. This blood was projected through a syringe."

That created an uproar and the cops wanted to know what the hell that meant. So did I.

"I'm waiting for the DNA report on this blood sample but I am sure it will indicate this particular syringe blood is not—cannot be—from victim #3. I assume it will be found to be blood from victim #1 or #2. If that proves to be the case, then we are not only faced with a very devious and brutal serial killer, but one who is apparently taunting us with his crimes."

The DNA report confirmed my findings. The detectives were not pleased. The press had to be notified and more manpower was authorized for the task force.

I went home exhausted. When I got to my apartment Ron was there waiting for me. Inside.

"Hope you don't mind. I let myself in," he said matter-of-factly, the usual charming Ron.

"I wasn't aware you still had a key?" I replied, testily, but too dog-tired to argue. He'd obviously made a copy of the key I'd asked for him to give back to me. "What do you want?"

"Just to be with you, Julie. This case, your work, is building a wall between us. I don't want that. You may not believe this, but you're very special to me. And I know, I'm special to you too."

He came over to me and caressed me with a softness I'd never seen from him before, then he smiled his winning smile and added, "And besides, the sex is great."

"Yeah," I muttered quietly.

"Oh, come on. You like our little games as much as I do. I don't hear you complaining. Sometimes you even egg me on with your own ideas. Maybe I went a little overboard the other night. Can't we put that behind us? I have some new ideas, something I think you'll really like."

I looked up at him, he looked so sincere, so sad and lost, and in spite of myself I couldn't help thinking about what was now on his mind. What new games he had planned? My juices began to flow with anticipation. I could feel the area at my crotch getting wet and saw Ron had noticed the tiny stain that had appeared between my legs now. He was smiling. In spite of myself I ran into his arms and in a moment we were naked and rolling around on the carpet down on the floor.

Ron's new kick was ritual bleeding. He wanted us to bleed each other, then mix small amounts of our blood together, rubbing it all over our bodies as we had sex. Ron knew me, see. He knew I was up for almost any freaky thing, especially if we'd never done it before. Well, we'd never done this before. Soon we both lost ourselves in the frenzy of it all. The cutting. The bleeding. Not deep cuts, but a lot of blood. We did some drugs, and that made it all easier, painless, all so dreamlike. I don't know what the pills were that he game me. I never asked. Ecstasy, probably. I felt like I was there somewhere above us, watching from overhead like in a film. It was ethereal, unreal. I never felt any pain. I don't remember too much of what happened. In the end I must have passed out.

When I woke up the next morning Ron was gone. I was there alone. That was so much like Ron, like most men I guess, to leave after he'd taken what he wanted.

I got up and showered. I was covered in dried and caked blood. I looked like one of my own murder scenes for christsakes. I was also weak, exhausted. I cleaned my wounds, most were nothing but mere superficial cuts, but a couple needed Band-Aids. My arm was also sore. I thought it was from a muscle pull—we'd been pretty crazy last night—but then I noticed a small black and blue bump that looked like an injection site on the inside of my right arm, by the vein.

Had Ron injected me with something? Some kind of drug? Meth? Heroin? I panicked for a moment, but I was a scientist after all, and I knew the signs of those drugs. It wasn't meth or heroin. Probably some kind of muscle relaxant or barbiturate cocktail to put me in that dreamy state I remembered. Something Ron gave me to feel no pain, only pleasure.

I was called to the task force early that morning for an emergency meeting. There had been another murdered woman discovered the night before. The woman, Shelia Smith, had been killed like the others, however, "Number Four" had been written in blood on the wall behind her corpse. I studied the blood spatter with dread, because it was projected blood and it appeared to have been done through a syringe again.

I knew we had a serious problem with this killer. He was vicious, intelligent and now taunting the police to catch him. The DNA report on this projected blood from the syringe however had me stumped. This time it was not blood from any of the four victims we knew about. So who was the blood from? The killer? It seemed improbable. We could never be that lucky. Or was it blood from a fifth, and presently unknown victim? That possibility sent a

chill through me, the realization that we could have another, unknown victim. I informed the police of my findings.

That night Ron was not in my apartment when I came home.
He wasn't waiting for me inside or outside. I was almost thankful
he was not there except I was so full of pent up emotions at what I
had discovered at the 4th crime scene that a good hard dose of wild
sex with Ron would have been the perfect drug to set me right.
Something to get me to sleeping like a baby that night, but it was
better he was not here.

Then Ron called. He was nervous, edgy. "I need to see you,
Julie," he said forcefully.

"Ron, can't it wait? I've had a hectic day and I'm totally out of
it right now."

"I'm coming over," was all he said.

"Ron . . .!" I replied curtly, but he wasn't on the line any
longer. I sighed, put down my phone, resigning myself to the fact
that he was coming over.

It was late and I was tired but the more I thought about him and
what he might have in mind for us, my anger lessened and my li-
bido grew. And that sexual appetite became a massive hunger fu-
eled by my fantasies of all the delightfully wicked things we had
done in the past—*and what we might be doing soon.*

By the time my doorbell rang I'd showered and was dressed in
sexy silk pjs, ready for my man to take me any way he liked. I
know it was wrong, sexist, slutty, maybe even dangerous, but
that's what excited me about it. I felt the wetness between my legs
growing, my anticipation building, as the bell rang. I knew it was
Ron at the door. As I got up off the couch to answer the door I
shivered from the tickle of one warm, solitary droplet of moisture
that ran down my inner thighs. I knew I was ready for Ron. I just
hoped he was ready for me.

He was.

No sooner had I opened the door than I felt the force of a large
body pushing me backwards hard, powerful hands held me down
and covered me with something—a dark blanket—or large plastic
garbage bag.

My head hurt. I struggled terrified, but Ron didn't pay any attention to my pleas. Or was it Ron? I could not see his face.
Maybe it was someone else? The killer? I began to grow fearful
now. I tried to cry out, but my face and mouth were covered so
tightly I couldn't make a sound. Whoever it was, he was so much
bigger and stronger than I.

Now it was getting hard to breath! Then I felt my pajamas ripped away with rude force followed by the hard joy of penetration. Now I knew it was Ron. He was mounting me from behind. I screamed in agony—joy—fear—lust—I couldn't even tell you what I felt just then. I lay back helpless as my body spasmed with multiple searing orgasms. Then I heard Ron scream wildly as he climaxed into me with a force I'd never felt before.

Finally we both fell to the floor, the bag removed from my head, the gag taken from my mouth. I gasped in exhaustion.

"Surprise!" was all Ron said, looking languidly into my eyes from beside me.

I punched his chest twice with my small balled-up fists. "You bastard! You scared the hell out of me!"

He laughed, "But you liked it. I know you liked it."

I never answered him but the truth was I did like it. It had been great, incredible—and just a little sick. I began to fear that I had become a slave to my desires and Ron was my addiction.

I watched him as he got dressed to leave. After all, he'd got what he wanted. He gathered his things, looking so confident, so superior. I watched as he collected his rope, duct tape, plastic garbage bags, a hammer and screwdriver.

Then a dreadful chill took me. I knew what I saw. It was quite plain. Ron had his own rape kit! The realization had my mind whirling.

And this kit of his hadn't been the result of our spur-of-the-moment sexual games either, quickly throwing together a few things, but a well thought out plan. Or even scarier, the result of long practice and experience!

"Ron?" I asked quietly.

He looked over at me as he continued to collect his things. He put them all in a large black gym bag near me on the floor.

"I think we should stop this. It's not right, not . . . healthy. I'm afraid we're going to go too far some day and one of us will loose control."

"Isn't this what you want, Julie? What you crave? I know it is. I know you only too well," he said, coming toward me now with that confident winning smile of his. "You live a well-ordered logical life in a well-ordered world ruled by science and reason. So do I. We need to escape and our games give us that escape."

"I don't think I want to do this anymore," I said slowly.

Ron just looked at me and laughed.

That got me angry, I shouted, "I'm serious, dammit!"

"Sure you are. You don't know what you want and now you're acting like every other damn bitch with a bug up her ass about sex."

"This isn't sex! This is sick. It's not right what we do."

"You like it. I know you do."

"Maybe, but I don't want to do it anymore."

"You don't know what you're saying."

"Don't tell me I don't know want I'm saying, dammit! I'm telling you . . ."

Then Ron slapped me hard. Twice.

I screamed and cursed him, "Get out! I want you out of here now!"

"You'll change your mind," he said with a confident smirk.

"Fuck you!"

His eyes focused on me then with an animal rage. Suddenly he came at me, pinning me down on the floor so I couldn't move. His hand grasping my throat and squeezing tight. This wasn't fun and games. This wasn't sex now. I was having trouble breathing.

My God, he was going to kill me!

I became frantic, and from somewhere, somehow, I gathered the energy to push him off me. He fell over to my left and I bolted to my right and fell into his gym bag. I remembered the hammer I'd seen him put inside it and frantically reached for it and pulled it out. When Ron came at me again, I hit him full on the forehead with the ball-peen hammer and he dropped down like a felled ox, unconscious, or dead. I didn't care which at that point.

I got up shaking, angry, infuriated with a rage I had never felt before, but surging through my body was another feeling I knew well but had never realized I could feel from such an incident—the release of incredible sexual energy.

I quickly looked at the other things inside Ron's gym bag. There I found my missing crime scene photos. And others from the crime scene, Polaroid's not from the department, but his own personal photos of *his* crimes. Ron was the killer! My mind reeled at the knowledge. Then I saw a vial of blood with a label marked with my name on it. Then I found the syringe! That made it all clear now.

I looked down at Ron, he was moaning softly but apparently unable to move. He was so helpless. The memory of my previous outburst of violence had turned me on like nothing else ever had. Now seeing Ron on the floor helpless only caused to stimulate my sexual desires even more. I touched my nakedness, my most intimate area was moist, soon dripping wet. My nipples were hard and sore, hypersensitive and burning to the touch. I was on fire. Now I was anticipating doing something with Ron that we had never done before.

I picked up the ball-peen hammer and hit Ron once on the head. The dull thud caused him to moan loudly. As he did so, I moaned louder in my sexual frenzy, hitting him again and again and again, faster, faster, faster—screaming in an orgy of sexual release culminating in a bloody orgasm of sheer violence.

I looked at the members of the task force and concluded my report. "This latest victim, a male, Ron Jackson, was a dump job. He was killed somewhere else and then left at the edge of the park. Blood spatter indicates blunt force trauma, I'd surmise a hammer of some kind." I smiled slightly, "Probably a ball-peen hammer."

WAR

STAPLETON IS A MOSTLY BLACK SECTION on Staten Island, which is a bedroom community of sorts, to New York City. Not a lot of white people come there at night, so when Robert Earl saw the big white guy at his doorway, he knew something was up. The man was not in any uniform, but he oozed 'cop' nevertheless.

Detective Howard Simmons looked like a tough cop, but old and tired these days. He was a 'Nam vet, a former Marine, and an NYPD detective about half an inch away from retirement. He had looked up Earl and was visiting him that summer evening to talk about Sergeant Manny Dunbar, or 'Dunny' as Sarge was called. They both knew Dunbar well, but from different eras. Viet Nam to Iraq and a lotta in-between.

Earl knew the official report said Sarge's death had been suicide—a bullet into the brain. Just another despondent veteran. A loner, recently retired, no family but the Corps. Sarge's fingerprints were on the gun and it had been *his* weapon. It was a death that had shocked Earl and all who had served with the Sergeant in Iraq. More so, because it had been ruled a suicide. But Earl knew Sarge. This just wasn't like him. 'Dunny' was a *pro*-war activist. Since he had retired from the military he wrote flyers that he handed out at anti-war and 'peace' rallies to support the Iraq War, and the overall War on Terror. He did it on his own time, at his own expense. He wasn't part of any group or party. He was just one American making his opinions known and trying to educate the public on what he knew was the truth.

"I don't give a damn what the official report says," Simmons finally told Earl that night as they sat in a local cop bar, "Sarge didn't blow his brains out with his own gun. I think he was murdered."

Earl nodded, what Simmons told him made sense. They both knew Dunny. The man was not the type to pull the plug, he was a fighter. But Earl knew his old Marine buddy and mentor had some

ideas that caused controversy and argument these days. Earl told
Simmons about his last conversation with Dunny.

"Dunny believed war could be a good thing. War can be just.
War can be right. That's what Dunny told me, proclaiming it with
his usual passionate pride. He said, war can be—sometimes—the
only proper way to settle a problem when all else has failed."

Simmons nodded, he'd also known the Sarge's opinions.

Earl remembered smiling at Sarge when they'd talked about
this back then, him bringing up how Quakers wouldn't see things
quite that way.

But Dunny had surprised Earl by saying he didn't have a problem with Quakers and the like. He said they never hurt no one, and
he recognized their feelings on the matter and respected them.
They were not hypocrites in his book. They lived what they believed. Like Marines.

"So what was his beef?" Simmons finally asked Earl.

"Mostly with what he called the America haters," Earl told the
cop, "retro 60s protesters and peacenik leftovers who never grew
up. He recognized the type from his Vietnam days. Dunny said
they didn't know what they were talking about being against our
war on the terrorists and their enablers. Like Saddam. He felt too
many were simply America haters, raging and spewing venom
against this country and our President. See, Dunny didn't care if
you liked the President or not, or even voted for him or against
him, he respected the fact the man is our president, and he is
president during wartime. Sarge said that means you support him,
you support the country, and you always support the troops. He
felt the America haters turned their disagreement with the war into
support of America's enemies, and he was sick of it."

"How did you feel about that?" Simmons asked Earl.

"I don't know. I'm not so political, I just ignore them," Earl
said simply.

"And Dunny?" Simmons asked.

Earl nodded, "Dunny would smile that crooked little grin of his
and explain how they had no plan to deal with the dangerous problems we face today. They don't have a responsible bone in their
body. They never consider how their anti-war rhetoric brings
down troop morale, emboldening our enemies. Dunny said they
give our enemies aid and comfort and that gets our guys and gals
killed."

Earl knew that much was true, he'd seen it first-hand in Iraq. A
far worse disgrace were American political leaders whose anti-war

and anti-America statements were actually used as recruitment posters on Al Jazirah for Al Qaeda and the insurgents in Iraq. Anyone who'd seen what Dunny and Earl and their comrades had seen in Iraq, knew that we were doing a good job there and should never leave until that job was done.

"So you think he was killed for his politics?" Simmons asked Earl, curious now.

"I don't know. Not his politics exactly, but because he was doing something about politics. He was doing what he believed in, and someone didn't like it. Dunny had been on a roll back then. I remember him telling me about how the left, liberals, the cynical media, 'Hollywood freaks', 'academic know-it-alls', were putting us in danger and getting our troops killed."

Detective Simmons asked Earl if he would look into the political end of it and keep him informed if he found anything.

"I'll give it a try," Earl said softly. "I guess I owe Sarge that much."

"Good, but don't do anything drastic, my captain is tight with our two Senators so he won't let me look into this myself," Simmons replied. Then he added in warning, "This could get dangerous. Let me know if you get any bites or leads. If I have something concrete, my captain will have no choice but to let me open the case as a homicide."

The next day Robert Earl went to work. Earl wasn't all that political, but he wasn't blind either. He knew Dunny had his views and he knew there were people who didn't want those views voiced. He opened an ice-cold Bud, drank the refreshing brew down in a few gulps and thought again of his friend, Sergeant Manny Dunbar.

"You were a tough critter, Sarge, and a hell of an opinionated bastard," Earl said thoughtful, remembering his friend with warm laugher. Dunny hadn't been perfect, but he was a good man, a fair man. "You know, you were loved by every damn jarhead in the outfit. You were a hard taskmaster and a general pain in the ass, but your hard ways kept us all alive in the thick of battle. I realize it now, you used every harsh word, body blow, and bully tactic to make us stronger, more alert, tougher. All to ensure our survival. And we did survive. Every one of us came back home alive from that damn desert. Then they found you dead in some tiny SRO in Manhattan. *Bullshit!*"

Earl found Dunny's journal in his effects. It told how Sarge often confronted opponents at rallies and events. He loved to debate but was never welcomed, never treated with respect, usually just shouted down or called names. Sometimes he was spit upon or feces and urine were thrown at him. When he proudly wore his old Marine jacket to honor his service to our country, he was called baby killer and murderer!

Earl didn't think these kinds of things happened in America these days, like they had during the Vietnam era, but they did. He was surprised when he saw first-hand the truth you never see on the TV news.

Dunny wrote how he was proud that he never let the terrible things they did to him provoke his temper. He never got angry, never took revenge. He realized the more crazy his opponents became, the more they just proved he was right.

Earl examined the flyers Dunny had handed out at recent anti-war marches and rallies. They were all unashamedly pro war. More than that even, they spoke of the outright honor and righteousness of war. That couldn't have gone over well with the anti-war crowd. Dunny's flyers lauded the long illustrious tradition of warfare throughout human history that had brought down evil and despots. War could be good. War could be just.

Dunny's flyers told of the American Revolution; a war fought by a colonial people yearning to be free from oppression. He wrote about the U.S. Civil War; a war that for many was a test of whether we would end the abomination of human slavery—or keep it! We rejected slavery, but with a high toll in blood and pain. But then, as Dunny wrote it, nothing really worthwhile is ever easy or cheap.

Sarge also wrote about the heroic wars waged and won to free the world of the twin scourges of Nazism and Communism. Then he added how today's War on Terror, and the accompanying battles in Iraq, were no exception to that long and noble fight for human freedom and progress.

Earl looked over the rest of Dunny's papers and flyers. He noticed that Dunny had collected notes on some of the protesters, what he called a professional political agitator class made up too often of silver-spoon, guilt-ridden, spoiled-rich brats. Storm troopers of the New Left. Cynical activists with no morals or ethics, who laughed at anyone who stood for honor or integrity. After the murder of 3,000 Americans on 9/11 they wasted no time in proclaiming how we had gotten what we deserved. How 9/11 was just the chickens coming home to roost. They are the same sort who've always hated this country, but now they were against us even during a time of war. And yet, their American citizenship guaranteed their freedom and rights—paid for by the blood of our veterans—which protected these people and their views. No matter what their views were. Fair enough.

But what disturbed Earl now was the problems Dunny encountered and wrote about, they were getting serious.

Earl started hanging out at anti-war events. There were a surprisingly large number of them, but after a while he always saw the same people attending. The usual suspects. These were the ones he took note of—and he noticed that they took note of him as well. He was being watched. Monitored. Sometimes followed. Some of these people weren't just protesters or demonstrators, they were activists and operatives.

Robert Earl took Sarge's old flyers and rewrote them in his own lingo, then copied them to hand out at events and rallies all over the Northeast.

That got him the attention he wanted.

He was surprised when so-called peace-loving, open-minded, free-thinking intellectuals and First Amendment advocates called him the vilest names for having the audacity to hand out his flyers. They shouted him down when he tried to explain or debate them. They balled up his flyers and flung them back into his face with venomous rage. They spit on him. They did dirty little tricks like pouring blood and urine on him. Then they screamed that they hoped he died of AIDS or cancer, admitting that the blood they'd poured on him was infected with the HIV virus. They threatened him with physical injury. They threatened his family, even his mother. They shouted with pure hatred how they'd track him down one day, find out where he lived, and then teach him a lesson. Then they called *him* a Nazi.

But what really hurt was when they called him 'Uncle Tom'. Earl had been a United States Marine, a war hero, a strong, proud man. He was a Black man with his own ideas. He was no less an American than any other American, and as such entitled to his own opinions.

What really pissed him off though, was when they called him 'Nigger'. They shouted the word as if channeled by some KKK cracker but of course *their* motives were pure—they were using the word to further what they considered 'the right things'. Of course they said it in the typical hit and run style, too scared to face Earl's anger, too quick for him to catch them. Yeah, he told them, "You better run!"

Earl realized the front lines in this war could be every bit as treacherous and vicious as Sadr City in Baghdad or central Filiujah. Now he thought he understood what Dunny was trying to do with his flyers. Dunny was still fighting the war, but this time on the home front, where it needed to be fought and won. But had he been murdered for it?

One of Dunny's hardest hitting flyers ran with a very provocative headline, *"Let's Give War A Chance!"*

Earl smiled, that was so much like Dunny. In your face. Not afraid to lay it right out in the open. It was a phrase Earl knew Dunny purposefully had used to play on the simplistic 60s antiwar slogan of, "just give peace a chance."

Dunny said the hell with that!

Instead, he proudly proposed the reverse, *"Let's Give War A Chance!"*

That had been Dunny's last flyer. So Earl figured that might be the flyer that had struck a nerve. He decided he'd use that one now, but he'd go his old buddy one better.

Robert Earl rewrote Dunny's last flyer and customized the title and fonts on his home PC, then printed the title in large red letters. Next day he took the flyers to the rally in the park and began handing them out to the demonstrators.

"All We Are Saying is . . .Give War A Chance!"

For a split second Earl was met with cold silence from the demonstrators. Most looked at the flyer, examining it closely as if their eyes were actually burning from the words written there. Some couldn't believe what they saw.

Earl smiled, his flyers were having the desired effect.

One of the group of thugs who'd been watching Earl the last few days, some sort of political operative or enforcer, tried to grab the stack of flyers out of Earl's hands. Meanwhile, a slip of a girl, looking like some neo-hippie, tried to outflank him and knock his flyers to the ground.

Earl body blocked the girl easily, then tripped the guy and sent him sprawling with a nudge into the bushes. That seemed to take care of them.

But suddenly Earl was blindsided, hit from behind by another of the guy's hippie wannabe operatives.

Then the riot began.

Earl stayed strictly on defense, he wasn't out to hurt anyone. Though it was obvious they were certainly out to hurt him. He was a well-trained Marine, so in a way he was actually enjoying what he considered a bit of exercise. Earl easily warded off the blows of his attackers, but was careful to make sure they didn't get behind him again. They played dirty and could be dangerous. The site of his Marine jacket only seemed to make his attackers madder, more reckless. They kept coming at him. A couple of old 'Nam vets and two African-American Christian senior citizen ladies joined to lend a hand, but Earl soon found he was protecting them more than they were protecting him. Soon dozens of 'peace' activists charged them in a headlong rush of hate, violence and righteous rage.

The cops were nearby and broke it up before anyone got hurt too badly, but by that time Earl's flyers were scattered all over the ground and the cops ended up writing him a ticket for littering. Once the cops separated the sides, things calmed down.

The girl came over to him later. The rally had ended by then, most people having gone home. Earl was still picking up the last of his flyers from the ground. Most of them had footprints all over them.

Earl noticed the girl was a little older than college age but still looked collegiate, white middle class, not dressed like the usual hippie wannabes. She was holding one of his flyers.

He smiled as she walked up to him and with a grudging shake of her head, held out his flyer. Earl only noticed that she was damn attractive, limp blond hair, but nice shape, blue eyes, maybe 20-25. Hard to tell for sure, but right in that age group that Earl at 29 years-young liked best.

"One you missed," she said, handing him the flyer.

"Thanks," Earl said, taking it and putting it into his pile. He had about 50-60 left, but he'd given out about a hundred. He would consider it a good day if one of those flyers stimulated the light of independent thought in the mind of just one of those protestors. But he wasn't expecting much. He'd discovered for all that these people talked about openness and freedom, their minds were shut as tight as a steel trap. He feared such attitudes could be dangerous to a free people, a free society.

The girl was still there, looking at him carefully. Earl didn't hide his surprise.

He said, "I guess you didn't read it?"

She said, "I read some of it."

She hadn't spit at him yet, or cursed him, so that probably was a good sign.

"So what do you think?"

"About what?"

"Well, about the flyer. What it says, for starters," he said carefully.

She smiled, then laughed, "I mean, you don't really believe that stuff, do you? I mean, this is a joke, right? I mean, you're a Black man!"

Earl was shocked.

"Or, are you some kind of spy?"

Now Earl smiled, shook his head, "No, I don't work for anyone. Only myself. I'm a vet, just back from Iraq. I was there and saw first-hand what we're doing. We've freed over 50 million people from the cruelest slavery in Iraq and Afghanistan. People are voting for the first time now, women have rights—so do minorities. We all—all of us serving there in the military—feel the same way. We see the truth of it every day. I don't know why none of it ever gets reported here on TV. Something is very wrong here. We're doing a good thing in Iraq. The only ones who don't seem to understand it are the terrorists we're fighting there—and the America-hating Americans here."

"Wow!"

"Sorry, but you asked, you got me started," he replied with a wry grin, figuring she'd leave now or start in with some typical shouting down tactic he'd seen too much of lately. Instead neither happened, and he noticed she was still looking at him.

She surprised him when she said, "I guess a few things you wrote make sense. I mean, 9/11 killed all those people but we weren't even *in* Afghanistan or Iraq back then."

"So you noticed that," he replied with a smile. She smiled back nodding. He was just about ready to leave, go home, have a few beers. Then pass out for the evening before he started it all over again the next day. There was always another rally, another meeting, some damn protest march somewhere.

"So what are you doing now?" she asked. At first he wasn't sure he heard her right. He couldn't figure it, but she did seem interested in him.

"I was gonna go back to my place, have a few beers, then pass out," he said, laughing. "I'm not a very exciting guy."

She smiled at that and he liked what he saw. "Oh, I don't know, I have a feeling there's much more to you than there appears to be."

Earl said, "Well, yeah. You, maybe, wanna go for a drink?" He said it boldy but hesitant and curious, figuring she'd slap his face, maybe call him some kind of imperialistic sexist-dog or capitalistic robber-baron lackey.

Instead, she said, "Okay." Then as an afterthought added, "Ah, maybe you could just roll up the flyers so no one can see them? You know?"

Earl nodded, he could do that. There was a time for politics and a time *not* for politics. They walked over to a local bar on the street outside the park. It was busy, but they found a small table in the back and talked all kinds of stuff, *except* politics. They enjoyed getting to know each other. He found out her name was Joy. He kind of liked that. He thought he could use a dose of Joy in his life just then.

She told him how she'd like to see his place and he told her he'd like to show it to her. Then he made a quick phone call, told her, "I share an SRO with another vet across the Park. I'll just give him a call to let him know not to come home *too* early."

She smiled, "That's fine."

A few hours later they were sitting on the couch, getting better acquainted. She was tilting back a beer and telling him how much she really liked sex, that she felt it freed her from the restraints placed upon us all by an over-bearing paternalistic civilization. He smiled, said nothing, and they began to undress each other.

Then she saw his gun.

"So you're ex-military?" She asked him, looking at the gun intently.

"Marines, but I just like guns. Weapons of all types, actually. They're beautiful objects in design and function."

"Like women?" she asked coyly.

Earl smiled, "Well, nothing comes close to a woman."

She liked that. She picked up the gun, a .32, looking it over carefully, then set it down again, quickly.

"I don't like guns, they're bad. People die from them."

Earl sighed inwardly. He didn't want to begin a debate now but he wasn't going to let her comment pass without offering the truth. He felt she deserved to hear the truth. "People live because of them, too. Guns save a lot of lives."

She didn't reply, it seemed she now had other things on her mind. Then they got down to it. Their lovemaking was fast but cumbersome. After they made love, they lay exhausted and sleeping like babies in each other's arms. He didn't move when he felt her get up from the bed, even when he noticed she'd gone over and picked up his gun.

She quietly came over to Earl's sleeping form, carefully placed the gun in his hand, then brought his hand up to his head.

So this is how Dunny got it, Earl realized sadly. The only way a man like the Sarge could have been taken out.

It happened so fast.

With her hand molded over his own, she quickly pressed his finger down to squeeze the trigger, firing the gun into Earl's head.

There was a loud click.

Then nothing.

Earl suddenly opened his eyes and smiled at her, grabbing the gun out of her hand. He pulled her down so she couldn't move and held her, "You didn't think I'd leave a loaded gun laying around, did you?"

At that point the front door burst open and Detective Simmons entered the apartment with two uniformed officers. They soon had cuffs on the girl.

"Nice work, Earl," Simmons said, carefully placing the .32 into an evidence bag.

"You got her on the video?" Earl asked. Simmons had allowed him use of an apartment the cops kept for drug deals that was wired with cameras.

"Good thing you made that call before you came over. We got it all. The gun to your head, her pressing the trigger. We also picked up her two friends, and they talked, spilled the beans on how she'd played the exact same 'game' with the Sarge."

"You lousy son of a bitch! You betrayed me! You used me!" Joy screamed at Earl, punching, whirling, trying to get away. Her balled-up fists struck him furiously. The two uniformed cops pulled her off Earl, then threw her clothing over her nakedness.

"No, you're the bitch, sister!" Earl growled as the cops took her out of the apartment. "You murdered an innocent American, a hero, because you didn't like what he said and you had no damn right! He was my friend, my sergeant. Then you were going to do the same to me!"

"Baby killer! Fascist murderer!" she screamed as they took her out of the room.

"What the hell is wrong with her?" Simmons asked Earl.

"It's what goes for peace, love and free speech these days with some people," Earl replied sadly, suddenly looking very tired as he left the room.

POLITICAL YEAR

T HERE WASN'T A CRAZIER BASTARD I'd ever known than Jack Rodriguez. We'd grown up together in Brooklyn. When I went into the cops, Jack went into the mob. Such are the choices you make when you're young, and they'll affect the rest of your life, setting it on a course that most people can never imagine. Jack and I hadn't seen each other for a dozen years, but we'd heard about each other over the years. And as those years passed we found ourselves both down and out, ground down by life and the system, back to where we'd started from so many years earlier. We were back to nothing again. Just older, more tired now.

I was another broken badge, trying to kick a drug habit, an ex-killer for hire and sometimes private dick, and an ex-married man. I was a widower now. Forever mourning the best thing I'd ever had, missing her, feeling lower than death. She'd been dead two years. So had I. Jack was just as bad, a too-wise punk kicked out of the mob for being too smart, too tough, and too damn crazy for anyone to whack.

Jack had made a big mistake. He'd fooled with his boss. Acted like a wise-guy made man, forgetting he was just a too-smart Puerto from Fourth Avenue. But, like I say, Jack was just too crazy to whack, and he had too many friends. So they set him up, got him sent upstate to rot away. They did it with his lawyer. This was a young, back-stabbing, ass-kisser named Thomas who had visions of political futures and a don't-give-a-damn do-anything-to-get-there attitude. Thomas was worse than the mob guys who owned him. At least you always knew where you stood with those creeps, but with a smile-in-your-face double-dealing shyster weasel like Thomas, Jack never had a chance. Of course, Jack found out about all this too late to do him any good. He was sent away to prison and told he'd never get out. And as the years passed it began to look like he really would never get out. There was heavy political influence behind it. The mob coughed up the bucks to bribe the judge, fired-up the perjured "victims" to fight against any release, influenced the parole board and the press. Jack was sent away from the world and no one gave a damn.

Meanwhile, Jack's lawyer became a big-shot political who parlayed the fame in a crooked election to buy a seat in the state Assembly. Two years later another crooked win and he became a freshman Representative sent to Congress in Washington. Two years later it was Senator. Once Thomas was in office, the people couldn't seem to get him out. Thomas made damn sure Jack Rodriguez would never get out of prison either, hefty campaign contributions from mob fronts flowed into his campaigns to ensure that.

Thomas ran unopposed in every primary. He ran in the general election for his seat just like everyone else in Congress. And like most Congressmen he ran unopposed. Either that, or the opposition was so weak, so inconsequential, so poor or disorganized, that the election process became a big joke. A rubberstamp. A big sham where only incumbents win, and no one else even has a chance. New York State, New York City, most of America just rotting away because it has become a mass of one-party states run by a ruling elite of politicians far removed from the people they are there to serve. They've all forgotten the reason they're in Washington in the first place. They're supposed to serve the people—not own them.

I remember it wasn't too long ago people used to complain about the old Soviet Union and Communism. All well and good, I say, but people haven't taken a long hard look at their own country in so long they wouldn't recognize it now if they ever opened their eyes to really see. It's been taken away from them. Thomas was just one of the takers.

Meanwhile, Jack Rodriguez rotted away. Doing the time, never having done the crime. Growing old and angry, while Senator Thomas grew rich and fat.

I came into it when I heard Jack had broke prison. After fifteen years, he'd had enough. It was weird. Him being in so long. A trumped-up charge with political weight behind it. I mean, no one goes to prison for fifteen years full time in New York State. Murderers and child molesters don't even get hard time like that most of the time. But Jack did. They had him good. Just where they wanted him. Jack was never getting out unless he broke out. I guess he finally realized that too and decided to do something about it. I wondered what else he'd decided. Knowing Jack, I got a bit concerned. There were others much more concerned.

They came to me. Scumbags in expensive suits and perfect smiles, promising whatever the traffic would bear, eyes like razors, but minds so corrupt and evil they fouled the very air with their presence. You see, I knew the type. Politicians. A breed of parasites we could all do without. So-called "public servants" who think they rule by divine right rather than at the behest of the people. Loud voices who shout about freedom, the power of the vote, free speech, and democracy—but only if your free speech agrees with them, only if your vote *goes* to them, only when your idea of freedom *agrees* with the particular brand of patent medicine they're hawking at the moment. These are the same people who always squawk about how they just love democracy—but that's because it's the perfect system where a useless parasitic demagogue can weasel his way into public office right under the radar. The gravy train doesn't get no better than a nice, comfy, political appointment or do-nothing seat in Congress these days.

These were the guys who knew I knew Jack. These were the guys who were concerned Jack might open his big yap and start to blab. After all, it was a presidential year. Nothing could be allowed to interfere with certain plans. These were the guys who wanted to pay me big money to find Jack and bring him back. To get him back safely behind bars where he belonged. Or kill him.

I said sure. I needed the money.

Figuring what Jack Rodriguez would do wasn't something I needed to consult a crystal ball about. I knew Jack, knew his ways. I was concerned. He hadn't broke prison just because he was horny and wanted to go out and get laid or something. You know, just for the hell of it. There was a reason and I figured that reason had to do with Senator William Thomas. So I took the shuttle to D.C.

An hour later I was loitering with a *Washington Post*, pretending to read the damn rag in the hallway outside the Senator's office. Snooping around, talking to people, keeping an eye open for Jack. I had some recent photos to go by, but fifteen years and Jack hadn't changed all that much, just thinner, almost gaunt, his eyes more piercing than ever. Eyes that saw through all the bullshit. One hell of an intense dude for a Puerto Rican. All the mob guys said he had the black heart of a Sicilian. That can be pretty damn black if you know the kind of Sicilians that I know.

I was getting nowhere fast. The place was busy, teeming with people, but no Jack Rodriguez. And no Senator Thomas by late morning either. I knew I'd made a mistake. I would have to get out to the house right away.

I got a cab and had the driver take me out to the Virginia suburbs where Thomas lived. I'd gotten the address from the Senator's handlers back in Manhattan, the mob guys who kept him in business, the guys who'd owned him since the first days he'd been a low-life shyster with a winning smile and delusions of grandeur, power, and laundered cash. Mostly small bills. He was just a WASP front man. The mob had tons of them.

The neighborhood where he lived was nice, full of big houses, well-tended lawns, so quiet you could hear the birds chirping like crazy in all the damn trees. The American dream bought with blood money.

I knew something was wrong right away. The front door was open. Just a speck, barely noticeable, only an inch, but no one kept their front door open like that out here. Unlocked maybe, not open. The kind of thing Jack might do, just to make things interesting. It didn't look right. I smelled Jack Rodriguez all over the place. I told the cabby to wait.

"I might be a while, buddy. Just sit tight. Don't get out of the cab. Don't come in the house. And don't leave. No matter what you might hear." I gave him a folded over fifty.

He stared at the fifty, pocketed it quickly, looked back at me.

I told him, "Close your mouth and sit tight. Do nothing. Don't worry. Just be here when I come out of the house."

Jack was waiting for me inside. Gun in hand.

"Vic? Vic Powers! Son-of-a-bitch! I can't believe it! You look good for so much wear and tear, my man."

"You knew I was coming, Jack." It was a statement, not a question.

"I got friends, Vic. Even after all these years. They still tell me things."

"That why you broke out?"

"I was set up, man. That scumbag, Thomas, set me up. He's a bought off fink for the mob. They didn't have the balls to send someone to whack me . . ."

I didn't say a word.

" . . . Until now, I guess. That's why you're here, isn't it, Vic?"

"I got a job, Jack" You know how it is when you got a job. You do the job. You just do it."

"That include killing me?"

"They want me to bring you back. That's all I'm getting paid for, Jack."

Jack laughed at that. "They wouldn't send Vic Powers just to put my ass back in the can."

"If you don't want to come back I'm supposed to persuade you."

"And if you can't persuade me, Vic?"

"You know how it is, Jack."

"They pay very well?"

"They pay too well. And I need the cash. They wanted me to take this case very badly. They insisted."

"Well, now you got me," Jack laughed, "or rather, I've got you."

"I'm not armed, Jack," I said, letting him get a good look at my empty hands.

"I'm not going back, Vic. No way."

"I don't care what you want, Jack. In the end you know how it will be."

For the first time since I'd known Jack Rodriguez I saw him grow a bit nervous, a bit unsure of himself. He wasn't stupid. He knew how things worked.

I said, "Where's Thomas? You didn't kill him already. Did you?"

"No, man, I figured I'd wait for him, then pop him. Something musta held him up." He looked at me. "You warn him off?"

"No," I said, "but you're not going to whack him. You're not going to whack anyone, Jack."

He didn't reply. He just looked at me, almost pleading. Like I was the guy holding the gun on him instead of the other way around.

"You don't know what this slimy bastard did to me, Vic. He took away fifteen years of my life! The best damn years! He was my lawyer, Vic! He was supposed to defend me! He knew I wasn't guilty. He suppressed evidence. He lied to the judge. He sold me out and set me up!"

"I believe you, Jack," I said quietly, "but you can't kill him. You've gotta come back with me."

Jack didn't hear me. He just went on about what it was like in prison. The hell he'd been forced to endure for fifteen long years. I felt for him. I knew it wasn't right what had been done to him.

"The years passed and I always kept track of that bastard Thomas, as he went from shyster to Assemblyman, to Congressman.

Then Senator. Now they say he's being considered as serious vice-presidential material. Can you believe it!"

I could believe it. In any toilet the shit always rises to the top sooner or later. In this case it took fifteen years and there was no telling how high it might go.

"There's no way, Vic. I've never been one of those flag-waving morons, but I can't let this happen. Not to the country I love. I had to get out to stop him. If this guy becomes vice-president, a heartbeat away from becoming president, this country will really go in the toilet."

I laughed now. "What makes you think the country ain't in the toilet already? What makes you think he'd be any worse than all the other crooks already running the government?"

Jack smiled. "That's just it, Vic. That's exactly what it says in the book."

"What are you talking about?"

"The book, Vic. You should see some of the stuff Thomas wrote about these guys. Terrible things. They're worse than the mob guys, Vic. The mob guys are all scumbags. Everyone knows that. But these other guys. No one knows how really bad these guys are, Vic. Liars, cheats, criminals of the worst kind. Not a one of them has an ounce of honor."

"Politicians," I said.

"Yeah, Vic. The book has them all pinned, man. Right to the wall. I guess it was Thomas' way of keeping score."

"What is this book, Jack?"

"I found it upstairs. While I was waiting I figured I'd crack the bastard's safe. I found the book inside. It's got almost every Congressman, every Senator, every damn politician in Washington listed. You wouldn't believe the names, Vic. Big names! Guys you see on TV every night! And the crimes! Terrible! Just terrible! Next to each name is the information Thomas had on them. Who owns what Congressman. The mob. The oil companies. PAC's and lobbyists. Some players no one's ever guessed. Rich guys that got away with stealing from the country's S & L's, economically raping the American people. Conflicts of interest you would not believe! But that's not all, Vic. There's even worse stuff. Sicker stuff. There's records of payoffs, everything from selling votes to contract murder. Cash Congressmen were skimming from their campaigns by check kiting through the House Bank and the House Post Office; hush money paid to witnesses. Congressmen lining their pockets with illegal campaign contributions. It tells which

Congressman is in the employ of what foreign government, and what secrets these guys have been funneling to those governments. Then there's much worse, Vic. Stuff about a couple of Congress-men involved in an underground sex club where there was a kill-ing. Another Congressman involved in a Satanic cult. There are child molesters and pedophiles, rapists, drunks, drug addicts, drug dealers, a number are involved in straight and gay prostitution rings. There's one man listed who had his wife killed. Contract killing. A Congressman so abused his daughter that the child died. Another Congressman beat his wife to death. All this and more was all hushed up. Witnesses were bought off. Some were killed. Hundreds of lives were destroyed. Then there are the rumors about companies driven out of business, the owners committing suicide. All true it seems. One businessman went on a rampage in Duluth killing five people in a shopping mall. It was a direct result of a Congressman taking over his company. Of course this was all done through dummy corporations or front men. The book says they've been getting away with this for years, Vic, enriching themselves like bloated pigs. And it goes on and on, dirtier and dirtier, and I don't doubt for a minute that it's all true."

"Let me see this book, Jack."

Jack surprised me by putting his gun down and handing me the book.

"Read it, Vic. You'll never believe it, but it's all true. Once I make this public . . ."

"No one will ever believe it, Jack."

His face dropped, "But . . . ?"

"But my ass! You think you'll live long enough to ever make this public! No way, Jack. You're dead already."

He got defensive then.

I laughed, "Not me. Don't you understand what you've got here?"

I looked through the book. Senator Thomas was a superb re-cord keeper, if nothing else. I could see him parlaying the informa-tion in his little black book into the vice-presidency, maybe even into the presidency itself someday. No Washington politico has had leverage like this since J. Edgar Hoover. Thomas was an in-credible weasel, but the people he had the goods on were far worse. The irony was that all their terrible deeds went unsuspected by the sleeping American public. Unreported. Unknown. I realized these guys were totally bent out of shape, so crooked they couldn't tell the difference between right and wrong anymore. And could care less. These were the people we trusted with the future of our country. The future of our kids. And now America had fallen into their greedy hands. It made me sick to see it, all neatly written right there in front of me in black and white. It had been happening for a long time, little by little, the public growing lazy and stupid and never doing anything about what was going on. Now America and her people were paying the price. The tote board ringing up the score on a daily basis: the S & L scandal involving billions, the budget deficit involving billions more, the rotting infrastructure, schools churning out illiterate children, riots in the cities, guns and drugs everywhere, bounced checks and illegal kiting by Congressmen, gridlock in government, recession, jobs leaving the country, no direction or leadership from anyone. The future looked grim and the loss of the American dream was just the down payment.

"I gotta go. I got a cab waiting for me outside," I said.

Jack looked surprised. So was I at that point, but I didn't give a damn after what I'd just seen in that book. I knew it was true. It was too damn sick not to be true. I figured Jack Rodriguez could do whatever the hell he pleased to Senator Thomas. I wasn't about to stand in his way now.

"I'm gonna kill him, Vic. When he comes home, I'm gonna pop him good for what he did to me. For what he did to all the people in that book by getting the goods on them."

"You fucking moron! If you had any brains, or some real balls, you'd know what to do. Thomas ain't the problem, Jack. It's the system. The people listed in that book aren't victims, they're the problem. They're the enemy! If you had brains you'd see that! If you had the balls you'd do something about it!"

"I don't know, Vic."

"Yeah, I know. No one ever wants to do anything."

I sat in a run down bar near the yuppie section of D.C. sipping a Daniels and coke. By myself. Talking to no one. Thinking. About Jack. About the people in that book. Jack wasn't going back to prison now. At least for a while. Until they caught up with him. I'd have nothing to do with that now. I was happy about that. Jack didn't deserve to be in prison. He didn't deserve to live either now. He'd originally went after Thomas to kill him, but he'd discovered something a lot more important. A lot more dangerous. The book.

The overhead TV was on. The latest politico talking to some news guy about the campaign for president. How the entire system was corrupt. How both parties, Republicans, Democrats, whether liberal or conservative were bought and paid for by big money. Special interests. The only constituency without a lobby or PAC in this town was the American people. The American people had lost their country. Freedom and democracy in the United States was a rapidly diminishing commodity. It was nothing everyone in that bar didn't already know.

But the bar was noisy. Full of people. Laughing. Drinking. Having a good old time. No one paid any attention.

This was a political year. All the stops were pulled. All that mattered was money and winning. Getting elected. Any way that you could.

I downed my Daniels and coke. Called for another.

Suddenly the screen went blank, the sound went off. It was only for a moment, but for some reason it got everyone's attention.

"BREAKING NEWS" filled the TV screen in big block letters. There was a long silence.

One of the yahoos shouted, "Now what the fuck is this!"

Someone else answered, "Shut up and you'll find out!"

A newsman's plastic face came on the screen. He looked tired, in pain. Shocked. He was silent for a long moment, as though not sure how to begin what he had to say. Finally he said, "There's been a terrible tragedy here today in the Halls of Congress.

This afternoon, at 4 PM EST an armed man, presumed to be an escaped convict, entered the chambers of the House of Representatives and opened fire with two Mach 10 machine pistols into a full session of Congress. Before the man was gunned down by House security police he had killed dozens of Congressmen and wounded dozens more in the worst spree of mass murder ever to occur in this country. This reporter saw dozens of the most prominent leaders of our country dead or wounded upon the cold stone floor . . ."

The newsman lost his voice for a moment.

The crowd was silent.

I didn't have to be told that it was Jack making his point. He was never going back to prison now. He'd found a way out, and he'd said what he wanted to say in the best way possible for him.

Then it happened. One or two voices began it, and others joined in, and it became a chorus of loud cheers and shouts ringing up from the crowd. It became ear-splitting. People clapped hands wildly. There were shouts of liberty. Independence. Freedom. Revenge.

"Good, Kill them all!"

"Throw the bums out!"

"That's the way to do it!"

"Fuck them!"

"Scumbags got what they deserved!"

I was silent. I didn't know whether to cheer along with them or cry. I wasn't even sure if I cared any longer or if it was worth it all anymore.

I ordered another shot of Daniels without the coke this time, drinking to the memory of Jack Rodriguez. A prisoner, a fool, a killer, a dead man, and maybe even a patriot. I guess they come in all types.

On the way out of the bar I dropped the package into the mailbox. It was addressed to *The Washington Post*. They'd know what to do with the book. Now that Jack had started the ball rolling, they'd have to believe what was written there. He'd died for what was written there. Now there was no telling where it might stop. Maybe, we'd even get our county back. But I wasn't betting on it. It was a political year.

You know what that means.

DO SOMETHING ABOUT IT!

WHEN RONDA CALLED ME she was angry and almost hysterical with rage.

"That son-of-a-bitch has been up my ass too damn long now. This is the last time, Vic. I want you to do something. Straighten him out, once and for all!"

I didn't say anything, I'd heard this all before. Ronda was a pint-size youngish gal who had had it with some two-bit moron neighbor who was causing her all kinds of grief. She told me daily stories about how he'd tail-gate her small Honda with his big truck, terrorizing her when she came home from work, then parking in front of her house instead of his own. Annoying certainly, but not deadly. Your generic Brooklyn big-mouth with shit-for-brains.

"You there, Vic?"

"Yeah," I said. "What do you want me to do about it, Ronda?"

"What do I want you to *do* about it! Are you a freakin' retard? I want you to kill the bastard! I know you've killed people before, and some of them a lot less deserving than this freak. I want him dead!"

I laughed, "I don't think I can do that."

"I can," she said and there was no doubt at all in her voice. "I hate him."

We were silent for one very long second. Then the second was over.

"Will you come over?" she asked.

"Yeah, I'll be right over."

It only took me fifteen minutes to drive from my rented dive in Canarsie to Ronda's small one-family cottage in Gerritsen Beach. She lived alone in the co-called new section, cute tightly-packed homes and bungalows on narrow streets by the water. The whole place looked more like a scene from a New England fishing village mistakenly dumped into the ass-end of Brooklyn.

I could see Ronda waiting in front of her house as I drove down the block. I saw there was only one parking spot, smack dab in front of Ronda's house like it was *Kismet* or something, and I headed straight towards it.

Out of nowhere a huge shiny black pick-up made a screeching turn from the other corner, cut me off, and shot into the spot like I didn't even exist.

"What the fuck!" I shouted. Where the hell had he come from?

The guy, your generic young muscle-bound moron-type parked in my spot and was about to get out of his truck when I pulled up beside him. Real close. My passenger side door was blocking his driver's side door from opening. He was trapped in his truck, just where I wanted him.

I lowered my passenger window. I looked at the big mook, trying to keep calm, wanting to keep it gentlemanly. I didn't want to start trouble with the guy. I figured, with the deepest respect, I'd say, *"Hey, fucking asshole, that's my damn spot!"*

Well, that's what I *wanted* to say, instead what I actually said was, "Excuse me, I think you took my spot."

The guy looked at me like I'd just arrived from Mars. His face twisted when he realized my SUV was blocking him from opening his door to get out.

"Fuck you!" he shouted. "Move your piece of shit out of my way!"

Well, this didn't seem to be the proper attitude to take at all and I was about to tell him so when he jerked open his door, smashing it into my door.

Now I saw red.

He just laughed viciously, like the big jerk he was, not even caring about whatever damage he had done to his own vehicle. Muscle-bound morons can be like that—all hyped up on ego, testosterone or steroids. I saw he had an old guy in the cab with him, most likely his father, and it looked like the relic was already passed out drunk. It wasn't even noon yet.

"You took my parking spot, now you smashed my door!" I shouted in disbelief.

"Too fucking bad! Now move off, asshole!"

I heard loud booms behind me and was amazed to see Ronda banging with her fists on the back of the guy's truck.

I sighed, *that Ronda*, what a gal, she was always ready for trouble. I knew it wouldn't be easy to calm her down, now that she was all revved up.

Suddenly out of the corner of my eye I saw another woman bolt out of one of the houses nearby and take Ronda down with a running tackle. Ronda was flung back and both women were on the ground, embroiled in a fierce fight on the small lawn in front of Ronda's house.

This was all turning to shit way too fast for me. I moved my SUV forward away from the guy's truck and double-parked up ahead. Then I got out and ran back to the two women to break up their fight.

I tried to find an opening where I could pull Ronda off the thin peroxide blonde. Ronda, while smaller was a spunky angry little bitch and was beginning to beat the crap out of the other woman, I was kinda proud of her, but I couldn't let her face a felony beef. I knew I had to stop this before it got too serious.

"Come on now . . . *ladies* . . ." I finally got a hold of Ronda and was about to pull her off the other woman when I felt a huge hand wrap itself around my arm.

"What the fuck!"

"Let them fight, asshole."

It was muscle-head.

I looked at him serious now, "Get your hand off my arm."

"Make me."

I smiled, ripping into the steroid-hulk and hammering him with my fists. He never knew what hit him. My knuckles smashed into his face and gut non-stop like a battering ram. His face was soon transformed into a bloody mess. In sixty seconds I had him on the ground and was knocking him senseless. He tried to fight back, but I wasn't no kid or woman, which I presumed was his usual beat-down partner. He never expected the force and fury of my attack. I was so relentless, so quickly, he never had a chance to get his breath, much less go on the offensive. My motto, 'never give an asshole an even break'!

Once he was down and out, I went over and pulled Ronda off the anemic blonde.

"Vic, let me finish her off!"

"Ronda, the poor girl's got no teeth left, enough is enough."

Ronda, smiled, "I'm glad you came over, Vic, it's always good to see you."

"Yeah, it's nice to see you again too," I said with a shrug. "Now that this shit is done with, why the hell did you want me to come here anyway?"

"You just did it."

"What do you mean?"

"Little Abner. Least ways that's what I call him. You gave him a beating he won't forget. Thanks, Vic."

"My pleasure," I said. "What about the wife?"

Ronda laughed, "Oh, Daisy Mae? She ain't nothing. I can take care of her myself."

"You sure as hell did. I never realized there could be so many problems owning a home in this neighborhood."

"You have no idea what I have to go through, Vic. No idea. I won't even tell you about the problems with all the spoiled out-of-control kids and the stray cats. But the worst is Little Abner. I hate Little Abner."

I smiled, Ronda could be like that sometimes. "I don't think you'll be having any more trouble with Little Abner and if you do I'll be glad to come over and give him another attitude adjustment."

"Thanks, Vic, you're the best. I knew I could count on you to do something about it."

GARY LOVISI is a Mystery Writer's of America Edgar Nominated author for his Sherlock Holmes pastiche, "The Adventure of the Missing Detective." He is an avid Sherlockian, as well as book collector. His latest books are *Sherlock Holmes and The Crosby Murders* (Linford Press, UK, 2009), *Dames, Dolls & Delinquents*, a collector's guide to sexy pulp fiction paperbacks (Krause, 2009) and the edited crime anthology, *Deadly Dames* (Boldventure Press 2009). His hard crime novels include *Hellbent on Homicide* and *Blood in Brooklyn* (Do Not Press, UK). Lovisi is the founder of Gryphon Books, editor of *Paperback Parade* and *Hardboiled* magazines, and sponsors an annual book collector show in New York City. To find out more about him, his work, or Gryphon Books, visit his web site at: www.gryphonbooks.com.

RAMBLE HOUSE's

HARRY STEPHEN KEELER WEBWORK MYSTERIES

(RH) indicates the title is available ONLY in the RAMBLE HOUSE edition

The Ace of Spades Murder
The Affair of the Bottled Deuce (RH)
The Amazing Web
The Barking Clock
Behind That Mask
The Book with the Orange Leaves
The Bottle with the Green Wax Seal
The Box from Japan
The Case of the Canny Killer
The Case of the Crazy Corpse (RH)
The Case of the Flying Hands (RH)
The Case of the Ivory Arrow
The Case of the Jeweled Ragpicker
The Case of the Lavender Gripsack
The Case of the Mysterious Moll
The Case of the 16 Beans
The Case of the Transparent Nude (RH)
The Case of the Transposed Legs
The Case of the Two-Headed Idiot (RH)
The Case of the Two Strange Ladies
The Circus Stealers (RH)
Cleopatra's Tears
A Copy of Beowulf (RH)
The Crimson Cube (RH)
The Face of the Man From Saturn
Find the Clock
The Five Silver Buddhas
The 4th King
The Gallows Waits, My Lord! (RH)
The Green Jade Hand
Finger! Finger!
Hangman's Nights (RH)
I, Chameleon (RH)
I Killed Lincoln at 10:13! (RH)
The Iron Ring
The Man Who Changed His Skin (RH)
The Man with the Crimson Box
The Man with the Magic Eardrums
The Man with the Wooden Spectacles
The Marceau Case
The Matilda Hunter Murder
The Monocled Monster

The Murder of London Lew
The Murdered Mathematician
The Mysterious Card (RH)
The Mysterious Ivory Ball of Wong Shing Li (RH)
The Mystery of the Fiddling Cracksman
The Peacock Fan
The Photo of Lady X (RH)
The Portrait of Jirjohn Cobb
Report on Vanessa Hewstone (RH)
Riddle of the Travelling Skull
Riddle of the Wooden Parrakeet (RH)
The Scarlet Mummy (RH)
The Search for X-Y-Z
The Sharkskin Book
Sing Sing Nights
The Six From Nowhere (RH)
The Skull of the Waltzing Clown
The Spectacles of Mr. Cagliostro
Stand By—London Calling!
The Steeltown Strangler
The Stolen Gravestone (RH)
Strange Journey (RH)
The Strange Will
The Straw Hat Murders (RH)
The Street of 1000 Eyes (RH)
Thieves' Nights
Three Novellos (RH)
The Tiger Snake
The Trap (RH)
Vagabond Nights (Defrauded Yeggman)
Vagabond Nights 2 (10 Hours)
The Vanishing Gold Truck
The Voice of the Seven Sparrows
The Washington Square Enigma
When Thief Meets Thief
The White Circle (RH)
The Wonderful Scheme of Mr. Christopher Thorne
X. Jones—of Scotland Yard
Y. Cheung, Business Detective

Keeler Related Works

A To Izzard: A Harry Stephen Keeler Companion by Fender Tucker — Articles and stories about Harry, by Harry, and in his style. Included is a compleat bibliography.

Wild About Harry: Reviews of Keeler Novels — Edited by Richard Polt & Fender Tucker — 22 reviews of works by Harry Stephen Keeler from *Keeler News*. A perfect introduction to the author.

The Keeler Keyhole Collection: Annotated newsletter rants from Harry Stephen Keeler, edited by Francis M. Nevins. Over 400 pages of incredibly personal Keeleriana.

Fakealoo — Pastiches of the style of Harry Stephen Keeler by selected demented members of the HSK Society. Updated every year with the new winner.

RAMBLE HOUSE's OTHER LOONS

The End of It All and Other Stories — Ed Gorman's latest short story collection

Four Dancing Tuatara Press Books — *Beast or Man?* By Sean M'Guire; *The Whistling Ancestors* by Richard E. Goddard; *The Shadow on the House* and *Sorcerer's Chessmen* by Mark Hansom. With introductions by John Pelan

The Dumpling — Political murder from 1907 by Coulson Kernahan

Victims & Villains — Intriguing Sherlockiana from Derham Groves

Evidence in Blue — 1938 mystery by E. Charles Vivian

The Case of the Little Green Men — Mack Reynolds wrote this love song to sci-fi fans back in 1951 and it's now back in print.

Hell Fire — A new hard-boiled novel by Jack Moskovitz about an arsonist, an arson cop and a Nazi hooker. It isn't pretty.

Researching American-Made Toy Soldiers — A 276-page collection of a lifetime of articles by toy soldier expert Richard O'Brien

Strands of the Web: Short Stories of Harry Stephen Keeler — Edited and Introduced by Fred Cleaver

The Sam McCain Novels — Ed Gorman's terrific series includes *The Day the Music Died, Wake Up Little Susie* and *Will You Still Love Me Tomorrow?*

A Shot Rang Out — Three decades of reviews from Jon Breen

Mysterious Martin, the Master of Murder — Two versions of a strange 1912 novel by Tod Robbins about a man who writes books that can kill.

Dago Red — 22 tales of dark suspense by Bill Pronzini

The Night Remembers — A 1991 Jack Walsh mystery from Ed Gorman

Rough Cut & New, Improved Murder — Ed Gorman's first two novels

Hollywood Dreams — A novel of the Depression by Richard O'Brien

Seven Gelett Burgess Novels — *The Master of Mysteries, The White Cat, Two O'Clock Courage, Ladies in Boxes, Find the Woman, The Heart Line, The Picaroons*

The Organ Reader — A huge compilation of just about everything published in the 1971-1972 radical bay-area newspaper, *THE ORGAN*.

A Clear Path to Cross — Sharon Knowles short mystery stories by Ed Lynskey

Old Times' Sake — Short stories by James Reasoner from Mike Shayne Magazine

Freaks and Fantasies — Eerie tales by Tod Robbins, collaborator of Tod Browning on the film FREAKS.

Seven Jim Harmon Double Novels — *Vixen Hollow/Celluloid Scandal, The Man Who Made Maniacs/Silent Siren, Ape Rape/Wanton Witch, Sex Burns Like Fire/Twist Session, Sudden Lust/Passion Strip, Sin Unlimited/Harlot Master, Twilight Girls/Sex Institution.* Written in the early 60s.

Marblehead: A Novel of H.P. Lovecraft — A long-lost masterpiece from Richard A. Lupoff. Published for the first time!

The Compleat Ova Hamlet — Parodies of SF authors by Richard A. Lupoff - A brand new edition with more stories and more illustrations by Trina Robbins.

The Secret Adventures of Sherlock Holmes — Three Sherlockian pastiches by the Brooklyn author/publisher, Gary Lovisi.

The Universal Holmes — Richard A. Lupoff's 2007 collection of five Holmesian pastiches and a recipe for giant rat stew.

Four Joel Townsley Rogers Novels — By the author of *The Red Right Hand: Once In a Red Moon, Lady With the Dice, The Stopped Clock, Never Leave My Bed*

Two Joel Townsley Rogers Story Collections — Night of Horror and Killing Time

Twenty Norman Berrow Novels — *The Bishop's Sword, Ghost House, Don't Go Out After Dark, Claws of the Cougar, The Smokers of Hashish, The Secret Dancer, Don't Jump Mr. Boland!, The Footprints of Satan, Fingers for Ransom, The Three Tiers of Fantasy, The Spaniard's Thumb, The Eleventh Plague, Words Have Wings, One Thrilling Night, The Lady's in Danger, It Howls at Night, The Terror in the Fog, Oil Under the Window, Murder in the Melody, The Singing Room*

The N. R. De Mexico Novels — Robert Bragg presents *Marijuana Girl, Madman on a Drum, Private Chauffeur* in one volume.

Four Chelsea Quinn Yarbro Novels featuring Charlie Moon — *Ogilvie, Tallant and Moon, Music When the Sweet Voice Dies, Poisonous Fruit* and *Dead Mice*

Five Walter S. Masterman Mysteries — *The Green Toad, The Flying Beast, The Yellow Mistletoe, The Wrong Verdict* and *The Perjured Alibi*. Fantastic impossible plots.

Two Hake Talbot Novels — *Rim of the Pit, The Hangman's Handyman.* Classic locked room mysteries.

Two Alexander Laing Novels — *The Motives of Nicholas Holtz* and *Dr. Scarlett*, stories of medical mayhem and intrigue from the 30s.

Four David Hume Novels — *Corpses Never Argue, Cemetery First Stop, Make Way for the Mourners, Eternity Here I Come,* and more to come.

Three Wade Wright Novels — *Echo of Fear, Death At Nostalgia Street* and *It Leads to Murder,* with more to come!

Eight Rupert Penny Novels — *Policeman's Holiday, Policeman's Evidence, Lucky Policeman, Policeman in Armour, Sealed Room Murder, Sweet Poison, The Talkative Policeman, She had to Have Gas* and *Cut and Run* (by Martin Tanner.)

Five Jack Mann Novels — Strange murder in the English countryside. *Gees' First Case, Nightmare Farm, Grey Shapes, The Ninth Life, The Glass Too Many.*

Seven Max Afford Novels — *Owl of Darkness, Death's Mannikins, Blood on His Hands, The Dead Are Blind, The Sheep and the Wolves, Sinners in Paradise* and *Two Locked Room Mysteries and a Ripping Yarn* by one of Australia's finest novelists.

Five Joseph Shallit Novels — *The Case of the Billion Dollar Body, Lady Don't Die on My Doorstep, Kiss the Killer, Yell Bloody Murder, Take Your Last Look.* One of America's best 50's authors.

Two Crimson Clown Novels — By Johnston McCulley, author of the Zorro novels, *The Crimson Clown* and *The Crimson Clown Again.*

The Best of 10-Story Book — edited by Chris Mikul, over 35 stories from the literary magazine Harry Stephen Keeler edited.

A Young Man's Heart — A forgotten early classic by Cornell Woolrich

The Anthony Boucher Chronicles — edited by Francis M. Nevins
Book reviews by Anthony Boucher written for the *San Francisco Chronicle,* 1942 – 1947. Essential and fascinating reading.

Muddled Mind: Complete Works of Ed Wood, Jr. — David Hayes and Hayden Davis deconstruct the life and works of a mad genius.

Gadsby — A lipogram (a novel without the letter E). Ernest Vincent Wright's last work, published in 1939 right before his death.

My First Time: The One Experience You Never Forget — Michael Birchwood — 64 true first-person narratives of how they lost it.

A Roland Daniel Double: The Signal and The Return of Wu Fang — Classic thrillers from the 30s

Murder in Shawnee — Two novels of the Alleghenies by John Douglas: *Shawnee Alley Fire* and *Haunts.*

Deep Space and other Stories — A collection of SF gems by Richard A. Lupoff

Blood Moon — The first of the Robert Payne series by Ed Gorman

The Time Armada — Fox B. Holden's 1953 SF gem.

Black River Falls — Suspense from the master, Ed Gorman

Sideslip — 1968 SF masterpiece by Ted White and Dave Van Arnam

The Triune Man — Mindscrambling science fiction from Richard A. Lupoff

Detective Duff Unravels It — Episodic mysteries by Harvey O'Higgins

Automaton — Brilliant treatise on robotics: 1928-style! By H. Stafford Hatfield

The Incredible Adventures of Rowland Hern — Rousing 1928 impossible crimes by Nicholas Olde.

Slammer Days — Two full-length prison memoirs: *Men into Beasts* (1952) by George Sylvester Viereck and *Home Away From Home* (1962) by Jack Woodford

Murder in Black and White — 1931 classic tennis whodunit by Evelyn Elder

Killer's Caress — Cary Moran's 1936 hardboiled thriller

The Golden Dagger — 1951 Scotland Yard yarn by E. R. Punshon

A Smell of Smoke — 1951 English countryside thriller by Miles Burton

Ruled By Radio — 1925 futuristic novel by Robert L. Hadfield & Frank E. Farncombe

Murder in Silk — A 1937 Yellow Peril novel of the silk trade by Ralph Trevor

The Case of the Withered Hand — 1936 potboiler by John G. Brandon

Finger-prints Never Lie — A 1939 classic detective novel by John G. Brandon

Inclination to Murder — 1966 thriller by New Zealand's Harriet Hunter

Invaders from the Dark — Classic werewolf tale from Greye La Spina

Fatal Accident — Murder by automobile, a 1936 mystery by Cecil M. Wills

The Devil Drives — A prison and lost treasure novel by Virgil Markham

Dr. Odin — Douglas Newton's 1933 potboiler comes back to life.

The Chinese Jar Mystery — Murder in the manor by John Stephen Strange, 1934

The Julius Caesar Murder Case — A classic 1935 re-telling of the assassination by Wallace Irwin that's much more fun than the Shakespeare version

West Texas War and Other Western Stories — by Gary Lovisi

The Contested Earth and Other SF Stories — A never-before published space opera and seven short stories by Jim Harmon.

Tales of the Macabre and Ordinary — Modern twisted horror by Chris Mikul, author of the *Bizarrism* series.

The Gold Star Line — Seaboard adventure from L.T. Reade and Robert Eustace.

The Werewolf vs the Vampire Woman — Hard to believe ultraviolence by either Arthur M. Scarm or Arthur M. Scram.

Black Hogan Strikes Again — Australia's Peter Renwick pens a tale of the outback.

Don Diablo: Book of a Lost Film — Two-volume treatment of a western by Paul Landres, with diagrams. Intro by Francis M. Nevins.

The Charlie Chaplin Murder Mystery — Movie hijinks by Wes D. Gehring

The Koky Comics — A collection of all of the 1978-1981 Sunday and daily comic strips by Richard O'Brien and Mort Gerberg, in two volumes.

Suzy — Another collection of comic strips from Richard O'Brien and Bob Vojtko

Dime Novels: Ramble House's 10-Cent Books — *Knife in the Dark* by Robert Leslie Bellem, *Hot Lead* and *Song of Death* by Ed Earl Repp, *A Hashish House in New York* by H.H. Kane, and five more.

Blood in a Snap — The *Finnegan's Wake* of the 21st century, by Jim Weiler

Stakeout on Millennium Drive — Award-winning Indianapolis Noir — Ian Woollen.

Dope Tales #1 — Two dope-riddled classics; *Dope Runners* by Gerald Grantham and *Death Takes the Joystick* by Phillip Condé.

Dope Tales #2 — Two more narco-classics; *The Invisible Hand* by Rex Dark and *The Smokers of Hashish* by Norman Berrow.

Dope Tales #3 — Two enchanting novels of opium by the master, Sax Rohmer. *Dope* and *The Yellow Claw.*

Tenebrae — Ernest G. Henham's 1898 horror tale brought back.

The Singular Problem of the Stygian House-Boat — Two classic tales by John Kendrick Bangs about the denizens of Hades.

Tiresias — Psychotic modern horror novel by Jonathan M. Sweet.

The One After Snelling — Kickass modern noir from Richard O'Brien.

The Sign of the Scorpion — 1935 Edmund Snell tale of oriental evil.

The House of the Vampire — 1907 poetic thriller by George S. Viereck.

An Angel in the Street — Modern hardboiled noir by Peter Genovese.

The Devil's Mistress — Scottish gothic tale by J. W. Brodie-Innes.

The Lord of Terror — 1925 mystery with master-criminal, Fantômas.

The Lady of the Terraces — 1925 adventure by E. Charles Vivian.

My Deadly Angel — 1955 Cold War drama by John Chelton

Prose Bowl — Futuristic satire — Bill Pronzini & Barry N. Malzberg .

Satan's Den Exposed — True crime in Truth or Consequences New Mexico — Award-winning journalism by the *Desert Journal*.

The Amorous Intrigues & Adventures of Aaron Burr — by Anonymous — Hot historical action.

I Stole $16,000,000 — A true story by cracksman Herbert E. Wilson.

The Black Dark Murders — Vintage 50s college murder yarn by Milt Ozaki, writing as Robert O. Saber.

Sex Slave — Potboiler of lust in the days of Cleopatra — Dion Leclerq.

You'll Die Laughing — Bruce Elliott's 1945 novel of murder at a practical joker's English countryside manor.

The Private Journal & Diary of John H. Surratt — The memoirs of the man who conspired to assassinate President Lincoln.

Dead Man Talks Too Much — Hollywood boozer by Weed Dickenson

Red Light — History of legal prostitution in Shreveport Louisiana by Eric Brock. Includes wonderful photos of the houses and the ladies.

A Snark Selection — Lewis Carroll's *The Hunting of the Snark* with two Snarkian chapters by Harry Stephen Keeler — Illustrated by Gavin L. O'Keefe.

Ripped from the Headlines! — The Jack the Ripper story as told in the newspaper articles in the *New York* and *London Times.*

Geronimo — S. M. Barrett's 1905 autobiography of a noble American.

The White Peril in the Far East — Sidney Lewis Gulick's 1905 indictment of the West and assurance that Japan would never attack the U.S.

The Compleat Calhoon — All of Fender Tucker's works: Includes *Totah Six-Pack, Weed, Women and Song* and *Tales from the Tower,* plus a CD of all of his songs.

Totah Six-Pack — Just Fender Tucker's six tales about Farmington in one sleek volume.

RAMBLE HOUSE
Fender Tucker, Prop.
www.ramblehouse.com   fender@ramblehouse.com
228-826-1783   10329 Sheephead Drive, Vancleave MS 39565